This special signed edition of
# THE CONSULTANT
is limited to 750 numbered copies.

This is number ___713___.

# THE CONSULTANT

# THE CONSULTANT

## BENTLEY LITTLE

**CEMETERY DANCE PUBLICATIONS**

*Baltimore*

❖ 2015 ❖

Cemetery Dance Publications
132-B Industry Lane, Unit #7
Forest Hill, MD 21050
http://www.cemeterydance.com

The characters and events in this book are fictitious.
Any similarity to real persons, living or dead, is
coincidental and not intended by the author.

ISBN-13: 978-158767-501-0

Cover Artwork & Design Copyright © 2015 by Elder Lemon Design
Interior Design by Kate Freeman Design

*For the Konefsky family:*
*Bob, David and especially Natalie,*
*who knows all about the horrors of the modern workplace.*

# ONE

IT WAS HIS OWN FAULT.

If Craig Horne hadn't checked his email immediately after waking up, if he'd simply left his work at work, the way Angie was always nagging him to do, he wouldn't have even known about the staff meeting. He would have showered, shaved and eaten a leisurely breakfast with his family, discovering only when he arrived at the office shortly after eight that he'd missed a meeting. Later in the morning, someone would have caught him up on what had been discussed.

But he *had* checked his email, and the message that greeted him when he signed on was: "Senior Staff Meeting at 7:30." So he hurriedly showered and dressed, downed a quick cup of coffee under Angie's hostile, disapproving gaze, and sped out the door.

Leaving early made a huge difference in the amount of traffic on the freeway, and with his commute clocking in at a half-hour rather than the usual forty-five minutes, Craig arrived at work with twenty minutes to spare. He probably *could* have wolfed down a quick breakfast before leaving home, he thought as he took the elevator up to the sixth floor, but he wouldn't let Angie know that or he'd never hear the end of it.

He got off the elevator, walking down the hallway to his office and saying good morning to Lupe, his secretary, who had obviously just arrived and was standing behind her desk, taking a croissant out of a bakery bag. She smiled back at him. "You're in early."

"Staff meeting," he said, and found himself wondering what was going to be discussed. It was unusual for Matthews to call a meeting on such short notice, and even more unusual for the CEO not to specify an agenda.

Craig sat down behind his desk, turned on his computer and accessed the sales figures for their newest software. He'd been sent the numbers several days ago but had avoided looking at them, as he was pretty sure he knew how they were going to lay out. He was disappointed but not surprised to learn that he'd been right; the new business package, OfficeManager, was not merely underperforming; it was a bona fide flop.

Was this what they were going to be discussing in the meeting? Sales figures? It was more than possible, and, just in case, he printed out a few graphs showing overall market trends that he could use should he need to play defense.

The buzzer on his phone console sounded, the red light flashed, and he glanced over at the clock. It was almost time for the meeting. Gathering up his materials, he walked out and told Lupe to hold down the fort until he returned.

He took the elevator down to the first floor and saw Phil Allen in the hallway on the way to the conference room. "You have any idea what this is about?" Craig asked.

"Damage control," Phil replied, shifting his briefcase from one hand to the other. Craig's confusion must have registered on his face, because his friend suddenly stopped walking and said, "Oh my God. You don't know."

"Know what?"

Phil motioned him over to the side of the hallway, next to the wall. There was no one around, but he leaned in and kept his voice low. "A.I.'s called off the merger. It's front page in the *Journal* today. They're not even willing to make a bid. Word on the street is that our stock's going to start dropping as soon as the bell rings. Anderson's already taken a golden parachute and bailed. Don't be surprised if some of the other names follow suit."

Craig's heart was racing. "What happened?"

"No one knows. Or no one's talking. Their independent auditors gave us a clean bill of health just last week, but some sort of discrepancy must have shown up because A.I.'s out."

"You thinking layoffs?"

"I don't know what to think. You don't have anything to worry about, though. Your department's on the creative end. If heads are going to roll, it's going to be in Finance. They're the ones who pursued this strategy."

"Yeah, but OfficeManager tanked. I just looked at the numbers five minutes ago."

"And *Zombie Air Force* is still number one in games. Trust me, you're safe. If anyone gets the blame for OfficeManager, it's Sales. We always take the fall. Besides, I don't think this has anything to do with individual products. There's no merger. Anderson's gone. The company's in freefall. *That's* what the meeting's about."

Vice-presidents, department heads, division heads, managers and supervisors were on their way down the hall, and Craig and Phil cut short their conversation in order to get good seats in the theater-like conference room. Matthews was already standing at the front, by the podium, and the fact that the wall behind the

CEO was bare, with neither charts nor PowerPoint screens in evidence, meant that this was definitely something unusual. Glancing over at Phil, Craig saw an expression of repressed worry that mirrored his own anxiety exactly. Matthews was meeting no one's eyes, keeping his gaze focused on either the podium before him or the clock on the wall. Not a good sign.

A stickler for punctuality, the CEO always started meetings precisely on time, and this morning was no exception. Some people had not yet arrived and several were still not seated when he announced, "Let's begin."

For the next twenty minutes, they were subjected to a withering assessment of the company's performance over the past year, culminating in the confirmation that, yes, as reported in *The Wall Street Journal*, Automated Interface was no longer interested in merging with CompWare. CFO Hugh Anderson and Senior Vice President Russell Cibriano, architects of the merger strategy, had fallen on their swords and voluntarily left the company, but that would cause as many problems as it was going to solve.

"At this juncture, the most important thing we need to do is reinforce public and industry confidence in the company. To that end, we have decided to hire a management consulting firm in order to get our internal house in order. BFG Associates come highly recommended, and they have a phenomenal track record, with work in both the private and public sectors. They'll be conducting a study of the entire company, top to bottom, and will have access to everything and everyone for as long as they require. Each of your departments and divisions will be given a briefing regarding the specifics as they relate to your work unit, but, basically, BFG has been tasked with studying the company, analyzing the data and making recommendations as to how we can consolidate staff, streamline practices and procedures, do everything we need to in order to stay viable in today's competitive market."

*Consolidate staff?*

Craig looked at Phil as a murmur of worry passed through the conference room.

"This is not to say that we'll automatically implement their recommendations," Matthews emphasized. "Their report is only a starting point. But we hope to use it as a blueprint for a reinvigorated CompWare, a roadmap for our continued future. Now, if there are any questions, I'll be happy to answer as many as I can."

There were. And Matthews's answers were as vague and generic as his speech had been. Craig left the meeting knowing only that consultants had been hired to study ways to cut costs and increase profits—most likely by laying people off. It was a depressing turn of events and not one he could have predicted upon waking this morning, but at least he'd gone to the meeting and Matthews had seen him. That might count for something when it came down to the wire. Van Do and Josh Halberstram hadn't shown up at all, probably hadn't checked their email before coming to work, and that was the type of thing the CEO might take into account when heads started to roll.

"Interesting meeting?" Lupe asked when he returned.

Craig decided to give her a heads up, though he knew Matthews expected everyone to keep a lid on what had been discussed until an official announcement was made. "The merger didn't go through. Anderson and Cibriano are out, and it looks like there might be layoffs."

Lupe's normally easygoing expression grew serious.

"He didn't tell us much beyond that, but a consultant's been hired, and they're going to be doing some sort of study before deciding what to do next."

She glanced around to make sure no one else was nearby. "What do you think…?"

He shrugged. "Phil assures me we're safe. I hope he's right, but we'd both better be on our best behavior, just in case."

Lupe nodded. "Do you need me to do anything? I could—"

"Save it," he told her. "We'll just continue on as is for now. We might have to come up with a strategy once the consultants get here, but we'll cross that bridge when we come to it."

"I don't have that much seniority," Lupe said worriedly.

"As long as I'm here, you're here," Craig assured her.

But that didn't ease her concerns as much as he thought it would, and as he walked into his office, he wondered if there was something she knew that he didn't.

# TWO

"THEY'VE ALREADY MADE THEIR DECISIONS," ANGIE said. "Who's going to be laid off, what departments are going to be consolidated: they've already decided. The only reason they're bringing in consultants is to justify what they're going to do and provide themselves with cover." She shook her head. "Is there a bigger scam on the planet than the consultant business?"

She was making dinner, heating up bottled spaghetti sauce in one pot while pasta boiled in another, and Craig was sitting at the kitchen table, nursing a beer. "I'm not sure about that," he said. "You didn't hear Matthews talk. I honestly think they're floundering. I think they're looking for someone to give them answers."

"That's even worse."

Dylan came in from the living room, perturbed. "Daddy! You said you were coming out! I've been waiting forever!" Craig smiled as his son walked up and grabbed his hand, trying to pull him out of the chair. "You need to read to me!"

Giving Angie an amused look, Craig stood, leaving his beer on the table and following the boy out to the living room. On the couch, in the spot where he usually sat, Dylan had placed the *Goosebumps* book they were reading. Craig knew that his son was competing with a girl named Karen in his class for the most amount of hours read each week, so the two of them read the book aloud, alternating chapters, until Angie told them to wash their hands for dinner.

They read some more after they finished eating, filled out the nightly reading log, then brushed their teeth together. Dylan put on his pajamas, then Angie read him a story and tucked him in bed.

Later, after the dishes were done and Dylan was asleep, they discussed what they'd do if Craig lost his job. Determined that their son not grow up in daycare and that there always be a parent at home, Angie had quit her full-time nursing position at St. Jude's and gotten a weekend job at an Urgent Care affiliated with the hospital before Dylan had even been born. So she was with him on weekdays, while Craig took care of him on weekends. Which meant that Craig was the primary breadwinner, and there was no way they could survive without his income.

"I don't think it'll come to that," he told her.

"You don't know."

She was right. In his mind, he went through their monthly expenses, mentally calculating how much they spent and what they could do without. The biggest chunk of change went to the mortgage, although if he were suddenly unemployed, they'd also have to worry about health insurance since they were insured through his work and her part-time job didn't come with benefits. *That* would be a major expense, and while they had some savings in the bank, he doubted that they could survive for even another year unless he quickly found a position somewhere else.

But he didn't say any of that to Angie.

"We'll be fine," he said dismissively. "Now be quiet. I'm trying to watch this show."

"Don't you tell me to be quiet."

"Hey, I shut up when you were watching *Top Chef*."

"Fine," she said. "Watch your stupid show."

And the subject was dropped.

---

Phil was waiting for him in the parking lot when he arrived at work the next morning, and the two of them walked up together. "Did a little research last night," Phil said.

"On what?"

"BFG Associates."

"And?"

"They're heavy hitters. Fortune 500 companies, the whole bit." He paused. "Very impressive résumé."

"But you're not convinced."

"Well… No, I'm not." He glanced around furtively, as though afraid of being spied upon. "The thing is, they leave a lot of destruction in their wake. Sure, they usually get stock prices up, but they also cut a lot of jobs and do what they refer to as 'reshuffling,' which, as far as I can tell, means placing employees in jobs for which they aren't really qualified. It's supposed to give them a broader background and greater perspective, which is supposed to make them better employees, but what ends up happening is that they're thrown into positions where they're over their heads. So they can be legitimately fired and replaced with new hires who come in at a much lower salary."

"That doesn't sound good," Craig admitted.

"And it's probably just the tip of the iceberg. I'm sure there's a lot more that I wasn't able to find out."

They were approaching the building, and Phil stopped before they got to the entrance. He waited while a group of women walked by. "What's your take on this?" he asked Craig when the women had gone inside.

"You mean the consultants? I have no idea. Angie says consultants just provide justification for decisions that have already been made. But you're the one who always has his ear to the ground. What have you heard?"

"Nothing."

"Yet," Craig said.

"Yet," Phil agreed.

As always, Lupe was at her desk when Craig arrived on the sixth floor. "Those consultants aren't wasting any time," she told him. "They're already here. I got an email. Sent at six-thirty. Meet-and-greets have been set up all day long. Department heads first, then division heads, managers, supervisors, all the way down to peons like me. Your meeting is scheduled for eleven. We secretaries go in at three-thirty."

He walked around the desk to read the email over her shoulder. "What's the mood?" he asked. "Around the building. Have you had a chance to talk to anyone?"

"Nobody knows anything, and everybody's worried."

"My take on it exactly."

Lupe's voice was uncharacteristically serious. "*Should* we be worried?"

"I don't know any more than I told you yesterday."

"But you'll give me a heads-up if you hear anything."

"I will," he promised.

Craig walked into his office, intending to read through to-day's emails before getting started on anything else, but he was distracted and swiveled his chair around to look out the window. He had always liked this office, had always liked this building. Angular and modern, with skylights and large windows and thick walls of unpainted concrete, many of them hung with equally angular, equally modern artwork, it had seemed to him perfectly suited for the work they did here. Now, however, it seemed unnecessarily ostentatious. Even staring out at the grounds below—the "campus," as it was called—he noted the perfectly manicured lawn, the exotic plants and flowers, the high-priced sculptures. They could have just as easily done their jobs in a simpler environment, an ordinary building with generic offices and cubicles. He hoped this was one of the things the consultants were going to look at, as it would not be fair for loyal, hardworking employees to lose their jobs because money had been wasted on extravagant furnishings and landscaping.

Swiveling back to face his desk—an expensive Plexiglas slab when a cheaper wooden desk would have been much more practical—Craig turned on his computer and began scrolling through his emails. There was a lot of spam; a couple of updates from the lead programmers working on *WarHammer III* and *Zombie Navy*, the company's next two game releases; a desperate note from Tyler Lang concerning proposed updates to the ill-fated OfficeManager, and a message with the bizarre subject line "Photos of CompWare Women Sucking Cocks at Christmas Party!!!"

He'd been at that party—one of the most staid gatherings he'd ever attended—and he knew that no such thing had happened. Frowning, he opened the email.

And read the single-line message: "This is not what you should be looking at during work hours."

Craig quickly exited the screen, his heart pounding. It was a trap, probably planted by the consultants, who were no doubt keeping track of each employee accessing the message. Now he was going to be questioned about it and would have to come up with a justification explaining *why* he had wanted to see "Photos of CompWare Women Sucking Cocks at Christmas Party!!!"

These guys were playing hardball.

Craig responded to the emails that required a response, then told Lupe he was going downstairs to see the programmers.

"You have that meeting with the consultants."

"That's not until eleven."

"Leave your phone on," she told him.

"I'll be back in plenty of time."

"Leave your phone on."

She knew him well. He was still watching a demo of *Zombie Navy*, gathered around a PC with a group of programmers, all shouting out instructions and suggestions to the technical writer, testing the recently debugged second level of the game, when his phone beeped, and he picked it up to see a message from Lupe: "Meeting in ten minutes. Third floor conference room."

"Gotta go," he told them. "Let me know if you find anything. And I need you to have that next level ready by Friday."

"It's done," Huell said. "I just need to clean up a few things and then we'll let John-Boy go at it."

The technical writer did not look away from his screen. "My name's Rusty, dillweed."

"Just keep me up to date," Craig said.

The third floor conference room was much smaller than the one on the first floor and was not set up like a theater but consisted of three large tables facing a freestanding white board set up in front of the bare concrete wall. Nearly all of the seats around the tables were taken, and Craig was forced to sit in a row of overflow chairs that had been lined up in the back of the room. Phil was nowhere in sight, but seconds later, he hurried into the room and sat down in the chair next to Craig. "I was on the phone with this jerk from IBM. Couldn't get off. I finally had to just hang up and bail. I'll call him when we're done here and tell him there was a glitch in the phone system or something."

There was no one standing at the front of the room, and Craig didn't see anyone unfamiliar who might be a consultant, but just as he was about to ask Phil if he'd heard any scuttlebutt regarding the morning's earlier meetings, Matthews entered through the back door, another man with him. Silently, they strode between two of the tables directly to the head of the conference room.

All conversation ceased as the gathered division heads faced forward. The man standing next to Matthews was tall, thin and wearing a red bow tie. His hair, an odd shade of brown so light it was almost orange, was cut into a flattop, rendering his already large forehead even larger. The expression on his face was blank, like that of an automaton waiting to be powered up, and he placidly surveyed the seated audience, his eyes taking in everyone without resting on anyone in particular.

"All right," Matthews said. "Let's get started. This is Mr. Patoff. As you may have already guessed, he will be coordinating the study for BFG Associates to help us determine how to proceed forward after our recent, ah, *misfortunes*."

The man smiled. *Warmly*, some might have said, but they would be wrong. Outwardly, his smile did appear warm, and Craig had no doubt that it could seem that way to a lot of people. But there was something underneath, the opposite, a *coldness* he detected and that left him feeling uneasy. There was nothing genuine there, only a calculated attempt to convince those in the room that he was a kind man who had their best interests at heart instead of a soulless shark who was here to decide whose jobs should be cut.

This man was dangerous, Craig decided. He needed to be careful from here on in. And on his best behavior.

"Mr. Patoff and the consultants working with him will be…" Matthews paused, smiling. "Well, why don't I let him tell you about it? Ladies and gentlemen, Mr. Patoff."

There was light applause.

"No need to be so formal," the consultant said, stepping forward and writing his name on the white board with a black marker. "You can call me Regus. Like the talk show host, only spelled with a U."

Polite chuckles.

"As Mr. Matthews said, we've been hired to take a look at your operations. I understand that your organization has had some recent financial setbacks, and it's our job to look for a way to ameliorate whatever losses you may have suffered and find a new way forward. Whether that involves merely streamlining procedures or revamping product lines remains to be seen.

"We look at each company in toto. Problems can trickle down from the top or percolate up from the bottom, so we study every facet of the organization before determining which approach to restructuring will be most appropriate."

Phil's hand shot up, though he didn't wait to be called upon to speak. "There's going to be restructuring?"

Matthews stepped in. "That's premature. We don't know what there's going to be. That's why we've hired Mr. Patoff's firm. They will study the situation and then we'll determine the best course of action."

"He said 'restructuring,'" Phil pressed.

The consultant smiled. *Coldly*, Craig thought again. "An inappropriate turn of phrase on my part. Mr. Matthews is correct: nothing has been decided ahead of time, and we won't make any recommendations until we conduct our study. What I meant to say was that each company is different, with different problems arising from different sources. So we talk to everyone, conduct surveys, perform research and investigate the particulars of each organization hiring us.

"In the case of CompWare, we will start out by conducting individual interviews with each and every employee. We will film these interviews, and then go over them with the appropriate supervisors, managers, division heads and department heads in order to make sure that senior staff is involved in the process every step of the way. It is not our intent to spring surprises on anyone. Our methodology is purposely transparent, and any recommendations we make will not only be backed up by relevant data but will be discussed at the appropriate level in the chain of command so that if there are changes to be made, those changes will not come out of the blue."

The consultant continued to describe in vague terms the process by which his firm examined the companies they were hired to evaluate, though his account did not really address the particulars of CompWare. He asked afterward whether there were any questions, and while there were quite a few and he answered them all, neither the questions nor the answers were particularly illuminating. Craig himself asked nothing, only watched and listened, and he came away from the meeting with the distinct impression that Angie was right, that Matthews and upper management had already made their decisions and were looking to the consultants to provide validation.

Leaving the meeting, he expressed his thoughts to Phil, and wondered aloud whether the consultants were truly independent and what would happen if they came to a different conclusion than Matthews wanted.

"I don't think that's going to happen," Phil said drily.

"I don't either."

Craig had some errands to run at lunch. Angie wanted him to pick up some stamps at the post office—"Cute ones," she told him. "Not those boring flag stamps you always get."—and he stood in a long line to buy some Disney cartoon stamps before walking next door and getting himself a burger and chocolate shake at Wendy's. On his way back, he filled up his tank with gas because he'd heard prices were supposed to go up this week, and stopped off at Target for some Drano and paper towels. He could have also picked up a SpongeBob Monopoly game, which was the present they'd decided to buy for Dylan's friend Jamie who was having a birthday party on Saturday. But Dylan liked to be there himself when they bought presents, and he needed to pick out a card as well, so Craig held off on that.

After lunch, he had a meeting scheduled with the programmers working on updates to OfficeManager. Tyler Lang was in charge of that project, and while he had lobbied Craig hard for the position, he was now behind the eight ball due to the software program's weak sales. The programmer was not only a good worker but a good friend, and now Craig felt guilty for giving him this assignment. It was more than possible that the consultants were going to blame Tyler and his team for OfficeManager's poor showing, and all of the programmers involved were worried about their futures. Craig tried to reassure them, promising that he would argue on their behalf if it came down to that, but the meeting was serious and by-the-book, and the programmers left early for their introduction to the consultant.

The rest of the afternoon was taken up with other meetings. Updates on each of the division's projects. He saw Lupe after the secretaries' encounter with the consultant and asked her how it went. She frowned. "Honestly? I didn't like him and I don't trust him."

"Me, neither!" Craig said.

"There's something about him that just rubs me the wrong way. Apart from the fact that he's here to figure out a way to downsize the company and get rid of my job."

"I feel the same way."

Lupe fixed him with an open look. "There are a lot of rumors flying around. What do you think's going to happen?"

He didn't want to lie to her—he *couldn't* lie to her; she knew him too well—so he told her what he really thought, an opinion he hadn't even let himself acknowledge up to this point. "I think we'll be okay. Maybe not the whole division, but most of it. We're the workhorses, after all. We're the producers. And you and me, in particular? I think we're safe."

The expression on her face was one of visible relief. He felt relieved himself, saying it, and he realized that despite everything that was going on, he really did think his job was secure. His and his secretary's. The thought was absurdly comforting amidst the chaos, and he and Lupe shared a smile.

After work, he went out with Tyler and a few of the other programmers for drinks, something that had once been a regular occurrence but in the past several years had become exceedingly rare. It was fun hanging out with the guys, so he stayed out a little longer than he'd planned, and when he got home, Dylan was steaming. "Where were you?" his son demanded. "You're supposed to read to me!"

Craig couldn't help laughing at the intensity of the boy's focused anger, and that only made things worse.

"I told you Daddy was going to be late," Angie reminded him.

"But he's not supposed to be!"

"Sorry, buddy." Craig picked up his son, hoisting the boy onto his shoulders, noticing that he was starting to get heavy. Dylan was growing fast, and in another year or so, Craig probably wouldn't be able to pick him up anymore. And Dylan probably wouldn't want him to. The thought made him sad, and while he'd had fun going out with the guys after work, he decided that he should spend as much of his spare time as he could with his son. "Let's read."

# THREE

AUSTIN MATTHEWS LEFT WORK EARLY WITH A SPLIT-
ting headache that had already beaten the shit out of the Tylenol
he'd taken two hours ago and was apparently kicking the ass of
the Advil he'd swallowed just before leaving. Although he'd always
been good at maintaining his game face, the stress of CompWare's
ongoing implosion was too much even for his hardened sensibil-
ities. But he'd helped found this company, damn it, and he wasn't
about to let it go down in flames. He'd do whatever he had to do to
keep the business alive, and if that meant restructuring and mass
layoffs, well, so be it. Sometimes you had to cut off a foot to save
the leg.

He closed his eyes against the pounding pain in his temples.
Even if the company came out of this disaster solvent, he'd probably come out of it with an ulcer.

It had been so much easier when they'd first started out, when
he and Josh Ihara had rented their first office in a partially abandoned industrial park. They'd had to borrow from their parents

to make the rent each month; the one programmer they had was working on spec, and for a whole week they'd been without power because both of them had forgotten to pay the electric bill. When someone had broken in one night and stolen their one newly purchased desktop PC, they hadn't been able to replace it because they didn't have insurance, and all three of them had had to time-share the remaining refurbished computer. But somehow they'd survived, and while the prospects of their continued existence fluctuated from week to week, and everything was always on the line, they'd had fun. With nothing to lose, they'd been able to take chances, and they had, and it had ended up paying off big time.

Matthews pressed the button on the dashboard of his Jaguar to open the driveway gate, watching through the windshield as it slid slowly to the side. As he had so often over the past fifteen years, he wished Josh was still with him now. But his former partner had cashed out early, eager to strike out on his own, and though none of Josh's subsequent ventures had been successful, he had not given up. He was still in the start-up trenches, hoping lightning would strike twice.

While Matthews remained here, trying to keep things together, carrying the weight of the world on his shoulders.

He pulled up the driveway, parking in front of the door rather than pulling into the garage. Inside the house, he announced that he was home, but there was no answer, and he assumed that Rachel was out somewhere with one of her friends. It was just as well. He wanted to lie down for a while, and he went into the bedroom, kicked off his shoes and closed his eyes.

When he opened them, it was clear from the diminished light outside that some time had passed, and his headache had subsided into a dull pressure behind his eyes. He went into the kitchen to get a drink of water, then wandered around both floors of the house, looking for Rachel. His wife, apparently, was still out, and when he found himself upstairs in his office, he sat down at his desk, opened his laptop and accessed his email.

There were over three hundred messages in his inbox.

*300!*

Scrolling down quickly, he saw that they were all from Patoff, the consultant.

How was that possible? He never left work with messages still pending, it was almost an obsession with him, and when he'd left his office less than—he looked at the time displayed in the corner of the screen—three hours ago, his inbox had been clear. Which meant that ever since he'd left CompWare, Patoff had sent an average of one hundred messages an hour, over one-and-a-half messages every minute. That was not merely obsessive; it was crazy.

And damn near impossible to do.

Maybe the messages were identical. Maybe the consultant had set up some sort of program to automatically resend the same message until an answer was received.

But they all had diverse subject names, and when he called up two at random, they were both completely different. Each was more than two paragraphs long.

The doorbell rang, and Matthews jumped in his seat.

Why had he jumped? Was he nervous?

*Yes.*

But what was he nervous about?

He didn't know.

The doorbell rang again. Matthews frowned. It couldn't be Rachel; she had a key. And even if she'd forgotten her key, he hadn't locked the door behind him when he'd come in. So it had to be someone else.

But the gates were closed. How could someone have gotten up the driveway?

The bell rang again, and he hurried downstairs. He reached the front door, opened it, and—

It was the consultant.

Patoff stood on the wide portico. There was no vehicle other than his own on the driveway, and Matthews wondered how the consultant had gotten here. Had he parked outside the gates, jumped over the fence and walked up the drive? It seemed the only logical answer, but why in the world would he do such a thing? It made no sense.

The consultant stood there, his expression flat. Matthews was more disconcerted by the man's presence than he wanted to admit or was willing to show, but he managed to affix a scowl to his face. "What are you doing here?" he said derisively. "This is my house."

The consultant smiled, and Matthews decided that he didn't like that smile. He had seen it before, at the office, in the context of work, and its meaning had flummoxed him then. But now, things seemed clearer, and while Patoff's expression was supposed to be obsequious, there was a mocking element in it as well. "I heard that you left early because you weren't feeling well," the consultant said smoothly. "I just wanted to check in with you and make sure you're all right. I also sent you a few emails, and I was wondering if you had a chance to look them over."

*A few emails?*

Uneasiness had given way to anger. "I went home because I had a headache. I *still* have a headache. That is why I am not at work. If I *were* at work, I would speak to you about work-related matters. But I am not. I am at home. And I did not *invite* you to my home, and if you want to continue consulting for CompWare, I suggest you leave these premises immediately."

The smile grew more obsequious. And more mocking. "I understand, sir. And I'm sorry for the intrusion." Patoff started to turn away, then turned back, as though he'd forgotten something. "By the way, just to remind you, CompWare has a contract with BFG Associates. You cannot actually fire us from the project." His smile grew wider. "Well, you *could*. But it would cost CompWare a lot of money." Still smiling, he nodded. "Hope you feel better."

The consultant, turned, walking away, and Matthews watched him, feeling unaccountably nervous.

*Why?*

He couldn't say, but he stood in the open doorway as the man strode purposefully down the drive without once looking back. When he reached the gate, the gate slid open, activated by the motion detector, and the consultant stepped through, turning right onto the street, where he must have a car parked.

He couldn't have walked all this way. It was over ten miles.

Why had that even occurred to him?

Matthews thought about the three hundred email messages awaiting him and shivered involuntarily. He wished now that he hadn't bullied the Board into hiring BFG. He'd done so out of panic, to reassure investors and the market, but he probably should have put together a team to conduct a search for the right consultant. He hadn't really had the time, though. He'd needed to act fast, to appear decisive, and the CEOs of several blue chip companies had sworn by the firm. In fact, every indication from the quick research he did was that BFG would be the perfect fit for CompWare and a solution at the very least to their perception problem.

Now Patoff was sending him hundreds of emails.

And showing up at his house.

The solution to his nightmare was turning out to be a nightmare in itself.

He closed the door, locking it this time before heading back up to his office to read through the consultant's messages.

Rachel arrived home shortly afterward, and he left off with the emails—all of which appeared to be dry descriptions of survey methodology that were of little use and no interest to him—in order to tell her that he was home early because he wasn't feeling well. As he'd known, as he'd wanted, she fussed over him and had him lie down on the couch while she made him some hot tea. She quizzed him about his headache and whether he had symptoms of anything else. He told her it was just the headache, but he did not tell her about the stress he was under or describe his strange encounter with the consultant. He wished he could talk to her, wished she were more involved in his professional life, but their relationship didn't work that way. His business was his business. Rachel would have made a great mafia wife: she cared about him, but she didn't want to know the details of his work.

If Josh were still here, he'd be able to talk to him about what was going on.

But Josh wasn't here. Everything was on *his* shoulders, and Matthews decided that the best strategy with the consultants was to just let everything run its course. Patoff was right; CompWare did have a contract with BFG. But that didn't mean that he had to implement any of the consultants' recommendations. He could tell Patoff thank you, then toss the entire report directly into the trash can. Or, more likely, he could take the raw data BFG had assembled and pass it on to *another* consulting firm to see what *their* recommendations would be.

CompWare had a whole host of options, and he didn't need to decide on any of them now. Just by hiring BFG, the freefall of CompWare's stock prices had stopped, and perception in the markets and among their business customers was that after restructuring, the company would re-emerge stronger and more competitive. In the meantime, their games were selling better than they ever had. So he had a buffer. He had some leeway.

But the consultant still made him feel ill-at-ease.

# FOUR

CRAIG WAS TEN WHEN HIS FATHER DIED OF A HEART attack, and while the loss was devastating, he'd honestly thought he could handle it. After all, his dad had been there not only for the important early years but for most of his childhood. At ten Craig was old enough to remember all the time they'd spent together, all of the things they'd done. He knew his father's memory would always be with him. So it came as something of a shock a few years later, in junior high, when the Social Studies teacher announced that they would be doing a genealogy project and he suddenly realized that he had forgotten the sound of his dad's voice. Sitting in class, he could not even remember with any clarity his father's face, although there were still pictures of him throughout the house. The realization frightened him, engendering a deep sadness that made him want to cry, and it left him feeling completely alone even in a room full of thirty kids. He went home that day after school and not only looked carefully at all of the framed photos displayed throughout the living room, family room, dining room and bed-rooms, but took out the albums from the hall closet and looked through the pictures in there as well.

It didn't help. The man in those photos was a stranger to him, someone he'd met in the past but didn't really know. Somehow, all of those memories of moments, all of those emotions and recol-lections that he'd thought would be with him always had slipped away, unnoticed, and now he was left with a hole in his history where his father should have been.

That hole had never really gone away, and it was probably why it was so important now for Craig to spend time with his own son.

So Craig resented it when Scott Cho called a department meeting Wednesday afternoon and told everyone that if consul-tants were going to be nosing around, judging the department, they all needed to protect themselves by coming in earlier, leaving later and putting in weekend hours. As far as Craig was concerned, his free time was his own, and while both he and Angie had gotten where they were by being overachievers, they'd both backed off after Dylan was born. Their priorities had changed. Angie worked only on weekends now, and last year when she was offered addi-tional hours on Thursday evenings, she'd turned it down flat. Yes, he still sometimes put in ten-hour days, and he was never far away from his phone or email, but he'd given up working Saturdays and he liked it that way and didn't want to go back.

He wasn't the only division head to object on family grounds, and when several of them brought up the fact that they would have less time to spend with their children, Scott told them, "I'm in the same boat. But we need to do this for the sake of the department. Just make sure you spend *quality* time with your kids."

"That whole 'quality time' argument is bullshit," Craig said. "Kids want quantity, not quality. They don't care *what* they do with their parents, they just want to spend time with them, and the more time the better."

"Not necessarily."

"Really? Do you remember when you were a kid? Would you rather have had a jam-packed two hours with your dad where you did fun exciting stuff, or would you rather have spent the entire day with him, just being together, going to get the oil changed on the car, stopping by the hardware store to buy some nails, mowing the lawn, doing whatever?"

"I see your point," Scott conceded. "But this is only temporary, until the consultants leave."

"And how long is that going to be?" asked Elaine Hayman, the lone woman among the division heads. "A week? A month? Six months? A year? Some of these consultants hang around and drag things out, trying to squeeze every last dime out of the companies who hire them."

Scott sighed. "Look, all I'm asking is that you make an effort to show your commitment to the company and put in some extra hours. This is not up for debate. I want every one of you to come in this weekend. I don't care what you do, but I want you here. It's non-negotiable."

That put an end to the meeting, and Craig walked out of the room with Elaine. He'd already decided that he wasn't going to inflict his own weekend requirement on Lupe, and Elaine said that she wasn't going to make her secretary come in either.

"I am," Sid Sukee said from behind them. "If I have to be here, Carrie has to be here."

"Jerk," Elaine muttered under her breath as he passed by.

"I heard that," Sid said, not turning around. "And I don't care."

Craig smiled. "What do you expect from someone in charge of phone apps?"

Elaine laughed.

Ahead, the consultant emerged from an office and strode down the corridor toward the elevator. Craig watched him. There was nothing loose or natural in the man's movements. Every step was deliberate, intentional, even when his gait gave the appearance of spontaneity.

"Hello, Mr. Patoff," said a familiar-looking woman whose name Craig didn't know.

"Hello, Natalie." He smiled at her. "But call me Regus." He waved to other employees as he continued down the hall to the elevator, greeting many of them by name.

He might have been friendly, but he was not anyone's friend, Craig thought, and he wondered how many people realized that.

"That guy's a creep," Elaine whispered. "I don't trust him."

"Thank you!" Craig said.

The consultant got into the elevator, smiling blandly out at everyone on the floor as the doors closed.

"What do you think's going to happen?" Elaine asked. "I heard that we might have to file for bankruptcy if there aren't major cuts."

"There are a lot of rumors floating around," Craig told her.

"Yeah, but what do *you* think?"

"If they hired consultants, there are going to be cuts. And, according to Phil, *these* consultants have done some serious damage to other companies they've been brought in to, quote unquote, *help*. He did a little research of his own and said BFG is known for recommending major layoffs. Among other things."

Elaine's mouth was a thin angry line. "I'm sending out résumés. I'm not waiting."

"I really think our department might be safe. I've been thinking about it, trying to analyze the situation, and they need us. I think they'll cut elsewhere."

"They don't *need* anyone. And who's to say they won't fire us and bring in newer, younger people for a fraction of our salaries?" She shook her head. "I'm sending out résumés."

It probably wasn't such a bad idea, he thought as they parted. It might even give him some leverage if his job was threatened. They might want to keep him if they knew someone else wanted him.

His stomach muscles were tight and tense as he returned to his office. He told Lupe that Scott had ordered all of the division heads to help the department put on a good face by coming in to work this weekend.

"When do you need me here?" she asked.

"I don't," he said. "I'm not asking you to come in."

"My job's on the line, too," Lupe said. "So if I have to be married to CompWare while they're doing their study, I'll do it. I'm coming in."

"It might not be such a bad idea," he admitted.

"What time?"

"Make it mid-morning. There's no real work for you to do. There's no real work for *me* to do. But we'll make sure we're seen, parade up and down until some higher-up notices us, then we'll bail."

"But Mr. Cho—"

"If Mr. Cho or anyone else has a complaint, I'll just tell them that we got our work done quickly and it didn't take us as long as everyone else because we're more competent and efficient."

Lupe giggled.

"Don't worry. We're not wasting our whole Saturday here."

At home, Angie fixed him with a hard stare when he told her he would have to put in an hour or so at work on Saturday. They were in the kitchen, and with Dylan close by in the living room, taking down the Hot Wheels tracks he'd set up earlier, she kept her voice low. "I know I'm off this weekend, but you promised to take him and one of his friends to the children's museum."

"I'll still have plenty of time."

"That's not the point. You *promised*. He's expecting to spend the whole day with you."

"Which friend did he pick?" Craig asked.

"Zack."

He grinned. "I guess I'm lucky I have to work."

She frowned at him. "That's not funny. You know Dylan's been looking forward to this all week."

"I know. But I told you, I'll go into work early and be back before the museum even opens."

"He expects you to spend the *day* with him. When you make a promise to your son, you need to keep it."

"What do you want me to do? Scott told me I have to come in. He wants the consultants to see how dedicated and committed we are."

"Are the consultants even going to be there on the weekend?" she asked.

"I don't know," he admitted.

"But you need to go anyway."

Craig took a deep breath. "He was also talking about coming in earlier and leaving later each day."

"Jesus Christ, Craig!"

Dylan poked his head around the corner of the doorway. "Are you guys fighting?"

"No, sweetie," Angie told him. "I'm just mad at Daddy's work."

"We're both mad at them."

"Well, I can't get all my Hot Wheels back in the box," Dylan said. "Can you help me?"

With a nod of her head, Angie gave him permission to leave, and Craig took it. "Of course," he said. "And after that we'll read, okay?"

"Okay!"

He *was* mad at CompWare. For screwing up that Automated Interface deal and ruining the company's reputation. For botching the release of OfficeManager, which was a damn good program. And, especially, for wasting who knew how many thousands of dollars hiring consultants who were going to decide the fates of hundreds of good workers who had dedicated their careers to the company. It wasn't fair, it wasn't right, and Matthews and the rest of upper management should have known better.

Of course, they were the same people who'd gotten them into such financial straits that they needed A.I. to bail them out in the first place.

He read to Dylan, went over his homework, and after dinner all three of them played the Cookie Game before Angie got Dylan ready for bed. Craig gave him a big hug and a kiss on the forehead. "Good night, sleep tight, don't let the bed bugs bite," he said, as he always did.

Dylan laughed, as he always did.

Angie had DVR'd one of last year's Academy Award-winning movies that they hadn't yet watched, but he didn't really want to see it, and he told her to go ahead and watch the movie herself; he had some research to do. Following Phil's example, he went online and looked up everything he could about BFG Associates.

Phil was right. The firm was a force to be reckoned with. Not only were there major corporations on BFG's client list (including Automated Interface!), but several municipalities had also hired its consultants to streamline their workforces in an effort to do more with less in these downsized times. He checked the websites of several companies for which BFG had consulted, then looked up statistics on earnings, staffing and other specific before-and-after financial information before perusing some of the ratings sites, where individuals could anonymously praise or criticize a business. BFG did indeed recommend serious layoffs for nearly all of the companies that hired them, but the surprise was that there were few corresponding complaints on the ratings sites. He'd expected to read excoriating denunciations, angry castigations, at the very least snarky critiques, but the few grievances he found were off point and off-the-wall, the work of disgruntled employees whose rants sounded so unhinged that they made the consultants seem sympathetic.

That was weird.

He wondered if BFG had a person assigned to reputation restoration, someone who sorted through websites of criticism, threatening retaliation against anything negative.

Or maybe they owned these sites.

He had no hard-and-fast evidence of anything, only a feeling that the people whose jobs had been eliminated were not as docile or accepting as the situation made it seem.

He told Phil about it the next morning as they walked in from the parking lot together.

His friend nodded sagely. "It's like *Quadrophenia* and *Tommy*," Phil said. "When I was younger, when I used to read *Rolling Stone* and all that, when music was the center of the cultural conversation, critics were always saying that *Quadrophenia* was a better rock opera than *Tommy*. They argued that the story was better, the music was better, the movie was better. I probably listened to that album twice as much as I listened to *Tommy*, trying to hear what everyone else heard in it, trying to recognize its greatness. But you know what? I never liked *Quadrophenia* much. I tried to force myself to like it, but I didn't. I'm a *Tommy* guy. It's a great album, a brilliant story, and I loved the movie."

"Your point being…?"

"Don't rely on what others are saying, don't second-guess yourself. Go with your gut reaction. It's probably right."

"That doesn't really follow from your long, involved and typically self-obsessed example, but okay."

"Fuck you."

Craig laughed.

"I agree with you, though. I certainly wouldn't be so complacent if my ass was fired. And I noticed that, too. It's hard to find anything negative about BFG. I've been trying to stock up ammunition ever since I heard they were hired, but it's nearly impossible to get details. I even tried emailing a friend of mine who works for Sprint. BFG cleaned house there a few years back, decimated the place, but he wouldn't tell me anything. Said there was a confidentiality agreement. Of course, his job was saved, so I'm sure he doesn't want to rock the boat. Still…"

They'd reached the building, and their conversation cut off instantly, without prompting on either of their parts, as though they were both afraid that they would be overheard. Or, more likely, spied upon. Craig looked up at the corners of the lobby. There were security cameras visible, and they'd probably been there forever, but he hadn't noticed them before and had no idea if there were microphones connected to the cameras and, if there were, how powerful those microphones might be.

*Big Brother's watching you*, he thought, and he might have smiled if the idea hadn't seemed so utterly plausible.

# FIVE

EVER SINCE THAT FIRST INTRODUCTORY MEETING, Craig had been receiving twice daily email messages from BFG, generic updates on the consultants' methodology. After the first few, he'd relegated them to spam and started putting them into his wastebasket without even reading them. Today, however, Matthews had sent out an email ordering everyone to pay attention to BFG's morning message, and Craig discovered that the consultants were going to be starting individual interviews with employees. Attached was an interview schedule for his division, listing the who-what-and-wheres, though there seemed to be no pattern to the schedule. Interviews were not going to be conducted based on any hierarchical or alphabetical order, and, for his division at least, all of them were going to be conducted by Regus Patoff. Craig's own interview was scheduled for noon, during his lunch hour.

So far, Patoff was the only consultant any of them had seen, and Craig was starting to wonder if "BFG Associates" was a sham, if there *were* no associates and Regus Patoff was the sole member of the firm. The idea bothered him. He didn't like the man, and he wanted to believe that the consultant had a boss, that there was someone above him, someone to control him.

*Why did he need to be controlled?*

Craig wasn't sure, but it was a sense he had, and that sense was strong.

Phil stopped by his office mid-morning. Craig was checking the schedule to see who was up—Tyler was currently being interviewed—when Lupe buzzed and announced that Phil was here. Craig went out to meet him. "I was just going to walk down to the break room," Craig said.

Phil looked him over. "Yeah. You could use some exercise."

"Hilarious." He turned to Lupe. "Do you want anything?"

"No, I'm fine, thanks." She held up a silver thermos bottle. "I brought my own tea."

"Okay. I'll be back in ten minutes," he told her.

"So," Phil said as they started walking. "When's your interview? Tomorrow?"

"Today," Craig said. "The whole division."

His friend seemed surprised. "Mine, too. Who's doing yours, Patoff?"

"Yeah."

"Mine, too. That fucker's busy, isn't he?" The corridor was empty, and they walked slowly, not wanting to get to the break room too quickly, wanting to speak freely without others around. "Have you thought about what you're going to say?"

Craig shrugged. "I'll just answer whatever questions he asks me."

"I know what I'm going to say."

"What?"

Phil grinned. "How to save the company."

"Here we go."

"I'm serious," Phil insisted. "That's the whole point of this consultant thing, isn't it? Saving CompWare? Well, it's also an opportunity for us to step up. There's no reason Matthews should be relying on the suggestions of outsiders. There are plenty of people here who have good ideas and who *know* the company. They're wasting who-knows-how-many-thousands of dollars on BFG, when there's salaried talent in-house who can do the same thing for free."

"You have a point," Craig admitted.

They reached the break room and were both glad to see that it was empty. Craig popped in a quarter and got himself some straight black coffee from the coffee machine, while Phil purchased some sort of cellophane-wrapped pastry from one of the other vending machines.

They sat down at one of the tables. Craig spotted a security camera in the corner of the room and instinctively lowered his voice. "So what's your big plan?"

"We start making things."

"Making things? We already do."

"I'm not talking about software. The future is in proprietary hardware. Look at Apple. They have the hype machine so well-tuned that every time they make some minor adjustment to one of their products, the sheep are lined up around the block to buy it. Look at smartphone makers. They inundated the airwaves with meaningless tech-sounding buzzwords like '3G' and '4G,' and now every student and secretary on the street is spouting that gobble-dygook to justify purchasing the latest version of phones they already have. What we need to do is tap into that market. We need to create some sort of mobile device that exclusively runs our games."

He grinned. "My idea? Out of the gate, we say it's '5G' to give it that must-have appeal."

"But it *wouldn't* be fifth generation."

"How many of the yokels even know that 'G' stands for 'generation'? And how many of *those* know the specific differences between generations of product? If they get a chance to lord it over the Joneses and tell everyone that they have 5G, they'll be happy."

"So, basically, you want us to make a DS."

"No. Not exactly. Ours would be connected. And this is only the basic template. I'm expecting everyone else to add their ideas, too."

Another duo entered the break room—two secretaries from another department—and by tacit agreement, they changed the subject. They started talking about TV shows, and Craig described a new cartoon that Dylan had been watching yesterday. "It reminded me of *Ren and Stimpy*. Remember that one?"

"That was kick-ass!" Phil said.

One of the secretaries frowned at them.

That was their cue, and they stood up to leave, Craig giving the security camera in the corner one last surreptitious glance before walking out the door.

"So what time's your interview?" Phil asked as they started down the hall.

"Noon."

"You're before me then. Why don't you stop by when you're through, tell me how it went down."

Craig nodded. "All right."

Curious himself about how the interviews were going, he went to see if Tyler was back in his cubicle immediately after leaving Phil. The programmer was indeed there, and when Craig asked him how it went, he did not look up from his monitor. "Fine."

There was nothing else forthcoming, and after an awkward pause, Craig asked his friend, "So what happened?"

"Oh, nothing much."

This was starting to get annoying. "Tyler," he said. "What did the consultant ask you?"

"I can't tell you." For the first time, the programmer looked up from his computer. "The interviews are supposed to be confidential. I had to sign a non-disclosure agreement."

That made sense, Craig supposed. But Tyler's attitude was defiant rather than apologetic, and something about the way his friend was acting seemed odd. It made him wonder if the consultant was going on some kind of fishing expedition, with himself as the target. He had no idea why that would be the case, but it did not seem nearly as far-fetched as it should have.

Craig wanted to ask Tyler if they had discussed him or the division as a whole during the interview, or if the consultant had merely wanted to know the specifics of Tyler's own job, but he knew that, even if he asked, the programmer would not answer, so he said goodbye and walked back up to his office. On the way, he passed a poster that had been placed on the wall of the corridor in the few minutes that he had been in the programmers' work area. It showed a comical cartoon vampire with a conversation bubble above his head saying "Give Blood!" Beneath the vampire were the dates next month of a company-sponsored blood drive and the statement "Participation Mandatory."

Mandatory? That was new. Was this one of the consultants' suggestions? Some sort of attempt to get them to come together as one big happy family? It didn't seem logical, but he could think of no other explanation.

Was this even legal? he wondered. Could a company force its employees to give blood? Not Christian Scientists, he assumed, or other people with religious objections.

It didn't matter to him—he usually gave blood anyway—so why should he care? Let the people who objected fight this battle.

He walked back to his office. *Battle*? When had he started thinking of work here as a battle? He loved his job, and he'd always been happy here. There was nowhere else he'd rather be working. But something had changed with the hiring of BFG, and it wasn't just his own mindset. When they'd had setbacks in the past, when they'd been scooped by Microsoft or been unable to come to a deal with Sony for device access, they'd always come together. In a crisis like this, they would ordinarily have been circling the wagons and rallying around the company. The insertion of consultants into the mix, however, seemed to have fragmented them, torn them apart. They were now competing for jobs and space. Rather than working together as one for the good of CompWare, they were working as individuals, against each other.

It had been a big mistake to bring in consultants.

Lupe was on the phone when he returned, and she covered up the mouthpiece with her palm, mouthing the name "Jet Hayes." Hayes was his counterpart at a rival startup and possibly the most annoying human on the planet. He was always calling up and inartfully trying to gather information about CompWare's upcoming game slate.

Craig shook his head, and Lupe nodded her acknowledgement. "I *know* it's important," she said into the phone. "But Mr. Horne is in a meeting." There was a pause. "I believe he's in meetings all afternoon, but let me check."

Smiling, Craig gave her the thumbs-up sign as he walked into his office.

"Yes he is," she was saying as he closed the door behind him.

Unsure of what he would be asked in the interview but wanting to make sure he was up to speed on everything the division was doing and able to address anything that might be mentioned, Craig reviewed all of the programmers' current projects, memorizing target dates and recent mileposts. He was getting hungry by the time noon rolled around—this *was* his usual lunch hour—and as he turned off his computer and prepared to go to his interview, he wished he'd had some sort of snack before going out to face the consultant.

There was some bottled water in the small refrigerator next to his printer, and he took a bottle out, bringing it with him. He was leaving five minutes early because he was curious to see whether Lorene Nikono, the programmer whose interview was directly before his own, would be with the consultant for the entire time allotted. "I'm going to my interview," he told Lupe. "Hold all my calls."

"Good luck. Let me know what to expect."

"I'll tell you all about it when I get back."

But maybe he wouldn't be telling her all about it. If the consultant was making employees sign confidentiality agreements, he and everyone else would have to keep their experiences to themselves and would not be able to share what happened with anyone. Such a scenario didn't sit right with him. It would seem to allow a manipulation of the process, and while he had no reason to suspect such a thing, no factual basis on which to suppose this would happen, his gut told him that the consultant could tell one person that someone else had said something bad about him and obtain negative information about both, pitting them against each other, with neither able to find out the truth.

But was that really probable?

No, but it was *possible*.

Why did he mistrust Patoff? Craig wondered. He had never been one to form snap judgments, so why had he so quickly developed an antipathy toward the consultant? Part of it was the nature of the man's job, the fact that he was here to suggest structural changes to the way the company was run and, most likely, cuts in staff. But not all of it could be put down to that. There was a more personal element involved, and he thought about the consultant's—

*cold*

—smile, and realized that even though he was in the middle of a crowded building in the middle of the day, he dreaded being alone in a room with the man.

Interviews were being conducted on the seventh floor, and Craig took the stairs up, not wanting to wait for the elevator. Opening the stairwell door, he stepped into the main corridor. He was supposed to go to Room 713, which, following the numbering scheme, should have been down the next hallway. He headed off in that direction, turned left and glanced at the numbers of the widely spaced doorways on both sides, stopping before 713.

Craig frowned. Although he'd been up here many times, he had never seen this door before. How was that possible? Was he so unobservant that he simply hadn't noticed it? No. Everything else he recognized, but the door was conspicuously out of place. It was not supposed to be here. In fact, the seventh and sixth floors of the building were laid out almost identically, and there was no corresponding doorway up on his own floor, no Room 613 (didn't architects and builders usually avoid the number 13 so as not to freak out people who were superstitious?). In its place along the analogous wall, the sixth floor had a bright red fire alarm next to a windowed square with a recessed ax and fire hose.

Already he had a bad feeling about this.

Craig knocked on the door. "Come in!" a voice called—Lorene *was* done with her interview—and he turned the knob, pushed the door open and stepped inside the room.

It was smaller than he'd expected, smaller than any other room he'd seen in the building save the supply closets, and it looked like the type of interrogation rooms he'd seen on police shows: narrow, with bare walls, and only a single metal table in the center of the open space. Patoff sat in a chair on the opposite side of the table, while an empty chair on this side was clearly meant for interviewees. There was a round black globe mounted in the upper right corner at the far end of the room: a camera.

The consultant smiled, motioning for him to sit. "This is going to be a good meeting, isn't it?"

"I thought it was an interview," Craig said, taking his seat.

"I like to call them meetings."

"Okay."

"And before we start, I think we should pray that all goes well, if that's all right with you. It's something I like to do before each meeting," he confided. "Offer up a prayer."

Craig examined Patoff's face for any indication that he was joking, but the man appeared to be completely sincere. Craig was not religious himself, and he was unsure how to respond. Was he being tested? Was this some sort of leadership assessment where he would be judged on whether he went along with the request or stood up to it? He didn't know, couldn't tell, and he sat there and did nothing as, on the other side of the desk, the consultant folded his hands together.

"Let us pray to God," Patoff said. "I like to call him Ralph." He closed his eyes. "Dear Ralph," he intoned. "Please let our meeting be successful. Amen."

The consultant grinned, opening his eyes and unfolding his hands. "That was easy, wasn't it? Why don't we begin." From his lap or somewhere beneath the table, he withdrew an electronic tablet. He touched the screen, reading. "You're married, I see. Have one daughter, Dylan—"

"Dylan's my son."

"Yes. You live at 1265 Monterey Street—"

"Wait a minute. What does this have to do with anything?" The litany of personal information was starting to make him feel uncomfortable. Of course, CompWare had his address, and it made sense that BFG would have access to that information, but it was still disconcerting to realize that Patoff knew where he lived.

The consultant didn't respond. "Favorite color: red," he continued, as though talking to himself. "Favorite food: Mexican. Favorite rock band: U2. Favorite position: missionary…"

"What the hell is this?" Anger had gained the upper hand.

Patoff put down the tablet, smiling brightly. "So," he said, "are you happy working for CompWare?"

Caught off guard, he was not sure if this was an ice-breaking question or a veiled threat. "Yes," he said.

"Good. Are you happy with the staffing of your division? If not, what changes would you make, given the chance?"

He was not prepared for these sorts of questions; he'd been expecting a more fact-based interrogation. "Staffing levels are fine," he said. "And I have a great team working under me. Off the top of my head, I can't think of any changes I'd make." Smiling, he joked, "I suppose some additional funding for the division would be nice."

Patoff had no reaction. "Are you satisfied with the way in which your division is integrated into your department?"

"Yes," Craig said.

The consultant stood, smiled. "Thank you Mr. Horne. You've been very helpful."

That was it? A few generic questions about how the division was doing? He'd been expecting to go over in detail the specific jobs of everyone within his division, and he'd planned out justifications for each staffing position and each budget allotment in an effort to keep everything intact. He'd been prepared to fight for the programmers, technical writers and secretaries, and the lack of any such discussion, the superficial nature of the shockingly short interview, left him feeling unsatisfied.

Craig stood, preparing to leave. He had not had to sign a confidentiality agreement—such a document had not even been mentioned—and he was tempted to ask about it.

But he didn't.

Either Tyler had been lying about that or the consultant was only having some people sign them—and those people would be in trouble if they mentioned the agreement's existence to anyone else. Either way, he didn't want to tip his hand, and he nodded to Patoff and walked out of the room, heading toward the elevators.

As promised, he stopped by Phil's office on the way back to his own. Phil's secretary was gone, taking her lunch, but the door to his office was open, and Craig walked right in. His friend looked up from the computer screen he was staring at, quickly clicking his mouse. "Oh, it's you," he said, relieved. "I should learn to shut that door when Shelley's gone. I was playing *Zombie Air Force*."

"To figure out a new promotional angle, I'm sure," Craig said.

Phil grinned. "Exactly." He leaned back in his chair. "So how'd it go?"

Craig told him everything, starting with the awkward conversation he'd had with Tyler, up through the room that wasn't supposed to be there, the weird prayer, and the minute or two of in-consequential questioning.

"And that was it?"

"That was it. I was dismissed."

"Huh."

"What exactly does BFG stand for?" Craig asked. "I was wondering on my way up here."

"Big Fucking Gonads?" Phil shrugged. "I don't know. A lot of times, these names are bogus anyway. They're just designed to sound good and give customers confidence. BFG could be the initials of the company's founder or just something they thought would look good on a letterhead. It doesn't really matter. What does matter is what they're doing with these interviews. I don't like the fact that your interview was so general and non-specific and it sounds like Tyler's was probably a whole lot different."

"I don't like that either."

"It makes me think they're trying some sort of entrapment strategy. Against you. They're probably quizzing the programmers about you, asking leading questions, trying to elicit negative responses, and rather than having you respond directly to whatever case they're building, your official reaction will be a general, 'Oh, everything's fine,' which will make you seem clueless and out of touch."

"You're just being paranoid," Craig said. But he didn't think that; he was just hoping for reassurance. Phil's analysis sounded dead on to him.

"I hope so," his friend said. "But my gut hunch is they're going to do the same to me. They're probably planning to cut down on middle management. Us. Maybe they'll get rid of the divisions and just have departments, with supervisors reporting directly to department heads."

"So what are you going to do?"

"In my interview? Same as you. I don't want to let on what I know. Besides, maybe they *want* me to know. Maybe this is just a tactic to get department heads to rat out employees underneath them." He shook his head. "Or maybe I *am* being paranoid."

"I think it's good to be paranoid right now. I think we need to be on our guard."

Phil grinned. "He really calls God 'Ralph'?"

"Apparently so."

They both laughed.

Lupe had not yet gone to lunch and was still holding down the fort when he returned. There'd been no calls in his short absence, and he told her she could leave if she wanted.

"So what happened?" she asked.

He told her the same thing he'd told Phil.

"That *is* weird," she said. "I'll tell you what happens when I go."

"Unless you sign a confidentiality agreement."

"At least I'll tell you that." She picked up her purse. "I'm going to Panera. Want me to bring you back anything?"

"No thanks," he said. "I'm going out myself in a while. If I'm not here when you get back, see if you can set up that meeting with Peter in Development. I still have some things I need to go over with him, and we've been playing phone tag for two days now. I think he's trying to avoid me."

"Will do, boss."

"Speaking of being your boss, if the consultant asks you—"

"You're the best boss in the world, and I never want to work for anyone else."

He laughed. "You'll go far in this business, young lady."

She waved at him as she walked away. "I'm counting on it!"

# SIX

"WE NEED TO TALK," ANGIE SAID.

Those four words were never good. Especially when they were spoken in a serious voice after Dylan had gone to bed. They usually meant that she thought Craig had done something wrong and that he was about to get a lecture.

Sure enough, Angie put down the magazine she'd been reading, picked up the remote and turned down the volume on the television. "You're spending way too much time at work. I don't like it and neither does Dylan."

"What are you talking about? I take one day off and go out with Tyler and some of the guys—"

"That's not what I mean and you know it."

He was silent.

"Even when you're here these days, you're not *here*. Where was your head at dinner? Did you even notice that Dylan ate all of the hummus I put on his plate? Dylan! Hummus!"

"That's great."

"Last night, you were online for nearly three hours. Lately, it seems like you're on that computer every night. I'm surprised you're here with me right now. And it wasn't just the one time you went out with your buddies; each day you've been coming home later and later, leaving earlier in the morning—"

"I told you, while the consultants are here I have to—"

"I get that. I do. But when Dylan was born, we agreed that we would take up the slack for each other. I make his breakfast, make his lunch, take him to school, pick him up, take care of him in the afternoon, *and* I cook dinner for all of us. You're supposed to help me out at night. You can't spend all your time hiding in your study."

"What can I say? Things are…up in the air right now. We had personal interviews today with the consultants. Or, rather, every-one *else* in the division had interviews; interviews so top secret that they were forced to sign confidentiality agreements promising they wouldn't talk about what they talked about. Me? I didn't have to sign anything. They asked me a few generic questions and sent me on my merry way. Phil, too."

"What does that mean?" Angie looked worried. "Do you think you're out?"

"I don't know. I don't know what it means. But it doesn't look good."

"Why didn't you tell me this?"

"I'm telling you now."

"But you weren't going to. You sat here in silence watching TV, and you wouldn't've mentioned a thing if I hadn't brought all this up."

He said nothing. She was right.

"We need to communicate," Angie said. "You can't just keep things to yourself. We're in this together, and we should be able to talk about it."

"You're right," he told her. "You're right. I didn't want to worry you, but that's no excuse."

She put a hand on his arm. "Should you be sending out résumés? How serious is this?"

He sighed. "I don't know. I *thought* I was safe. But this weird interview thing threw me for a loop." He shook his head. "The problem is, it's a bad time in the industry to be job hunting. That's why CompWare's in trouble. It's not just that *our* market share is down—the whole market is contracting."

"Yeah, but you have great qualifications. And you look good on paper."

"Hopefully, it won't come up," he told her. "Right now, I'm just going to ride it out and see what happens." Smiling, he patted her hand. "And I'll be there more for you guys. I promise"

"I don't think that's too much to ask."

"It's not," he said. "And I'm sorry."

She picked up the remote and turned off the television. "Why don't we go to bed."

"Why? It's kind of early. Are you tired?"

She looked into his eyes. "No."

Grinning, he stood, pulling her up and off the couch. "Let's go."

---

Angie was still asleep when he awoke on Saturday morning, but Dylan was already up and in the living room, watching cartoons. Craig put on his bathrobe and slippers before heading down the hall to the front of the house. The carpet in the hallway was getting worn in the center, he noticed. The carpet had come with the house, and Angie had mentioned several months ago that she wanted to get it replaced, but he'd put it off because he was a procrastinator. Now he didn't want to do it because he didn't know whether he would still have a job, and until the situation at work was sorted out, he thought it better to act conservatively and save money just in case.

"Hey, bud," he said, walking up behind Dylan and affectionately squeezing the boy's shoulders. "You want to help me make pancakes?"

It was one of their weekend rituals, and Dylan jumped up excitedly. "Yeah!" he said, and the two of them went into the kitchen. Craig dumped some Bisquick into a bowl, cracked two eggs, then let Dylan pour in some milk and stir. When the frying pan was hot enough, he allowed his son to ladle the batter in a roughly circular shape. With his hand over Dylan's, the two of them used a spatula to flip the pancake. A moment later, they did it again.

"Go wake Mommy up," Craig said. "Tell her it's seven-thirty."

By the time he'd spread butter and poured syrup over Dylan's pancake, the boy was back. "She's up," he said matter-of-factly. Craig heard the bathroom door close and the shower go on.

He made the rest of the pancakes himself, piling them up on a plate, then sat down to eat just as Dylan finished drinking the last of his orange juice and got up to go back into the living room.

"Hey, sport?"

Dylan looked over at him.

"You want to come to work with me this morning?"

Dylan's eyes lit up. "Really?"

"Sure. I have some things I have to do, but you can play games on my computer while you're waiting."

"Can we go on the elevator?"

"Of course. And afterward we'll go out for lunch and maybe see a movie."

"All right!"

Angie had walked into the kitchen. "What are you all-righting about?"

"Daddy's taking me to his work!"

Angie smiled approvingly.

"Even when I'm not here, I'm here," Craig said, and she gave him a kiss on the cheek. "If we're not home when you get back," he told her, "we'll be seeing a movie."

"Yeah!" Dylan said.

"You boys have a fun day," Angie said, pouring herself some orange juice. "And if you're going to the movies, bring some Purell. It's flu season. Those theaters are disease incubators."

She'd awakened later than they had, but she ate a quick breakfast and was off to the Urgent Care before either of them had finished getting dressed. Craig *did* pack a small bottle of hand sanitizer, as well as one of They Might Be Giants' children's CDs, and he and Dylan sang along to a song about balloons as they drove over to CompWare.

"I like your building," Dylan said as they pulled into the parking lot. "It's *secret*."

Craig smiled. The exterior of the building—and the interior, for that matter—did resemble the hideout of some old James Bond villain, and though his son had never seen any of those movies, it was a perceptive observation, and he was proud of the boy for making it.

Craig let Dylan swipe his ID badge to open the door, and the two of them rode the elevator to several different floors before stopping finally at the sixth. "This place is so cool," Dylan said admiringly as they stepped off the elevator.

"It *is* cool," Craig agreed.

"Daddy? Do you still have that refrigerator in your office?"

"Yes I do. And I have some bottled water in there. Are you thirsty?"

"Yeah." Dylan smiled happily.

Scott Cho was in his office when they walked by, obviously and ostentatiously looking through a printout whose information he could have no doubt easily perused online. Craig waved and said hello, smiling to himself, reminded of a scene in *How to Succeed in Business Without Really Trying* where Robert Morse came into work on a weekend, spread some empty coffee cups over the top of his desk, dumped a bunch of cigarette ashes in an ashtray, unrolled reams of adding machine paper and then pretended to be sleeping at his desk as though he'd been there all night—just in time for the boss to walk in and see him. Scott was pulling the same sort of kiss-ass ruse, and Craig realized that bringing Dylan in this morning might accidentally give him a similar sort of cachet, making people think he was so dedicated that he was coming in to work even though he had to take care of his child. While that was probably a good career move, part of him regretted it, because he did not want to be playing this game at all.

"There's your office!" Dylan said, running over.

"Yep. There it is." They walked past Lupe's work station and through the open doorway into Craig's office—

Where Regus Patoff was seated at his desk, waiting for him.

And smiling.

"Good morning, Mr. Horne. I'm glad you decided to join us today. I was just looking through your papers here and thinking that you have an awful lot of work still outstanding. I wasn't sure you'd be able to complete it all during your normal hours, so I'm very impressed that you've taken the initiative to come in today."

"I didn't give you permission to do that." He was trying to control his anger.

"What? Look through your desk? I know it may seem a little intrusive, but I assure you, it's all part of the process. How can we be expected to render an objective judgment and make viable recommendations if we don't have access to all the information we require?"

Craig was trying to remember whether he had any personal items on his desk. "I'm talking to Mr. Matthews about this."

The consultant stood. "I understand your trepidation. And go right ahead. But, as I said, it's standard procedure, and BFG Associates does require access to work product." He walked around the desk. "And who's this?" He nodded toward Dylan. "Your daughter?"

"My son," Craig said coldly.

The consultant mussed Dylan's hair. "Cute girl."

"I'm a boy!" Dylan insisted, pulling away.

Patoff smiled tolerantly. "Of course you are."

Craig stepped protectively between the two of them. "Leave my office," he said.

"Certainly, certainly." The consultant walked past them. "I'm glad you came in today, Mr. Horne. Your dedication will not go unnoticed."

And then he was gone.

Craig did not realize he'd been holding his breath until he exhaled.

"Why did that man think I was a girl?" Dylan asked.

"He didn't really."

"Then why did he say he did?"

Craig didn't know, but it was a red flag if he ever saw one, and he wondered if it was enough to get Patoff dismissed. Where exactly *was* Patoff in BFG's hierarchy? He was clearly in charge of this project, but was he the president of the firm or merely a consultant? Could he be fired from BFG for inappropriate behavior? If not, could CompWare sever ties with the consulting firm because of the pedophilic overtones of his conversation with Craig and Dylan?

He was going to look into all of it.

But right now, he needed to take care of Dylan, and he changed the subject. "Are you still thirsty?" He pointed to the other side of the office. "You can check out the fridge if you want."

Dylan immediately ran over and opened the small refrigerator door. "You have Propel!" he said. "Can I have a grape one?"

"Sure," Craig said. He smiled as the boy took out a plastic bottle, unscrewed the cap, took a drink and, as he always did, let out a dramatic, "Ahhhh!"

He'd been planning to set Dylan up with a game on Lupe's computer while he worked on his own computer in the office. But after the encounter with Patoff, he didn't want his son out in the open where the consultant could see him, so he decided to switch, and he let Dylan play on his office computer while he stood guard outside at Lupe's desk and did his work from there. Time passed quickly, and when he looked down at the corner of his screen and saw that it was almost noon, he saved what he'd done and shut everything down. He'd only been planning to work for an hour or so, and he felt guilty that he'd made his son sit there for nearly three.

But Dylan didn't seem to mind. The boy was happily engrossed in whatever game he was playing, and when Craig told him to close up shop, it was time to go, Dylan did not even look up from the screen. "Wait 'til I die," he said. "Or I make it through this level."

*Wait 'til I die.*

It was something he said whenever he was playing games and one of his parents asked him to quit, but listening to those words here, at this moment, made Craig focus on their literal meaning, and in a voice that was perhaps too harsh, he said, "Dylan. Turn off the computer now."

Startled, Dylan exited his game and turned off the machine, looking up at his dad anxiously. Craig immediately felt guilty, and he went around to the other side of the desk, picking up his son and holding him tightly. "I'm sorry," he said. "I'm tired and hungry and I didn't mean to snap at you."

"That's okay, Daddy." Dylan patted his shoulder, and the combination of words and gesture was so adult that it made Craig laugh.

"Come on," he said, putting the boy down. "Let's go get something to eat."

Holding his son's hand, Craig led the way down the corridor to the elevators. Scott Cho looked up as they passed by his office, and Craig waved at the department head, who nodded in acknowledgement before turning back to what looked like the same set of printouts he'd been examining earlier.

The nearest elevator arrived just as Dylan was about to push the call button, and Tyler Lang stepped out. Dylan pushed the button anyway. Several times.

"Tyler. What are you doing here?" Craig lowered his voice. "Did Scott wrangle you into this, too?"

"No. I wanted to catch up on something. I had an idea about one of the updates and wanted to try it out."

"Hi, Mr. Lang," Dylan said.

Tyler smiled. "Hey, Dylan. How are you?"

"We're going out to lunch and then we're going to a movie!"

"What are you going to see?"

Dylan frowned. "What *are* we going to see, Daddy?"

"Whatever you want."

There were several children's movies out in theaters, and Dylan seemed to know all of them. He quickly described the basic premises of each, then proceeded to debate out loud with himself over which one he wanted to see the most.

Tyler motioned Craig closer. "What do you think of these consultants they've hired?" There was worry in his voice…and something else. Nervousness? Guilt? Fear? Craig wasn't sure, but it seemed completely out of character for his friend, and he wondered what had prompted the query.

"First impressions?" said Craig. "Not good. That Patoff seems creepy to me, and my interview with him was just plain weird. He prayed to some god named Ralph, ticked off a list of extremely personal information about me, asked a couple of generic questions and that was it. I did not have to sign any confidentiality agreement. Neither did Phil. Why? What do you think of the consultants?"

Tyler was *definitely* nervous. He looked around as though afraid of being overheard. "I gotta go," he said.

"Wait—" Craig began.

"Goodbye Mr. Lang!" Dylan called out, and Tyler was gone.

Craig watched him hurry down the hall toward…toward where? The programmers' offices and work area was on the fifth floor, not the sixth.

Was he going to see Patoff?

That made sense. And it would explain the programmer's worries about the consultant.

"Come on, Daddy!" Dylan's constant pushing of the call button had kept the elevator door open, and Craig took one last look down the hall as the two of them stepped inside.

"Can we eat at McDonald's?" Dylan asked. "They have good toys this time."

"Sure," Craig said, smiling down at his son.

Dylan was chatting happily about movies and McDonald's as they walked out to the nearly empty parking lot and their car, but Craig could not help looking back up at the building. Although his own office window was facing the opposite direction and not visible from here, he wondered if Patoff was behind his desk once again, snooping through his stuff. Was there anything personal on his computer or on his desk that he wouldn't want anyone else to see? Craig wasn't sure, but he was going to check everything thoroughly on Monday and make sure there was nothing in his office that could be used against him. He didn't trust the consultant, and he didn't like the new rules he was being forced to play by, and until all of this blew over, he was going to make sure he was very, very careful.

# SEVEN

LUPE WAS WAITING FOR CRAIG WHEN HE ARRIVED Monday morning. "I was about ready to call you," she said. "There's a meeting of division heads right now in the third floor conference room."

Frowning, he looked at his watch. "What time is it? Am I late?"

"No. They're early. Mr. Patoff emailed me that the meeting was to start at eight sharp. I would've called you about it before, but I just got here myself five minutes ago."

Craig sighed. "Take a message if anyone calls. I'll be back when I'm back."

"Let me know what happens!" she called after him.

The door to the third floor conference room was closed, which probably meant that the meeting had already started. Slowly, carefully, so as not to disturb anyone, hoping to attract as little attention to his tardiness as possible, Craig pulled open the door.

There were no other division heads present, only Patoff, Matthews and the four remaining members of senior management. They were all seated at a long table in the front of the room, facing him like judges at a hearing, their expressions seemingly set in stone. The other tables had been removed from the room, and the only chair left was positioned directly in front of the table. Meekly, feeling more self-conscious than he ever had in his life, he walked forward across the uncarpeted floor, his shoes tapping loudly on the hard surface.

Was he going to be fired? It felt that way, though he could think of no earthly reason for such a decision, and in his mind he began preparing a defense of his position. Casually, as though unconcerned and suspecting nothing, he glanced at each of the faces in front of him, maintaining a pleasant, friendly smile. His gaze kept coming back to the consultant, in the center next to Matthews, and he thought of that farcical "interview" he'd had, readying himself to rip that sham apart and, by extension, the consultant's entire efforts up to this point.

"Thank you for coming," Patoff said as he approached.

Craig looked into the man's blank unreadable face and saw an opportunity to embarrass him in front of the company bigwigs. "Are we going to pray to Ralph?" he asked.

"We have already done so," the consultant said. "Now on to other business."

Craig hazarded a look at Matthews and the other executives, seeing no discomfiture there, only grim purposefulness on their faces.

"I was told this was a meeting of division heads." He hated the note of defensiveness in his voice but was powerless to prevent it.

Patoff answered. "We're meeting with all of the division heads individually. You're the first. Have a seat." He glanced down at a laptop in front of him and tapped a few keys. "As you know, we recently finished the initial interviews with employees in your division. They all went fairly well, with the exception of—"

*Yours*, Craig expected to hear, and he was already planning a rebuttal when, to his surprise, the consultant said, "Tyler Lang."

Craig was taken aback. "Tyler?"

"Yes. As you know, we taped each of the meetings—"

"No, I did *not* know that."

"Well, we did," Patoff said shortly, "and I'd like you to view Mr. Lang's here and give us your opinion." He typed something on his laptop and pointed to the wall on the right side of the room, where a screen had been set up. "Watch."

It was the same room where he had been interviewed, the mysterious 713, and from the angle of the shot, it appeared as though the camera had been set up at about eye-level on Tyler's left side, though the only camera Craig remembered seeing had been stationed in the upper right corner of the room. Patoff and Tyler were both sitting down, and the consultant was reading aloud from his tablet, "Favorite position: doggie style…"

Patoff smiled. "We'll pass up the preliminaries."

He sped up the recording, the two figures moving in those infinitesimally jerky motions that signified fast-forwarding. A moment later, the interview resumed at normal speed. "What do you think of Mr. Horne?" Patoff was asking.

"Craig?" Tyler snorted. "He's totally out of his depth. He doesn't know what he's doing. OfficeManager was a bust, and it's his fault that it didn't work. We tried to tell him that times had moved on, but he insisted on that clunky interface and those outdated page designs, and the whole thing looked like something from 2005."

Craig felt as though he'd been kicked in the stomach.

"But he was smart enough to tap you to fix those conceptual flaws with updates to the original program," the consultant offered.

"Yeah. Right." Tyler rolled his eyes. "He's pissed at me 'cause I called it. This is his attempt to get me out of the picture. He's set me up to fail and is going to blame me when I don't pull gold out of my ass and save his stupid program."

The consultant stopped the recording and the screen went blank. "We all know that, in addition to whatever other remedies CompWare must take, there need to be reductions in staffing if the company wishes to avoid financial collapse. What we have here is an opportunity to get out in front of things with preemptive action even before we do any in-depth analysis. This is a no-brainer. We have here an ungrateful and disgruntled employee who is obviously not giving the company his best and whose negative attitude could prove infectious. One of the easiest and most obvious decisions you will ever make is to fire Tyler Lang."

Although Craig felt hurt by what he'd seen and heard on the recording, he refused to show it. All eyes were on him, he knew, and he did not want to give Patoff the satisfaction of an emotional reaction. Besides, irrespective of his personal feelings, he knew that Tyler Lang was one of the best and most creative programmers they had. He could think of five or six employees in his own division that he would let go before Tyler. Although he had no idea why his friend had not brought up reservations about management style or program specifics to his face, and while he was caught completely flat-footed by the hostility Tyler apparently felt for him, he still thought, objectively, that Tyler was an asset to the division and to the company.

Patoff faced him. "Before I formally recommend to these gentlemen here that Mr. Lang should be terminated, I'm afraid I need your approval as the head of his division."

Craig felt a web being spun ever more tightly around him. First the ridiculous "interview." Now, it was suddenly his decision whether or not to fire Tyler. The consultant seemed to be rigging the game in such a way that he would later be able to point to Craig's choices and actions as justification for letting him go. This Tyler situation could be used against him either way, and though he had no idea why Patoff would want to set him up like this, why the consultant should have any animosity toward him, he had the sneaking suspicion that he was on the man's hit list.

He chose to take the high road. "Tyler's a good worker."

Patoff pressed a key on his laptop and the recording started up again. "Craig Horne's a douche." The frame froze on Tyler Lang's expression of contempt.

"We need him," Craig said, unfazed.

The consultant shrugged. "It's your call. But we're going to have to trim the workforce somewhere, and if you want to keep Mr. Lang on, we're going to have to find somewhere else to cut." He brightened. "I think what we need to do is conduct a work management study."

Craig had no idea what that was, but he wasn't going to give the consultant the satisfaction of admitting as much. "Fine," he said.

Matthews and the other members of his management team nodded.

Patoff smiled. "Very well, then."

Matthews stood. "Thank you for coming," the CEO said formally. "And thank you for your input, Craig. We all appreciate it."

He was being dismissed, and it was like something out of a movie. Matthews had always been precise and punctual, well-organized to a fault, but this sort of theater, with the single chair facing the row of executives and the high-handed dismissal, was not like him at all. Patoff had staged this, and as Craig stood and walked out, hearing the consultant talk about Bob Tanner, the next person to be summoned, he wondered if the other division heads would be faced with choices similar to the one he had been urged to make.

"Isn't it going to be awkward working with him now?" Lupe wondered once he had told her what happened in the meeting. "I mean, you're still his boss. Isn't that going to make things…weird?"

"A little," Craig admitted. "It'll definitely be harder for me to be objective now. But maybe it was hard for me to be objective before, since we were friends." He shook his head. "I don't know."

"I just think it's going to be tough for you two to work together. It's going to be tough for *me* when I see him. I used to like Tyler. Now he seems like a two-faced rat."

"He doesn't know that I know. That *we* know. We keep acting the way we always have, pretend like nothing's changed, and things should be fine."

"Do you think you made the right decision?"

"He's a good programmer. And it's my job to fight for my team."

Lupe smiled. "That's what I like to hear."

"I told you," he reassured her. "As long as I'm here, you're here."

"I like to hear that even more. Oh, by the way, I need to take an early lunch today. Rebecca's setting up a *Biggest Loser* thing and we all need to weigh in and chip in ten bucks. The person who loses the most weight gets the cash."

He looked at her. "Rebecca I can understand. But why are you doing this? You're thin."

"I'm starting to get a belly. I want to nip it in the bud."

"You're not going to win, you know. And those other women are going to hate you. Some of them need to *lose* as much as you *weigh*."

She laughed. "I know. But it's an incentive. I need the pressure or I won't do it."

"Take whatever time you need," he told her.

"Thanks, Boss."

Craig spent the rest of the morning doing very little work, mostly staring out the window and thinking about the changes coming to CompWare. Always before, he had viewed corporate downsizings and restructurings from the outside, but it was quite another thing to be in the middle of it, and even if he didn't have such severe reservations about the consultants the company had hired, he was not sure he would agree that CompWare needed to undergo any drastic transformation. Yes, they'd had a few flops, but those weren't *structural* problems. In fact, as several people had suggested, if they gradually shifted focus from business software to gaming, the financial situation would probably take care of itself. But Matthews and the other executives, panicked after the failure of the merger, had opted to focus not on their products but on their procedures and had seemingly put the company's fate in the hands of a consulting firm known for gutting the workforces of their clients.

There was no way this didn't end with blood on the floor.

It was an overcast day, and the grayness of the sky outside mirrored the gloom he felt here in his office. Down on the campus, he saw a woman carrying a box in two hands, heading toward the front of the building and the parking lot. Had she been fired? He doubted it—the next division head was probably just getting to the conference room right now; there'd been no time to fire anyone—but Craig definitely saw her as an omen of the future, and he watched as she made her lonely way along the path and moved out of his sight.

He had a late lunch with Phil, the two of them heading over to a Chipotle several miles away from CompWare so they could speak freely. On the way, Craig described his early morning meeting.

"He pulled the same exact shit with me. Tried to get me to fire Isaac Morales."

"You didn't fall for it?"

"Hell, no." Phil was driving and pulled into a parking space. "But then again, they didn't have Isaac on tape trashing me." He shook his head. "What's up with that? I thought you and Tyler were buds."

"I did, too. And I've been racking my brain trying to think of why he might be mad at me or resent me or whatever, but I can't come up with a thing."

They got out of the car. "I'm just wondering how he kept it so hidden," Phil said. "You didn't even have an inkling?"

Craig shook his head. "I just talked to him yesterday. Everything was fine. Or I thought it was."

"I blame BFG."

"I wish I could, too. But I've looked at it from every angle, and I just don't see how they could be behind this. For sure they're exploiting it, but I don't think they caused it."

"I still blame BFG."

They went inside, ordered, then found a table by the window and sat down.

"Regus Patoff," Phil mused. "I know that name from somewhere. I tried searching it the other day but didn't come up with anything. The only references to him I found involved BFG."

"Did we ever figure out what that stands for?"

"No clue."

Craig took a sip of his iced tea. "I need to ask you a question. And answer me honestly. Do you think we hate BFG because they're consultants and their word could end up getting us laid off, or do you think there's something particular about BFG that bothers us? I've been thinking about this. I mean, would we hate *any* consultants who CompWare hired or just them?"

"Them? The only person I've seen from BFG is Patoff. As far as I know, he's the only one *anyone's* seen. And remember what that asshole said to Dylan? No, it's definitely not just consultants in general that we hate. It's *him*."

"Maybe we should complain."

"To who?"

"You don't think Matthews would want to know?"

"Honestly? I don't. He's looking to pull this company's wiener out of the fire, and if some toes get stepped on along the way, I don't think he cares. He's the one who brought in BFG. He knows their reputation, and he's all in. This is the way he's decided to go, and my guess is that anyone who rocks the boat will be thrown overboard. The goal is to downsize anyway."

"What if we catch him in some unethical behavior?"

"It has to be cut-and-dried, and we have to have proof. I mean, what do we have so far? Acting creepy and conducting some odd interviews? He hasn't actually done anything wrong. You saw those executives this morning. They're behind him."

Craig picked up his burrito. "This isn't looking good."

"No," Phil said, "it's not."

---

"Tyler?" Angie said incredulously after Dylan had gone to bed and Craig had told her about his day. "I don't believe it."

"I can't believe it either. And I *saw* it. I keep trying to figure out if there was some way the consultant could have goaded him into it or tricked him into saying what he did."

"Do you think that's what happened?"

Craig sighed. "No. I want to think that. But no, I don't."

"I thought he was your friend. Why would he trash you like that?"

"I have no idea."

"At least they're taking your side instead of his."

"Unless they're trying to build a case against me."

Angie smiled. "Now you're just being paranoid. They didn't want to get rid of you; they wanted to get rid of him." She paused for a second, looked into his eyes. "Maybe you should have let them."

He shook his head. "Even if Tyler for some reason hates my guts, he's still one of my strongest programmers. And I need him on that OfficeManager project."

"Well, you don't need to be bosom buddies to work together. You just need to be professional."

"And I think we both can be."

"Speaking of consultants," Angie said, "they're hiring some to look at the Urgent Care."

"What for?"

"That's what we want to know. We're already making do with half the budget we had five years ago—and we have twice the number of patients. They got rid of half of the salaried employees in favor of the per diems, who flake out on us almost every weekend. If they're looking to cut, I don't what more they can do. And it's a complete waste of money. We don't have to hire consultants to 'study' the Urgent Care. All management needs to do is talk to the doctors and nurses who work there. *We* know what needs to be done."

"You think they've already made their decisions and are just looking for consultants to back them up?"

"You know I do. Those gutless wonders obviously plan to screw things up even more than they already have, only they need to have a 'study' they can point to in order to justify their actions when we raise hell." She sighed. "Their mission statement is that everything is for the patients, but they compromise patient care every time they cut our budget or do things like waste money by hiring consultants."

Craig was silent for a moment. "You don't know the name of the consultants they're using, do you?"

She smiled. "I knew you would ask that. And I wondered myself. So, yes I do. I asked Pam when she called, and she said it's some healthcare-related consulting firm called Perfect Practices."

He let out an exaggerated sigh of relief. "At least it's not BFG."

"That doesn't mean these guys are any better," she pointed out.

"I think it does," he said.

Something was up.

Craig knew it even before he went upstairs to his office. He didn't talk to anyone while coming in from the parking lot, but there was a weird energy in the lobby, an almost tangible tension that reminded him of the day the A.I. merger hadn't gone through and half of senior management had jumped out of the crashing plane with golden parachutes.

As he rode up the elevator to the sixth floor, sharing part of the journey with a silent woman he didn't know who got off on the fourth, the feeling did not go away, and when he saw half of the programming staff crowding the open area in front of Lupe's desk, he realized that whatever had happened, it obviously in-volved his division. His mind began running down scenarios as he approached. Mass layoffs was the scariest, and not one he could automatically dismiss.

But he was not prepared for the news that greeted him.

"Tyler Lang's dead," Lupe announced before anyone else could say anything.

He looked from his secretary to the programmers, part of him hoping irrationally that this was some sort of prank, though he knew it wasn't, and he asked, "What happened?"

Lupe started to talk but was drowned out by the programmers, who all answered at once. "He was electrocuted—" "It was a freak accident—" "—at his desk." "He was—" "—the OfficeManager up-dates—" "—working after hours."

Craig raised his hands. "Hold on a minute. Hold on. One per-son at a time."

Lupe pointed to Huell Parrish. "Huell talked to Tyler's wife."

The programmer was apologetic. "I'm sorry. I know I should've called you first, but—"

"Don't worry about it," Craig interrupted him. "It's fine. Just tell me what happened to Tyler."

"Well…" Huell took a deep breath. "I guess he stayed late yesterday to work on those OfficeManager updates. Lorene and I had come up with some code that we gave him to look over, and I guess that sparked something because Bev, his wife, said that he called to tell her he wouldn't be home until seven or eight. He still wasn't home by eight-thirty, so she tried calling his cell phone but got his voice mail. She tried his office number, same thing. Then, around nine, she got a call from, I don't know, the paramedics, the police, the hospital, *someone*, saying that Tyler was dead. She thought it was a joke at first, but obviously it wasn't. One of the nighttime custodians had found him at his desk, slumped over, and it looked like he'd just fallen asleep, but when he got closer, the janitor smelled something burning. He's the one who called 911. Tyler had been electrocuted."

"Oh my God," Craig said.

"Yeah. Somehow, he'd knocked over a pitcher of water on his desk—maybe he *had* fallen asleep—and the water puddled on the floor, where the power cord to his desktop had been worn through and live wires were exposed. Tyler had kicked off his shoes and was barefoot, and…he was electrocuted."

"He was dead when the janitor found him?"

"Yeah."

Craig turned to Lupe. "How did you hear about it?"

"From him," she said, nodding toward Huell. "But I called Human Resources, and they were already aware of what happened."

Craig realized that he didn't know the protocol for death. Was it his responsibility to inform the higher ups in the company if one of his employees died? No one had called *him*. How was he supposed to find out? Via email? Like he had here, from office gossip? Nothing like this had ever come up before. Maybe, if someone in his division died and he was the first person in management to learn about it, he was supposed to call Scott and let the department head take it from there, pass the buck up the ladder. He *would* call Scott after he got through here.

"I hate to be crass at such a moment," Jason said, "but that OfficeManager deadline's coming up soon, and Tyler had all the updates. We're going to need to get into his computer. Do you know his password and ID? 'Cause none of us do."

"We'll figure out something," Craig told him, and after several more moments of shocked commiseration, the programmers left, most of them heading over to the elevator, a few taking the stairs.

"I can't believe it," Lupe said.

"I can't either."

"Should we send a card to his wife?"

"And flowers," Craig said.

"I'm not sure flowers are appropriate for a death. Aren't they usually for celebrations?"

"I don't know," he admitted. "I know nothing about funeral etiquette. Why don't you research that, find out what we should do, and go ahead and do it. Maybe one card just from me and another from the division."

"I'm on it," Lupe said, sitting down and turning on her computer.

Phil was striding down the hall toward them. "I just heard. Holy shit."

"Yeah." Craig walked into his office, Phil following.

"That is freaky."

Craig had been thinking of the interview with Tyler that the consultant had recorded—

*"Craig Horn's a douche"*

—and was ashamed that he felt more shocked than saddened by the programmer's death. He'd always thought that Tyler was his friend, but over the past twenty-four hours had come to realize that he did not know the man at all. Now he never would.

How well did he really know anyone? he wondered.

"Conflicted, huh?"

Phil certainly knew *him*. "Yeah," Craig admitted. "Well, not really. I mean, not about him dying. That's horrible. But, apparently, we weren't friends, even though I thought we were. So I'm wondering if I should even go to the funeral or memorial service—*if* I'm invited—because I'm not sure he would have wanted me there."

Phil was silent for a moment. "I don't know how to say this," he said.

"What?"

"I'm not some wacky conspiracy theorist, but it seems more than a little coincidental that the guy they wanted to fire had a fatal 'accident.'" He put air quotes around the word "accident."

Craig shook his head dismissively. "Even I don't buy that."

Phil shrugged. "I'm just saying."

"Who was it they wanted to fire in your division?"

"Isaac Morales."

"Well, if something happens to Isaac, *then* I might concede that you have a point." He looked askance at his friend. "You're not serious about this, are you?"

Phil didn't answer.

"Spit it out," Craig told him.

Phil looked toward the door to make sure they weren't overheard. "You heard how he died, right?"

"Of course. He was electrocuted."

"Because he'd knocked over a pitcher of water. *And* he was barefoot. *And* there were exposed wires. And and and…"

"What are you saying?"

"Who has a pitcher by their computer? A plastic water bottle, yeah. But a *pitcher*? And who takes their shoes off at work? Has Tyler ever done that before? And is he in the habit of keeping *pitchers* of water around? And what about that conveniently exposed power cord? How much do you want to bet that it's the only cord worn down that far in the entire building? How does a power cord even *get* worn down? It certainly doesn't happen naturally."

It did seem kind of suspicious when spelled out like that, and it made Craig not quite so inclined to discount Phil's speculations. Still, Matthews had the authority to fire anybody he wanted at any time he wanted, and it strained credulity to believe that it was easier to do away with Tyler than lay him off. That seemed a stretch even for Patoff.

"He could've just had him fired," Craig pointed out. "Killing him, or arranging for him to die in some sort of elaborate Mousetrap way, seems way too complicated and just flat-out unnecessary."

"Maybe," Phil conceded. "But I say we keep our eyes open. My hunch is that this is only the beginning."

# EIGHT

IT MIGHT HAVE BEEN A FRIDAY, BUT FOR THE FIFTH day in a row, Austin Matthews left work after eight and did not get home until nearly nine o'clock at night. Jack Razon, his vice president in charge of Advertising, had threatened to quit this afternoon, and while he would be happy to see that selfish prick out the door, Patoff had told him that for the moment it would be better if everyone in management remained in place. Once the new plan had been decided upon and implemented, then the chairs could be rearranged.

So he'd spent the last two hours trying to sweet talk that pouting baby into staying, and Jack had finally had his ego massaged enough that he'd agreed not to quit.

Lights were on in nearly every room in the house when Matthews drove up, but the porch light was off, which told him that Rachel was mad at him again. It was his own fault—he should have called to tell her he was going to be late—but there was nothing he could do about it now except face the music, promise not to do it again, and hope that her hormones weren't kicking in today.

He got out of the Jag, locked it, and, ignoring the growing knot in the pit of his stomach, walked up to the darkened front porch and used his key to open the front door.

Rachel met him in the entryway. "Hello, dear. I'm glad you're home." There was no sarcasm in the greeting, which seemed suspicious until she leaned in close and whispered, "I want that man out of here."

Before he could ask who, she was leading him into the living room. "One of your coworkers dropped by. I guess he has some business to discuss with you."

Sitting on the couch was Patoff.

Why was he always on edge when he saw the consultant? He didn't know why, but he was, and Matthews entered the room with a fake smile plastered on his face. "I thought I was through with work for the weekend." He found himself wondering how the consultant had gotten here. The gate had been closed when he arrived, there was no car in the driveway, and he could not remember seeing any vehicles on the street in front of the house.

Patoff stood. "I'm sorry to bother you at home," he said, although Matthews could tell that he was not sorry at all. The consultant had *wanted* to come here; otherwise, he would have said whatever it was he was he needed to say back at the office. Even if something new had come up, there was nothing so important that it couldn't wait until Monday.

Did the man ever stop working? Matthews was beginning to have his doubts. It was difficult to imagine the consultant relaxing at home and watching a football game. On the other hand, it was very easy to envision him staying indoors all weekend analyzing data and plotting out spreadsheets on his computer.

"What do you need?" Matthews said curtly. He wanted to get this over with as quickly as possible.

There was a clipboard in Patoff's hand, though there had not been a moment before. He walked around the low coffee table. "I need you to sign this," the consultant said.

Matthews accepted the extended clipboard and looked down at the densely printed form attached to it. "What is it?"

"You can read it for yourself, but, basically, it gives BFG Associates the right to collect employee computer IDs, passwords, and email addresses for the purpose of monitoring work product. It has been our experience that when employees know their computer time is being monitored, productivity increases. They are less likely to search private interest items, update their Facebook pages, play games, do online shopping or otherwise use company time and company property for personal use. Instead, they concentrate their time and energies on completing work assignments."

Matthews was hesitant. "Isn't that a little Big Brotherish? Invading workers' privacy? It seems to me that you get more work out of a happy worker than a disgruntled worker, especially in a creative business like ours. Allowing them a little leeway and giving them a little freedom seems like good policy to me."

"If it was good policy, I wouldn't be here," the consultant said. "You hired us because CompWare is having troubles. As I'm sure you know, the courts have ruled that employees do not have an expectation of privacy in the workplace. Allowing us to monitor employee computer usage over a set period of time will allow us to more thoroughly analyze your company's work patterns and help enable us to forge a comprehensive plan for getting CompWare back on track."

Matthews glanced down at the printed form, then handed the clipboard back. "I don't want to think about this right now," he said. "Show it to me on Monday. We'll discuss it then."

"There's nothing to discuss. I just need you to sign—"

"It's—" Matthews glanced at his watch. "—nine twenty-three on a Friday night. My weekend has started."

"I understand. But if you would just—"

"Look," Matthews said. "It's been a long week. Forgive me if I need a little R-and-R, but we suffered a tragedy in our midst, and I think we deserve a little breathing room, some time to absorb it and get over it."

"Yes," Patoff said without conviction. "A tragedy. Although— not to be too mercenary about it—Mr. Lang's death does save us from having to lay him off and pay him a severance package. And, as I understand it, the company is freed from its pension obligations, as those benefits as currently defined are nontransferable in regard to spouses and families. So basically, it's a win-win."

Matthews was shocked. "A *win-win*?"

The consultant held up his hand. "I'm sorry. I didn't mean that the way it came out. All I meant to say was—"

"I'll see you on Monday," Matthews said firmly. He leaned forward. "I told you before, and I meant it: I don't want you coming to my house." He stepped aside, motioned for Patoff to pass, and followed him to the front door. He did not relax until the consultant was outside, the door shut and locked behind him. Looking through the door's peephole, he watched the man walk down the drive and out to the street, the gate opening before him. Matthews breathed an inward sigh of relief when the consultant's tall thin form was no longer visible.

He turned to face his wife. "Sorry," he said. "I didn't mean to bring work home."

"You didn't bring work home. He came here on his own." She shivered involuntarily. "I want you to know that things were getting very uncomfortable before you arrived. That man…" She shook her head, letting the sentence trail off.

"What? Did he try anything with you?"

"No." There was a pause. "Not exactly. But there was a *feeling* I got from him. Like…like…I can't really describe it. All he talked about was work, but there was something *icky* about him. I didn't like being alone with him. He's not a trustworthy man, Austin."

"He's all right," Matthews told her, though he felt exactly the same way himself. *Icky.* It was the perfect word to describe the consultant.

"I don't want him in my house."

"I told him that," Matthews said. "He won't be coming back."

She shivered again. "He'd better not."

Matthews had to go to the bathroom, but before he'd made it halfway down the hall, Rachel called out, "Austin!" He hurried back into the living room.

"One of my snow globes is missing!"

"No it isn't," he said.

"Don't tell me. I know if something's missing or not."

"Well, it couldn't have been him, if that's what you're implying."

"Why are you taking his side over mine?" Rachel demanded.

"I'm not," he protested, but in fact he was. *Why?* he wondered. He wasn't sure, but it probably had something to do with the fact that he didn't want to confront the consultant.

Was *afraid* to confront the consultant.

"What does it look like?" he asked. "Maybe you just misplaced it."

"How could I misplace it? I never move it. It's supposed to be right there on that end table."

"What does it look like?"

"A snow globe. Medium size, like the one next to the lamp there. Gold base."

"Is that it?" He saw, with relief, one matching that general description on the floor next to the couch, and he moved forward to pick it up. "See? It's not even stolen."

Rachel walked over, peered into the glass and jerked back, horrified. "That's not mine!"

"Of course it is." But as he looked more closely himself, he saw that it could not be. For within the water-filled globe was a graphic scene of naked men and women engaged in acts of sickening debauchery.

"I want that out of this house!" Rachel ordered. "And I want you to call the police!"

"I can't call the *police*," he told her.

"And why not?"

"I just can't. Not at this point. We have a contract with this guy. CompWare is shelling out major money for his firm's services, and, the situation being what it is, I can't afford to alienate our consultants by sending in cops after them. Especially when it might all turn out to be nothing."

"So you're going to let that creep steal my stuff and replace it with this...*filth*?"

"Of course not," he promised. "I'll talk to him tomorrow—I mean Monday—and get this straightened out. Don't worry. I'll lay down the law with him, and if I don't get some satisfactory answers, I *will* call the police. But I'm not going to do it now on such a flimsy premise."

"Flimsy premise? He stole one of my antique snow globes and replaced it with *that*. In my book, that's a crime, and if you're not going to call the cops, I am."

"I'll talk to him, I said."

"I want my snow globe back."

"I'll get it."

"You'd better."

"I will," he said, "but right now I have to go to the bathroom," an exit line that could not be argued with. Once again he started down the hall. He didn't like the fact that Patoff had once again shown up at his house when he had specifically forbid him from doing so. It showed that the consultant was not afraid of him, and Matthews wondered if that was the whole point of the visit.

What would he do if it happened again?

He didn't know, but just the thought of it made his palms sweat, and he thought that he'd *better* confront the man before this situation got too far out of control.

———◦∞◦———

Monday morning, Matthews told his secretary Diane to have Regus Patoff come to his office; he wanted a few words with the consultant.

Ever since waking up, he'd been thinking about what he was going to say, rehearsing in his mind the delicate matter of asking the man whether he had stolen Rachel's snow globe and replaced it with another one. It was hard to accuse someone of stealing when confronting them face-to-face. Especially someone like Patoff.

But despite what he had said to Rachel, he was certain that she was absolutely correct about what had happened. What other explanation could there be?

Why would he do such a thing, though? And where in the world had he gotten that pornographic snow globe?

How had he even known that Rachel collected snow globes?

The whole situation was unsettling.

Matthews had brought the globe to work with him, hidden in a Neiman Marcus tote bag, and now he took it out, placing it on his desk. The small figures directly before him were doing something so unnatural and disgusting that he could not bear to look at it, and with a grimace, he twisted the object half a turn to the right until he at least saw a perversion that he recognized.

"Nice object."

Matthews looked up to see Patoff standing in the doorway. If Diane had announced his arrival, the CEO hadn't heard it. Pretending as though he had not been surprised, Matthews motioned the consultant into his office. Patoff smiled, but there was no friendliness in it, no humor. It was a calculated affectation, something he wore, like his geeky and ever-present bow tie, which today matched the oddly orange-brown shade of his close-cut hair. Rachel was right. There was a *feeling* one got from the man, a feeling of wrongness, and Matthews was glad the door was open because he felt uncomfortable being alone in a room with the consultant.

*Icky*

Although he had co-founded this company, had been at its head since the very beginning, had steered it from a two-person startup into the major corporation it was today, he had never felt less in charge of CompWare than he did when he was with Patoff.

Uninvited, the consultant sat down in the chair in front of Matthews' desk.

"It is *not* a nice object," Matthews said, gesturing toward the globe. "And we did not appreciate you bringing it to our house. In fact, my wife demands that you get rid of this and give her her original one back."

The fake smile remained in place. "I'm afraid I don't know what you're talking about."

"You most certainly do." It was time to get tough. "My wife collects snow globes. And after you left on Friday, one of them was missing. This one was left in its place." He could feel himself starting to get worked up. "My wife was kind enough to invite you into our home, after I specifically told you not to come over to my house, and how did you repay her? By stealing one of her antiques and replacing it with this!"

"I told you. I didn't take it. And I've never seen this before in my life." The consultant bent forward, peering through the glass into the watery world. He pointed. "Interesting. I think that fat woman bit off that gorilla's penis."

"There were only three of us there."

"I didn't do it."

"My wife wanted to call the police. I was the one who convinced her to wait."

The consultant straightened. "I can guarantee you that they will find no evidence that I had anything to do with this. But if she really wants to find out what happened, calling the police is probably a good idea." He met Matthews' gaze, and Matthews knew that there *would* be no evidence found linking Patoff to the theft, though the man was most certainly responsible.

What kind of game was the consultant playing?

"I *am* calling the police."

"Good."

"And I forbid you to come to my house anymore," Matthews said.

"You forbid me?"

The consultant's tone was mocking, but Matthews ignored it. "Yes," he said angrily. "I've already told you that. And if you don't pay attention this time, you will be prosecuted for trespassing. Do I make myself clear?"

The smile was back, and this time there *was* humor in it. "Of course. It's my fault for assuming that you weren't just a nine-to-fiver and that you took your work home with you. I thought, since you hired us, you were the type of man willing to do whatever it takes to bring this company back from the brink. I apologize." He stood, bowing formally.

There was no way to answer that have-you-stopped-beating-your-wife statement, so Matthews didn't even try, and he stood there ineffectually as the consultant left his office.

It had been a mistake to hire BFG. He knew that now. But there was nothing he could do about it. He was hemmed in not only by the contract CompWare had with the consulting firm, but by market perception, which could torpedo the company's stock if investors got any inkling of unsteadiness. At this point, in fact, he'd probably be *willing* to pay the charges and penalties stipulated by the contract in order to get rid of Patoff. But even if he could get the Board to agree to that drastic action, such a move would send their stock straight into the toilet, and with things as precarious as they were, he doubted that even the best PR campaign would be able to turn the situation around.

He might be able to get Patoff reassigned, however. He had no idea whether there was anyone above Patoff in the consulting firm, but if he could interface with someone else, that would go a long way toward making his life easier.

On second thought, maybe it wouldn't be so bad if Patoff was arrested for theft. That sort of internal problem wasn't something he had any control over, and if CompWare remained with BFG despite the scandal, thereby minimizing its importance, they'd probably be able to ride out the storm.

The phone on his desk buzzed. Diane. He pressed the intercom button. "Yes?"

"Your wife is on the line," the secretary told him.

"Thanks." He picked up the phone. "Hello? Rachel?"

"I found it," she told him, and he could hear the relief in her voice. "My snow globe. It was in the cupboard under the sink in the guest bathroom, where we keep the toilet paper."

"Under the bathroom sink?"

"Yes."

"Did you put it there?" He already knew the answer.

"Of course not!"

"Did *he* go in that bathroom?"

"That's the weird thing. No." She sighed, indicating that it was all a mystery to her. "I don't know *how* it got there."

He didn't know how it got there either—but he was pretty sure he knew *who* had put it there.

They talked for a few more moments, deciding jointly that it would be pointless to call in the police over such a small matter, and when he asked what he should do with the globe in his office, she told him to throw it away. "Don't donate it or anything. No one should have the disgusting piece of trash. Throw it away. Better still: break it and throw it away so it can't be rescued."

"Okay," he said. "I will."

He hung up, looking for a moment at the object on his desk. It was just possible that the consultant hadn't had anything to do with hiding Rachel's snow globe, but he was the only one who could have brought in this perversion ball.

Unless it was one of the help.

The more he thought about it, the murkier things seemed, and he realized that there was no way he could prove to the satisfaction of the Board, let alone BFG, that Patoff had done anything necessitating his removal. On impulse, he decided to call Morgan Brandt, the CEO of Bell Computers and one of the men he'd relied upon for the initial recommendation, to see if Brandt had had any problems with the consultant. Brandt said he hadn't, begging off when Matthews asked for details by saying that he was really busy and didn't have time to talk. He and Brandt were contemporaries, had come up about the same time and were allies rather than rivals, and to his knowledge the Bell CEO had never lied to him. But Matthews didn't believe him now, and he hung up the phone, troubled.

Looking into the snow globe on his desk, he saw a miniature man bent over and trying to fellate himself.

Disgusted, he picked up the object and dumped it into the wastepaper basket on the side of his desk.

# NINE

ANGIE KISSED BOTH CRAIG AND DYLAN GOODBYE BE-fore heading off to the Urgent Care. Still eating breakfast, they waved to her from the table.

Sometimes she resented having to work on the weekend. She knew they needed the money—especially these days, with everything up in the air at Craig's company—but Dylan was six now, and she felt increasingly guilty about missing weekends with him. This should be family time. They should be doing things together, all three of them, and each passing Saturday made her realize that these were not days she could get back; once they were gone, they were gone.

Life was passing quickly.

Still, she did enjoy her job, and it gave her great satisfaction to know that she was helping people, that she was making a difference, that what she did mattered.

There was a traffic jam on the way—road construction that had been going on forever and that she should have known enough to avoid—but she still arrived earlier than any of the other nurses, and as she pulled around to the employee's parking area at the rear of the building, she saw that there was already a line of patients in front of the closed front entrance. She let herself in the back door, and turned on the lights and computers. Dr. Bashir arrived, followed by two other nurses who were scheduled to work this morning. Nina Tranh phoned in and said she wouldn't be able to make it today—at least she *called* this time—but by the time Angie had logged on and clocked in, everyone else had arrived and was setting up.

Before they opened the doors to the patients, another man came in through the employees' entrance, accompanied by Pam, the Urgent Care's office manager. They all knew instantly who the man was, and Angie shared a glance with the other nurses. *This was the consultant who would be deciding their fates?* He looked like he'd been beamed directly out of *Revenge of the Nerds*. On his head was the worst toupee since William Shatner's *T.J. Hooker* rug, and he was dressed in clothes so geeky that they had *never* been in style. Skinny and nervous, he wouldn't meet anyone's eyes but stared down at the clipboard in his hand as Pam introduced him.

"This is David Morris. He's with Perfect Practices, the consultants that have been hired to study our operation here. He'll be with us for the next several weeks." The man nodded in assent. "Today, though, he's just going to get a feel for the place, observe what everyone does, find out how everything works, so I want you all to pretend he's not there and go on about your business as usual. He won't get in your way, and you probably won't even notice that he's there."

Pam then asked if there were any questions. Angie didn't have any, but even if someone else did, there was no time to have a discussion about it because they were already a minute late opening up, and they could all see through the thin window of smoked glass on the right side of the front door that there was quite a crowd out there. It was going to be a busy day.

And it was.

The consultant started out by parking himself in a corner of the waiting room and observing the admittance procedures, but Angie had no idea what he did after that. Nor did she care. She had her own work to do, and as long as he stayed out of the way and remained inconspicuous, she didn't give him another thought.

All of the exam rooms were occupied and stayed occupied throughout the morning. She dealt with a dog bite, an ear infection, strep throat, hives, an allergic bee sting reaction and two cases of stomach flu before carving out a minute to herself for a quick cup of coffee in the oversized closet that acted as the break room.

Sharon, the nurse who usually acted as her second, poked her head around the corner. "Dr. London needs you in room six."

Angie gulped down the rest of her coffee. "Coming."

The woman in exam room six had a hemorrhoid so swollen that it needed to be pierced and drained. Sharon wasn't there, but Dr. London was, and he left for a moment while Angie helped get the woman into a gown and into the proper position for an examination. The woman was young and thin—which was unusual in such a case—but she was in considerable pain, and when Angie saw the size of the hemorrhoid, she understood why. The doctor determined almost instantly that it required lancing, and he prepped the necessary instruments and anesthetic while Angie had the woman lay on her side, facing the wall.

Without warning, the door opened, and the consultant walked in, holding a clipboard and pen. After taking in the situation, he had to have known that his presence here was inappropriate, but he made no move to withdraw. Standing awkwardly in the center of the small room, he stared at the patient's buttocks as though transfixed, and Angie was horrified to see that the crotch of his pants conspicuously tented outward.

The doctor said nothing and made no move to have the man ejected, so Angie, moving to block his view, took it upon herself. "You need to leave," she said firmly. "This is private."

"I'm sorry," the consultant apologized, stumbling as he backed into the closed door. "I didn't mean to..."

His face was red with embarrassment and his attempt to open the door so clumsy that she almost felt sorry for him. But then she thought of the intrusive way he'd stared at the patient's exposed rear end, her eyes flashed downward for a second, and she was disgusted to see that he still had an erection.

Herding him out into the corridor, she closed and locked the door behind him before once again assisting the doctor with the patient's hemorrhoid treatment.

Pam had specifically said that they were to ignore the consultant and allow him to observe their practices and procedures, so Angie half-expected to be called into the manager's office and chewed out, but that didn't happen, and she continued to work nonstop until there was a slight lull and she was allowed to take her lunch shortly after two. Not having packed anything, she planned to walk across the street to Subway, and when she saw Sharon in the break room, pouring a cup of coffee, Angie asked if she wanted anything. Sharon hadn't taken a lunch yet either, but said she was fine.

"What's up with that consultant?" Sharon asked. "*He's* supposed to tell us how to run the Urgent care? I get creeped out everytime he even looks at me. You know, he came in to watch us examine this woman, and I think he was checking her out. Very unprofessional. I mean, if this is the best they could find…"

"I know what you mean," Angie confided. "We had a woman with a hemorrhoid, and he wasn't just checking her out, he had an erection."

"Oh my God."

"Yeah." She looked at her watch. "Anyway, I've got to get going. I only have a half-hour. You sure you don't want anything?"

"I'm good."

"Okay." Angie walked out the door, turned left—

And ran into the consultant.

His face was red, and he immediately looked down at the floor, mumbled an apology and hurried around her. He'd heard them talking! She wasn't sure whether he'd been spying on them or had accidentally overheard their conversation, but either way, he was obviously embarrassed, and she felt bad that they had hurt his feelings. *She* felt embarrassed, and she was grateful that after she returned from lunch and for the rest of the busy afternoon, she did not see him.

At home, Craig and Dylan surprised her with a pizza for dinner. The treat was more for them than her, but she was tired and not in the mood to cook, and she appreciated the gesture. She would have appreciated it even more if they had tried to make something themselves, but Craig was not one of those spouses who was into cooking, and his *very* occasional culinary efforts were always unqualified disasters.

Pizza was fine.

She talked about the consultant as they ate but left out the details in front of Dylan, only telling Craig what had happened after their son had left the room. He chuckled. "Well, it looks like we got both ends of the spectrum when it comes to consultants, didn't we?"

"I'm not worried about my job or anything," Angie said. "I have seniority and I'm an RN. But I do worry that they're going to reduce staffing, which will definitely affect my workload. And I do feel bad for that guy. He's all shy and nervous. Kind of a Barney Fife character. This is probably his first job, and now I've made it uncomfortable for him…"

"He was being inappropriate."

"Yeah, but he's probably, like, an accountant, who doesn't see things like that everyday."

Craig grinned. "Her ass was that good, huh?"

She slapped him playfully, but she could tell from his train of thought that he wanted sex tonight. She did, too, and after putting Dylan to bed and catching up on a couple of TiVoed shows from earlier in the week, they both decided to retire early.

She fooled him, pretending she wasn't in the mood, but once they were under the covers and next to each other on the bed, she pulled down his underwear, reaching for him. Her hands were cold, which made him shrink, but she liked that. She preferred to start when he was small. She enjoyed feeling it grow in her mouth, and, as always, she experienced a feeling of accomplishment and satisfaction as he hardened under her oral ministrations. When he was ready, she pulled away, lying back and spreading her legs, and he entered her roughly, grabbing her buttocks and thrusting with increasing intensity until they both came simultaneously, moaning into each other's open mouths as they kissed.

—⊗—

The consultant was supposed to be at the Urgent Care on Sunday as well, but he wasn't, and Angie wondered if he had chickened out after overhearing their conversation yesterday. She definitely resented the presence of a consultant in their midst, but she still felt sorry for him after what had happened, and she was determined to treat him fairly and decently despite her prejudices.

Things weren't quite as hectic as they had been on Saturday, but the Urgent Care was still pretty crowded, and Angie was kept busy. There was a small rush at midmorning, the waiting room full to standing, and Elise at the admissions counter asked her to check if any of the exam rooms were open so they could get a few more patients in. One through four were in use, as were six and eight, but room seven was clear. The door to exam room five, weirdly, was not only closed but locked. There was no chart in the slot, and she asked Cindy when she walked by whether anyone was in the room.

Cindy frowned. "Not that I know of."

The door opened, and the consultant came out.

Had he been hiding in there all morning?

*Had he been masturbating in there?*

That was mean, and she was ashamed of herself for even thinking it. Her antipathy to the entire idea of consultants was making her pick on this pathetic guy who was only doing his job, and she felt guilty about treating him so badly. Red-faced and mumbling, he tried to skirt around them, but Angie stepped in his way, stopping him.

"Listen," she said, apologizing. "I'm sorry if any of us have been rude to you while you've been here. Part of it, as I'm sure you can see, is that we're so busy we don't really have much time to socialize. But part of it, I admit, is because we don't like the fact that they've hired a consultant to spy on us and then make recommendations about changing the Urgent Care."

"Observing," he said quietly. "I'm observing, not spying."

She smiled. "I know. But it's just that… Well, we don't need anyone to tell us what's wrong with our operation here. We know. We know better than anyone. And we resent the fact that they've hired someone else to find out instead of just asking us." She shrugged. "At least, that's how I feel. But it's not your fault, and we shouldn't take it out on you, and I'm sorry if we were…mean."

It was his turn to smile. "That's okay. I understand."

"No hard feelings?" she asked, holding out her hand.

He shook. "None at all."

"All right, then." She pulled away without making it too obvious. His grip was limp and sweaty, and while she wanted to wipe her palms on her uniform, she restrained herself—though the minute he was out of sight she was going to rub on some hand sanitizer.

"Thanks," he told her. "I need to see Dr. Bashir." He was still smiling as he walked toward exam room eight, but it was a sad kind of smile, and Angie couldn't help feeling sorry for him.

She hurried back up to the admissions counter. "Five and seven are both open," she told Elise.

# TEN

IT WAS THE MIDDLE OF THE MORNING AND LUPE, BACK from break, knocked once on the doorjamb before walking into Craig's office. "I have something for you. A message. Special delivery."

He saw that she had in her hand a blue sheet of paper. She handed it to him across the desk. "It's from Austin Matthews himself, and it's not just an email but an official memo. You don't see those much anymore."

Craig read it over. It was addressed to all department and division heads.

In an effort to assist BFG Associates' comprehensive study of CompWare's staffing, practices, processes and procedures, each employee is hereby required to provide BFG with work-related email addresses, computer IDs and passwords so that consultants can access all of the information they need to construct a complete picture of our operation. It is the responsibility of each division head to record and collect these addresses, IDs and passwords, and pass them on to the appropriate department head, who will be responsible for providing them to a BFG consultant upon request.

He looked up. "Did you read this?" he asked Lupe.

She nodded. Glancing behind her to make sure they were alone, she lowered her voice. "Is it even legal?"

"I don't know," he admitted. "I assume so, because anything this all-encompassing would have to get a pass from the company's lawyers."

"I don't like this."

"I don't like it either. I don't want those consultants to have access to my personal information. Not that I use this computer for anything personal," he added. "I'm too paranoid for that. Everything on here's strictly business. But…" He let the thought trail off.

"I know," Lupe said. She lowered her voice even further. "Besides, I still don't like Mr. Patoff."

Craig smiled. "Join the club."

She shifted uncomfortably on her feet. "So do we have to do it?"

"I don't know. Probably. But, hey, who needs privacy, right? It's overrated anyway."

"As long as I can keep my guns. That's the only right I need."

He looked at her, surprised. "You have guns?"

"It's a joke," she told him.

"Oh. Anyway, don't do anything about this yet. Not until I call around and make sure what's what. I know a couple of people who'll make waves and definitely won't take this lying down."

"Mr. Allen?"

Craig chuckled. "Yeah, Phil would be one of them. So let's make sure it *is* legal before we start goose-stepping. And don't tell any of the programmers about this yet, either." He thought for a moment, reconsidering. "I take that back. *Do* tell them. Just in case they need to…"

She smiled. "Erase some evidence?"

"Well, I wouldn't put it that way."

"You're a good boss, Boss."

"I try." Craig read the memo again as she walked out to her desk. He was tempted to call Phil right now, but he really *was* feeling paranoid and wouldn't be surprised to learn that Patoff had had all of their phones bugged. He and Phil were already meeting for lunch, however—away from CompWare at what was quickly becoming their weekly Chipotle strategy session—and he decided to talk over the memo with his friend at that time.

Meanwhile, there was work to be done, and he quickly read through today's accumulated emails. Once again, his inbox was filled with subject lines like "Learn the Secrets to Good Anal Sex" and "Download Real Snuff Videos Free!" and he was glad he'd stopped having Lupe sort through his messages after that first trap the consultants had set. He answered his few legitimate emails, then accessed the latest updates to OfficeManager. While Tyler's death had been terrible and shocking, this was big business and the cogs still had to turn, so Craig had handed over control of the OfficeManager updates to Huell, senior programmer on the project. Obviously seeing this as his chance to grab the brass ring, Huell had been adding changes almost daily, surpassing even Tyler's impressive output. Today, two buttons and a page were gone, making three separate functions more intuitive and easier to use, and Craig thought they were pretty close to being able to show Scott where they were at. They were at least a week ahead of schedule, and in this environment, that would be a big feather in the department head's cap.

And in his own.

He started to write an approving email, then decided instead to go down to the programmers and tell Huell in person, but before he could even get up from his seat, Lupe was back in his office. "You're wanted in the first floor conference room."

"What for?"

"Mr. Matthews has called a meeting of senior staff."

"Another meeting? Jesus Christ. That's all I seem to do now is go to meetings."

She smiled at him, but there was worry in it. "Let me know what happens."

"I don't think it's going to be—"

"Let me know what happens."

She was more worried than she'd been letting on, and he said, "Of course I will."

They hadn't talked in detail about BFG and the future of CompWare, he realized, other than the occasional oblique reference and some laughing-in-the-face-of-danger jokes, and he wondered what the scuttlebutt was amongst the secretaries. Theirs was a network of information-sharing far more broad and accurate than the circumspect conversations he had with other members of management, and it was long past time that he sit down with Lupe and find out what rumors were being spread. When he returned from this meeting, he was going to tell her everything that went on, and they were going to have a real discussion about what was happening at CompWare. It was condescending of him to tell her only the information that would reassure her or that he thought she should know. They were in this together, and he was going to make sure that he was more open and honest from now on.

At least half of the supervisors, managers, division heads and department heads were already in the conference room when he arrived. Matthews stood in front of the room, next to the podium. Beside him stood Regus Patoff. On the other side of the consultant was a bearded man Craig had never seen before.

"Do you have any idea what this is about?" Craig whispered, sitting next to Phil.

"No clue."

Elaine Hayman sat down on the other side of him. "Kind of weird that he called it at the last minute, isn't it?"

"Again," Craig said.

Phil shrugged. "I think this might be the new normal."

Matthews started talking. There was no preamble; he didn't wait until the room had quieted down. Craig wasn't even sure everyone had arrived. The CEO simply began speaking: "I started CompWare twenty-three years ago with a small group of friends and colleagues. It has since grown far beyond my wildest imaginings. But something was lost in that…" He grasped for the right word. "…*diffusion*. What was lost? Camaraderie. We're a business now rather than a family, which I guess is the way it's supposed to be, but…" He trailed off, didn't resume immediately, and people began looking around at each other.

Matthews glanced over at Patoff, then cleared his throat. "The Board and I have decided that, in an effort to get to know one another better, all members of middle and upper management will attend a mandatory weekend retreat. This will give us a chance to spend some time together outside of work, quality time, and allow us to get to know one other. Reacquaint ourselves, perhaps."

Hands in the audience immediately went up, and rather than continue on, the CEO pointed to someone in the front row. "Yes."

"Why are we doing this?" It was Neal Jamison, head of the Finance department. "We've never done it before."

Patoff answered, stepping forward. "We are only in the preliminary phase of our study, but one thing we've noticed so far is a lack of communication among senior staff. In an effort to combat this, we have proposed some bonding exercises, and we suggested to Mr. Matthews and the Board that a weekend retreat would be the fastest and most efficacious way of addressing the situation."

"*We?*" Phil whispered.

Craig raised an eyebrow, taking his point. Patoff was still the only consultant either of them had seen, leaving them to wonder whether BFG even *had* any other employees. Apparently they did, and Craig studied the man standing next to Patoff as the consultant fielded another question about where the retreat was located and what the "bonding exercises" actually entailed. Patoff explained that BFG had access to an off-season student science camp that they often rented just for this purpose, and that there were games and collaborative activities specifically designed by psychologists to bring together people who ordinarily interact only within a corporate setting.

The bearded man remained unmoving, not looking at either the consultant or the CEO, not looking at the audience, not looking anywhere in particular. He didn't seem like a consultant, Craig thought, and he definitely didn't seem like a psychologist. With his black beard, leathery skin and rugged mien, he had the look and affect of a park ranger or lumberjack, someone who worked outdoors, and Craig was about to raise his hand and ask who the man was, when Patoff said, "Maybe I should introduce you to the person who's been assigned to lead this little expedition." He nodded toward the other man. "Dash," he said.

"Hi," the man said. "I'm Dash Robards."

Craig glanced over at Phil to see his reaction. *Dash?* his friend mouthed silently, and the raised-eyebrow look on his face was so comical, it was all Craig could do not to laugh.

"A little bit about myself: I've been an avid sportsman my entire life. Grew up tracking and hunting in the rugged pine country around Juniper, Arizona. I served as an Army Ranger, and after that spent several years as a wilderness guide, leading Elk hunting expeditions in the Yukon. Five years ago, I went back to school and received training in conflict resolution and therapeutic group dynamics. Upon graduation, I was hired by BFG to conduct wilderness exercises and to facilitate bonding excursions such as the one you will be going on. What we'll be doing this weekend—"

"*This* weekend?" Jack Razon exclaimed.

Robards looked over at Patoff, who nodded. He turned back to face the crowd. "Yeah, this weekend."

"I can't go this weekend!"

There was sudden cacophony as a chorus of voices protested the timing of the retreat.

Matthews took charge again. "This isn't voluntary," he reminded them. "This is mandatory. You are all going on the retreat. I'm not asking you—I'm *telling* you. Reschedule what you have to reschedule, rearrange your plans as necessary, but make sure you get this weekend off. We'll be leaving Friday afternoon and returning Sunday evening. I will accept no excuses, not even illnesses. Anyone who does not attend will no longer be working for CompWare. Do I make myself clear?"

The room was silent.

"Good." Patoff was grinning. "Go on, Dash."

Craig tuned out the rest of the discussion, already trying to calculate the logistics in his head. Angie would have to take the weekend off, which she wouldn't be happy about, but she was never voluntarily absent and had almost perfect attendance, so that was probably doable. What concerned him more was Dylan. He wasn't sure how he was going to break the news to his son. Despite the hours he spent at work, all of the early mornings and late evenings, he had never before taken any sort of business trip, and since Dylan's birth, they had spent every night under the same roof. The thought of not doing so for the first time filled him with a piercing melancholy, and if breaking their streak bothered *him*, he could imagine how hard Dylan was going to take it. He had to come up with a gentle way to tell the boy the news. *Maybe a bribe*, he thought, and decided that the Saturday after the retreat, they would go to Disneyland. That meant Angie would have to take *another* day off—but this one even she would consider worth it.

Convinced he had enough good news to balance out the bad, Craig felt better, and he listened to descriptions of role-playing games and crafts projects and what was apparently going to be the main activity of the weekend: a "wilderness expedition." They all sounded stupid and pointless, but he nodded along with everyone else to show he understood the plan, and on the way out of the meeting shared a silent look with Phil that told him his friend felt exactly the same way.

It was too risky to talk here, too many ears, so they split off in the corridor with the unspoken understanding they they'd discuss it all at lunch.

Lupe was at her desk when he returned, filling out some paperwork for HR regarding Tyler's position, and he asked her to join him in his office, shutting the door behind her. Offering her a chair, he described the meeting, told her about the weekend retreat, then said that he was worried about the direction BFG seemed to be steering the company and the impact it could have on employees.

"So what have *you* heard?" he asked her.

"Why?" He could hear the worry in her voice. "What have *you* heard?"

"Nothing really. That's why I'm asking you." He smiled. "Everyone knows secretaries have the best gossip."

There was a pause, a hesitation. Was that a flicker of suspicion in her eyes? Did she think he was asking in order to test her loyalty to the company? Or because he was trying to ferret out a leak? Or because he'd been asked to spy on her?

He quickly disabused her of any such notion, and she claimed that nothing like that had even occurred to her, but he knew that it had, and the fact that BFG had managed to drive even a small wedge between them, and do it so quickly, left him feeling vulnerable.

"Look," he said, "I'll be honest with you. They're not telling the division heads anything. And with the way my 'interview' went, I'm pretty sure I'm on the outs with the consultants."

"I thought you said we're safe." The worry was back again.

"I don't think my job's on the line. Or yours. I was honest about that. I'm not even worried about funding for our division, really. It's just…I don't know. I don't like the way things are going, and I'm trying to get a handle on it."

"You're a good boss, Boss."

Maybe she *hadn't* been suspicious of his motives, maybe she'd always believed him. But if that was the case, *he* was the one who'd been suspicious of *her*. Either way, Patoff had come between them, and the ease with which that had been accomplished worried him.

"I wasn't joking about secretaries' gossip. I hear things you don't, but they're mostly the party line. You hear things I don't, and I think they're probably a lot more accurate. If we pool our information and act as each other's eyes and ears, I think we'll be ahead of the game."

"Okay," she said, and stood. "So you want me to go out and do a little recon?"

He laughed. "That's my Lupe."

"I have an idea. It's about those passwords and everything. But I may be gone for a little while. Do you want me to let calls go to voicemail or…?"

"Just transfer everything from your phone to mine. I'll take care of whatever comes up."

Nothing did come up, and she popped back a half-hour later, closing the door behind her. "I just talked to Pauline—Pauline Praeger? In Legal?—and she said that as soon as they got the memo, the attorneys immediately started looking to see if they could be required to comply."

"So what's the verdict?"

"It's legal. I guess the Supreme Court issued some sort of ruling about privacy in the workplace, and…well, there really isn't any. Employers hold all the cards and employees pretty much have to do as they say."

"We all better be careful," he told her. "And make sure your IDs and passwords on personal devices, even at home, are totally different than the ones here at work. I don't trust those guys, and I wouldn't put anything past them."

Lupe didn't question that assumption—which told him a lot.

"Pauline asked about that 'work management study' they're supposed to be doing. Are they still going to do it? Did they already start? What's going on with that?"

"I don't know," Craig admitted. "But I don't think that's underway yet. From what I understand, they're going to assign people to observe us at our jobs. I'm not sure how that's going to work, exactly, but there'll probably be someone sitting in a chair in my office and by your desk, watching us and taking notes."

"That's going to be uncomfortable."

He sighed. "Yeah."

"So we should probably try to look busy, even during down times."

Craig allowed himself a small smile. "I'm sure Scott will be sending us a memo to that effect in the very near future."

"At least we found out that Mr. Patoff's not the only consultant they have. I was beginning to think he was."

"Me, too," Craig said.

"Did Mr. Matthews tell you guys how long this is going to go on, how long they're going to be here?"

"No. In the back of my mind, I'm thinking it's a six-month contract, but I don't know where I got that from. For all I know, the consultants are here indefinitely."

"So we'd better just get used to living under the occupation."

"For now," he said.

He was hoping to discuss things with Phil, but his friend called just before Craig was about to head out to lunch to let him know that he was unable to get away. "Garrett just asked me to put together a sales report in time for a meeting this afternoon."

He was being circumspect on the phone—just in case—so Craig was, too. "All right," he said casually. "Later."

But as he left alone to grab a burger at In-N-Out, he could not help wondering if someone had noticed that the two of them usually went out to lunch together—and if Phil's assignment had been specifically timed to put a stop to that.

———— ∞ ————

"*You're* breaking it to him," Angie said after Craig told her about the weekend retreat. "I'm not doing it."

He nodded and glanced into the living room, where Dylan was writing treasure hunt clues on Post-It notes. He understood why she was annoyed, but it wasn't his fault. He didn't *choose* to go on this retreat. Emotion trumped logic every time, however, and even though he had emphasized that this was a requirement, she still blamed him. Dylan would, too, he knew, and he tried to think of the best way to explain it to his son.

Looking up from his writing, Dylan waved at him with a go-away motion. "Stay in the kitchen!" Dylan yelled. "Don't come out 'til I tell you!"

"Okay. Sorry." Craig backed away, moving over to the sink, where he picked up a glass and got a drink of water out of the faucet.

"You're not here all week," Angie said, keeping her voice low. "The least you can do is be there for him on the weekend."

"You think I want to do this?"

"You could call in sick, you could—"

"I can't," he said. "I have to go." Although he wondered what would happen if he really *was* sick. Could he get out of it that way? No. Matthews had specifically said that anyone who didn't go on the retreat would no longer work for CompWare.

They heard Dylan moving from the living room to the hallway, hiding his treasure clues.

"Besides," Craig said, "this is the first time this has ever happened and, hopefully, the last. I'm *always* there for him. And even though I work during the week, I'm home every night to tuck him into bed."

He knew how defensive he sounded, but he felt surprisingly emotional about this issue. Angie must have been able to tell, because she sighed. "I know," she said. "I just don't like the fact that I have to call in sick to cover for you."

"This is a one-time thing."

"Can you guarantee that?"

He couldn't, and she knew it. Luckily, Dylan ran excitedly into the kitchen at just that moment, saving the discussion from deteriorating back into an argument. "Time for your treasure hunt, Daddy!" He handed over a Post-It, and though Craig had intended to talk to his son about the weekend, he decided to do the treasure hunt first. He looked down at the note in his hand. "Go to the bookcase." He did so, and saw a yellow Post-It stuck to the third shelf that said, "Go to the bathtub." He did, and found another yellow square telling him to check under "Mommy's pillow." Ten notes later, he was crouched down on the floor, looking under Dylan's bed, where a final note attached to a single square of Starburst candy leftover from Christmas announced: "Here is your prize!"

He unwrapped the Starburst, popped it into his mouth and gave the boy a hug. "Thanks, little buddy."

Dylan grinned. "I knew you'd like it. Can we read now? I wanna finish the book before Friday."

Craig smiled. "So you can beat Karen?"

"I beat her three weeks in a row! Now she says she's gonna beat me. But if we finish the *Droon* book and then speed through the next *Bailey School Kids*, there's no way she'll win."

"Sounds like a plan." Craig sat down on the bed, patting the mattress next to him to indicate that Dylan should sit, too. "But we need to talk about this weekend."

"Are we going to go miniature golfing? You said we could! Can I invite Toby?"

"Uh… not this weekend."

"How come?"

Craig looked down into his son's innocently hopeful face. Now that the time was here, he was finding it harder to explain than he'd thought it would be. "I have to go somewhere this weekend. For work."

Dylan didn't seem as upset as he'd expected, although maybe it was just taking time to sink in. "Where?"

"It's kind of a camp. In the mountains. Mr. Allen's going, too. And most of the people I work with."

"Mr. Lang?"

They hadn't told Dylan that Tyler was dead, and Craig wondered now if they should have. "No, not Mr. Lang," he said simply.

"Can I go?"

*Here it comes.* "No. It's only for grownups."

Dylan was silent for a moment. "How long is this camp?"

"The whole weekend. I'll be gone Friday night, all day Saturday, and won't be back until Sunday afternoon."

"You won't be here to brush with me?"

They brushed their teeth together each night, a ritual for both of them.

"No. I'm sorry."

"I don't want you to go."

The honesty of the plea made Craig's heart ache. He felt guilty, and he put an arm around Dylan's shoulder and brought out his big gun. "Why don't we go to Disneyland next weekend? Me, you and Mommy. All three of us."

"What if you have to go to another camp?"

He hugged his son's shoulder more tightly. "I won't." And he repeated the hopeful sentiment Angie had not let him get away with. "It's only this one time."

"I still don't want you to go."

"I know. But it's only this weekend, and the time'll be over before you know it. And next weekend we'll go to Disneyland."

"Okay, Daddy." It was resigned acceptance, but it was still acceptance, and it was a more mature response than he'd been expecting. The two of them got off the bed and walked back out to the living room, where Angie was turning on the TV to watch the local news.

"Daddy's going to be gone this weekend," Dylan told her.

Angie nodded sympathetically. "I know, sweetie."

"But at least we get to go to Disneyland next week."

"What?" Angie shot Craig a look over their son's head that made him realize he should have talked it over with her first.

"That's what Daddy said." Dylan looked back at him with an expression of worry.

"We are," Craig assured him.

"Good! Oh, wait, I forgot my book! Me and Daddy are going to read!" he told Angie. He turned and ran back down the hall to his bedroom.

Angie fixed him with a hard stare. "Disneyland?"

"We haven't been for over a year. I thought it would be nice."

"You're not getting any tonight, mister," she told him.

But he knew he would, and he did, and afterward they both fell asleep, tired, sated and content.

# ELEVEN

THEY LEFT FRIDAY AFTER LUNCH, ON A CHARTERED bus. The retreat was in the San Bernardino Mountains, a good three hours away, and the fun started almost immediately after they pulled out of the parking lot. Bonding exercise number one was a participatory sing-along. Not "99 Bottles of Beer on the Wall" or "John Jacob Jingleheimer Schmidt," but an equally simple, equally repetitive, equally annoying song that involved making each person sing a verse alone before joining in with everyone else on the refrain. Craig felt obligated to participate, but Phil, sitting next to him, felt no such obligation, and, when it was his turn to chime in, he continued to play *Angry Birds* on his phone, ignoring the high-pressure silence around him until the song moved on to Jack Razon across the aisle. Inspired by Phil, more and more people dropped out, and by the fourth round, there were only a handful of diehards still singing. By the time they reached Pomona, the bonding exercise was history and everyone was reading, texting, talking to friends or otherwise doing his or her own thing.

Craig stared out the window at the passing scenery as they headed up into the mountains. It was supposed to be spring, but the landscape outside looked like winter. There were patches of snow on the rocky ground, and the only trees that didn't look dead were stunted asymmetrical pines growing from cracks in the cliff.

Twenty-two people were on the bus, including Matthews. Dash Robards had gone ahead and was preparing the camp for them. Patoff was not coming, and Craig found himself wondering what the consultant was going to do while they were gone. Granted, the retreat was taking place over a weekend, but he had the sneaking suspicion that they'd been scheduled to leave Friday afternoon so the consultant could do...*something* in their absence. He still didn't like the fact that BFG had access to all of their passwords and email addresses, and he imagined Patoff moving from office to office, snooping through computer files, reading saved emails.

He himself had nothing to be ashamed of, nothing private on any of his work machines, but he could understand why other people might. They all spent so much time at CompWare that sometimes it was probably necessary to conduct personal business during office hours. Hell, if he didn't have Angie and she didn't have the work schedule she did, he'd probably be doing exactly the same thing.

He felt a nudge in his side, and Phil passed over his cell phone. On the screen was a Googled image of the place they were headed. Neither Matthews nor anyone else had revealed the name of the camp where they were going to spend the next two days. It was as if the location of the retreat was purposely being kept secret, and more than a few conspiracy theories about that had spread around CompWare over the past few days. But Phil had accessed satellite photos of the road they were on, had cross-referenced any student science camps that might be located in the area, and had come up with an aerial photograph of a log cabin compound in the woods. There seemed to be a large main building, a lodge, and, arranged in a square behind it, twelve smaller cabins bordering an open area that featured a wooden stage and a rock-ringed fire pit.

Phil took the phone from him, called up another screen and handed it back. "*Camp Ponderosa,*" Craig read, "*was established in 1959 and has provided generations of Southern California school-children with the opportunity to study geology, botany and zoology in a natural setting. Sleeping in comfortable cabins, hiking on well-maintained trails, eating freshly prepared food in a communal dining hall, students are able to experience life in the mountains for an unforgettable weeklong adventure!*"

Craig handed the phone back to Phil. "I guess that's where we're going, huh?"

"I believe so."

"Looks nice."

"Yeah." Phil didn't sound convinced.

The road continued to wind up the mountain. Twenty minutes later, they were passing through a small hamlet filled with ski shops and tourist traps, and twenty minutes after that they were on a one-lane road winding through the trees toward Camp Ponderosa.

The photo Phil had accessed must have been taken some time ago, for while this was indisputably the same location, the buildings looked considerably the worse for wear, and their dilapidated state was reflected in the poorly maintained grounds. The camp looked abandoned, and Craig wondered exactly what Dash Robards had been doing up here to get the place ready.

Nothing, so far as he could tell.

There was a car parked in the small lot in front of the main lodge, and the bus pulled next to it. Craig stood, along with most of the other passengers, but before they could gather their belongings, the driver said, "Listen up!" Addressing them as though they were children, he explained that he would return to pick them up on Sunday. "I will be here at one o'clock sharp," he said. "I expect everyone to be ready and on time. We will depart at one-thirty. If you are not on-board at that time, you will be left behind and will have to arrange for your own transportation back."

"No one will be left behind," Matthews promised them.

"Yes they will."

"No," Matthews said, and there was steel in his voice. "They won't."

"I don't know who you think you are…" the bus driver began.

"I am the CEO of this company."

"Well, I don't work for you. I was hired by Mr. Patoff, and his instructions were very specific."

Matthews was angry now. "Mr. *Patoff* works for me. I hired him to consult for my firm."

"And he hired me. Piss and moan all you want, old man. I arrive at one, I depart at one-thirty and anyone late will be left behind. Now get the hell off my bus. I'm leaving."

There was shocked silence. Craig had never heard anyone talk to Matthews that way, and obviously, the CEO hadn't either. He didn't know how to respond other than to order everyone off the bus. Gathering his own luggage, he pointed a finger at the driver. "I'm making a phone call," he said. "I'm having you fired."

The bus driver snickered. "Yeah, good luck with that."

Matthews and the four remaining members of senior management got off the bus first, everyone else following, passing by the unmoving driver who stood staring at them with a smirk on his face. "Wow," Phil said as they stepped off the steps onto the ground.

Craig hazarded a look at the CEO who was off to the left, in a huddle with the Board and angrily gesticulating. Craig was disturbed by what had just happened, though he was not immediately sure why. At first he thought it was just ordinary tribalism, a variation of the old I-can-criticize-the-people-in-my-group-but-outsiders-can't attitude, and it took him several moments to realize that what really bothered him was the fact that the encounter made Matthews seem diminished. He'd been under the impression that the CEO was the ultimate authority at CompWare, but all of a sudden Patoff seemed to be the man in charge. Matthews may have hired BFG, but, here, at least, the consultant was the one calling the shots, and the thought of Patoff having such power chilled him.

Reasserting his authority, Matthews called out, "Everyone follow me! We're checking in at the lodge!"

There was no TV here, Craig learned almost immediately, and no internet access. Even their phones didn't work, although it wouldn't have mattered if they had, because Robards—*Dash*—confiscated everyone's electronic devices as they entered the building. "You won't be needing those crutches," he said. "We're going to be spending some *real* time together."

The main lodge did have electricity from a generator, although the cabins housing their individual sleeping quarters did not and relied on battery-powered camping lamps for light.

They checked in by signing a guestbook page that had already been pre-printed with their names. The guestbook was located on top of an expansive oak desk, and once a person found his or her name on the list and signed on the line next to it, Robards would hand over a laminated nametag with the person's first name in white letters on a red background.

The lodge was divided into two main rooms: the one they were in now, sort of a cross between a hotel lobby and a living room, and a larger mess hall filled with rows of picnic tables and flat unuphol-stered bench seats. Unlike the exterior of the building, the interior was kept up nicely. There were rustic throw rugs on the wooden floor, comfortable-looking chairs and couches, polished wooden coffee tables and end tables, and a rock fireplace.

Once all electronic devices had been collected and everyone had signed in, Robards directed them to a bulletin board on the wall to the right of the desk where cabin assignments had been posted. Craig moved forward through the crowd to find his and saw that he was in Cabin 3 and paired up with Elaine Hayman. The pairings were purportedly random, but he noticed that no friends had received cabin assignments together. Moreover, it appeared that people had invariably ended up with individuals who were either their temperamental opposite or were of the opposite sex. There were only three female division heads out of all of the de-partments, and none of them were assigned to bunk together. At least he and Elaine got along, which was more than could be said for Phil and Parvesh Patel, who were going to be spending the next two nights with each other.

A chorus of complaints greeted the cabin assignments, but Matthews held up his hand and said that this, too, was part of the bonding experience and was a way for his management team to broaden their social horizons within the company and get to know co-workers with whom they might otherwise not associate.

Elaine smiled at Craig somewhat queasily. "I hope you don't snore."

Each cabin had a small bathroom containing a sink, toilet and tiny shower stall. "There is no hot water," Robards warned them. "So be prepared. The water's *cold*."

Their bathroom door did not have a lock, which probably wouldn't be a problem, but it contributed to the sense of uneasiness Craig felt. He let Elaine pick the bed she wanted, and she chose the one closest to the bathroom, which meant that he got the one by the window, although the glass was so dirty and dusty that he could barely see out of it. He placed his single small suitcase on the floor and sat down on the bed, feeling awkward. They were to get settled and then meet everyone else in the lodge in an hour, but until then they were on their own, and the room felt small and cramped to him, the space too intimate. "I'm going to check outside," he said, and when Elaine, opening her suitcase, nodded acquiescence, he could see the relief on her face. She wasn't enjoying this any more than he was.

He wished he could call Angie and Dylan. He'd suspected there might not be cell phone coverage out here, so he'd warned them that he might not be able to talk to them, but he hadn't suspected that his phone would be confiscated. He wondered if that was legal. Even if not, he didn't plan on making waves about it. He had the feeling that there were going to be a lot of other things coming up that he objected to, and he needed to pick his battles carefully.

The air was cool and crisp, the sky bluer than it ever got in the Los Angeles basin, the trees almost tall enough to be redwoods. It was like something out of a PBS nature show. The area was beautiful, and he thought that maybe some weekend he'd bring Dylan up here. Especially when there was snow on the ground. The boy had never seen snow outside of a picture book.

A few other people emerged from their cabins. Scott Cho wandered over to the fire pit, lighting up a cigarette.

"I didn't know he smoked," Elaine said behind him, and Craig turned around.

"I didn't either," he said.

Elaine smiled. "Another reason not to like him." She took a deep breath, though he couldn't tell if she was enjoying the clean air or having a hard time breathing because of the altitude. He could definitely feel the lack of oxygen up here.

"Kind of a small cabin," Elaine said.

He nodded. "It's weird," he admitted. "Do you want to switch with someone else?"

She shook her head. "I'm not sure we can. Besides, there aren't a lot of people in management I get along with." She motioned toward Scott, ostentatiously exhaling smoke. "I might get stuck with him."

Craig chuckled. "We'll make it work," he said.

"I never doubted it."

More people were emerging from the cabins—there wasn't a lot to do inside—and some were making their way toward the lodge. Phil came out of Cabin 6, yelling something at Parvesh, who remained within.

"God, that guy's an asshole," he said, walking up. "I'm done bonding. Let's get the hell out of here."

Elaine smiled. "Only forty six hours to go."

Phil sighed. "I've died and gone to hell."

Jack Razon and a couple of other people from Advertising were already walking across the overgrown grass toward the lodge. Craig nodded in their direction. "Shall we?"

The three of them made their own way through the open square. Inside the main building, Elaine excused herself and walked over to Robards to ask if there was a restroom she could use. Garrett Holcomb, Phil's department head, waylaid him to ask about sales projections for a product Craig was not involved with, and Craig wandered around the big room, looking for something to do.

Although he hadn't noticed it before, a primitive record player sat on the floor underneath a picture window that looked out on the cabins. Next to the record player was a stack of LPs. He crouched down. The album on top, by Randy Newman, was titled *Good Old Boys*, and the cover featured a blurry photo of what looked like John Belushi and Tammy Wynette with their arms around each other. Randy Newman was one of those guys Craig didn't know much about. He'd heard of him, and knew he was supposed to be a respected songwriter, but the only music of his that Craig could remember hearing was the theme from *Monk*.

Flipping through the stack of remaining records, he finally found one that he recognized: U2's *The Joshua Tree*. It was the second CD he'd ever bought, though he'd never seen the vinyl version before, and he picked it up, intrigued by the size and heft of the album.

Phil came over, having extricated himself from the conversation with Garrett. "What are you—?" he began, then his eyes widened as he saw the stack of records. Dropping down next to Craig, he started sorting through the pile. "CCR!" he exclaimed, pulling one out.

It was a greatest hits collection, with multi-colored foldout silhouettes of the band members' faces on the cover. Craig looked at a list of song titles on the back as his friend withdrew the album from the inner sleeve. "Oh. Those guys," Craig said. "All their songs sound the same."

Phil was putting the record on the turntable. "You don't like Credence?" He seemed astounded that anyone could hold such a view.

Craig shrugged. "I don't know. They're all right, I guess."

"Well, you gotta listen to 'Proud Mary.' I want you to tell me if I'm crazy. Because everyone thinks it goes, 'Big wheel keep on turnin'/Proud Mary keep on burnin,' but what John Fogarty really sings is 'Big wheel keep on *boinin*'/Proud Mary keep on *boin*.' It makes no goddamn sense, but I swear to God that's what he says. No one believes me. I've told this to a million people, and they all think I'm full of crap, but now I have a captive audience, and I'm going to prove it."

Turning on the record player and placing the needle in the groove, he held up a hand as the song began, pointing to the spinning album as the line approached. "See?" he said immediately afterward. "See?"

"Could be," Craig admitted.

"Could be? It is!" He picked up the needle, moved it back and put it down. "Listen again. That's no 'T' sound. That's a 'B.' *Boinin'*. And the second time he says '*boin*.' Listen."

Craig wasn't sure if he was simply buying into his friend's delusion, but it *did* sound like the singer was singing "boinin'" and "boin."

"He's right," Dash Robards said from behind him, and Craig nearly jumped. He stood up. A crowd had gathered around, and Phil happily played the section of song again, telling everyone what to listen for. He asked if they'd heard what he heard, and they all seemed to agree that he was right.

"Victory is mine!" he declared.

The last few stragglers, including Matthews and the four remaining members of the Board, had arrived, and Robards moved to the center of the room, holding up his hand for everyone's attention.

"We're going to play a little game before dinner," Robards announced.

There were audible groans.

"No, this'll be fun. It's Speed Conversation, a game where everyone gets a chance to talk to everyone else—for twenty seconds. It's quick, but it's personal, and this will enable you to get to know one another in a way that you probably have not during your encounters at work. What I'm going to do is separate you into two groups. You will stand in concentric circles, with the inner group remaining stationary and the outer group moving clockwise. Each participant from group one will ask a question of a corresponding member of group two, who will answer that question in twenty seconds or less. Then group two will move on. Afterward, the circles will switch places. Everyone is to answer honestly and no one is to take offense. There will be no repercussions for anything said here tonight. This is your chance to say whatever you want. So," he announced, "if I tell you that you are in Group One, please move to the right side of the room. If I place you in Group Two, please move to the left side of the room."

Robards hadn't been quite correct, Craig realized. They wouldn't actually be interacting with *everyone*, only those on the opposite team. He watched as Robards started separating people into the two groups and noticed that he did so by looking at nametags and then at a sheet of paper in his hand. Was there a strategic reason for each placement? he wondered. Had Patoff ordered Robards to place specific people in a specific group for a specific purpose? He wouldn't put it past the consultant, and when he saw that he and Phil and Elaine were all part of Group Two, he started looking at who else had been chosen, trying to see if he could detect a pattern. He couldn't. There was no consistency of department or managerial level or anything that he could detect—although the fact that Matthews was in Group One led Craig to believe that his own team consisted of those who were on the outs.

Or the whole thing could be completely random.

What was with Robards' sheet of paper, then?

He didn't know. Maybe this was a head game Patoff was playing. Maybe he *wanted* them to think—or overthink—the stability of their positions.

Following Robards' direction, Craig's group formed a circle in the center of the large room, each of them facing outward. Around them, Group One formed a larger circle, facing in.

Craig found himself opposite Matthews, and when Robards blew his coach's whistle, the CEO asked him, in an unexpectedly reflective voice, "What do you think of the decision to hire consultants?"

He had to answer immediately, didn't even have time to wonder why Matthews would ask such a question, and he said, "I don't think they were necessary. I think the Board could have made decisions about the company's future based on information gathered in-house."

What did he see in Matthews' eyes? Affirmation? Agreement? Craig didn't know, but he couldn't ask his own follow-up because the whistle sounded again, and a second later, the CEO was gone, replaced by Garrett Holcomb.

Eventually, he would have a chance to ask a question of everyone in Group One, and Craig bided his time until the groups switched places and he was once again face-to-face with Matthews.

"Are you sorry you hired the consultants?" Craig asked.

"I don't know," Matthews said, and there was a pause. "Maybe."

The answer was honest, and Craig wondered if he had shared that with anyone else, if the CEO had canvassed the room, trying to get a sense of his management team's opinions of the consultants.

But there was no time for him to follow up, no time for Matthews to elaborate, and the whistle blew again. He moved to his right and found himself facing Sid Sukee. "What are you thinking about?" Craig asked.

"When I was a teenager. The first time I came in a girl's mouth. I'd only jerked off before that, and it was so amazing to me that there was no mess! I didn't have to aim it or think about it or hold back or anything. I just let it happen. I spurted and spurted, and she swallowed it down, and that was it, done, all clean."

The whistle blew, and Craig nodded politely and moved on, remembering why he never spent much time with Sid. Or, indeed, most of the other members of management. These were people he worked with, not his friends, and the truth was that he saw no real reason for them to bond emotionally. They didn't need to be buddies, they just needed to do their jobs and interact in a professional manner when necessary.

After the game ended, he was hoping to find a moment to speak with Matthews further, but this retreat seemed to have been scheduled down to the second, and they were all ushered into the mess hall, where a wrinkled gnomelike old lady, barely four feet high and wearing a patch over one eye, was placing a final plate of food on the farthest picnic table in the last row. She shuffled toward the open door that led to what had to be the kitchen.

"As you can see," Robards announced, "my wife has prepared dinner." He smiled at the stooped old woman. "Thank you, Edna."

Craig glanced over at Phil.

*Wife?* his friend mouthed.

"Please find a seat and begin eating," Robards instructed. "You have an hour."

There were no set seating assignments, so Craig pulled out the nearest bench and sat down at the end of the table. Phil sat next to him. Dinner consisted of fried chicken, french fries, a small salad and a roll, all on a metal plate more suited to a mining camp. The food was cold, and the water in the tin cup next to the plate was warm. He wished they had something stronger to drink, or at least something with more flavor than water, because he was having a hard time getting the odd taste of the salad out of his mouth, though he'd had only a single bite.

Bob Tanner was on the other side of Phil—Craig wasn't sure where Elaine was sitting—and that made him leery of speaking freely, but he had to tell Phil about his speed conversations with Matthews. Keeping his voice low, he explained that the CEO had brought up the subject on his own, asking if CompWare should have hired BFG. "And on the next round," Craig whispered, "when I asked him if he was sorry he'd hired the consultants, he said, 'I don't know. Maybe.'"

"So even he's having second thoughts. That's a good sign," Phil said.

"What's a good sign?" Bob Tanner asked.

They changed the subject to something vague and boring, let it die off, then got down to eating the truly god-awful food.

After dinner, after chores had been assigned ("What is this?" Phil asked, *sotto voce*. "Betty Ford?"), after two of the department heads had cleared the tables while two others performed dishwashing duties, Robards led everyone outside to where benches had been set up around an already lit bonfire. Craig expected a pep talk or a seminar-style lecture, but instead Robards told them a horror story (Phil again: "Are we ten years old?"). It wasn't very scary, but it was site specific, the tale of a boy who had been left behind at the camp some fifty years ago, had disappeared and become a cannibal, and who now snuck into the cabins of unsuspecting visitors to kill and eat them while they slept. The story seemed designed to be interrupted by someone jumping out at a prepared moment to frighten the listeners, but that didn't happen, and the story ended, and they all dispersed.

On his way back to the cabin, Craig looked at his watch. Dylan was in bed by now, and he felt sad that he hadn't even been able to call and say goodnight.

In the dark of night, it seemed even more awkward and uncomfortable to be sharing the small room with Elaine. He turned on the light while she locked the door behind them. The beds seemed closer together than he remembered.

"Do you need to use the bathroom?" Elaine asked.

He shook his head.

"I shower at night," she informed him.

"That's fine," Craig said. "I take mine in the morning."

"Do you mind if I…?"

"Go ahead," he told her.

She opened up her suitcase, took out some clothes, presumably pajamas, and went into the bathroom, closing the door. A moment later, he heard the water turn on.

He had always liked Elaine, but she was a work friend, someone he only saw at the office, and then only occasionally. If pressed, he probably wouldn't have even had an opinion as to whether or not she was attractive. But hearing the water run in the shower, knowing that only five feet away, behind the thin wall and the door without a lock, she was naked, made him realize that, yes, she was attractive. It was a random thought and completely natural under the circumstances, but merely acknowledging to himself that she was naked and so close made him feel creepy. And disloyal to Angie. The fact that Elaine was unmarried didn't help, and he quickly opened his own suitcase, changed into his pajamas and got into bed. The water turned off, and he closed his eyes, pulled the blanket tight, rolled over to face the opposite direction and tried to fall asleep before she emerged from the bathroom.

# TWELVE

IN THE MORNING, WHEN CRAIG AWOKE, HIS BOWELS were full to bursting and he desperately had to go to the bathroom. He didn't want to do it here, just a few feet away from Elaine's bed, where the entire process could be heard—and smelled—so he tried to hold it until she got up and went out for breakfast. She was a late sleeper, though, and the pressure was building, and finally he was forced to give in. Trying not to awaken her, he picked up the jeans he'd been wearing yesterday, took a clean shirt out of his still-open suitcase and crept around the foot of her bed, opening and closing the bathroom door as quietly as he could. He turned the shower on, hoping the noise of the water would cover him, then sat down on the toilet and did his business quickly. Taking off his pajamas and hopping into the stall immediately afterward, he cried out at the shocking coldness of the spray. There was no way he could survive a shower this freezing, and he turned off the water immediately and patted himself dry with the bathroom's lone towel, still damp from Elaine's shower the night before.

He'd forgotten to bring his razor and comb into the bathroom, and, after dressing, when he opened the door to get them, Elaine was awake. "Are you through in there?" she asked. "I need to change."

Acutely conscious of the smell, Craig closed the door behind him. "Almost," he said. He hurried over to grab his bag of toiletries, and after shaving and combing his hair, liberally sprinkled his aftershave in the corners of the small room to cover up the stench.

"All yours," he said, coming out.

Breakfast was made not by Robards' wife but by three division heads, who had been assigned to cook and serve oatmeal and orange juice. Phil was going to be one of two people on cleanup duty. Craig's assigned chore was to help prepare lunch. There wasn't a lot of conversation as they ate, though whether it was because people were sleepy and grumpy or whether it was because they had nothing to say to one another, he could not tell. He, Phil and Elaine kept their conversation to a minimum as well, pressured into silence by those around them. There'd been little or no shoptalk on this retreat, Craig reflected, and that was surprising to him. At the very least, the weekend would seem to offer the opportunity for everyone to discuss practical work matters in a pleasant setting and in a leisurely manner.

While Phil helped clear tables, Craig went into the kitchen with Jenny Yee from Accounting and Alex Mendoza from Promotions. Waiting for them, on the opposite side of the room from the sink and dishwasher where bowls, glasses and utensils were being carefully stacked, was the stooped and wrinkled old lady who'd cooked and served their dinner last night.

Robards' wife.

This close to the patch-eyed woman, the pairing of the two seemed even more odd and impossible. She was old enough to be his grandmother, and her voice when she spoke was a mannish croak. "I'm going to teach you how to make a sandwich," she said. "If you listen, you'll learn something. If not, the Lord will damn you to hell." She let out a cracked glass chuckle, though whether because that was a joke or because she found it amusing to think of them burning in hell, Craig could not tell.

The old lady's instructions were exceedingly easy and the resulting sandwich extremely unappetizing, but she made them repeat the steps in unison over and over again before allowing them to try and make sample sandwiches of their own. Grimacing, Craig placed a slice of white bread on a plate, put a thin slice of head cheese on the bread, spread a knifeful of liverwurst on the head cheese, then placed another slice of white bread on top before slicing the sandwich in half.

There was no way Craig was going to eat that sandwich, but luckily it was to be accompanied by a snack-sized bag of potato chips. Since he was going to be one of the people preparing the lunches, he could probably snag himself an extra bag or two. Not much of a meal, but definitely better than that god-awful sandwich.

Their work was inspected by Edna, who informed them that she might not be here at lunchtime and they could be on their own—which was why she was drilling the instructions into their heads.

"Don't think I won't hear about it if you make them wrong," she warned. "And if you do, the Lord will damn you to hell." This time, she didn't laugh, but grunted and hobbled away, leaving them to walk, bewildered, back to the dining room.

Everyone else was already outside, gathered in the open area between the lodge and the fire pit. Robards was laying out the day's schedule.

"Today," he announced, "we're going on a wilderness expedition. It's a character-building exercise that requires trust and cooperation. Together we will explore the local terrain while engaging in goal-oriented tasks that, believe it or not, will improve your interpersonal skills back at your office and will help you immeasurably in your everyday life."

Craig had sidled next to Phil. "Yeah, right," his friend muttered.

"You will be divided into the same groups as yesterday. Each group will be out for approximately four hours. I will take Group Two in the morning, and Group One in the afternoon. Those remaining behind will participate in a scavenger hunt. Afterward, each of you will be required to write a story incorporating the items you've scavenged."

A chorus of groans and complaints greeted the news.

"I'm not going to do it," Jack Razon announced.

"That is a decision you will have to make for yourself," Robards said, and from his tone of voice Craig understood that there would probably be repercussions for those who did not participate, particularly once the news had been reported back to Patoff.

"I'm going to write a story about fucking his wife's ass with the objects I find," Phil whispered, and Craig could not help laughing. "Wait 'til he reads the pinecone scene."

"The scavenger hunt will be overseen by Mr. Matthews, who has agreed to help out today. He won't be going on the hike or participating in the scavenger hunt himself, but I've trained him to conduct the session, and since this retreat is his baby in the first place, he knows what he wants from you."

The CEO nodded, although he did not look as though he was enjoying this.

*What do you think of the decision to hire consultants?*
Craig was feeling cautiously optimistic.

Robards clapped his hands. "It's getting late and we'd better get going. Group One, follow Mr. Matthews back to the lodge to obtain your list of scavenger items. Group Two, get yourselves some canteens or water bottles and meet me back here in five. Move out!"

It was closer to fifteen minutes than five by the time everyone had procured enough water for the hike and Robards had checked to make sure they were all wearing appropriate footwear. He had strapped on a backpack, and they followed him up a dirt path that led up a gently sloping hill between tall pine trees and spreading manzanita bushes. The ground gradually flattened out, the trees grew thicker and more varied, and the trail disappeared under an encroaching blanket of dead leaves.

An hour later, they stopped under a sycamore to rest for a few moments and drink from their canteens and water bottles before continuing on. Moments later, Robards stopped again. "Here's where we leave the trail," he announced. "Follow me."

He led them around an outcropping of lichen-covered rock and through a closely growing copse of bushes. "Watch out for stickers," he said. "Those branches have thorns."

"Where are we going?" Elaine asked.

"We're looking for spoor and scat. I'm going to teach you how to locate an animal in the wild."

"What exactly *is* spoor?" Phil asked.

"Tracks," Robards answered simply.

"I can guess what scat is."

"Droppings," Robards responded.

"I was going to say shit, but same difference."

"Keep your eyes open," Robards said. "And trained on the ground. Do any of you see anything?"

Parvesh Patel, who had wandered a bit off to the right, pointed. "That looks like dog poop," he said.

Robards walked over, motioning for everyone else to follow him. "It is, indeed."

"Do you think it's a wolf?" asked Jenny Yee, nervously looking around.

Robards touched his finger to the excrement and sniffed it. Craig looked immediately away, willing himself not to gag. Purposefully staring into the trees and focusing only on that, he heard someone making aborted retching sounds. Next to him, Phil chain spit, as though trying to get a terrible taste out of his mouth.

"Not wolf," Robards announced. "Dog."

Still not brave enough to look back, Craig heard Elaine utter a phlegmy groan of disgust. She was the one who'd almost vomited.

"Anybody see tracks?" Robards asked.

"There?" Parvesh said uncertainly.

"No. There," Robards said, and Craig finally turned around to see him pointing off to the left. *Was he pointing with the same finger he'd…?*

Craig spit, the accumulating saliva in his mouth suddenly making him feel like throwing up.

*Where had he wiped off that finger? On his pants?*

He forced himself to derail that train of thought and concentrated on the dog tracks. Although he couldn't really see them, he believed they were there, and he and the others followed Robards deeper into the woods for at least another half mile, zigzagging this way and that, steered by bent branches and disturbed leaves, until the guide stopped them with a raised hand. "There it is," Robards whispered, pointing ahead.

They were on a flat stretch of ground, and the dog, a Labrador obviously *very* far from home, was sniffing in the underbrush. The animal turned to look at them, panting happily, its tail wagging.

Robards withdrew a handgun from an easily accessible pouch on the side of his backpack. "Who wants to take it down?" he asked.

Craig looked around in horror at his fellow employees. They all seemed equally shocked by the suggestion, save for Parvesh who stepped forward, hand extended. "I'll do it."

"Asshole," Phil said angrily.

"No, that's good." Robards smiled at Parvesh, handing him the gun, butt first. "I'm proud of you."

"What do I do?"

"This is a valuable lesson." He looked around. "For all of you." He put a hand on Parvesh's shoulder. "Move forward slowly. Keep the weapon in your right hand behind your back, and keep your left hand outstretched to show you're friendly. It'll approach you, lower its head to be petted, and when it does, place the gun next to its head, pull the trigger and blow its brains out."

"No!" Elaine protested.

"Shut the hell up." Robards fixed her with a glare so menacing she backed up, lapsing into silence. "That's going in my report," he told her.

*What report?* Craig wondered.

"That's not a wild animal," Phil said, coming to her defense. "That's obviously someone's pet. It even has a collar."

"Out here, it's prey," Robards responded, and his tone was as hard-edged as a scalpel. Craig suddenly wondered if BFG conducted any background checks on its contract employees. It did not require much of a leap to imagine Robards serving time in prison for a violent crime.

Everyone was silent.

"Move toward it," Robards instructed Parvesh. "Slowly... slowly..."

The division head approached the Labrador, left hand extended. Happily, tail still wagging, the dog hurried forward, padding across the open ground.

"Take it out," Robards coached.

Parvesh patted the Labrador's head.

"Do it."

The blast was so loud and sudden that it hurt Craig's ears, piercing into his brain. The dog's head exploded in a rain of blood, and the animal fell to the ground as an echo of the shot diminished in the distance. Elaine and Jenny screamed. He wasn't sure he hadn't shouted out himself.

"Excellent!" Robards pronounced with a grin, walking over to Parvesh and clapping him on the back. "You did great!" He reached down and took the gun out of Parvesh's hand.

The division head was staring down at the bloody body and trembling.

Robards reached behind himself and pulled a rough cloth sack out of his backpack. "We'll put it in here," he said, "and bring it back with us as a trophy. Who wants to help me?"

No one volunteered. In fact, Craig was not the only one to take an involuntary step backward.

Robards shrugged. "Guess I'll do it myself." He placed the sack on the ground, opening up the neck. Rolling up his sleeves, he reached down, picking up the Labrador's body. There was no head left to speak of, and several chunks of wet red flesh dropped to the ground. Blood was flowing now instead of spraying, but it was still leaking out of the dead animal's ragged neck as Robards dropped the dog into the sack and tied the opening in a knot. The guide's hands and forearms were coated with blood, and he bent over, grabbed two handfuls of dirt and began rubbing the dirt over his skin. The dirt turned brownish black and muddy, and Robards opened his canteen and poured the water over his hands and arms, which emerged from the ordeal surprisingly clean.

He picked up the heavy sack, slinging it over his shoulder. "Let's go!" he said. "Move out!"

Robards whistled a happy tune, but the rest of them were silent as they followed him back through the woods and down the long trail to the camp, where Matthews was in the lodge, collecting papers from those who had remained. Before him was a box filled with what looked like branches, rocks and debris. Once inside, the entire group, with the exception of Parvesh, hurried over. They were all speaking at once, but it was Elaine's outraged voice that carried above the others. "He made Parvesh kill a dog!"

"I know," Matthews said quietly, looking down, and that shut everyone up.

He had known.

He didn't seem happy about it, though, and like the incident with the bus driver, the reaction left the CEO diminished in Craig's eyes, leaving him to wonder once again who was really in charge of CompWare.

*Regus Patoff*, he thought, and the idea sent a chill down his spine.

Elaine had said after the weekend meeting with Scott that she was sending out résumés, and for the first time he seriously considered whether he should do the same.

It was nearly lunchtime, and while the others remained behind to discuss what had happened, Craig accompanied Jenny and Alex to the kitchen, where Robard's wife was waiting for them. "Make da sandwiches," she said in an appallingly offensive yet indefinable accent and cackled to herself.

The sandwiches were as bad as Craig knew they'd be, and, as planned, he ate chips instead. Around him, employees were complaining about the food and leaving most of their lunch on the plate. The dog hunt was the primary topic of conversation, but Robards was not there to hear it, having grabbed a sandwich from the kitchen and taken off to…what? Bury the dog's body? Stuff it?

He didn't know and didn't want to know.

Even as he, Phil, Elaine and the other division heads around them discussed and relived their horrible experience in the woods, Craig kept one eye on Austin Matthews. The CEO spoke to no one and actually ate his entire lunch, wearing an unhappy expression all the while. It was probably too much to hope that he would fire the consultants, cancel their contract or do whatever it was he needed to do to get rid of them, but the man's dour demeanor, and his question and response during last evening's game, gave Craig hope.

The scavenger hunt was poorly planned and amateurish. They were expected to find everything on the list each of them were handed, but the items were all generic objects easily rounded up in an environment such as this: five pinecones, a piece of granite, two twigs, a wildflower. It reminded him of Dylan's treasure hunt, only not as fun, and thinking about his son made him realize what a complete waste of time this weekend had turned out to be and how much he would have rather been at home.

Nearly everyone finished quickly, and when they were done, a distracted Matthews handed each of them a pencil and lined notebook paper on which they were to write a story that mentioned the objects they'd gathered. Craig's was a horror story about a science camp that turns into a prison run by a torturing psychopath.

He had long since turned in his story and was outside next to the stage, talking with Phil, Elaine and Alex Mendoza. They were discussing getting a group of senior staff together to complain to Matthews and the Board not only about the retreat but about BFG in general, when Group One returned to the camp, Robards carrying a heavy burlap sack over his shoulder.

Another dog?

The expressions on the faces of those behind the guide told him that it was, and Craig turned away, sickened, but not before seeing a dark stain on the bottom of the sack.

Blood.

There were no houses nearby, no sign of civilization out this way save for the camp. So how did the dogs get out here? He was suddenly certain that the animals had been kidnapped by Robards and brought up to the mountains specifically to be hunted. Somewhere in a Southern California neighborhood, children were looking for their missing pets.

Once again, Robards was whistling happily, and he nodded in greeting as he passed by.

"We've gotta do something," Alex said.

Phil smiled thinly. "Mayday, mayday. Company going down."

Robards took his sack somewhere and reemerged ten minutes later washed and wearing new clothes. He gathered everyone from both groups into a standing circle around the fire pit and said they were going to work on their communication skills. He whispered something to Scott Cho, and told him to whisper it in the ear of the person to his right, who would then whisper it into the ear of the person to *his* right, until the message had gone all the way around the circle, at which time it would be spoken aloud to see how close it was to the original.

*Really*? Craig thought. This grammar school party game was their communication exercise?

He stood there, shaking his head at the uselessness of the activity, until Alex said something in Phil's ear and Phil, grinning, leaned over. "I have a big dick," Phil whispered.

"Asshole," Craig whispered back and turned to his right. He had no idea what the real message was, but he knew it was nothing close to this. Phil was just fucking with him.

He turned to Elaine. "The quick brown fox jumped over the lazy dog," he whispered, and she passed the message on.

It finally came full circle, and Jack Razon, the last link in the ring, was urged by Robards to speak the message aloud. "The quick brown fox jumped over the lady dog," he said, and Robards grinned. "See what happens when we don't listen? What I originally said was, 'I scream, you scream, we all scream for ice cream.' Twenty-two retells later, it's changed into 'The quick brown fox jumped over the lady dog.'"

Phil was still chuckling to himself.

"We're going to do it again, this time from the opposite direction, and I want all of you to listen carefully and repeat what you hear exactly. Let's see if we can get this right."

The new message came around, and Elaine whispered in his ear, "Now is the time for all good men to come to the aid of their country."

Craig passed along to Phil, "Your mama gives one hell of a B.J."

As if he'd said nothing out of the ordinary, Phil nodded and turned his head to the left. Moments later, Scott Cho said loudly, at Robards' prompting, "Your mama gives one hell of a B.J."

There were snickers among the employees, as well as expressions of shocked outrage. Phil was staring calmly straight ahead when Craig turned to look at him.

Robards was furious. "How did that happen?" he demanded. "Who changed it to that?" He looked around the circle and when no one responded, he said, "Fine. We're going to keep doing this until you get it right. You are going to learn how important communication is in business and in life, and you will stay here as long as it takes you to figure that out. Do I make myself clear?"

Elaine nudged him with her elbow. "I know it's you two," she said under her breath. "Knock it off or we'll be here for hours."

Craig kicked Phil's shoe in turn, and though there was no outward reaction from his friend, this time the exercise proceeded smoothly and the message repeated at the end was identical to the one spoken at the beginning.

"Good," Robards said. "Now we'll do it again."

It was late afternoon by the time they finished, and they were given two hours of free time before dinner. Elaine went back to the cabin, but Craig and Phil headed over to the lodge, where Phil sorted through the records until he found one that he wanted to play: an album called *Caravanserai* by Santana. Craig had been hoping to talk to Matthews about the consultants, but the CEO was on dinner duty and was working in the kitchen. Phil sat cross-legged on the floor in front of the record player, listening to the music, and Craig looked around for someone he could talk to about the dog hunt, thinking he could recruit some brave souls to his side. No one wanted to discuss it, however, and he ended up sitting glumly on the couch flipping through a decade-old *Time* magazine.

Phil put on a new album, something Craig didn't recognize, and came over, sitting on the opposite end of the couch. "I've been thinking," he said. "I don't think it's legal to kill someone's pet. And that dog definitely had a collar."

"Yes!" Craig said. "That's what I'm talking about."

"We could probably report this to the cops or something."

The conversations nearby had stopped, the department and division heads who had wanted nothing to do with any talk of the hunt, now listening carefully. Before Craig could bring them into the discussion, Robards appeared in the entrance to the dining room. "Dinner is served!" he announced loudly.

Reluctantly, Craig stood up from the couch. Phil went over to turn off the record player, and everyone made their way into the dining room. The lights seemed dimmer than they had yesterday, and Craig wondered if the generator was going.

They sat down on the benches, and Garrett Holcomb, the head of Phil's department, brought plates of food to their aisle. Even in his peripheral vision, Craig could see the wide grin on Phil's face as the department head served him. "Uh, Garrett," he said, "can I get some coffee to go with this?"

"I'm not in charge of drinks," Holcomb informed him.

Phil leaned over. "It's so hard to find good help," he told Craig.

The food on the plate was supremely unappetizing. Soggy string beans sat between an overcooked biscuit and a chunk of deep fried meat approximately as big as a hamburger. Craig took a bite of the meat, which was chewy, tasteless and almost impossible to get down.

"What are we eating?" he asked suspiciously.

Robards, nearby, overheard and answered the question. "You should know. You hunted it today."

There was a clatter of silverware as shocked diners dropped their forks on the table. Matthews and Jack Razon, who, along with Robards' wife, had been responsible for making the meal, had made no attempt to eat the food, and neither of them looked up, both staring guiltily down at their plates.

Had *they* butchered the animals? Craig wondered. Or had they merely watched while *Edna* did it?

He stared out the window. This retreat had turned violent and ugly. There were no skills they had learned here, they hadn't grown closer, and there was nothing any of them would take away from the experience that they would ever use in their jobs or in their real lives. Not for the first time, he wondered about the *real* reason BFG had sent CompWare's senior staff into the mountains. It was obviously a pretext for something—but what?

They would find out when they returned, he assumed, but he did not think it was information he was going to be happy to learn.

There was a talent show scheduled after dinner. Each person was supposed to get up and do some sort of act: recite a poem, sing a song, tell a story. But no one was in the mood, and it was Matthews who got them out of it, saying, "I think we'll skip the talent show tonight." Craig was grateful, and once again he was hoping to have an opportunity to talk to the CEO about this whole bizarre weekend, but Matthews announced, "I'm going to bed. I'll see you in the morning," and headed off toward his cabin. He sounded tired.

Somewhere nearby, a dog howled, a lonely sound that made Craig think of an animal that had lost its mate.

Craig and Phil were the last two remaining, everyone else going into their cabins for the night. "Parvesh is going to be impossible to live with now," Phil said. "I dread going in there."

"We're heading home tomorrow."

"Thank God."

"I wonder if Matthews is going to rethink the consultants after this," Craig said.

"I wonder if he'll be allowed to."

"You noticed that, too, huh?"

Phil nodded. "It's like, after the merger fell through, he panicked and handed over all power of decision to BFG. Maybe he regrets it now, but I'm not sure what he can do about it at this point. CompWare's probably locked in by contract, and if we hope to stay alive in the shark-infested waters of Wall Street, we'd better not show any weakness."

"You sound like Matthews."

"I'm just taking it from his point of view."

Craig smiled wryly. "And on that dispiriting note…" With a lazy wave, he started toward his cabin, leaving Phil to decide whether to hang by himself for a while or go back in with Parvesh.

"Bastard," Phil muttered.

"Sorry," Craig said. "I'm tired." And he was. It had been a long fucking day, not one that he wanted to remember but one he knew he wouldn't forget. He knocked on the door of the cabin to make sure Elaine was decent. "Elaine?" he called. He heard no response, and used his key to unlock the door.

The room was dark and empty, but the bathroom door was closed, a sliver of yellow light outlining the edge of the frame. She was obviously in there, and immediately after he'd stepped into the cabin, she called out, "Craig? Is that you? I forgot my underwear and pajamas." She opened the door a crack and held out her hand. "Could you hand them to me?"

He closed and locked the front door behind him, turning on the battery-powered light. He couldn't pretend to be asleep; she'd heard him come in. And now she'd seen the light go on. Besides, he didn't want her to come out naked or partially wrapped in a towel in order to get her clothes. So he said, "Okay. Hold on." He looked around, frowned. "I don't see them. They're not on the bed."

"Just open up my suitcase. They should be on top."

They weren't on top. What *was* lying on the carefully folded clothes was a bright red vibrator in the shape of an erect penis. Embarrassed, he moved it aside, picked up the folded pajama top and bottom, then grabbed a pair of lacy silk panties. The panties, he saw instantly, were crotchless.

Moving the vibrator back into place, he closed the suitcase, making no mention of any of this as he handed her the bundle of clothes and said, "Here you go."

"Thanks," she told him, closing the door.

As soon as she saw the underwear he'd given her, she would know that *he* knew they were crotchless. She already had to know that he'd seen her vibrator. Had she *wanted* him to see it? He wasn't sure. But he didn't want to deal with any of this, and for the second night in a row, he quickly changed into his pajamas, turned off the light, got into bed and closed his eyes, facing the wall, pretending to be asleep.

"Craig?" she whispered when she came out of the bathroom. "Are you awake? Craig?"

He didn't answer, didn't move, kept his breathing believably even, and, eventually, he drifted off.

He awoke shortly after midnight, prompted into consciousness by an exterior noise that broke through the artificial world of his dreams. He opened his eyes, staring upward into the darkness, hearing a shuffling in the gravelly dirt outside the cabin. Though the window next to his bed was closed, the silence was so all-encompassing that, even through glass, the smallest noise seemed amplified.

The shuffling sound was very clear.

A person was outside their cabin, and Craig listened, assuming it was Robards doing some sort of nightly rounds. But the shuffling did not go away, did not move on. Instead, it circled around the cabin until it was back again, and against his will, he thought of that stupid story Robards had told last night about the abandoned boy who became a cannibal and broke into cabins searching for victims.

The sound was close, seemingly right on the other side of the wall, and he sat up to see what he could through the dirty window.

A horrible wrinkled face stared back at him from the other side of the filthy glass.

Startled he sucked in his breath but, luckily, did not cry out. It was the old lady from the kitchen, he realized instantly, Robards' wife—*Edna*— although what she was doing staring in at his room in the middle of the night he did not know. He glanced over at the other bed to make sure he had not awakened Elaine, and when he looked back, the face at the window was gone. He waited a moment to see if she would return, but the sound did not reappear and neither did that terrible visage.

Craig lay back on the bed. Robards was a strapping young guy. Could that hideous crone really be his wife? It didn't make sense, something about it didn't add up, and Craig wondered if the scenario was part of some elaborate psychological test, if BFG had brought them up here to monitor them under artificial conditions in order to gauge their reactions to certain purposefully introduced stimuli.

He was getting as paranoid as Phil.

He closed his eyes, trying to fall asleep, but though there were no more sounds, sleep did not come easy, and when it did, it was marred by dreams of dark forests and old ladies and a fiendishly grinning Regus Patoff eating a dead dog at an indoor picnic table while wearing a blood-stained bib.

# THIRTEEN

EVEN IF THE BUS DRIVER HADN'T GIVEN THEM A LEC-ture about being on time when they first arrived, no one was about to miss the ride back. They were all packed and ready to go after a sad breakfast of cold burnt toast and runny scrambled eggs prepared by two of the division heads from Finance, and the remaining hours were taken up with subdued conversations, and filling out a survey form about the retreat that was so carefully and precisely worded that there was no way possible to criticize their experience here.

Before leaving, they finally got their phones, tablets and iPods back. Craig tried to make a quick call to Angie, but there was still no service.

The problem continued for the entire return trip, and Craig wondered aloud if the bus was equipped with some sort of transmission blocker or scrambler.

"The guy reports to Patoff," Phil noted, "so I wouldn't be surprised."

Dash Robards had seen them off, standing in the parking lot and waving goodbye, a handgun in a shoulder holster conspicuously visible. Craig had turned away, glad to be leaving, and was gratified to see that no one else was returning the man's wave either. The weekend had been a disaster. None of them had had a good time, none of them had learned anything, and they were returning disgusted and demoralized—which was exactly the opposite of the retreat's intent.

The bus driver was not the same one who had dropped them off on Friday, but he was equally hostile, and at a stoplight in San Bernardino he threatened to kick Phil off the bus for being disruptive and unruly. "You try it, and I'll kick your ass," Phil said to a chorus of cheers, and the bus driver, recognizing that he was outnumbered, seethed silently for the rest of the trip.

It was great to be back in the city. They got stuck in traffic on the Pomona Freeway as a result of an overheated car on one of the middle lanes; the day was so smoggy that the buildings of downtown had lost all detail and were little more than gray shapes in the white air…and it was wonderful. Already, the events of the weekend seemed fantastical and far away, as though they'd happened in a dream.

It was Sunday, but Regus Patoff was waiting for them when the bus pulled into the CompWare parking lot. He was standing in front of the building, wearing a bright blue bow tie, and his suspiciously colored flattop seemed even flatter than it had before. If his appearance was odd in the office, in the open air it looked positively clownish, and Craig wondered how anyone could take him seriously. They did, though. Not just at CompWare but at all of the other companies who'd hired BFG to streamline their operations.

Craig grabbed his suitcase from beneath the seat and was caught for several moments in the slow-moving stream of people trudging toward the exit at the front of the bus. From outside, he heard Patoff announce to the departing employees, "No one is to leave. Remain in front of the bus until you are told what to do."

"Who does he think he is?" Phil said angrily. "He's not my boss."

Nevertheless, he stepped off the bus and moved to the side, waiting with everyone else. Craig did the same. The consultant was speaking in low tones to Matthews and the members of the Board, and a moment later, the visibly shaken CEO stepped back while Patoff called a meeting in the first floor conference room. "This will be quick," he promised, "and afterward you may go home, but first there are some matters that need to be discussed."

"Jesus," Phil sighed. "Will this weekend never end?"

As they walked into the building, Craig tried to call Angie on both their home phone and on her cell, but the land line was busy, and he was forced to leave a message on the cell phone's voicemail, telling her he would be there soon.

Both Matthews and Patoff walked up onto the stage, standing next to the podium, and as soon as everyone was seated, the CEO cleared his throat. "You're going to hear this on the news tonight and read about it in the paper, but we thought you should learn about it here first." Matthews took a deep breath. "Our recently resigned CFO Hugh Anderson and Senior Vice President Russell Cibriano both committed suicide yesterday."

There were several gasps of surprise, as well as widespread whispering.

"It is indeed tragic. As you know, both men recently resigned after the Automated Interface merger did not go through, but they were both extremely competent professionals with extremely bright futures. I have no idea why either of them would do some-thing so…drastic. Their deaths are a loss to their friends and fam-ilies, their coworkers here at CompWare and our entire industry."

"The upside," Patoff offered, "is that, according to the terms of their resignations, the company is no longer on the financial hook for their retirement benefits. The golden parachutes given to these former employees—which, by the way, I would have advised against offering if BFG had been consulting for CompWare at that point—are cancelled. So, while I'm sure their loved ones and even some of you may be saddened by their departures, from a fiscal standpoint, their deaths are quite fortuitous for the company, par-ticularly at this time."

His remarks were greeted with shocked silence. Even Mat-thews and the members of the Board seemed stunned by the ex-traordinary callousness of the consultant's words.

"As to how they died," the consultant continued, "in case you all are wondering, Mr. Anderson hung himself, while Mr. Cibriano slit his wrists."

Craig could not believe anyone, even Patoff, could be so heart-less and unfeeling.

The consultant pressed a button on the podium, and a screen began lowering behind him. "A lot of you are probably wondering why you had to come into the building and into the conference room to hear this news. After all, we could have announced it to you either while you were on the bus or when you had just gotten off. The reason is that I put together a little PowerPoint presenta-tion that I thought you might like."

The lights dimmed.

"As you can see, I was able to obtain police photographs of both men."

158

On the white screen behind him flashed a full color photo of Hugh Anderson hanging from an open beam in a neatly ordered garage. He was wearing a suit, and there was a large stain on his pants where he had wet himself. His head hung at a disturbing angle, his neck obviously broken, and both his face and his hands, at the ends of his loosely dangling arms, looked unnaturally dark.

"Here's Mr. Anderson. He was found in his garage by a gardener, who had come to do the lawn. The gardener told Mr. Anderson's wife, who called the police."

The photo onscreen shifted to a close-up of the ex-CFO's face, his purplish skin bulging and swollen; his tongue lolling between slack blackened lips; his bloodshot eyes so wide open they were practically popping out of their sockets.

"And here is Mr. Cibriano."

The screen changed again.

"Mr. Cibriano, uncharacteristically unclichéd, from what I've learned of his personality, did not do the deed in the bathtub, but rather bled out in his marital bed, where he was discovered by his wife and daughter, who had just returned home from a shopping trip to Nordstrom's."

It was the most gruesome sight Craig had ever seen, an image he did not think he would ever be able to get out of his mind. Russell Cibriano, face contorted in agony, body twisted in anguish, lay on a bed drenched with red, severed veins visible in the sliced sections of wrist that gaped open and still appeared to be bleeding.

There were more pictures, but he could not bear to look and stared at the side wall instead of the screen, a tactic that more than one person in his sightline seemed to be following.

The lights came up again, and Craig turned his attention back to the podium, where a visibly upset Matthews told everyone to go home. "See you in the morning," he said.

Phil was silent until they were back in the parking lot, walking toward their cars. Craig knew what his friend was going to say, and he wasn't sure he disagreed. "Doesn't it seem a little *too* coincidental that both Anderson and Cibriano happened to commit suicide on exactly the same weekend?" Phil asked. "And that all of our cell phones were confiscated so that we couldn't find out this information for ourselves, leaving Patoff to control the message and determine exactly when and how we were told?"

Craig nodded. It was paranoid thinking, but it was also plausible. More than plausible. "And what was with those pictures?" he wondered aloud. "What was the point of that?"

Around them, others were talking in hushed tones about what they'd seen.

"A warning?" Phil said quietly.

Craig frowned.

"How else are we to take it? We're herded in there to look at *Faces of Death* photos of two men Patoff told us were a drain on CompWare's resources. I think he wanted us to know that if we cross him or step out of line…" He didn't finish the thought.

"I don't think so," Craig demurred.

Phil shrugged. "Think what you want."

The suggestion wasn't as outlandish as it should have been, and Craig was still thinking about it as he and Phil waved goodbye to each other and split off, walking to their separate rides.

He'd been slightly worried about leaving his car in the CompWare parking lot for three days. Even in the nicest parts of Los Angeles, an unmoving vehicle was an invitation to thieves. But despite the fact that the lot was open and had no guard, his car was unmolested, and, grateful that something had finally gone right, he tossed his small suitcase on the passenger seat, got in and drove home.

Pulling into his driveway, he saw movement behind the front window, and by the time he'd gotten out of the car, the front door of the house was thrown open and Dylan was speeding in his direction, Angie striding right behind.

"Daddy!" Dylan yelled, running up and throwing his arms around him. Craig picked the boy up and hugged him back, his eyes welling. He hadn't realized until this moment how much he'd missed his son, and though he'd only been gone since Friday morning, it felt as though they'd been apart for a month. It was impossible for him to have grown in such a short amount of time, but Dylan looked bigger, and while it was probably unrealistic, Craig vowed that he would do everything in his power not to spend another night away from his family.

He put Dylan down. Angie gave him a quick perfunctory hug and kiss. "Thank God you're back!" she said.

"What is it?"

"I just got a call from work. They want me over at the Urgent Care. Now."

He looked at his watch. "They're closed already."

"I know. But Pam called a mandatory meeting. I have to go. I was going to bring Dylan with me, but now that you're here…"

"Don't worry about it. Go."

She kissed him again. "I hate this," she said.

"Wait until I tell you about our little hunting exercise."

"You went hunting?"

"Did you kill animals, Daddy?" Dylan sounded worried.

"No," he reassured his son. "I'll tell you when you come back," he promised Angie.

"Why didn't you call?" she asked.

"I couldn't. No reception up there. Besides, they confiscated our phones for the weekend so we'd have to rough it." He shook his head. "I'll tell you all about it."

"Okay."

"Go," he told her.

Angie dashed back inside to get her purse while Craig unloaded his suitcase from the car. "I'll be back as soon as I can," she told him, coming out. Her Acura was parked on the street instead of the driveway, and she waved goodbye to both of them as she hurried over to it.

They waved back, watching her leave, then went inside. He was hungry, Craig realized. He hadn't had a decent meal since breakfast Friday morning. He carried his suitcase into the bedroom, dropped it on the bed, then returned to the living room, where Dylan hadn't moved.

"Hey, buddy. What's wrong?"

"I missed you," Dylan said honestly.

Craig was touched. "I missed you, too."

"I brushed my teeth with Mommy but it wasn't the same and I cried."

Craig couldn't help smiling. He put an arm around his son's shoulder. "Well, I'm back now, and I'll brush with you after dinner."

Dylan looked up at him. "Can we read until then?" he asked, holding a *Secrets of Droon* book in his hand. "Karen's two chapters ahead of me, and I need to catch up."

Craig smiled, squeezing the boy's shoulder affectionately. "Sure," he said. "But let's get a snack first. I'm starving."

⸎

The employee parking lot was empty, and for a moment Angie thought that she'd arrived too late for the meeting. But she glanced down at the clock in the dashboard and saw that she was right on time.

That was strange.

There were no cars in the rear lot, and she turned around and drove back out to the front. The Urgent Care shared its parking lot with a travel agency and a beauty supply distributor, and she wasn't sure at first if the smattering of cars was connected to one of those businesses. But then she recognized Pam's Altima and pulled next to it. The sky was dimming but not yet dark, and she made sure her car was locked before going in, knowing it would be night before she came out. She hoped the meeting would be short, but knew that was wishful thinking. She should have defrosted something for Craig and Dylan to eat in case things ran long.

The front door was unlocked, and she walked into the Urgent Care, surprised to find that the waiting room was empty and dark, although lights were on in the area behind the admittance desk.

"Hello?" she called.

It was not only dark, it was silent, and Angie frowned. Staff meetings were usually held before or after hours in the waiting room, and although occasionally Pam convened them all in the central corridor, particularly if she wanted to lord things over them and make them stand the entire time, Angie should have been able to hear voices.

"Hello?" she called again. "Anybody here?"

Nothing.

She wasn't a person who was easily spooked, but her Spidey-sense was telling her something was wrong. Half-tempted to leave, she decided instead to call Pam's cell phone. Her mind ran through possible scenarios as she pressed the preset number—the meeting had been cancelled and not only had Pam forgotten to call and tell her, she'd forgotten to lock up; everyone mistakenly thought it was her birthday, and they were throwing her a surprise party, lying in wait to jump out at her. She stopped right there. That was already too outlandish to be true.

The number dialed, and she heard a ringing in her ear.

And heard the office manager's distinctive Neil Diamond ringtone from somewhere in the back.

She closed her phone. "Hello?" she called, walking through the admittance area. "Pam?"

She saw no doctors and none of the other nurses, but Pam was in her office, working on the computer.

"Pam?" she said, but the office manager didn't respond, and Angie suddenly noticed that, although the computer was on, the monitor displayed not a work page but a kitten-and-puppy screen-saver, which meant there'd been no keystrokes for a while.

The woman's hand, on the armrest of the chair, had not moved. At all.

Angie sucked in her breath. "Pam?" she said cautiously.

Forcing herself to move forward, she reached out and touched the office manager's shoulder. "Pam?"

No movement. No response.

She stepped to the side, nervously craning her head around to see the figure in the chair and finding what she expected to find. The office manager was dead. What she did *not* expect was the look of horror on the woman's face, a wide-eyed, gaping mouthed expression that made it appear as though she had seen a monster and died of fright in mid-scream.

Angie ran back the way she'd come in, down the corridor, past the admittance desk, through the waiting room and outside. She had time to wonder where everyone else was, why she was the only one who had shown up for the meeting, but overriding all of her thoughts was the necessity of calling the police, and she was punching in 911 even while she sprinted toward the parking lot, telling the dispatcher what she'd found as she was getting into her car and locking the door.

"Send! Someone! Now!" she yelled, cutting through the dispatcher's questions.

It was thirteen minutes later before the police finally arrived.

# FOURTEEN

MONDAY MORNING, CRAIG WAS SUMMONED TO work early by the programmers sending a torrent of surreptitiously sent text messages. There weren't many details, but the tone was frantic, and though he'd planned to call in sick today after last night's excitement, Angie assured him that she was fine and told him to go. Skipping breakfast, and with messages still coming in, he sped over to the office before Dylan was even awake.

Craig was not prepared for the fury that Scott Cho was unleashing upon the programmers when he arrived on the fifth floor. He could hear the department head yelling as soon as the elevator opened, and he hurried down the corridor to try and diffuse the situation.

Scott was standing before the gathered programmers, pacing, his face red, pointing finger jabbing the air as he shouted accusingly. "Again, which one of you was it?"

"What's going on?" Craig said, trying to keep his voice calm.

Scott whirled to face him. "I'll tell you what's going on! Someone here released a working demo of *Zombie Navy* and now it's all over the internet!"

Craig felt as though he'd been punched in the stomach. None of the texts had mentioned the reason for Scott's tirade, and he scanned the blanched faces of the programmers.

This couldn't be possible. The game was under tighter security than any other CompWare product in history. It was their summer blockbuster, their one sure thing, and the prime directive had been to keep everything about it, from the graphics to the through-line, under wraps. How could it have gotten out?

"Not only that, but it's getting trashed on all the gamer rating sites!"

Craig found it suddenly hard to breathe.

"I told him, none of us did it," Huell said.

"And I told you to shut the hell up!" Scott bellowed.

Craig didn't know what to do or where to start. Since none of the frantic texts he'd been sent had mentioned the reason for Scott's blowup, it made him wonder if one of the programmers *had* uploaded the demo. None of them looked guilty, however, and as he observed each of them and thought about those who were not yet here, he realized that he believed Huell's denial. He knew these men and women. They were all good people, good workers, loyal and honest. None of them would jeopardize their jobs with such a stupid move.

He thought he'd known Tyler, too, though.

"What do you think happened?" Craig asked the programmers.

Scott whirled to face him, angered by the interference, but before he could voice his displeasure, Rusty spoke up. "You know those consultants have access to everything."

Craig looked at Rusty, the situation suddenly sharpening in his mind.

"We've kept this under wraps for nearly a year. No one outside the loop even knew it was in development. Now, a couple of days after they get access to our passwords, it's out in the world? Seems a little suspicious to me."

"More than a little suspicious," Craig agreed.

"Stop right there," Scott ordered. "I don't want to hear any of this talk—"

"You don't want to find out the truth?" Craig stared him down. There was a weird dynamic between them after the weekend retreat. It was almost as though they were equals instead of boss and subordinate, and he wondered if that had been the consultant's intention or if it was merely a coincidental side effect.

Scott backed off.

Maybe the weekend *hadn't* been a complete waste of time.

"We need to find out how this happened," Craig said. "Now. Whoever did it needs to be fired, and we have to make sure it never happens again. This is major." He scanned the faces before him. "We'll need to work with someone from Operations on this. Who's good at—"

"I can track the leak," Benjy Goldfarb offered. "If Operations can get me access to everyone's computer, I can scan the internal records and find where and when it went out. It may take me awhile, but I'll catch the consultant who did it."

"What did you say?" Scott demanded.

Benjy tried to hide a smile. "Guy," he said. "I'll catch the *guy* who did it."

"Do it," Craig told him. "This is our top priority. I'll tell Fistler in Operations and get someone to work with you. In the meantime, I'm going to talk to Legal and get this thing pulled from any site it's on. What I want the rest of you to do is find out who has *Zombie Navy*, who's commenting on *Zombie Navy*, who's seen *Zombie Navy*, who's even *thinking* about *Zombie Navy*. Email me everything you find and don't wait until you have a list. The second you find a site, let me know. We have to stop this in its tracks.

"Everyone get to work. I'll be talking to each of you individually, so be thinking also about ideas on how the game might've been leaked. No theory's a dumb theory until we find out what went down. Got it?"

Nodding, they hurried back to their work stations, and he caught the looks of gratitude on the faces of those who'd texted him. Surprising even himself, he'd neutralized Scott, protecting his people, though he knew that was something the department head would *not* forget. Instead of mindlessly blaming the programmers, he'd shifted the focus to finding out who had done it using all logical means at their disposal.

He turned to the department head. "You'd better tell Mr. Matthews what happened. He's going to want to know."

Scott shot him a look of supreme irritation. "I'm well aware of that, *Horne*."

Knowing when to back off had always been one of his strengths, and Craig did so now. Certain that Scott would follow proper channels, dotting I's and crossing T's all the way, Craig took his leave. It was going to be one hell of a busy day, but he was pretty sure he could cover this *Zombie Navy* situation from home through telephone and email. Angie needed him. She *couldn't* be all right after finding Pam's body, and he wanted to be there for her. He'd stop off and see Lupe first, tell her what was going on, and let her know that he'd be gone for the day.

On his way to the elevator, he called Angie to tell her that he would be coming home, but she didn't answer the phone, and when he called her cell, he discovered that she was on the way to the Urgent Care for a meeting.

"I'll be there when you get back," he told her.

"Don't bother," she said. "You're already there. Might as well stay. Save those hours for some other time."

"Tomorrow?"

"Sounds good," she admitted.

"It's a date. Are you sure you're all right?"

"I'm fine. Call you later."

"Love you," he said.

"Love you, too. Bye."

In front of his office, Craig found a clean-cut young man sitting in a swivel chair to the right of Lupe's desk. Dressed impeccably in black pants, white shirt and tie, the man had the look of a Mormon missionary. In his lap was some sort of electronic tablet. He smiled at Craig and nodded.

Before he could ask who the man was and what he was doing here, Lupe came hurrying down the corridor from the direction of the elevators. "I'm not late!" she announced. "I'm not late!"

She was clearly addressing the young man in the chair, and when Craig shot her a quizzical look, she plopped down in her own chair and explained, "The work management study. It started Friday afternoon, right after you left." Dropping her purse on the floor and pushing it under her desk with her feet, she turned on her computer. "I'm working," she told the man. "I'm already at work. I'm answering my boss' questions, which is part of a secretary's duties."

This was getting ridiculous. "Time out," Craig said. "Everyone hold up a minute. No one informed me about this at all. Walk me through it, step-by-step." He turned to the man in the chair. "Now who, exactly, are you? And what is it you're doing here?"

"My name's Todd." Standing and smiling, the young man held out his hand to shake.

He wanted to ignore the outstretched hand, but he knew it would be better for both Lupe and himself if he acted like a team player, so Craig shook.

"My job is to account for every minute of every hour of Ms. Ferrera's work day. I am to make note of how long it takes her to perform each task listed in her job description, and to note how much time she spends each day on non-work-related items. BFG will eventually analyze this information to determine what can be done to improve efficiency." It was a prepared speech, and it sounded like a prepared speech, and it reminded Craig not to be too hard on this kid. He was only doing what he'd been told to do. He was following orders, not giving them.

"How long is this going to last?" Craig asked.

"I'm here for the week, at least. Beyond that, I don't know. I haven't been told."

Lupe was already on her computer, trying to show how hard she worked, and Todd was watching her, typing into his laptop even as he spoke to Craig.

"Well, have fun," Craig said. He half-expected to see someone waiting for him in his office, but there was not, and he understood that the study would be conducted in stages, apparently from the bottom up. A consultant would be coming in to monitor him soon, though, and he was almost sorry that it wasn't starting today. With this *Zombie Navy* disaster, he had a lot to do.

The morning flew by quickly. He talked to Legal about going after the sites that were offering the game, got Fistler in Operations to grant Benjy access to computer records, waded through a seemingly unending stream of emails, and had a chance to meet with about half of the programmers. He was pretty sure before he talked to them that they hadn't sabotaged the program, and nothing he heard made him change his mind. After lunch, he'd meet one-on-one with the rest of them, but as far as he was concerned, it was only a formality. He did not think any of his people had released the game.

He was pretty sure it was BFG.

But why?

That he did not know.

At noon—exactly—Lupe buzzed him on the intercom. He hadn't gotten out of his chair for over two hours and was tired of sitting down, so instead of answering, he got up and walked out the door. "What is it?"

Lupe stood. "I'm going to lunch," she announced. She looked tired and stressed out.

Todd stood behind her, tablet in hand.

Craig frowned. "Is he following you to lunch?"

Her mouth tightened. "Apparently so. He also followed me to the bathroom earlier and helpfully stood outside the door, timing how long I spent in there."

"Jesus Christ! Why didn't you tell me?" Craig moved around to confront the young man, who was now looking down at his tablet, typing. His cheeks were red with embarrassment.

"What the hell is this?" Craig demanded.

"I'm just doing my job," Todd said defensively.

"You don't follow someone to the bathroom."

"I have to."

Craig fixed him with a hard stare. "How long have you been working for BFG?"

"I don't work for BFG exactly," Todd said. "I've just been hired on a contract basis. Temporarily."

"Well, I'm going to make sure it's *very* temporary," Craig told him. He turned back toward Lupe. "Go to lunch," he told her. "If this little robot tries to follow you, I'll tackle him."

With a grateful smile, Lupe picked up her purse and walked purposefully down the corridor toward the elevator.

"Mr. Patoff—" Todd began.

"I don't give a shit about Mr. Patoff," Craig said. "If you want to do your job properly, sit there, note the time she left and write down the time she returns. You are allowed to document how much time she spends at lunch, but that is her free time, and you are not allowed to monitor or intrude upon what she does on her lunch hour."

"Mr. Patoff is not going to like this."

"Tell him to talk to me," Craig said. "And, by the way, you are *not* to follow my secretary to the restroom. Do you understand me? That's an invasion of privacy."

"Mr. Patoff says—"

"Fuck Mr. Patoff."

Todd's face hardened. "I'm going to tell him you said that."

"You go right ahead." Craig strode back into his office. "And stay out of my way!" he shouted over his shoulder. "You might be assigned to monitor my secretary, but you're nothing to me, and if you do anything to impede work in this division, I'll have your job!"

He slammed the door behind him, breathing heavily. Part of him felt guilty for being so hard on the kid, especially since he was just a temp, but the little puke had stepped way overbounds. Craig wasn't about to let *anyone* treat Lupe that way.

Slamming the door had been a bit too dramatic, though. He had never been good at confrontation, either avoiding it completely or overcompensating by acting like a bully. He wasn't going to apologize—his feelings were true, and he *wanted* Todd to be a little afraid of him—but he opened the door to show that he wasn't unprofessional.

The consultant was gone.

Craig walked out of his office, looking around. Lupe's work area was empty, as was the hallway.

Maybe, Craig thought, Todd had gone to complain to Patoff. Maybe.

But maybe he was following Lupe to lunch.

---

There was an eight o'clock meeting at the Urgent Care for all shifts—weekend and weekday—in order to talk about Pam. Angie was late for the meeting because Craig had had to rush off early to work to confront a crisis, and she could not drive over until she had dropped Dylan off at school. When she arrived, nearly fifteen minutes late, the meeting was already in progress, though it stopped cold the second she walked through the door, everyone instantly gathering around to hear her version of what had happened.

The consultant was nowhere in sight, and Angie wondered if he had been invited to the meeting. The Urgent Care didn't officially open until nine, and she thought it highly likely that no one had told him to come in early. It was just as well; she felt more comfortable without him there.

Very quickly, she was able to ascertain that she was the only person Pam had ordered in yesterday for a "staff meeting," which made her wonder why the office manager had *really* called her. Causing even greater confusion was the fact that, according to Dr. Bashir, who had been in touch with the coroner, the time of death had been placed at 4:00 p.m., a full hour before Pam had called her. The police were still trying to reconcile that with Angie's story, and for a brief horrifying second she wondered if that meant she would be a suspect if foul play was presumed. The second she voiced that fear aloud, however, her coworkers shot it down with a logic so unassailable that she was immediately reassured.

But why had Pam called her?

*Had* it been Pam?

She tried to think now if there had been anything off about the voice, any little giveaway that would indicate she'd been talking to someone else. She wasn't sure. That was not something for which she'd been on the lookout, and if it had occurred, it had been so subtle that she had not caught it. She took a deep breath. The entire situation was confusing. Everything about it seemed more than a little off, and it was not only the nurses but the doctors who were tense and on edge. Until a coroner's report came back with a specific cause of death that was simple, rational and easily explainable, Pam's demise would remain a mystery—and no one here liked mysteries.

Angie thought of the terrified expression on the office manager's frozen face and shivered.

The consultant walked in, blinking nervously at the sight of the gathered crowd. It was clear he was startled by their presence, and it was equally clear that he didn't know how to react. Angie could tell from the look on his face that he thought he had stumbled onto a meeting where they were probably discussing *him*.

He tried to smile. "Hey," he said nervously by way of greeting.

Angie decided to just blurt it out. "Pam's dead," she said.

Now he looked confused. "What—? I mean, are..." He took a deep breath. "Huh?"

"I found her. She called me in, told me there was a staff meeting, but I was the only one she called, and when I came in I found her in her office, dead."

The consultant looked panicked. "You don't think *I* was responsible?"

"No," Angie assured him. She heard stifled laughter from some of the other nurses, and though she, too, felt an impulse to smile, she felt sorry for the consultant. "No one thinks you had anything to do with it, Mr. Morris. In fact, it was probably a heart attack or a stroke…" She recalled Pam's horrified face. "Probably."

The meeting was rudderless without Pam. The office manager was the one who usually kept them on point, and with no designated leader, the gathering's focus meandered. The doctors were distracted, already checking out mentally, most of them on their phones, and the nurses endlessly chewed over every detail Angie shared with them. Nothing was going to be resolved here today, and as soon as she could, Angie left. She needed to clear her head.

It was almost time for the Urgent Care to open, and outside, patients were already lining up. *Had* it been Pam who'd called last night? The thought haunted her. She was more unsure now than she had been before the meeting, and none of the possibilities seemed plausible. Either Pam had lied to her and called her in for a secret one-on-one meeting and had died in the interim, or Pam had *intended* to call everyone in and had called her first but had died before phoning anyone else, or someone had killed Pam and then called, imitating the office manager's voice.

What did it say about her that the last scenario seemed the most likely?

Why, though? Why would someone do that? Because they wanted Pam's body found immediately? Because Angie had also been a target, and she had only escaped a similar fate after something went wrong?

Every solution brought up more questions than it answered.

The building had exterior security cameras, and there was one in the waiting room. If anything could shed a light on what had happened last night, it should be the surveillance tapes. She assumed the police had looked at them, and she was tempted to drive by the station and see if they could tell her anything.

Were there cameras in Pam's office? There weren't in the exam rooms—for privacy reasons—but she didn't know if there were any surveillance devices trained on the hallway or the offices. She'd never had any reason to notice or check before.

Back at home, Angie felt restless. She wanted to call Craig, but he had his own problems to deal with today. She did call her friend Irma, but Irma was busy with her mother, who had Alzheimer's, and could only talk for a few moments.

Seconds after hanging up, the phone rang, and Angie answered.

"Hello!" a cheerful recorded voice greeted her. "Thank you for participating in our Perfect Practices quality control survey."

It was the Urgent Care consultants.

"To continue in English, please press one now..."

She pressed the one button.

"Using your touchtone phone, please indicate whether you work at a hospital, a doctor's office or an urgent care facility. Press one if you work at a hospital. Press two if you work at a doctor's office. Press three if you work at an urgent care facility."

Angie pressed three.

"Please type in the zip code of the urgent care facility at which you work, followed by the pound sign."

Angie did so.

There was a pause and a click before the recorded voice spoke again. "The following questions pertain to the consultant assigned to evaluate your facility. On a scale of one to five, with five being extremely unlikely and one being extremely likely, how would you rate the chances of the consultant murdering his mother and keeping her body in a basement freezer?"

What kind of survey was this?

Angie hung up. Rattled, she stared for a moment at the phone. She'd acted instinctively, but maybe she should have stayed on to hear what else was going to be asked. This couldn't be real, could it? It had to be a joke.

The thing was, it seemed legitimate. It wasn't just some kid making a prank call but a prerecorded series of questions that were integrated into a working automated system.

Did the consultant even know that this survey was being conducted? Angie wondered. Was he aware of the type of questions being asked? Whether he was or wasn't, she felt sorry for him. He was a creep, no doubt about it, but his nearly crippling awkwardness made him somewhat sympathetic in her eyes, and the fact that he was at the mercy of the consulting firm for which he worked, a firm that was conducting a truly bizarre survey in what was probably an effort to oust him, made her more predisposed toward his position. She had no compassion for companies to begin with, and when they behaved toward individuals in such an obviously hostile manner, she automatically opposed them.

It was time to do a little research, Angie decided. She needed to find out more about Private Practices. In the back of her mind was the idea that the firm was a subsidiary of BFG or was in some way connected to the consultants engaged by Craig's company, but going on the internet, checking out their own website, Wikipedia and several consumer sites, she could find nothing to back that up. She read through the information: Founded in 1990 by two physician brothers…Mission: to help streamline business practices of medical facilities…No complaints filed with the Better Business Bureau…References and recommendations from over 40 satisfied clients…Moved base of operations from Chicago to Los Angeles in 1999…Supports several charities providing medical care to Third World countries…Favorable press in both medical and business journals…

As far as she could tell, the firm was clean.

Angie shut off her laptop, staring at the screen as it shut down. In her mind, she saw the terrible look on Pam's dead face and heard the outrageous question voiced by the telephone survey.

She didn't want to think what she was thinking, but she couldn't help it.

The consultant *did* look like someone who would kill his mom and keep her body in the freezer.

# FIFTEEN

PATOFF HAD CALLED A MEETING, AND MATTHEWS was glad that the rest of the Board was going to be there, because he no longer felt comfortable being alone with the consultant. The weekend retreat had been a disaster, and while he'd gone along with the fiction that it had been his desire to foment some sort of interpersonal bonding between employees, the truth was that the consultant had pushed him into it. "We don't need to do this," Matthews had argued. "It's a complete waste of time. Everyone works fine together."

"If everything was working fine," the consultant countered, "you wouldn't have had to call me in."

So they'd gone on the retreat and Patoff had remained behind—and Hugh Anderson and Russell Cibriano had committed suicide.

Matthews didn't think that was merely a coincidence.

He didn't think the suicides had just *happened*.

What did that mean, though? Did he think the consultant had killed them?

No, he didn't believe that.

But he didn't disbelieve it, either.

Last night, he'd had a nightmare where the consultant was standing in front of a long line of CompWare employees. The man was dressed in black and wielding an ax, and as each employee stepped forward docilely, he chopped off that person's head, laughing happily as the head rolled to join dozens of others on the ground at his feet. Matthews had never been one to put much stock in dreams, but it was clear what was occupying his subconscious mind, and the nightmare imagery correlated perfectly with not only his personal feelings about Regus Patoff but his opinion of the consultant's impact on his company.

Why had he hired a consulting firm in the first place? And how could all those other CEOs have recommended BFG? Their experiences must have been completely different than his, because he wouldn't recommend BFG to *anyone*.

Matthews entered the conference room. Everyone else had arrived ahead of him, and the members of the Board were crowded around Patoff, laughing and joking. All conversation stopped as soon as he walked into the room, everyone moving to their proper places, and he wondered when he had become such a killjoy that people made a conscious effort to avoid his company.

*When Patoff arrived*, he answered himself.

At the retreat, after the debacle of the bus ride, during the first Speed Conversation exercise, he had asked the people on the opposite team what they thought of the decision to bring in consultants after the merger fell through. Most of the employees had been wary, had hemmed and hawed with non-answers or told him what they thought he wanted to hear. But Craig Horne said he thought the Board could have made decisions about the company's future based on information gathered in-house. And on the next go-round, when the roles were reversed and it was Horne asking questions, the division head had asked whether Matthews was sorry he had hired the consultants. It emboldened him to know that others seemed to have the same reservations he did.

Even if the Board obviously did not.

Patoff stood at the front of the room as Matthews sat down next to the members of the Board.

"Since we're all here," the consultant said, "let's start. This is the first of what will be weekly status summaries; regular meetings to discuss our progress. We've found that our clients are happiest if they are kept in the loop, and sessions such as these allow us to report on current operations, explain the next steps we will be taking and address any concerns you may have.

"Senior management has just returned from a very successful weekend retreat—"

*Very successful?* Matthews thought.

"—and we have started to conduct our work management study. Obviously, the study is still in its infant stages, but we will be expanding its scope very shortly. In the meantime, there are rules and procedures that can be implemented which will not only begin to boost your productivity but will enable you to begin transitioning your staff."

"To what?" Matthews asked.

"That's what our research and analysis will determine."

"But how will we know if they are *transitioning* in the right direction," he said, exasperated, "if you don't know what we'll be transitioning *to*?"

Patoff smiled. "BFG has gone through this same scenario literally dozens of times. We know what we're doing."

"What *are* you doing?"

"You hired them," the gruff voice of Mitchell Lockhart intoned. "Let them do their job."

Matthews looked over at the members of the Board. Lockhart was scowling, and the other three were nodding in agreement. "They know what they're doing," Don Chase told him.

Matthews forced himself to remain calm. "It is our job to provide oversight, so we have a duty to ask questions. And since I'm the one who started this company, I think I've earned the right to have some say in its direction, don't you?" He turned away from the Board, dismissing them. "It is not your job to implement anything," he told Patoff. "Everything has to be run by me first, is that understood?"

The consultant stared back at him with a flat unreadable expression, and Matthews tried to maintain a similarly even mien, hoping his nervousness didn't show. Even in a roomful of people, the man made him uneasy. "Actually," the consultant said, "that's not true. If you read your contract, you will see that we *are* empowered to implement short-term measures that we deem appropriate. After we have completed our mission, then it is up to your discretion whether to adopt our long-term recommendations. But in the interim, we are *required* as per our signed agreement to address any problems we encounter within your organization in the manner that we see fit. And our experience with organizations of similar size and scope tells us that by gradually phasing in targeted rules and procedures, we can not only address some of your concerns immediately but can help position you to more readily adapt once final recommendations are made." A chilly smile graced Patoff's long face. "Now, if we may proceed with our meeting…"

There were only Matthews and the members of the Board, but the consultant had prepared for this meeting as though he were giving a presentation to the entire company. There was a Power-Point slideshow, a series of handouts with graphs and spreadsheets to back up BFG's assertions, and copies of the first memos and emails to send to employees. Matthews was the only one with any questions or concerns, and after a while, even he gave up arguing in the face of the consultant's implacability and the complete acceptance of the Board.

"You hired him to do a job," Lockhart repeated. "Let him do it."

Matthews spent the rest of the day in his office, fuming and feeling trapped, though he had no one to blame but himself for the situation he was in. At this point, if it were solely up to his discretion, he would fire BFG, consequences be damned. But he was in this with the Board. He needed their approval, and it was pretty clear he wouldn't get it, so it was probably best to bide his time.

Why the hell had he ever let the company go public?

Matthews left on time for once, and in the lobby saw Patoff chatting with a group of sales associates. Their eyes met accidentally, and Matthews forced himself to wave, but the consultant turned away, laughing at something one of the salesmen said. Maybe it was unintentional. Maybe Patoff *hadn't* seen him. But he knew that wasn't true, and he strode out to the Jag, rebuffed and angry, honking at two lower level employees to get out of the way as he sped out of the parking lot.

At home, he swam laps to relax and de-stress. He'd had a pool room built next to the gym last year when they remodeled, promising Rachel that he'd swim twenty laps each day to keep his gut down, but he couldn't remember the last time he'd actually used the pool. The water felt soothing, however, the swim invigorating, and he decided that perhaps he *should* do this every evening when he got home. Or maybe early in the morning before he went to work.

He got out, toweled off and found himself with an unprompted erection. When was the last time *that* had happened? Not bothering to put on clothes, he padded around the house looking for Rachel, but his erection was gone by the time he found her in the kitchen, and she just looked at him and said, "What are you doing? Get dressed."

They did make love that night, for the first time in over a month, and he didn't even need any Viagra. He just wined her, dined her, sixty-nined her, as the old saying went, and though he wasn't able to hold out that long, they both managed to have an orgasm.

He fell asleep almost immediately afterward.

It was still dark when he was awakened by the ringing of the phone next to his bed, and he answered with eyes still closed. "Yeah?" he managed to croak.

"Hello, Mr. Matthews."

It was Patoff.

"I know you forbade me from coming over to the fine house that you share with your lovely wife, but I had a few ideas I wanted to run by you, so I thought I'd give you a call."

"Do you know what time it is?" Matthews demanded.

"It's two-fourteen," the consultant replied, and the preciseness of the answer made Matthews open his eyes. There was a hint of rebuke in the response, maybe even a threat. He wasn't sure how that was possible, but it was.

"I'm hanging up," Matthews said. "You can tell me your ideas in the morning. During *business* hours."

"If you don't want me to share with you the ideas that will save your company, that's fine," the consultant said smoothly. "I understand. Apparently, that's not a priority for you, and you'd prefer to put it off to a later time that's more convenient. But when CompWare is in Chapter Eleven, I want you to remember this phone call and the chance I gave you. I want you to realize that you could have saved your company if you *weren't so fucking lazy*!"

There was a click as the consultant hung up, and Matthews was gripped by a feeling of panic. The panic was unfocused—was he afraid that CompWare *would* go bankrupt? Was he afraid that the consultant, once angered, would somehow take revenge on him?— but it left him shaky and nervous. He placed the handset back in the cradle.

"Who was it?" Rachel asked groggily.

"Nothing. Go back to sleep."

She was suddenly wide awake. "Was it that man?"

He pretended he didn't who she was talking about. "What man?"

"The consultant. The one who came over. I had a dream about him. He was chopping off people's heads and replacing them with those horrible snow globes."

*Chopping off people's heads?*

Matthews shivered. "No," he lied, "it was a wrong number."

"But weren't you talking to them?"

"No. You must have been dreaming. Go back to sleep."

She did, easily and quickly, but he remained awake for some time, staring up into the darkness, muscles tense. When he finally drifted off, he ended up in a nightmare, and in the dream, it was *his* head the consultant was chopping off.

The next morning, Matthews decided not to go into work. It was the first time he'd ever done anything like this—ordinarily, he went in even if he was sick as a dog—but he deserved to take a day off after years of such unrelenting dedication.

Besides…he was afraid of seeing the consultant.

That was ridiculous. The man worked for *him*. CompWare was BFG's *employer*. But the fact remained that the consultant seemed to be the one calling all the shots lately. Patoff was the dominant one in their relationship. Especially after that phone call last night.

If he didn't go in today, though, it would make it that much harder to go to work tomorrow. He could feel his grip on Comp-Ware slipping, and if he had any hope of holding onto his company, he needed to fight for it. He needed to *be* there.

Matthews forced himself to get out of bed. He couldn't back off now; he couldn't give up. And he couldn't hide in his office the way he had yesterday. He had to remain engaged, and he decided to visit all of the departments on all of the floors, to get out there and talk to people. Maybe he'd call his *own* meeting, without the consultant present, and find out what his employees were thinking. He wasn't by nature a democratic man, but desperate times called for desperate measures, and if he needed to let workers think that he was basing his decisions on their input instead of autocratically issuing edicts, then he would do so.

He couldn't let Patoff walk all over him.

But as he looked at his face in the mirror while preparing to shave, he could see the truth in his own eyes.

No matter how tough he might talk, he was still afraid of the consultant.

# SIXTEEN

TO:      All Employees
RE:      Proper Foot Attire

    Beginning this Monday, April 15, tennis shoes and other types of athletic footwear will no longer be considered acceptable attire at CompWare. Boots and sandals are likewise prohibited. This interdict applies not only to those employees who come in to work each day but also to those who have been temporarily granted permission to telecommute. If you are telecommuting and do not have a webcam on your communications device, you must install one at your own expense and submit a photograph of the shoes you are wearing each morning before you sign in.

Brown or black dress shoes are the only proper foot attire for males.

Closed-toed shoes with heels of less than a half-inch in height are the only proper attire for females.

Any questions regarding this change in policy must be submitted in writing to CompWare's Human Resources department before the end of business hours today. Reading this email constitutes acknowledgement and acceptance of the policy change.

Thank you.

*Regus Patoff*

Regus Patoff
BFG Associates
For Austin Matthews, CompWare CEO

# SEVENTEEN

"So," PHIL SAID, LOOKING DOWN AT CRAIG'S FEET AS they met on the outside steps, "are you wearing the right shoes?"

"Very funny."

Phil laughed. "It is, actually. Can you believe how ridiculous this is getting? Next thing you know, they'll be telling us what kind of hair styles we can have."

"I see that *you're* wearing black shoes instead of your usual sneakers," Craig noted dryly.

"Yeah, well, you have to know when to pick your battles."

Walking into the CompWare building, Craig couldn't help noticing everyone's footwear. Male or female, all shoes were regulation, and he realized how easy it was for an employer to change and control the lives of its employees. Corporations were governed from the top down, and an autocrat didn't have to contend with the messiness of democracy. Edicts were issued and obeyed, and people's appearance and behavior were instantly altered. Companies were little fiefdoms, which explained why business owners were so relentlessly anti-regulation. They wanted to dictate everything under their jurisdiction, and they didn't want the disorder of the real world intruding into their domains.

Phil was right. CompWare really could tell them what type of hairstyle to have. There were employers who didn't allow beards or mustaches or who regulated hair length—and no one blinked. Society had tacitly agreed that a company paying for work could determine the physical appearance of its workers, even away from the job. Their influence was insidious.

"Look above the elevators," Phil said, his head down and his voice low. "New cameras. They're popping up everywhere, a few more each day."

"I've noticed that, too."

"Where do you think those feeds end up? What system do they run on?"

"You mean, can they be accessed?"

Phil shrugged. "Well…"

"I think I can get someone to find out."

"Be careful."

"Always am."

On the way up to his office, Craig stopped off on the programmers' floor. After what had happened with Tyler, he wasn't sure who he could trust—or if he could trust anyone—but Rusty had already expressed his displeasure with the consultants, blaming them for leaking *Zombie Navy*, and Craig thought if there was anyone who'd be willing to look into the new surveillance equipment for him, it was the technical writer.

He was right, but, as he should have known, Rusty did not have the specialized expertise needed to conduct such an investigation. "Ang might be able to check it out," Rusty said. They were both speaking low so as not to be overheard. "He used to work for AT&T, and he's good with hardware *and* software. We'd need to trace those feeds back to their source but not let the trace be traced back to us. He can probably do that. Want me to ask him?"

"No, I'll do it," Craig said. "No need for you to put your ass on the line." He thought for a moment. "Do you think Ang…?

"He hates the consultants, too. *Everybody* hates them."

That was a relief to hear. It had occurred to him that maybe some employees approved of hiring BFG, although with everyone's jobs potentially on the line, he didn't see how that was possible. It heartened him to know that they were all on the same page.

"Is Ang in yet?" he asked.

"I don't think so." Rusty stood and peered over the edge of his cubicle. "No. You want me to have him call you when he gets in?"

"Tell him to come up to my office."

"You got it, chief."

Craig couldn't be sure his office wasn't bugged, but it was definitely safer to talk there than on the phone.

Upstairs, Lupe was already at her desk. Alone.

"Where's Todd?" Craig asked, looking around.

"I believe he's in the bathroom."

"You should mark that down."

"Oh, I am. I'm keeping score. Yesterday, he arrived a minute later than me, and I was exactly on time. Which meant that he was late. I'm keeping track of everything." She smiled. "Don't mess with me."

At that moment, Todd returned. Craig saw him striding briskly toward them. Smiling slyly, Lupe met his eyes, then reached into her desk. As the consultant sat down, Lupe made a big show of staring at him and writing something down in the notebook she removed from her drawer, making sure he was aware that *she* was keeping track of *him*. Reddening, he looked down at his tablet. She put her notebook away and went back to whatever she'd been doing on her computer.

Craig wanted to laugh, but he kept a straight face as he walked into his office, closing the door behind him.

He sat down at his desk and turned on his own computer.

There were forty-three email messages in his queue, all of them from the consultant.

The first was an email about how to write and send emails, with six pages of attachments containing do-and-don't examples. The second concerned phone etiquette within the company and without. This one also contained an attachment: audio clips of correctly and incorrectly conducted phone conversations. The third email involved new company-wide restrictions on the use of printer ink.

Craig paused. This was ridiculous.

And there were still forty more to go.

He would have emailed Phil to see if his friend had received the same messages but was afraid that written communications were being monitored. Ditto for the phone.

Quickly, he scanned through the rest of the messages, all of which were attempts to micromanage daily office routines, then told Lupe to hold his calls because he was going to Phil's office for a few minutes.

Todd, seated behind Lupe, duly typed something onto his tablet.

"I thought you were supposed to be watching her, not me," Craig said.

"I am," the consultant said.

"Then what were you entering there?"

"You gave her a specific duty, and I noted it."

Not wanting to get into an argument and already feeling irritated, Craig shared a glance with Lupe, then headed down the corridor toward the elevators.

Upstairs, Phil's secretary, Shelley, was sitting stiffly at her desk, an observer seated to the right watching every move and typing on the electronic tablet in his lap.

"Is Phil in?" Craig asked.

Shelley's greeting was uncharacteristically formal, but he understood why and did not fault her for it. In a single smooth move, she picked up the handset of her phone and pressed one of the buttons on the console. "Who may I say is calling?"

"Craig Horne."

She relayed the message, then informed him that he was approved to enter Phil's office. Getting up from her seat, she led him the five feet to Phil's doorway, stepping aside to allow him entrance. "Sorry," she whispered.

Phil rolled his eyes. "Close that door, will you?" he asked Shelley. "Thanks."

Craig motioned toward the door and the observer beyond. "I see you guys have one, too."

"What a pain in the ass this is turning out to be."

"Tell me about it."

"Do you have any idea how long they're going to be disrupting our lives?"

He shook his head. "No one's confiding in me."

"Well, I hope it's quick."

"Don't hold your breath. Hey, the reason I'm here is that when I came in this morning I found forty-something emails from Patoff telling me how to write email messages, and how to make professional phone calls, and how to save money on printer ink, and a whole host of helpful hints. I was wondering if you'd gotten anything like that."

"Oh, indeed I have." Motioning Craig closer, Phil swiveled his monitor and typed something on his keyboard. Up popped an Inbox filled from top to bottom with messages. "I guess my skill set deficiencies are somewhat different than yours. Look! Now I can learn how to describe a product to a prospective buyer in the most positive manner possible. Something I've been doing for *half my goddamn life!*"

Craig shook his head, scanning the subject lines. "These are all completely different than mine. How can he write so many? Where does he find the time?"

Phil waved his hand. "They're probably generic. Every client they have probably gets the same emails. I get the Sales ones, you get the Programming ones…"

"Maybe," Craig said doubtfully.

Phil sighed. "Well, as if that weren't enough, I'm down one man."

"What does that mean?"

"I got here this morning and found out that Isaac Morales had been fired for cause."

"They wanted you to fire Isaac, didn't they? After the interviews?"

"Indeed they did."

"So what'd he do?"

"Apparently, he'd been charging personal items to our department account. And not just an occasional flash drive or ink cartridge but …a flat screen TV…a new laptop…clothes…"

"Really?"

"Yeah. Except…"

"Except you don't think he did it."

196

"The evidence is there. In black and white. He's not only been fired, he's being criminally charged, and I'm told the case is airtight."

"But you don't think he did it."

Phil shook his head. "No. I don't think he did it. I *know* Isaac. He's not that kind of guy. Sales is sometimes a shady business, and we get all types here. But he's an anomaly, like a virgin in a whorehouse. He's an honest sales rep. That's why his numbers are so good. Clients trust him because they know he won't steer them wrong. Besides, some of those purchases…a flat screen TV? Isaac doesn't even *watch* TV."

"Maybe his wife—"

"His *boyfriend* doesn't, either."

"Oh."

"There's just a lot of shit that doesn't add up."

"So he was framed?"

"That's my guess. I have no way to prove it, but I hope he finds a smart lawyer who can."

Craig believed him. It made no logical sense to sideline a good employee, not from a consulting firm supposedly trying to shore up CompWare's business, but there seemed nothing logical in the decisions that had been made recently, no method to BFG's madness.

He thought about the weekend retreat, Tyler's freak accident, Anderson's and Cibriano's suicides.

Maybe he and Phil were reading undeserved import into unrelated events, seeing malevolent conspiracies where none existed.

But he didn't think that was the case.

"So what's the plan?" Craig asked.

"I don't know." His friend sounded tired, his usual fight in abeyance. "Keep our heads down and wait it out? They're not going to be here forever. I don't know what the time frame is, but for all we know, they could be halfway through already. It's probably easier and faster to wait them out than try to go against them."

"Matthews—"

"If he really wanted to, he could get rid of them today. He might be having second thoughts, but he's obviously not willing to scrap this consulting thing completely."

Craig was silent for a minute. "I'm not sure there *is* a time frame. Those new cameras don't make it seem like they're leaving anytime soon. I wouldn't be surprised if there was an open-ended contract and the consultants are here for as long as they want to be here, for as long as *they* say it's going to take them."

Phil nodded soberly. "Highly probable."

Craig stood. "Well, it's been fun. Thanks for the pep talk."

"Anytime."

He started for the door, turning before grabbing the handle. "We *might* be halfway through this 'work management study.'"

"But what comes after that?"

"Exactly."

He'd been gone less than ten minutes, but Lupe passed him a handful of pink While-You-Were-Out messages when he returned. Neither of them spoke in front of Todd, but Craig sorted through the notes as he walked into his office. As he'd hoped, one was from Ang, and he shut his door and called the programmer, at first asking Ang to come to his office, then changing his mind and telling the programmer to wait at his desk, he'd be coming down.

Rusty had always had a mouth on him—in retrospect, maybe he shouldn't have revealed so much to the technical writer—and as soon as Craig approached Ang's desk, a group of programmers gathered around, all wanting in on the action. There were no BFG fans in his division, and Craig felt a certain pride at that.

But he was already thinking that maybe Phil was right, and the best approach was just to go along to get along, and wait the consultants out. What good, really, would it do him to know where the growing number of video feeds led, especially since, if word of their investigation got out, they could all be fired? Tony Hernandez had once worked for TRW, was more versed than the rest of them in workplace privacy issues, and he said that consistently upheld court cases had gutted employee privacy and allowed employers to monitor workers on job sites with almost complete impunity. That put the nail in the coffin. "You know what?" Craig said. "I changed my mind. We're not going to do this. Just let it lie."

"Got it," Ang responded, but it was said almost with a wink, and Craig knew they all thought he was just trying to institute some plausible deniability.

"No, I'm serious," he said. "It's too dangerous. It's not worth it, and there's nothing we could learn that would help us in any way."

That seemed to get the point home. "They're *spying* on us," Rusty said.

"And, apparently, they're allowed to do so."

In order to make their retreat more palatable, Craig added a "for now" to his prohibition against investigating the cameras, and that seemed to placate everyone, even Rusty. It was a feeling of helplessness they had, that he shared, and they all wanted to do something about the consultants, though there was not really any-thing they *could* do.

He went back up to his office.

Found twenty new emails from BFG.

Deleted them all without reading a single one.

Feeling restless, feeling antsy, he stood and paced around his office. Getting a bottle of water from his little fridge, he stood near the window, drinking as he stared down at the campus. Below, two men dressed in black hoodies were making their way along the winding concrete path toward the parking lot, carrying a long covered bundle between them, a bundle that looked like…

*A body?*

No. It couldn't be.

*Yes, it could.*

He probably should have called Security but instead sped down to the campus. Taking the stairs rather than an elevator, he held onto the railings on both sides, using leverage to swing over multiple steps in an effort to get to the ground floor as fast as he could. But by the time he ran outside to the spot he had seen from his window, that area was empty. He followed the path in the direction the hoodied figures had been moving, ending up in the parking lot, but saw no one on foot and no moving vehicles. Wherever they'd gone, he'd missed them, and now he'd never know what they were carrying.

In his mind, the contours of the covered shape still looked like a body, and he tried to think of who it might be. *Isaac Morales?* The idea was ludicrous and crazy—only it wasn't. Not after Tyler. Not after Anderson and Cibriano.

Turning, he walked back into the building, this time taking the elevator. What the hell was going on here? If people were actually dying, he needed to tell the police or quit his job or…do something. But he had no proof that anything had even occurred, and the uncertainty and the incrementalism of it all left him feeling lost and helpless as he returned to the sixth floor.

"Mr. Cho called," Lupe told Craig when he reached her desk. "He's in a meeting with all of the programmers. He wants you there." From her tone and expression, he understood that Scott was angry, but she said nothing aloud, glancing meaningfully at Todd to her right.

"Where?" Craig asked.

"In the conference room." She motioned down the hall.

Thanking her, he walked purposefully to the conference room, which was already filled.

"Where were you?" Scott demanded. "When I call a meeting, you're supposed to be here."

Craig didn't respond. What could he say? *I thought I saw two men carrying a body?* Any excuse would just prolong the department head's tirade. He sat down silently in the nearest chair.

"As I was *saying*," Scott said, looking pointedly at Craig, "the investigation has determined that Jack Razon was the one who leaked a version of *Zombie Navy*. We're now in full damage control mode. Mr. Razon, of course, no longer works for CompWare, and criminal charges will be brought against him. *Our* job is to continue to make sure that no sites, corporations or individuals have *any* version of our game. Legal is also sending out threatening letters and working to get all reviews wiped since they were obtained using illegally copied prototypes, although you know how that goes, the First Amendment and all that." He fixed Craig with a hard stare. "How are you doing with the containment effort?"

Craig was still having a difficult time processing the information. *Jack Razon?* The vice president hadn't even been shown the game yet and was nowhere in the development chain of command. It was also well known that Jack Razon was not exactly the most tech savvy vice president the company had. Craig found it hard, if not impossible, to believe that Razon had independently wound his way through the tight security surrounding *Zombie Navy* and then uploaded a copy of the game onto the web. Even if he *had* had the expertise to do such a thing, what would be the point?

"I think we've got them all," Craig told Scott, "but we're still checking to make sure."

"Good."

He shook his head. "Jack Razon? Really?"

"Really," Scott said, his voice hard.

Craig still didn't believe it, and he thought of Isaac Morales, who had probably been framed by BFG. He wouldn't be surprised if this was the same situation.

He wouldn't be surprised at all.

# EIGHTEEN

LUPE HEATED UP HER LEAN CUISINE, TOOK A DIET
Snapple out of the refrigerator and went down to the weight loss
meeting. Last week, they'd tried convening in the break room on
the sixth floor, but too many people had shown up, so this week
they'd decided to book the third floor conference room. Today was
the official weigh-in, and a doctor's scale had been obtained from
somewhere and set up against the wall opposite the door.

Lupe was one of the first to arrive. She sat down at the center of
the long table in the back, eating her lunch as other women gradually filled up the empty spaces around her. Rebecca from Finance
was organizer of the gathering, and she walked in last, striding
straight to the front of the room.

"Thanks for coming," she said. "We'll make this quick, since
I know some of you have abbreviated lunch hours. But before we
weigh in, I've asked Mr. Patoff to give us a little pep talk.

Patoff?

Lupe instantly regretted coming here today. The last thing she wanted to do at lunch was listen to the consultant. Why was he even involved with this? It was an extracurricular activity, arranged by employees for employees on their own time. Shouldn't he be doing what he was hired to do? Looking for ways to keep the company viable? She filed that away for future reference.

Besides, Craig was right. She didn't really need this meeting. While she might want to take off a few pounds, she was by no means overweight, particularly in comparison with some of the other secretaries. But she was halfway through her lunch, and it would be awkward to walk out now. Like it or not, she was committed.

The consultant entered, beaming, nodding at women as he walked by. "Hello, Liz. Shelley! How are you today?" He seemed to know everyone by name, and by the reaction he was getting, most of the other secretaries were thrilled by his presence. How was that possible? Lupe glanced over at Pauline Praeger, who caught her glance, shook her head and shrugged her shoulders to indicate her own confusion.

At the front of the room, Rebecca was smiling broadly. "Mr. Patoff," she said. "Thank you so much for stopping by. We are truly honored by your presence."

He moved next to her. "It's my honor to be here."

"We were about to have our first weigh-in, and I was hoping you could give us a little encouragement and inspiration."

"Be glad to," he said, and spread his arms to include all of the women in the room. "You're *all* overweight," he told them. "Most of you are fat. Some of you are obese. And that is not acceptable. You might fool yourself into thinking you're a ton of fun, but the truth is that men find you disgusting." He pointed to a woman at the front table. "Olivia," he said. "I know you're unmarried. Do you think you'll ever be able to get a husband looking like *that*?"

The woman reddened, looking down at the remains of lunch in front of her.

"Even those of you who are married, you know your husbands aren't into you anymore. How often do you have sex? Twice a month? Once? You know that's not satisfying him. He has to be going elsewhere." He turned to Rebecca. "And when's the last time you could even look down and see your bush beneath that blubber? You think a man likes to look at a gunt when his woman takes her clothes off? Show a little pride.

"In short, you all better lose some weight. Because this is your last chance, your last hope. If you don't get yourself in shape now, you never will. You'll end up dying alone, and it'll be a miracle if they don't have to take out a wall in order to forklift you into a piano box." He smiled, bowed. "Thank you."

Lupe was horrified, but Rebecca led the applause, which was surprisingly enthusiastic. "Thank *you*, Mr. Patoff. Very inspirational. Very inspirational, indeed." She addressed the seated women. "Now everyone stand and line up on this side of the room." She pointed to the wall on the right. "We're going to weigh in. I will fill out a card for each contestant, and we'll update it every week for the next six weeks. After that, we'll see who lost the most, and that person will win the money."

"We need to make this fair," the consultant chimed in. "Everyone needs to strip down before stepping onto the scale so we can get an accurate weight."

"Good idea," Rebecca said.

"Everything off," the consultant said. "Underwear included."

Lupe left.

Gathering her Lean Cuisine tray and her iced tea bottle, she deposited them both in the trash can by the door as she walked

out. She expected a mass exodus behind her, but only Pauline followed in her wake. Everyone else remained.

"What the hell was that?" Pauline said in the hallway.

Stopping to turn around and look at the closing door, Lupe
shook her head. There were squeals and giggles from inside the
room, and she didn't even want to *think* about what might be happening in there.

"Maybe he's a chubby chaser," Pauline said.

Lupe's eyes met those of the other secretary, and instantly they
both burst out laughing. The laughter felt good.

Until she looked to her left.

And saw Todd standing there, tapping away on his tablet.

She stopped laughing. At least a dozen other consultants were
lined up by the wall next to him, and as Lupe strode angrily toward
the elevator, Todd broke away to follow her. Another man trailed
Pauline, heading in the opposite direction.

"Chubby chaser!" Pauline called out, and Lupe could not help
smiling as she pushed the Up elevator button.

⁙

Once again, Huell Parrish stayed late to work on the Office-
Manager updates. He knew this was his big break, which was why
he wasn't even putting the hours down. If he could kick ass on
this project, and they thought he was doing it within regular work
hours, without accruing overtime, it would show the powers-that-
be that he was ready for more responsibility, that he deserved a
promotion. At any other company, he would already be a supervisor based on experience and seniority alone, but CompWare was
run differently. He was hoping the consultants would change that,

although his work on this project should help him advance no matter which way the wind was blowing.

After running a compile, he exited, shut down his computer and came back in, calling up the main menu.

*Underage Diddlers.*

Huell stared in horror at the banner title of the website that appeared on his computer. Beneath the words, photos of young girls masturbating were displayed on the page. Quickly, he exited the screen, but instead of returning to one of CompWare's internal networks, another website showed up.

*Dick Loving Daughters.*

He shut off the machine, his palms sweaty. How in the hell had that happened? He could probably find out easily enough by tracing the route, but in the front of his mind was the fact that the consultants had everyone's password and ID. No doubt they were tracking all employees, and to them it was going to look like he'd been accessing kiddie porn sites.

With CompWare's computers.

And if he did trace the route, they would probably think he was trying to erase the evidence of his own misdeeds.

Ever since that "Photos of CompWare Women Sucking Cocks at Christmas Party!!!" scam, neither he nor anyone else he knew had even *thought* about accessing an outside site, particularly a porn site. But this had been automatic, as though a command had been inserted that forced his computer to go to specific locations no matter which key was pressed.

That was impossible, though. He'd been working on this machine for hours. No one else had had access to it, and he'd experienced no glitches, seen no indication that anything was amiss.

Could a rogue command have been inserted into the compile?

It was possible, and for the first time, he thought that maybe this wasn't the consultants.

Maybe Lorene had done it in order to get her hands on Office-Manager.

The idea gave him pause. The two of them had been working together pretty smoothly, but he knew how much she'd wanted to be in charge of the project, and he wouldn't put it past her to sabotage him in order to make herself look good. She was a sneaky one, as ambitious as he was, and she was more than capable of pulling off something like this.

Well, two could play at that game.

Moving to a different terminal, *her* terminal, he logged in under the department's generic sign-on, then created a new password and produced a quick and dirty program that would automatically erase any OfficeManager updates created on this machine. He hesitated briefly in a moment of uncertainty—*could it really be Lorene?*—but then submitted the program, signed off, shut down the terminal and walked away.

Let the bitch try and talk her way out of this one.

— &#10082; —

Jack Razon had no idea where he was.

He had closed the door to his office after lunch for his usual early afternoon catnap, had nodded off at his desk...and had awakened in darkness, tied to a chair, arms bound behind him, legs strapped together. He felt disoriented, but only because the world around him was pitch-black; it didn't feel as though he'd been drugged or hit on the head.

How had he gotten here, then?

And where *was* here?

"Help!" he called, but his throat was dry, his voice was weak, and his cry for help ended in a coughing jag that almost made him vomit. Closing his mouth, he tried to generate some saliva, then made another attempt. "Help!"

"No one can hear you."

It was impossible to tell, in the darkness, from which direction the voice came, but Jack recognized its owner immediately.

Regus Patoff.

An overhead light switched on, a blinding harsh white after the gentle softness of gloom, and it took his eyes a moment to adjust. When they did, he saw that he was in what looked like the same narrow bare-walled room where he'd had his initial interview with the consultant. In front of him was the same metal table, and sitting in a chair on the other side of the table was Patoff. The only difference this time was that Jack was bound.

"What the hell's going on here?" he demanded, hoping he sounded more angry than scared.

"You know very well what's going on." The consultant fixed him with a stony gaze.

"This is illegal. You're not only going to be fired, but I'll make sure you go to jail."

There was no response.

"Let me out of here now!" he ordered.

The consultant smiled indulgently. "Jack, Jack. You know we can't do that."

For the first time, he felt the taste of real fear.

"You need to be punished for what you've done."

"I haven't done anything!"

"Yes, you have."

"What?"

"Do I need to spell it out?"

He was becoming frustrated. "I guess you do, because I don't know what the hell you're talking about."

The consultant's eyes were flat, hard. "In direct violation of your employment contract, you released over the internet a test version of the game *Zombie Navy*, potentially costing CompWare millions of dollars in lost profits."

"I didn't do that!"

"With users able to download and play a version of the game for free, why would they shell out money to buy *Zombie Navy*? You may have single-handedly bankrupted the company. At the very least, you have caused significant financial harm during a fragile rebuilding period."

"I didn't do it!" Jack insisted.

"You keep saying that, but we know you did."

"I don't even have access to new games! I *couldn't* have done it!"

There was a significant pause and Jack jumped on it. "Maybe I've been set up," he told the consultant, "maybe there's been a mis-understanding. I don't know. But check it out. I swear it wasn't me."

He could see that he'd gotten through, and Patoff looked at him for a moment, then stood. "I'll be back," the consultant promised.

The lights remained on as Patoff walked around the table, past him and out the door. The second he heard the door click closed, Jack started trying to wiggle his way out of his bonds. He'd been tied to the chair with not rope or twine but some type of coated electrical wire, like the kind used in old radios and tele-visions. The wire had much less give than rope, was much more effective at keeping him bound, and he was unable to gain even an inch of slack.

His eyes were now completely adjusted to the light, and he looked around the room, hoping to spot something he could use to free himself. The table before him was completely empty, as was the area around his feet, but on the far side of the narrow room, past the chair where the consultant had been sitting, on the floor next to the right wall, were two poles, each about three feet long.

One of them ended in a pointed spearhead, the other in a barbed hook.

Jack began jerking his hands and feet violently back and forth, trying desperately to escape.

There was a loud click behind him as the door opened once again. The consultant passed by him on the right and stood on the other side of the table, not sitting down. "You're right," Patoff said. "You didn't do it." He waved his arm magnanimously. "You're free to go."

The wire, somehow, had become untied and lay on the floor beneath Jack's suddenly loose hands and feet.

He stood. His first impulse was to yell at the consultant, to threaten the man with jail time for capturing, confining and restraining him against his will, but common sense won out, and he decided it was better to bring that up when he was safely out of here and around other people. He exited the room, not saying anything to the consultant or even looking in his direction.

He strode purposefully down the hall, and it took him a moment to realize that he didn't recognize where he was. The corridors looked like CompWare corridors, the doors looked like CompWare doors, but...something was off. Everything he saw was not quite right: the color of the floor, the shape of the lights, the font of the numbers identifying the rooms. He saw no other people, and that was odd, too.

Disconcerted, he hurried over to the elevators.

Only...

Only the elevators weren't there. Instead, a bare wall stretched over that space, its color a slightly *whiter* white than the ones he was used to in this building.

*Was* it this building?

Jack was not sure. He decided he needed to find a window. If he could look outside, get his bearings, maybe it would help him figure out where he was and how to get out of here. At CompWare, the offices on the opposite side of the corridor from the elevators overlooked the campus, and he walked across the hall, trying three doors before he found one that opened.

It had no window.

It was also not an office. It looked more like a living room, and, frowning, he peered into the enclosed space. On the walls were old-fashioned paintings in elaborate wooden frames: a sailing ship, a New England town, a race track with horses and jockeys milling about. In front of an ugly brown couch was a long low coffee table, and on the side of the couch was a smaller, higher end table.

On the end table was a bottle of pills.

Jack stood there, staring. He recognized that end table. It was the same as the one in his grandmother's house, the one next to her sickbed where she'd kept all of her medicine. She'd died when he was twelve, overdosing on the medication that was supposed to help her through the worst side-effects of the chemo, and no one in his family had ever been sure if her death had been accidental or intentional. On the one hand, the bottle holding the high-dose medicine had been almost identical to the one holding the low-level aspirin-based pain reliever. On the other hand, she'd spent over a month in that bed and had never made the mistake of confusing the two.

How could that table and medicine be here, though?

And why?

*He was supposed to kill himself.*

Jack slammed the door shut and ran down the hallway, away from the room. He had to get out of here. In the normal version of CompWare, the *right* version, he would be running toward the north stairwell, but the corridor didn't end where it was supposed to, it continued on, and other corridors branched off to the sides, all of them lined with closed doors that *looked* like CompWare doors—but weren't.

He hadn't been merely hurrying down the hallway, he'd been *running*, and he slowed, then stopped, out of breath. Was there any way out of here? There were doors to either side of him, and he tried opening the one on the right. It was unlocked, and inside the windowless and otherwise empty room a bottle of pills sat atop his grandmother's end table.

Closing that door, he tried the other one on the opposite side of the corridor.

The end table and pills were right next to the entrance.

He tried to slam the door, but the hinges wouldn't allow it, and the door closed slowly.

"Help!" he called out, feeling weak and pathetic as he did so. "Help!"

There was no response, but he thought he saw movement out of the corner of his eye, up the corridor in the direction he'd been running. "Hey!" he yelled, and though he was still short of breath, he sprinted up the hallway. He saw no movement ahead of him, but down side hallways, in his peripheral vision, there always seemed to be a figure. Blurry, out of focus, too ill-defined for him to even ascribe it a shape, it moved out of sight before he could focus on it.

He chased the elusive form for over an hour before finally giving up and trying yet another door.

There again, this time in a hospital setting, was his grand-mother's end table and the pills.

*Was there any other way out?*

He was beginning to think there wasn't, but there was no way in hell that he was going to kill himself. He'd run through these hallways forever if he had to, but he was not giving up, and if it was the last thing he ever did, he would find that consultant and make him pay.

Jack closed the door.

And ran farther down the corridor.

# NINETEEN

"I WISH I COULD QUIT," ANGIE SAID AFTER PUTTING Dylan to bed.

Craig, on the couch, looked up from the television, surprised. "Why? What happened?"

"Nothing happened." She sighed, sitting down next to him. "Well, nothing specific. But ever since…Pam, I just don't feel comfortable there anymore."

"You *can* quit," he said, though he sounded dubious.

She smiled. "Thanks for the enthusiastic support."

"No, I mean—"

"I understand. But we both know that with your situation so shaky, it would be stupid for me to give up my job."

"It doesn't mean you can't look around. What if you find something better? As long as you have something else lined up before you resign…"

"Yeah, but I have seniority here. And they let me have the schedule I want. Someplace new, I'd be bottom person on the totem pole."

"I don't know what to tell you."

She shrugged. "There's nothing to say. Unless we win the lottery, we're pretty much stuck."

"I'll buy a ticket tomorrow," he promised.

Smiling, she kissed his cheek. "The drawing's tonight," she said. "But it's the thought that counts."

"Next time, then."

The next day was Sunday, and Craig and Dylan were going to go to a Pet Expo at the L. A. Convention Center. That sounded like fun, and Angie almost called in sick to join them, but she decided at the last minute to tough it out and head to work.

The consultant was waiting for her outside the Urgent Care, next to the alcove that housed the employee's entrance, holding a sheaf of papers in his hand. Above his geeky clothes and below his atrocious toupee, his eyes stared intently at her with his usual needy nervousness. She smiled politely as she approached, nodding a generic greeting, intending to walk by him, but when he said her name, she stopped.

The consultant glanced awkwardly down at his feet, holding out the sheaf of papers. "We're out," he said. "Private Practices has been replaced. But I already started on my report, and you were always nice to me, so I thought I'd give you a copy anyway. You can look at it, compare it to what the new consultants say. Maybe… maybe it'll help."

"What happened?" Angie asked.

"You were poached. Apparently, this other company's really aggressive. They started doing polls and surveys, trying to prove that we weren't efficient—"

"Oh my God!" she said. "I got one of those calls! I hung up on them. That wasn't you? I thought it was you guys."

He shook his head. "No, it was BFG."

She suddenly felt cold. "BFG?"

"That's the company taking over from us. Apparently, there was some sort of clause in our contract that they managed to exploit. If your management determined that we weren't effective, the agreement could be voided and other consultants found to do the job. So BFG bombarded them with polls and studies purporting to show that they were wonderful and we were terrible. And now...we're out."

"I'm sorry," Angie said.

The consultant sighed. "It wouldn't bother me so much if I hadn't already started writing the report. But I put a lot of work into this—we all have—and I think our suggestions are pretty good. Just throwing it all away seems like such a waste. Besides, I've *heard* things about BFG," he admitted, and the way he said it sent goose bumps surfing down her arms.

"What have you heard?" she asked.

"I probably shouldn't say."

"What?"

He spoke carefully. "Well, I've heard, second hand, maybe third hand, that their methods... sometimes...are not always... that they, ah, don't just observe and report, that they get *involved*. Like most consultants, we study and scrutinize each workplace we're hired to survey, and we make recommendations based on what we've seen. But BFG...I've heard they're more hands-on—and a lot of people don't like it. They look good on paper, and maybe they have some references, but a lot of their customers...they don't end up happy."

"Do you have any more...?"

"Details? No. I've already said more than I should. Anyway, you have my report, or the rough draft of it. Maybe it'll help you." He looked at his watch. "I'd better go." The consultant gave her an awkward hug, leaning in too close, and she felt a hard penis press against her stomach. She pulled quickly away, disgusted. If he were still monitoring the Urgent Care, she would have taken some sort of action, gone up the ladder to his superiors. But as this would be the end of their contact, she made the decision to ignore the incident and let it go.

Red-faced, he turned away and hurried into the parking lot. At least he had the decency to be embarrassed.

From what Craig said, she doubted that BFG would be as human.

Angie opened the door, walking into the building and looking down at the pile of papers in her hand. The pages were held together with a clip at the top, and the cover page was blank, probably to disguise what was beneath. Part of her was afraid to open the report, fearing some sort of Jack Torrance manuscript: the same phrase repeated over and over again, single-spaced, double-sided. But when she walked up the hallway, reached the front desk, sat down in an empty chair and flipped up the cover page, she saw a flow chart of the Urgent Care's weekday and weekend staffing.

"What're you reading?" Sharon asked, walking up and stashing her purse under the counter.

"Apparently, we're getting new consultants. The old one gave me this. It's his initial report."

"He's gone?" Sharon said. "Thank God. That weirdo gave me the creeps."

"He *is* a weirdo, and he *is* creepy, but I'm not so sure these new guys are going to be any better." She gave the other nurse a short rundown of Craig's experience with BFG at CompWare.

"Why do we even need consultants at all?" Sharon asked. "*We* know what works and what doesn't. All they have to do is ask us."

"My point exactly." Angie flipped through the report, skimming a section marked "Conclusions" at the bottom of one of the pages. The suggestions seemed reasonable and much more astute than she would have guessed, based on the consultant's demeanor. But she didn't have time to read the whole thing. The doctors and other nurses were arriving, and it would soon be time to let in patients. She needed to get ready for this morning's shift.

She turned on the computer in front of her, logging on and clocking in, while Sharon did the same on the next machine over. It was her turn to inventory the exam rooms for supplies, so she stowed the report on the same shelf under the counter where Sharon had put her purse and headed back down the hall, wondering when the consultants from BFG were going to arrive—

*I've* heard *things about BFG.*

—and what would happen when they did.

———

When Craig walked into work Monday morning, there was a man seated in the guest chair in his office. The chair had been moved from in front of his desk to the wall next to the refrigerator. Young and clean-cut, like a *Sound of Music* Nazi, the man did not bother to look up, and even if he had not been typing on an electronic tablet resting on his lap, Craig would have known why he was there.

"What's your name?" Craig asked.

"Martin," the observer said, still focused on his screen.

"Well, Martin. Stay out of my way and don't annoy me, and we should have no problems."

He'd intended to sound commanding and authoritative, wanting to intimidate the young man, but the consultant was having none of it. "Arrive on time, work your allotted hours, do your job, and *then* we should have no problems."

Martin finally looked up and met his gaze. There was hostility in his expression, and the unexpected belligerence threw Craig off guard for a second, but anger quickly replaced surprise. "Put that chair back where you found it."

"I put it here because—"

"I put it *there* because that's where it belongs," Craig told him. "You will move it back in front of my desk. You may sit on it until I have visitors, at which point you must either sit on the floor or stand. I don't really care which."

"I am authorized to—"

"I don't give a shit what you're authorized to do," Craig declared. "Do it or get the fuck out of here."

"You can't—"

"I can kick your ass," Craig said.

Smiling, the observer entered something on his tablet, and Craig knew that he'd stepped in it. Still, his anger had not abated. "I'm taking this up with your boss," he said.

"Mr. Patoff's in a meeting," Martin said.

"We'll see about that." Craig stormed out of his office. "Get me Mr. Patoff," he ordered Lupe. "Now."

Todd looked up. "Mr. Patoff is in a meeting," he said.

Craig ignored the observer. "I want to talk to him," he told Lupe. "Put it on speaker."

She pressed a button. He heard a dial tone, then four beeps as she called the consultant's extension. A woman answered. "Mr. Patoff's office."

Lupe gave him a questioning look, and Craig nodded. "Hold for Mr. Horne, please," she said.

Craig moved next to her desk, leaning over. "This is Craig Horne in Programming. I'd like to speak with Mr. Patoff."

"I'm sorry, sir," the woman said. "Mr. Patoff is in a meeting,"

Todd smirked. "Told you."

"I told you, too," Martin said from the doorway of his office.

Craig ignored them. "Do you know when he will be in?"

"His schedule's full today."

"Well, please have him call me back when he gets a chance. My extension's 358."

"I will relay the message," the woman said. Was there a smirk behind *her* voice? He didn't get a chance to probe further as the connection was cut and the dial tone returned. Lupe pressed a button, and it was gone.

Craig grabbed one of the chairs near his secretary's desk and placed it next to Todd. "This is your chair," he told Martin.

The observer stared at him, unblinking.

"Do I have to physically move you?" Craig threatened.

Typing on his tablet, Martin emerged from the doorway and sat down. "I will report what you're doing," he said, still not bothering to glance up.

"You can report when I'm in my office and when I'm not," Craig told him. "That's *all* you can do." He met Lupe's eyes, shooting her a look of apology, but she smiled back, understanding, and he left her out there with the two of them, closing the door behind him as he returned to his office.

⤜⧂⧂⧂⤛

After his mom gave him a quick hug, dropped him off at school and, as always, told him to "have fun," Dylan ran immediately to the playground. But because he'd taken too long to eat his breakfast, he was a little late this morning, and the bell rang before he even found his friends. Disappointed, he walked over to his classroom and lined up with everyone else in front of the door. Andy and Brian shoved themselves behind him.

Mrs. Higgins was usually right on time, but the classes on both sides of them had already gone inside by the time the door opened and their teacher came out. Distracted, she ushered them into the room, where they each took their seats. After attendance and the pledge, instead of starting on math, the way they usually did, Mrs. Higgins stood next to her desk and asked for their attention.

"I want you all to be on your best behavior," she told them. "For the next few days, there will be a man coming in to watch our class. He'll be taking notes on what we do and how we learn. He may even ask you questions. During the next three weeks, he'll be visiting all of the classes in school."

"Why?" Laurie Connor asked.

"The district wants to help us become better teachers, so that all of you will learn more."

"*I* think you're a good teacher!" Juan Florez piped up.

Mrs. Higgins smiled. "Thank you, Juan. But remember, next time raise your hand."

Behind them, the door opened, and the principal walked in, followed by a tall, thin man wearing black pants, a white shirt and a rainbow-colored bow tie.

The man from his dad's work.

The one who'd thought he was a girl.

Dylan stared straight ahead, unmoving, but the man placed a hand on his shoulder on his way to the front of the room.

"Hello, Dylan," the man said, and he was smiling. "Nice to see you again."

# TWENTY

TO:      All Employees

RE:      Blood Tests

As you know, drug testing is mandatory
for all of CompWare's new hires. Beginning this Monday, April 22, quarterly blood
tests will be required for all salaried,
hourly and temporary employees. Blood will
be tested for drug use, alcohol abuse and
infectious diseases. A temporary clinic
will be set up on the campus for this purpose, and employees may arrange appointment
times or line up on a first-come-first-served
basis during open testing periods.

Any questions regarding this change in
policy must be submitted in writing to

CompWare's Human Resources department before the end of business hours today. Reading this email constitutes acknowledgement and acceptance of the policy change.

Thank you.

*Regus Patoff*

Regus Patoff
BFG Associates
For Austin Matthews, CompWare CEO

# TWENTY ONE

"ALL RIGHT, JENNY. WE'RE UP."

Jenny Yee shut off her terminal. She'd asked members of the accounting unit she managed to let her know when it was time for the blood test, and now all six of them stood in front of her cubicle. Picking up her purse, she gave the go-ahead and followed them out the door and down the hall. She remembered seeing a *Seinfeld* episode where Elaine tested positive for opium because she'd eaten a poppy seed muffin, so she'd done some online research and for the past two days had made sure to eat nothing that could mimic the presence of any illegal substance. She'd never taken drugs in her life—she did not even drink—but Jenny was paranoid that the results of this test would be used as an excuse to get rid of her.

She didn't trust the consultants.

No one from BFG had done or said anything that would lead her to believe she was a target, but ever since the retreat, she'd been walking on eggshells around the consultants. Murdering a dog and then serving it to them for dinner? That was seriously sick and had completely freaked her out. She'd had nightmares every night since. Last evening, she'd dreamed that Mr. Patoff, the head consultant, had been slinking through her apartment like a snake, or, more accurately, like the Grinch when he was stealing personal effects from Cindy Lou Who's house. The consultant had been whispering a series of numbers, and they were Hurley's numbers from *Lost*, and somehow she knew that if he repeated those numbers fifty times, she would die in her sleep, and if he repeated them a hundred times, she would never have existed and all traces of her would be wiped from the earth. It had scared the hell out of her, and the emotional response generated by the nightmare had stayed with her, even as she recognized that its specifics were ridiculous.

The blood tests were being given in a room on the seventh floor, and Jenny and the other accountants went up in the elevator.

"You know," she said, watching the floor numbers light up as they rose through the building, "we already had to take a drug test. So what are they testing us for now? Are they looking for genetic markers so they can lay us off before we get sick and they won't have to pay for insurance?"

"That's illegal," Jim Rodman said.

"That's my point. This is an invasion of privacy. Has anybody checked with Legal to see if we really have to do this?"

"It wouldn't've gotten this far if it wasn't legal," offered Francis Pham. "They vet all this stuff before it filters down to us."

"But what if they didn't? What if people are walking in like lemmings to be tested because no one made the effort to question it? You know, about a year ago, my apartment building had a blackout. I did what I always did and waited for the lights to come back on. They didn't, and I eventually fell asleep. When I woke up in the morning, the power was still out, so I called the electric company. They didn't even know about the power outage. *No one had called it in.* Everyone had assumed that someone else would do it, so no one did it."

Jim looked at her. "So you want us to—?"

Jenny shook her head. "No. But I'm going to ask about it before we let anybody take any blood."

The elevator had reached the seventh floor, the doors sliding open. The corridor looked dim, though all of the overhead lights appeared to be on, and she wondered if it was due to some sort of power-saving program. They walked down the hall to the left, seven of them, on the seventh floor, looking for room 777. The accountant in her couldn't help but notice the unlikely probability of such a correlation, and it triggered in her mind nonsensical associations. *The seventh son of a seventh son... the seven seas...the Seventh Voyage of Sinbad...the Seventh Seal...*

"That's where I had my interview with the consultants," Francis said, pointing to a door marked 713. Her voice was subdued, and Jenny remembered the unpleasant oddness of her own interview—the negative things Mr. Patoff had tried to get her to say about her team.

They all walked quickly past the closed door. Something about the seventh floor seemed different than the other floors in the building. She wasn't sure whether the corridor was too wide or the doors were in the wrong places or the walls were painted the wrong shade of white. Maybe it was just a trick of the dim lights. But something was off here, and the askew perceptions they shared made each of them walk more quickly and silently down the hall, looking for room 777.

They found it halfway down a side corridor that dead-ended in a flat wall where there should have been a window overlooking the campus. The door was open, and the room behind it, large and high-ceilinged, had been subdivided into smaller sections separated by white sheets and curtains. Mr. Patoff himself greeted them at the entrance, and before Jenny could say a word, he spoke up: "The blood test you are about to take is mandatory and entirely legal. It is *not* an invasion of privacy, and any employee who does not consent to be tested will be terminated."

She thought of the cameras that had been popping up all over the building. Had there been one in the elevator? There must have, because he knew exactly what she was going to ask. She met his eyes and saw nothing there, only a flat blankness.

"In order to *maintain* your privacy, in fact, each of you will be issued a number corresponding to the blood sample taken. If there are any issues or concerns on our part, you will be called in for an individual conference using that number."

Jenny was expecting to receive a printed number at the conclusion of the test, one copy given to her, one affixed to her blood sample, but Mr. Patoff motioned her forward, then leaned in, his mouth next to her ear. "Four, eight, fifteen, sixteen, twenty-three, forty-two," he whispered to her.

*Hurley's numbers.*

Gasping, she took a step back. He smiled knowingly, and she was paralyzed by the thought that he knew about her dream.

*How was that possible?*

She didn't know.

But it was.

Shaken, she stepped forward as Jim moved up behind her. Mr. Patoff whispered his number, and, looking back, she saw the accountant's face blanch.

What number had he been given, and what did it mean to him?

A woman in a nurse's uniform lightly grasped her wrist and pulled her further into the room, down a makeshift passageway formed by two hanging sheets, until she was in a small square space containing a chair and a table, atop which sat a row of syringes, a box of Band-Aids and a pile of large adhesive bandages.

Behind the table stood a man in a bloody butcher's apron, holding a rusty knife.

The floor and the surrounding sheets were spattered with splashes of deep red, some dried, most wet.

"What's—"

*—going on here?* Jenny intended to say, but the nurse's grip tightened on her wrist, her other hand grabbing Jenny's elbow, straightening the arm and presenting it to the blood-splattered man, who used his rusty knife to slice the skin. The nurse collected some of the welling blood in a vial she withdrew from a pouch in front of her uniform, then capped it, dropping it back into the pouch before picking up a bandage and slapping it on the wound. She grabbed one of the syringes and gave Jenny a shot. "Tetanus," she explained. "So you don't get infected." The nurse let go of her. "You're through, now. Get out of here."

Stunned and in pain, holding the bandage on her arm in place, Jenny walked back between the sheets until she was out of the room. Seconds later, Jim emerged, dazed and holding onto his own bandage. Within five minutes, all of the accountants were finished with their tests.

"We'll let you know," Mr. Patoff said once they were all out of the room and in the corridor. He slammed the door behind them.

"What the hell?" Jim said.

On the way here, Jenny had worried only about incorrect test results. Now she was worried about…other things. Diseases, for one. She thought of that rusty knife and the man in the bloody butcher's apron. The entire scene seemed unreal, and she decided then and there that she was through. She wasn't going to put up with any more of this. She was quitting. She wouldn't tell anyone, not even her team; she'd just go back to her desk, clean out what she needed and leave. It might take her awhile to find another job, but even if she ended up at 7-11, it would be better than here. This was wrong. And she was no longer going to be a part of it.

Her only regret was that she'd participated in the blood test. If she had refused to do it, she would have been fired, and then she could have collected unemployment. She couldn't get unemployment if she quit.

No matter. The important thing was to get out of here.

"Jenny?" Francis was saying. "That man can't be a nurse or a doctor, can he? He cut me with a dirty knife."

"I don't know," she replied.

They reached the elevator, and she was silent as she pressed the bottom button, the one marked *Down*.

———❀———

Austin Matthews pushed the intercom button on his console. "Get me Morgan Brandt at Bell Computers," he ordered his secretary.

"Right away," Diane replied.

Matthews leaned back in his chair, looking at the circular adhesive bandage on the back of his hand. A nurse had come into his office this morning to take a blood sample ("No one is above the rules!" she cheerfully informed him), but instead of withdrawing his blood using a needle and syringe, the woman had taken out what looked like a plastic bottle opener and started scraping the skin on the back of his hand. It seemed primitive and barbaric, and it hurt like hell, but the nurse assured him that this method was new and state of the art. Once her scraping had drawn blood, she'd pinched the skin and squeezed a drop onto a glass slide, immediately covering it.

The procedure still seemed wrong, and, looking at the bandage, he decided that after he called Brandt he was going to find out a little bit more about this new process of collecting blood samples to see if it was legitimate.

"I have Mr. Brandt's office on the line," Diane announced. "Please hold."

There was a click on the speakerphone and Matthews said, "Morgan?"

"I'm sorry," the woman said in a flat voice that indicated she was anything but. "Mr. Brandt is not here."

*Damn.* "Well, can you tell me when he'll be back?"

"I'm afraid Mr. Brandt is no longer with the company."

*Brandt was out?* Matthews' internal warning system went off. He switched off the speakerphone and picked up the handset. "Where is Mr. Brandt?"

"I cannot say."

"Well, why is he no longer with the company?"

"I cannot say."

"Well, who's the new CEO?"

"The *interim* CEO is Mr. Nelson."

"I would like to speak with him, please." The secretary was getting uppity, and he put enough authority in his voice to make sure he was obeyed.

There was a click, a pause, a snippet of generic instrumental music, then a man's voice came on the line. "This is Nelson."

"Hello." Matthews introduced himself. "My name's Austin Matthews. I'm the CEO of CompWare."

"What can I do for you?" The man was all business.

"CompWare does a lot of business with Bell, and I worked very closely with Morgan Brandt."

"Brandt no longer works here."

"I was just informed of that."

"He was replaced as part of the phase two restructuring."

"I just talked to him a couple of weeks ago."

"He signed off on it back in January when the plan was first implemented." Nelson sighed heavily, clearly bored with the conversation. "Listen, I don't have time for idle chitchat. Is there a reason for your call?"

Matthews had intended to pump Brandt for some honest information about BFG, but it was pretty clear that he would not be able to do that with this guy, so he said, "Would it be possible to get a home or cell phone number for Morgan? We're friends, and I'd like to—"

"If you were friends, you would already have his number. And you would have known that he no longer works here. Good day."

The line went dead.

Matthews slowly hung up the phone. Brandt had signed off on his own ouster? How did that happen? Was he doing the same thing himself by going along with these incremental edicts Patoff was issuing under his name? He looked at the bandage on the back of his hand. Was he paving the way for his own expulsion?

No. He was not Morgan Brandt.

Not yet.

But he'd better start putting his foot down and exerting some authority if he expected to ride this out.

His office door flew open, hitting the wall with a sound so sharp it made him jump.

Patoff stormed in, his normally placid face distorted with rage. Behind him, Matthews could see a frantic Diane anxiously attempting to signal him. Then the consultant slammed the door shut. "Jenny Yee in Accounting just quit! *Quit*! Damn that little bitch!"

Matthews was not sure how to respond, or if he was even expected to respond. He had no idea what was going on here.

The consultant paced around the office. "I wanted her gone, but that's not the way she was supposed to go! She screwed up the plan, that slant-eyed slut!"

Was he talking to himself? It seemed so, but at the same time he was addressing Matthews, so it was hard to tell at whom the diatribe was directed.

Patoff slammed a hand down hard on the desk, making Matthews jump. "Meeting! I'm calling a meeting!"

Matthews had slowly, carefully scooted his chair back from the desk and away from the consultant. "Okay," he said, placatingly. "Who do you want to meet with?"

"You! You and me, we're the meeting!" He paused for a moment, clasping his hands together beneath his chin and lowering his head. "Dear Ralph, Bless this meeting. Amen." Immediately, he resumed pacing. "These are your people, Austin. You have to get them in line."

"People quit all the time…"

"No one *quits*!" the consultant shouted. "Not until we want them to!" He stopped pacing, took a deep breath. "A company is like a machine. Everything is delicately balanced, everything has a specific function, and when changes are made, they need to be done so carefully, surgically, so as to leave that machine more finely tuned. We have a *plan* here. And that plan needs to be *followed*!"

He hit his closed right fist against his open left palm for emphasis. "We can't let it get derailed by nobodies and nothings like that little yellow twat!"

Matthews kept his eyes on the man. He did not understand the consultant's tantrum, but he was glad to see it. Patoff had always seemed so unflappable, so completely in control, that it was gratifying to see him lose it over a minor deviation in his ultimate plan.

*Ultimate plan.*

The phrase had a James Bond ring, like something hatched in the mind of a supervillain.

Which seemed apropos.

"Things are going well," the consultant said. "Not just here but everywhere. Businesses are becoming more efficient, doing more with less. The economy's coming back, and they're not hiring, not wasting money on *people*. They're staying lean and mean, boosting profits but not payrolls. It's part of the overall strategy, and we've been working on it for a long time. Why do you think we came up with email? Why do you think we invented smart phones?"

"Who's 'we'?" Matthews asked, frowning.

The consultant didn't reply, just kept talking. "We've got them checking their email at home, on vacation, at night, on weekends. They're working even when they're not at work. And all those overtime hours are free! It's why we can keep cutting staff and raising profits. We keep them off guard by making them think they're always about to be fired or outsourced, and we've *got them*!" He clenched his fist so hard it was shaking as he held it in front of him. Matthews saw a drop of blood drip down the edge of the scrunched palm from beneath Patoff's pinky.

This was getting out of hand. Matthews stood. "So what if Jenny Yee quit? We'll hire someone else for her position. It's not the end of the world."

"That's not the point!"

"Then what is the point?"

"Look, we're *going* to reduce staff. That's the goal."

"I thought the goal was—"

"Shut up!

Matthews stiffened. "Excuse me?"

"Shut up!"

He glared at the man, infuriated. "No one tells me to shut up in my own office. Get out of here right now. You're fired. Your services are no longer needed."

The consultant leaned forward, two hands on the desk. "Who do you think you are? You can't fire me. I have a contract—"

"I'm voiding that contract."

"Oh, no, you're not."

"Oh, yes, I am."

The consultant straightened, said nothing, closed his eyes.

A low hum vibrated through the room. With a sharp crash, a framed painting flew off the wall, glass shattering on the floor. The pens and pencils in a Lucite holder atop his desk floated into the air, hovering in a staggered pattern that made Matthews think of stars in a constellation. As though he had suddenly ascended in altitude, his ears plugged up, the pressure building, turning into a piercing headache that made him want to cry out in pain.

What was going on?

He stared at the consultant. *What was he?*

"All right!" Matthews said. "All right!"

The pens and pencils fell onto the desktop. The consultant opened his eyes. "We are here to do a job. The job you hired us to do. When we have completed that job, we will be gone. But, until that time, we require the freedom, access and resources that are stipulated in our contract in order to carry out our mission. Do I make myself clear?"

*Our mission*

Matthews nodded dumbly.

Patoff smiled. "Good. Then let me sort out the Jenny Yee situation and you go back to doing—" He waved a dismissive hand toward Matthews' desk. "—whatever it is you do."

The door opened on its own, and the consultant strode out. Diane instantly rushed into the office. "I'm sorry," she apologized. "I tried to get him to stop, but he just walked right past me and—"

"It's all right," Matthews assured her. He felt numb.

The secretary was looking at the fallen painting and the shattered glass on the floor. "What happened in here?"

"Nothing," he said.

"I'll call a custodian and get this cleaned up."

He nodded as she hurried out. Opening his mouth wide as if to yawn, he got his ears to pop, and the thick wall of pressure that had been muffling his hearing abated. He took a deep breath and held his right hand level with his eyeline. It was shaking. He glanced at the empty Lucite holder, and the pens and pencils scattered about the top of the desk, and looked toward the doorway through which the consultant had left.

The thought occurred to him once again: *What was he?*

# TWENTY TWO

"OH MY GOD," ANGIE SAID.

Dylan, who'd been pushing the cereal around in his bowl, looked up. "What?"

"Eat your breakfast." She held the folded section of the newspaper she'd been reading out to Craig. "Do you know someone from CompWare named Jenny Yee?"

"Not well, but I know her. Why?"

Angie tapped a small article below the fold. "Read that."

The headline made him catch his breath: *West Hollywood Woman Dies in Freak Accident*. He read the article:

> Jenny Yee, 31, of West Hollywood, was killed late Tuesday evening when she was struck in the head by one of the original Maltese Falcon statuettes that was used as a prop in the 1941 Humphrey Bogart film of the same name.

An accountant at the software company CompWare, Yee was on her way home from work at the time of the accident. In a series of unlikely coincidences, she had gotten out of her car on Wilshire Boulevard to inspect her two front tires, which had been flattened by a police nail strip that had been thrown onto the street as a prank by three juveniles who had stolen it after a high-speed chase in a nearby neighborhood. A honking horn reportedly caused Yee to jump onto the adjacent sidewalk, where she knocked over Damon Harrison, an employee of the Academy of Motion Pictures Arts and Sciences. For reasons yet to be explained, Harrison was hand-carrying the falcon statuette, which was to be part of an exhibit at the Academy headquarters on the next block. In an attempt to protect the object, Harrison threw the falcon into the air as he fell, intending to catch it before it struck the ground. The statuette hit Yee on the head, knocking her out. She fell backward onto the sidewalk, slamming her head on the concrete.

Yee was rushed by ambulance to Cedars-Sinai Hospital for emergency treatment but was pronounced dead on arrival.

"Jesus," Craig said.

*Unlikely coincidences.*

That was an understatement. The interlocking actions were like the game *Mousetrap*, or, more to the point, like one of those killings from the *Final Destination* movies, and reminded him of what had happened to Tyler. A chill passed through him, and he looked across the table at Angie, who met his gaze with an expression of disquiet that mirrored his own.

"What happened?" Dylan asked.

"Eat your cereal," Craig told him.

"Accident?" Angie said.

He handed back the paper. "I'm sure it is," he lied.

His cell phone beeped twice, signaling an incoming message, and Craig quickly dug the device out of his pants pocket. Angie shot him a laser look. "I thought you were going to keep that thing off during meals."

"Yeah, Dad!" Dylan chimed in.

"Well..." Craig trailed off, not answering the accusation. He looked down at his phone, reading the text message. "There's an early meeting for all supervisory staff," he announced. "I need to go."

Angie's voice was hard. "I thought this was going to stop."

"I told you, not as long as the consultants are still there. Once they're gone, everything'll be back to normal. Better than normal," he corrected himself.

"You're not going to be late tonight, are you?" Dylan asked worriedly. "I need to write that story."

"Mommy can help you."

"But you said *you'd* help me!"

Angie gave him a warning look from across the table.

"I'll get off early," Craig promised. "How's that?"

"Really?"

"Really."

Dylan smiled, satisfied. "Okay."

He kissed the top of Dylan's head. "See you later."

"Good-bye, Daddy!"

He tried to give Angie a kiss, but she was having none of it. "Go," she said.

Lupe's car was not even in the parking lot when he arrived, but senior staff was already gathering in the first floor conference room. Phil was seated on one of the aisle chairs, and he motioned Craig over.

"Any idea what this is about?" Craig asked, sitting down.

"None whatsoever."

Craig looked around, lowered his voice. "Did you hear about Jenny Yee from Accounting?"

Phil frowned. "No. Why?"

"She was killed last night. By the Maltese Falcon, of all things. One of the original props from the movie. It hit her in the head. It had nothing to do with CompWare, was just a freak accident…"

"Right," Phil said grimly.

"That's where I was heading." The conference room was getting more crowded. A frowning Scott Cho passed in front of Craig, moving to the center of the aisle, obviously not wanting to sit near them, and Craig lowered his voice even more. "I wonder if that's what the meeting's about. Letting us know what happened. A veiled warning, maybe?"

Phil's voice was even lower, a whisper, and Craig leaned to the left to hear it. "I think we'd better not talk here," he said. His eyes moved up, and Craig followed his friend's gaze to see new cameras installed at the juncture of wall and roof.

Craig nodded his acknowledgment, and they both sat silently, staring straight ahead as they waited for the meeting to begin.

They didn't have to wait long. Matthews was as punctual as ever, though he did not take charge of the meeting as usual but merely introduced Patoff and sat back down. The CEO looked tired, Craig thought, and there was something in his body language that suggested a man defeated.

As confident as ever, Regus Patoff stepped forward. From where, Craig was not sure, since he had not noticed the man until that moment. *The shadows*, he thought, and that felt right. The consultant smiled out at the gathered staff. "I am here today to discuss an important issue that involves everyone in the CompWare family."

*The CompWare family?* Phil mouthed.

Craig stifled a cynical laugh.

"As you may or may not be aware, this is the one month anniversary of BFG's association with CompWare. A lot has already been accomplished, and we have many new initiatives that are being undertaken, even as our comprehensive study is ongoing. One of the most important of these involves saving money on supplies, which is what I am here to discuss today. I have a short video I would like you to watch that helps illustrate my point."

The lights in the room darkened, and the consultant stepped aside as a screen lowered from the ceiling. On the large white square, an overweight woman Craig did not recognize was seated on a toilet, red-faced and grimacing.

"What is this?" Elaine demanded from somewhere off to the right.

"This is the part I want you to watch," Patoff said. "Look."

The woman stood awkwardly, unspooled a length of toilet paper from the roll, wadded it up and wiped herself. She looked at the paper before dropping it into the toilet, then unspooled some more and wiped herself again. She did this two more times before flushing.

Patoff froze the picture at a particularly unflattering moment as the lights went up. "This is but one example of how misuse of supplies costs this company money on a daily basis. Look how much toilet paper she's using. That should be enough to supply three or four people. And she's not the only offender. This, we have discovered, is the most common way in which CompWare materials are incorrectly used. "It is a complete…waste." The consultant smiled "So to speak."

He walked across the stage. "There are several ways to address this issue. The first and most obvious, and the one we will be following, is to instruct all employees in proper wiping technique. To this end, we will be setting up a series of tutorials for all divisions within each department, using this video as part of a side-by-side contrast in order to illustrate what should and should not be done."

Phil spoke up. "This is illegal."

The consultant fixed him with an insincere smile. "How so, Mr. Allen?"

Phil motioned toward the screen and the overweight woman frozen in the act of pulling up her pants. "I'm assuming you didn't get her permission to show this to all of us, and if you didn't, it's an invasion of her privacy and probably punishable by law."

The smile remained. "First of all, your assumption would be incorrect. We did indeed get the young lady's permission on a signed release to use this recording in any matter we deem fit. Secondly, even if we had not done so, as stipulated in *our* contract, there is no guarantee of privacy in this workplace for the length of time that we are conducting our study. We would be perfectly within our rights to show this to anyone and everyone."

Elaine was shaking with anger as she stood. "This *is* an invasion of privacy. You need permission to even *do* this, not just to *show* it." She confronted the consultant. "Are there cameras like this in *all* of the women's bathrooms or just that one?"

"Oh, all of them," he replied cheerfully. "The men's, too."

"That means—"

"Yes." He smiled. "And if I may say so, you could use a little prudent trimming." He wiggled his index finger at the lower half of her body. "Down there."

Elaine stalked out of the conference room, and the consultant faced the staff, completely unfazed. "Now be honest," he said. "How many of you really know the most efficient way to wipe your ass?"

It was Craig's turn to stand up. "I think there are more important things going on and better ways to save money than monitoring people's bathroom habits," he said disgustedly. He glanced over at Matthews, who was remaining suspiciously silent. The CEO stared down at his shoes, not looking up. "You're telling me that with all of the printed reports we churn out here, with all of the computers and lights that are left on all night, the best way to save money is to cut down on the use of toilet paper?"

"Yes."

The answer was so simple, direct and unexpected that Craig did not have an immediate response.

The consultant moved on. "Any more questions or comments? No?" Patoff clapped his hands. "All right. Time to wrap up here." He made a show of looking at his watch. "I have another meeting in ten, and you all have work to get back to." He winked. "At least I hope you do. We'll be sending out a schedule for the toilet paper tutorials, men with men and women with women, for each division within each department. As other concerns arise throughout this process, additional meetings will be called to discuss the topics with those affected. Thank you for coming this morning and please share the information we went over with your staff."

Hesitant and confused, people stood, looked around and gradually made their way out of the conference room.

"Who's in charge of this place?" Craig wondered as he and Phil headed down the hallway. "Matthews or *him*?"

"Keep that question between us," Phil said in a low voice as the consultant hurried past them, greeting people by name on his way to the elevators.

"Ken! Good to see you! Marcie! How's the cold? Looking good, Hu!…"

"I'm taking the stairs," Craig said.

He stopped by Lupe's desk on his way into his office, ignoring Todd and Martin, who were both seated in their usual spots, typing away on their tablets. "There are cameras in the bathrooms," he told Lupe. "We just watched a video where an employee used too much toilet paper."

She sucked in her breath, shocked.

"I thought you should be aware of it." He wanted to talk to her in more detail but not in front of the observers. He walked into his office, ignoring Martin, who stood and started to say something to him. Craig closed the door on the observer and sat down at his desk. He'd go out to lunch with Lupe today, tell her what had happened. Maybe she had some news for him as well.

His mind kept coming back to how uninvolved and disassociated Matthews had looked up there on the stage. After the retreat, he'd had hopes that the CEO would fire BFG or at least get more involved in what was going on. But now…

Craig turned on his computer.

There were five hundred emails in his inbox, all from BFG.

He started deleting.

———— ✇ ————

Dylan's reading group—the *good* reading group—sat in a semi-circle at the front of the class while the other students worked on their history projects. Mrs. Higgins was having them each read a paragraph aloud while the others followed along silently in their own textbooks. Karen was reading now, and Dylan knew that he would be next, but he still looked up from the story to see what Mr. Patoff was doing.

The man, seated awkwardly on a chair far too small for his frame, was staring at him.

And smiling.

He always seemed to be staring. Every time Dylan hazarded a glance in his direction, the man seemed to be watching him, and it made him feel very uncomfortable. He didn't look at Dylan the way an adult usually looked at a kid, but stared at him in a creepy way, as though he could read Dylan's thoughts and was *thinking* about them.

Most of the kids in his class thought Mr. Patoff was pretty funny. Even though Mrs. Higgins said he was only supposed to be watching her teach, sometimes he participated, telling jokes or stories or helping out, although Dylan always thought he was faking, *pretending* to help out, *pretending* to like the students, and it made him mad that no one else seemed to realize it. "That smile's fake," he told Josh Kaplan. "No it's not," Josh said. "It's funny." And that seemed to be everyone's attitude.

For Art, they were supposed to use colored pencils and draw a humorous picture. After all the reading groups had met, Mrs. Higgins passed out paper, told them to get out their pencils, and asked them to draw something they could see here in the classroom but to make it funny. Mr. Patoff jumped up in a goofy way that made everyone laugh. "I'm a wiggly man!" he announced, waving his arms in a rubbery manner. "I'm a wiggly, wiggly man!"

Dylan froze.

He had dreamed last night about a wiggly man, a terrifying nightmare in which he'd found himself at home, alone, his parents gone. It was night, but he'd been seated in front of the living room window, like the boy and his sister in *The Cat in the Hat*, looking outside. Only it wasn't a humanoid cat he saw in the bluish moonlight. It was a wiggly man, a wild-haired figure with spindly legs and impossibly long arms that were undulating in time to a noise that sounded like a stretched rubber band being plucked. The wiggly man was approaching the house, his face in shadow because of the moon's overhead light. Dylan did not want to see his face, did not want to see those rippling elastic arms and legs, so he shut the drapes and ran away from the window—

—and heard that rubber band noise from down the hall.

Turning in panic, he saw the wiggly man emerge from his parents' bedroom, hands at the ends of those long supple arms flapping against the walls, feet moving forward in exceptionally long strides on bendy legs. The wiggly man was looking at the floor, and just before he reached Dylan, the man looked up. He had no eyes, no nose, only a huge hole of a mouth ringed with black rubber teeth.

It was the scariest dream he could ever remember having—he was not usually one for nightmares—and Dylan knew instantly upon awakening that it was one he would never forget.

Now Mr. Patoff was standing in front of the class, wiggling his rubbery arms.

And staring at him.

Many of the kids were already starting to draw, giggling as they did so, and even Mrs. Higgins was smiling. But Dylan didn't find anything funny about the man with the fake smile imitating the monster from his nightmare, and he looked quickly away, down at his paper, picking up a random pencil from his pack—a red one—and drawing not Mr. Patoff but the class turtle in its terrarium, putting a "For Sale" sign on the back of its shell. Exchanging the red pencil for a brown one, he hazarded a quick glance at the front of the class. Mr. Patoff had once again sat down in his too-small chair, making a show of it, causing other students to laugh, but there was no humor in the eyes that were still looking in his direction.

Dylan immediately grabbed the brown pencil out of the pack and focused on his paper. He hadn't told his parents about what was going on in class, but now he thought that he should have. His dad didn't like Mr. Patoff, and he'd probably want to know that the man was now here at school.

Recess was after Art, and as soon as the bell rang, Dylan hurried outside. Even on the playground, however, he felt the man watching him, and though Dylan tried not to look in the direction of the classroom, he couldn't resist the pull and finally glanced over.

Mr. Patoff was standing next to the closed door, smiling at him.

Dylan looked quickly away. He and Raul were alternating between slide and swings, both of them trying to impress Allison Woolridge, but just knowing that Mr. Patoff was watching him put Dylan off his stride, and when he hazarded another glance in that direction, he saw the man, still smiling, striding across the playground toward him.

Welling panic caused him to run instinctively in the opposite direction, but the playground was small, and even the adjacent field was fenced in, so there was no place to which he could escape. He turned to look over his shoulder. The man was still coming, and Dylan decided at the last moment to run over to the area by the monkey bars. There were more kids here, it was more crowded, and Mrs. Ruiz, who was on recess duty, was standing nearby with her whistle in hand. She could protect him if he needed it.

Dylan climbed quickly to the top of the bars, looked around, didn't see Mr. Patoff, and slid down the center pole. Squeezing out of the jungle gym, he found himself behind the metal structure, next to the fence, away from swarming kids…

And facing Mr. Patoff.

The man smiled broadly, but, as usual, the smile did not reach his eyes. "I've been wanting to talk to you, Dylan. Could we talk for a minute?"

He didn't respond, tried to ignore the crazy pounding of his heart.

"I just have a quick question. What do you think of uniforms? We're thinking that it might be good for everyone in school to wear uniforms."

Dylan shrugged his shoulders, desperately looking around, hoping one of his friends would bail him out.

The man leaned closer. "What do you think about a uniform with a short skirt? Would you like to wear a short skirt? A frilly pink one?"

"Get away from me!" Dylan yelled and ran away. Behind him, the man's booming laughter sounded above all the other playground noises.

It followed him across the blacktop and all the way back to class.

That night, he told his parents about Mr. Patoff. They both assured him that there was nothing to worry about, but he caught the look that passed between them and knew that *they* were worried, and that frightened him.

After recess, he'd wanted to tell Mrs. Higgins what had happened, but didn't know how to bring it up so it would make sense. He couldn't tell her, couldn't tell the principal, and even though he had told his parents, they advised him not to worry about it. There was no adult, it seemed, who could protect him, who could understand what was really going on.

"He asked me if I wanted to wear a *dress*, Daddy. Remember how he kept calling me a girl at your work?"

Another look passed between his parents, but his dad put on a not-very-reassuring smile and told him to just ignore the man. He put a hand on Dylan's shoulder. "He'll be gone pretty soon. What did your teacher say? The end of the week? You can survive that long, can't you?"

He could, but he didn't want to, and for the first time in his life, Dylan thought about telling his parents that he was sick so he could stay out of school for the next three days. The man would know, though, why he wasn't there, and Dylan couldn't let him win. You had to stand up to bullies, and even though Mr. Patoff was an adult, he was still a bully.

Dylan would just have to stay away from him, ignore him in class, and stay close to the lunch monitors, and the teachers and moms on recess duty. But he would not back down. He would not run away.

"Okay, Daddy," Dylan said.

His dad smiled at him, and it was a real smile. "That's my little buddy."

But his parents gave each other that look again, and he realized that his mom and dad weren't just worried and concerned.

They were afraid.

He went to bed that night and dreamed that Mr. Patoff was the wiggly man and was coming down the hallway toward his room, smiling and holding a pink dress on a pink coat hanger.

# TWENTY THREE

TO:      All Employees

RE:      Clothing Color Preferences

Although CompWare has not had and does
not have official uniforms, it has been determined that a differentiation in the col-
or of employees' attire will foster a more
professional attitude among company personnel, and will make it easier for both
employees and members of the public to dis-
tinguish between individuals of management
and non-management status. Beginning this
Tuesday, April 23, vice-presidents, department heads, division heads, managers
and supervisors will be requested to wear,
in a style of their choice, shirts/blouses

of a gold or muted yellow color similar to the one shown in the attachment herein. All other employees are requested to wear, in a style of their choice, shirts/blouses of a red color similar to the one shown in the attachment herein.

Any questions regarding this change in policy must be submitted in writing to CompWare's Human Resources department before the end of business hours today. Reading this email constitutes acknowledgement and acceptance of the policy change.

Thank you.

*Regus Patoff*

Regus Patoff
BFG Associates
For Austin Matthews, CompWare CEO

# TWENTY FOUR

MARTIN HAD BEEN REPLACED.

When Craig arrived at his office, a hard-looking middle-aged woman was sitting in the chair where his observer was supposed to be.

"I am Mrs. Adams. I will be here for a week," she announced, staring straight at him with a stony expression. "Do not talk to me. I will not talk to you. I am conducting your work management study and will note your required duties, extra duties, all peripheral actions, and the amount of time you spend on each. This will be part of the aggregate data used by BFG to formulate a master plan for your company. I trust I have made myself clear."

"Perfectly," Craig said. He looked at his watch. "I'm two minutes late," he told her. "Better note that down."

"I already have," she informed him.

Craig walked past Lupe's desk into his office, sharing a glance with the secretary as he closed the door behind him. One by-product of this work management study, he realized, was that, because of the presence of the observers, he and Lupe had very little time to talk anymore. The paranoid part of his mind wondered if that was intentional, and the rational part of his mind answered yes.

Mid-morning, he went down to see the programmers, and Mrs. Adams silently followed along, staying behind him down the corridor and on the stairs, parking herself in an unobtrusive position against a wall in the programmers' work area. Craig had come down to get quick updates on both OfficeManager and *WarHammer III,* and to talk about adjusting milepost timetables, but the moment he approached Huell's work station, a group of programmers immediately began gathering around him. Accompanying them were *their* observers (how many did BFG have working here? Dozens? Hundreds?), and while a few programmers cast distrustful glances in the consultants' direction, it didn't stop them from bringing up what was on their minds.

"Our computers are being monitored," Huell told him. "At *home.*"

Craig frowned. "Are they CompWare—?"

"No," Rusty interjected. The technical writer looked angry. "*Personal* computers. And, I suspect, our phones."

"That's illegal," Craig said.

"That's what we're saying." Huell cocked a thumb back toward the observers. "Someone needs to tell *them* that."

"There was also that thing I told you about last week where someone inserted a program on my computer *here*," Lorene said, "and it automatically erased anything I created."

"I'll see what I can do," Craig promised them.

"Well, let those assholes know that they're supposed to be helping us get *more* work done not *less*," Rusty said. "If CompWare's going to dig out of its hole, we need to start pushing out product."

Craig had been watching his observer—

*Mrs. Adams*

—while talking to the programmers, and though the expression on her face was flat and unreadable, he knew where her sympathies lay. She was a direct conduct to Patoff, as were all the other observers auditing this scene, and he cut the dialogue short, not wanting his employees to get themselves in trouble because of their complaints. There would be time for a more honest discussion later. The programmers seemed to sense this, and while their anger was still palpable, they began drifting back to their work stations, letting the matter drop, apparently satisfied that they had let him know their concerns and that he would do what he could to address the problem.

Although, there was not really much that he *could* do. The thread that seemed to run through everything these days was that the employee had no rights while the employer and the consultants were given free rein to do as they pleased.

Shadowed by Mrs. Adams, he spent the next hour discussing OfficeManager and *WarHammer III* with the programmers while staying away from more personal topics. When he was finished, in order to make it tough for the observer, he took the stairs and walked down to the first floor instead of going back up to his office. He got a drink from the drinking fountain in the lobby, then took the stairs back up to the sixth floor. He knew she would note this bizarre behavior, but he didn't really care. He wanted to make the bitch walk, and he experienced a small sense of satisfaction when he heard her breathing loudly behind him as he strode down the corridor toward Lupe's desk.

He spent the rest of the morning behind closed doors in his office, on the phone for the most part, going up the CompWare chain of command in an effort to find out what he could about the surveillance situation. Scott was an asshole as usual and no help at all. He couldn't get through to Matthews, and the vice-president to whom he talked toed the party line and claimed there was nothing intrusive going on. Craig knew the programmers weren't taking this lying down. As brave as they were to even bring it up in front of the observers, they weren't stupid enough to come clean about everything, and he knew that one or more of them must be surreptitiously trying to disable the devices that were spying on them.

The problem was that they didn't know if the consultants were using *other* means to snoop. It was his job to find that out, and so far he'd been a failure.

He needed to talk to the tech guys in his division after work, coordinate some kind of plan with them.

For the first time in over a week, he and Phil were able to get off at the same time for lunch, and they hurried from the building before something came up to delay one of them.

"So," Craig said as they walked through the parking lot. "Did you see the new memo?"

"Yeah, I saw it." Phil snorted. "Gold shirts and red shirts? What'd they base this plan on? *Star Trek*?"

Craig smiled. "I think we'll survive the trip to the planet. We're gold shirts. I am worried about the fate of Yeoman Jones, however."

"You think this is funny?"

He sighed. "Not really."

"Neither do I. I'm starting to wonder if we shouldn't be sending out résumés."

"You're not the first one to mention that."

"I think you'd better drive," Phil said as they approached his Honda. "My transmission's making weird noises again. I don't trust it."

"Are you going to take it in?"

"Yeah. After work. Josie's going to follow me and drive me home or to the rental car place if the dealer won't give me a loaner."

They walked past Phil's car to the end of the lot, where Craig's Prius was sandwiched between two minivans. The fit was so tight that he had to crack open the driver's side door, slide into his seat and back out of the parking space before his friend could even get in the car. His satellite radio was tuned to CNN, and as they pulled onto the street, two commentators on opposite sides of the political spectrum were agreeing that, war on terror or not, the federal government was abusing its power to a frightening *1984*-ish degree and destroying individuals' right to privacy with its telephone surveillance techniques.

Phil laughed derisively. "They just learned that they lost their right to privacy?"

"Well, it's gotten more publicity lately."

"Yeah? Well, we're in the thick of it. We *know* there's no privacy. The Great Unwashed might get their panties in a bind over NSA data gathering, but their grocery stores know more about them than the government does, thanks to that little scanned card that gets them such tremendous savings. And their browser not only tracks what sites they visit, but how long they spend on each, then sells that information to marketers. Not to mention the fact that morons are keeping personal data on easily hacked servers instead of on their own privately held storage material."

Craig smiled. "Well, in their defense, those servers are white, puffy and completely unthreatening 'clouds.'"

"As opposed to *Colossus: The Forbin Project*, which is what they really are." Phil shook his head. He was silent for a moment, thinking. "You know, even by the Limbo Jack standards of today, BFG is pretty fucking scary. Big Brother is definitely watching *us*."

"The programmers are freaked out," Craig admitted. "I went over there this morning, and got an earful about illegal surveillance at work *and* at home."

"You think that's bad? I checked in on my corporate sales team, and the place was *silent*. Ordinarily, you've never heard so many complainers in your life. But they're completely cowed. As far as they're concerned, the walls are bugged, their computers have cameras and their every conversation is either recorded by hidden devices or monitored by those damn work management drones. Which means, from my perspective, that not a lot of work is getting done. Fear is not conducive to a productive work environment."

"Those consultants are doing more harm than good."

"Kind of makes you wonder if our cars are bugged," Phil said as they pulled to a stop at a red light.

They were both silent for a moment, looking at each other.

"Maybe we should eat…somewhere else today," Phil suggested.

Craig nodded, understanding. Any type of routine could leave them open. If the consultants knew they usually ate lunch at Chipotle…

Better too cautious than not cautious enough. Neither of them said a word as Craig cranked up the radio and drove straight instead of turning right, heading toward a Rubio's that he remembered seeing near the freeway.

They did not speak again until they were out of the car and in the parking lot of the Mexican fast food restaurant.

"This is getting ridiculous," Craig said, locking his door.

Phil smiled wryly. "Just because you're paranoid doesn't mean they're not out to get you."

Walking inside, they ordered, then took their food to a table near the window, away from the smattering of other diners, most of whom were seated close by the salsa bar or the drink refill station.

"Went to a meeting this morning," Phil said before biting into his taco. "You know how Patoff loves meetings."

"What was it about?"

"What do you think? They want to get rid of someone in my department."

"Who?"

"Jess Abodje."

Craig looked at him blankly.

"The guy in the wheelchair?"

"Oh, yeah. I know who you're talking about. Why do they want to get rid of him? What's the rationale?"

"Who the hell knows? But he's a good guy, and I need him, and I refuse to give in to those fucks, so I framed it as a discrimination issue and hinted that the only reason they wanted to get rid of Jess was because he was disabled." Phil grinned. "All of a sudden, the Americans with Disabilities Act was being quoted right and left. Apparently, it's CompWare's and BFG's favorite law, and we were pioneers in setting up an accessible workplace."

"So they're not going to fire him?"

"They're not even going to furlough him. Victory is sweet." He took a long sip of Dr. Pepper.

"I guess they're rearranging some chairs of their own," Craig noted. "My trusty observer Martin is gone, replaced by a fascist woman."

"I still have the same guy," Phil said. "And he doesn't seem too bad. I don't think he toes the party line as much as your watchers do."

"'Watchers' now, are they?"

"It seems less Orwellian."

"I'm sticking with 'observers.' By the way, whatever happened with those blood tests? Did anyone get fired or test positive for… whatever they're looking for?"

Phil shrugged. "You got me. But there were supposedly *inconsistencies* in the testing. Did you hear anything about that?"

Craig shook his head. "No, but you're always more up on things than I am. What'd you hear?"

"When I got *my* blood test, a nurse used a needle and syringe to draw blood."

"Of course."

"Well, apparently, some people had their arms cut with a knife to draw blood."

"Jesus."

"Others were poked with rusty ice picks."

"That can't be true."

Phil just looked at him.

"Okay. It could be true. But why? What would be the point? It makes no sense."

"What does these days?" Phil wiped his hands on a napkin, then walked over to refill his drink. "That reminds me," he said, coming back, "how goes their effort to take over the healthcare system and access all of our medical information?"

"Angie says they haven't started. Or at least haven't shown up onsite. They might be combing through emails, computer files and phone records for all anyone knows, but there are no boots on the ground as of yet."

"Small favors."

"I'm curious to see what they do there. If it's different than at CompWare."

"Leopards don't change their spots."

"You're just a font of clichés today, aren't you?"

"What I don't get is how they've gotten all these big clients and how they keep getting good recommendations."

Craig sighed. "Like you said before: they make the companies money. People get laid off, employees get harassed, people *die...* but stock prices go up and profits do, too. How are we supposed to fight that?"

"I don't know," Phil admitted. "But we will."

Driving back to work, they were almost to the entrance of the CompWare parking lot when a rolling contraption came speeding out into the street in front of the car. Craig slammed on his brakes so hard that the shoulder harnesses locked up. He didn't hit the fast-moving object, but he had time to see that it was a man in a wheelchair, a wheelchair that seemed to have been shot out of a cannon, and then there was the screeching of brakes, the honking of horns, and a terrible sound of crashing metal as a pickup truck in the southbound lane smashed into the speeding chair. The man must have been strapped into the seat as the momentum of the collision should have sent him flying. Instead, it buckled him under the collapsing chair as the truck rolled over him.

Craig threw the car into Park, got out and dashed across the double yellow lines to see a broken body tangled up in rods and wheels, blood and bits of brain spread in a sickening smear across the pavement.

"I not see him!"

The driver of the truck had leaped out and was running back and forth in confusion, hands in the air, looking from the mess on the ground to Craig to the other people who were beginning to gather. "I not see him!" the man kept repeating. "He just speed out in front of me!"

Craig looked back toward the CompWare parking lot, at the spot where the wheelchair had come flying out onto the street. It had had to jump a curb, cross a sidewalk, pass over a thin strip of grass, then go off the curb onto the street. The fact that it had done so at such a speed seemed a complete impossibility, and Craig could not figure out what had propelled the chair.

By this time, Phil had come over, and Craig did not even have to hear him speak to confirm what he already knew.

"That's Jess Abodje."

His friend looked numb, and Craig felt numb, too. No doubt, this would be classified as a freak accident, and while it was definitely freaky, he was sure it was no accident. The consultant had wanted to get rid of Jess, the same way he'd wanted to get rid of Tyler. Like Craig, Phil had objected to that decision, and, like Tyler, Jess had been killed. There was no way to prove it, nothing that would stand up in any court, but it was true nonetheless. They looked at each other, then looked across the CompWare parking lot toward the building where they both worked. People around them were shouting, screaming, talking, and someone must have called 911 because, from far away, came the sound of sirens. The front of the building was mirrored glass, so nothing could be seen within, but Craig had no doubt that if the windows were clear and he was looking through a pair of binoculars, he would be able to see Regus Patoff looking out at the scene.

And smiling.

# TWENTY FIVE

CAUGHT IN AN ATYPICAL SATURDAY MORNING TRAF-
fic jam caused by a localized power outage that had taken out
three consecutive traffic lights, Angie was late for work. The minute she walked into the Urgent Care, she could tell that something
was different, something had changed, though it took her a moment to figure out what it was. *The lights*, she realized. The lights in
the waiting room were dimmer than usual. Someone had turned
them down, probably to save money.

*The consultants were here.*

The knowledge arrived with a shiver. Suddenly, the Urgent
Care, which she knew like the back of her hand, seemed foreign to
her, the placement of doors slightly off, the sink alcove smaller than
usual. It was wrong to let Craig's experiences color her perspective,
but she couldn't help being affected by what he'd told her, and in
an instant, the homey familiarity of her longtime workplace disappeared, replaced by a feeling that was far less welcoming. Walking

up the poorly illuminated hallway to the front desk, Angie was struck by the abundance of shadows swaddling the nurse's station, the eerie gloom that seemed almost a solid entity and wrapped around the perimeter of the waiting room.

She jumped when Sharon said her name. She hadn't seen the other nurse sitting there.

"Heads up," her friend said in a low voice. "The new consultant's here. Was here when I arrived. He already asked about you: why you were late, if you called in to tell us, if this is part of a pattern."

"There was a traffic jam. And it's only been ten minutes!"

"I know. I told him this was a first, that you're our most re-liable nurse, but…" She shook her head. "He had a look on his face." She motioned Angie closer. "I can't believe I'm saying this, but I think I liked the other weirdo better. This one…I don't know. I don't trust him."

Reaching down to the computer next to Sharon, Angie signed on and signed in. "Where is he now?"

"Room four with Dr. London."

Angie patted her friend's shoulder. "Thanks for the warning."

The Urgent Care was busy. So busy that it was fifteen minutes before she even saw the consultant, almost half an hour until they were in the same room and introduced to one another.

Craig was right, she thought, looking at him. There was defi-nitely something *off* about the man. Despite the geek chic impri-matur granted to bow ties by *Doctor Who*, the consultant's neck-wear looked not merely out of fashion but out of time, as though it could easily have come from a century ago. He was tall and un-nervingly thin, and his peculiarly tinted hair was cut into an un-flattering flattop that would not have been in style during any age. He smiled at her, bowed his head slightly in greeting, but the smile did not touch his eyes, which were hard and cold.

They had no time to speak with one another. Angie had to help Dr. Bashir with a young girl who'd been bitten by a neighborhood dog and was on the verge of crying again after stopping only moments before, and the consultant was monitoring the interchange, typing notes into an electronic tablet. Angie spoke calmly to the girl, explaining to her what the doctor was doing, and once the tetanus shot was given—without an accompanying scream or prolonged crying jag—the doctor explained to the mother what was to be done, handing out a prescription, while Angie dressed the wound.

Cleaning up after the patient and her mother had left, and after the doctor and the consultant had moved on to another exam room, Angie noticed something she hadn't before: a video camera installed in the upper left corner of the room, cattycorner from the door. Her first reaction was shock—*This wasn't right. It wasn't even legal*—but then she started thinking about the logistics of such an installation. The Urgent Care had closed last night at six and had reopened this morning at eight. So someone had come here in the middle of the night to mount and wire the camera. Which meant that the consultants had keys to the building and could let themselves in at any time.

She was upset as she walked out to inform Sharon that the room was ready for another patient. It was another ten minutes before her path and the consultant's crossed again, and by this time, she had discovered that there were cameras in *all* of the exam rooms. So when she encountered the consultant by the coffee machine as he scoped out the tiny break room, she confronted him.

"Why?" she asked, "are there cameras in the exam rooms?"

"Because we put them there."

She could feel her face getting hot with outrage. "The patients are entitled to privacy. *By law.*"

He gave her a flat stare. "This is not our first rodeo. We have consulted for many hospitals and healthcare companies, and, inevitably, we find that someone within the organization is stealing."

"Stealing what?"

"Supplies…drugs…who knows?"

"So you think you're going to catch me shooting up or shoving prescription painkillers in my pockets?"

"We don't know what we'll learn. But when everything is under surveillance, we are provided with a fuller picture of the workplace and are better able to make informed decisions as to its future."

She thought about everything Craig had told her and about the fact that the consultant had keys to the Urgent Care. She wouldn't put it past him to steal from the office and blame it on someone else. She didn't want to say anything to him about it, but she was going to talk to the doctors and other nurses. Before they closed up each evening, she was going to suggest, two of them should either take a quick inventory of all medications onsite or, at the very least, use their phones to photograph the supplies in all of the drawers, cabinets and closets, so the consultant couldn't frame anybody for anything.

"As you no doubt know," Patoff said, "BFG is also consulting for CompWare, the firm at which your husband works. We have not yet decided whether it is a conflict of interest for both of you to be working for organizations being studied by BFG. But if it's determined that there *is* a conflict of interest, I'm afraid that one of you will have to resign your position."

"What? That makes no sense whatsoever!"

"It's important to avoid even the appearance of impropriety."

"Impropriety? What are you talking about? If anything's improper it's the fact that *you* are passing judgment on the two of *us*. If you have a problem with Craig, you might take it out on me, or vice versa. I think you need to recuse yourself from one of these jobs."

Patoff laughed, though the mirth did not touch his eyes. "Feisty! I like that." He patted the top of her head as though she were a dog. "We'll be seeing more of each other."

And then he was walking away, out of the break room and into the hallway.

For the rest of the day, he was in *every* exam room in which she assisted, and it appeared to Angie that the consultant was paying more attention to her than he did to the doctors. It might have been self-consciousness, might have been paranoia, but the result was an increased ratcheting up of tension throughout the rest of the morning and the afternoon. She had the feeling he was waiting to catch her in a mistake, and though she tried to keep her focus on the patients, his unwanted attention had the effect of compromising her ordinarily unimpeachable standard of care.

As soon as she got home, Angie told Craig everything that had happened. She assumed Dylan was in his bedroom, playing, but he poked his head around the corner of the kitchen after she finished talking, a worried expression on his face, and she quickly reassured him that she had merely had a long day at work and was tired. Her eyes told Craig something else, however, and she waited until later that evening, when their son was asleep, before talking to him about it. They spoke in the kitchen, on the opposite side of the house from his bedroom, and purposely kept their voices low. He tried to calm her down by reminding her that BFG had stayed only a week at Dylan's school and probably wouldn't spend much longer at the Urgent Care, but she could tell that he didn't believe that himself. The consultants' engagement at CompWare was open-ended, had already lasted nearly two months and might very well have several more months to go, and there was no reason to assume the same thing couldn't happen at her work.

Despite all of his complaints over the last weeks, Craig seemed to go out of his way to try to minimize her concerns. It didn't make her feel less anxious, only pissed her off—she didn't want to be placated—and Angie broke off the discussion, turning away to do the dishes. He attempted to help, but she wouldn't let him, and after he'd retreated to the living room, she stood in front of the sink, staring at her ghostly reflection in the window, her pale face superimposed above the patio furniture against the blackness of night. She was afraid, she realized, and a part of her thought it would almost be a relief to be fired, because then she wouldn't have to encounter the consultant again. She thought of the night she'd found Pam's dead body, the way the office manager had looked, that terrible expression of horror on her face, and Angie found herself wondering if the consultant had had anything to do with that, if that was when he'd started to make his move on the Urgent Care.

In bed, Craig wanted sex, but she wasn't in the mood. He pulled his underwear down and began masturbating next to her, and at the last minute, before he came, she took him in her mouth so there wouldn't be any mess to clean up.

She fell asleep almost immediately after and dreamed that she was on duty at the Urgent Care when Craig came in with a horrible case of hives that covered his entire body. She took off his clothes and got him into a gown, in preparation for the doctor's arrival, but instead of one of the doctors, the consultant showed up. He was holding a hatchet in one hand, a small video camera in the other, and as soon as he walked in, the room went dark. The camera in the corner of the room was no longer a camera but a spotlight and it illuminated Craig's body which was now naked. The consultant chuckled. "Nurse, watch and learn while I film your husband's death."

The alarm woke her in the morning, but Angie had no desire to go to work and promptly shut it off, crawling back into bed.

"Get up," Craig said next to her, prodding her shoulder with his.

"I'm calling in sick," she told him.

Suddenly he was wide awake. "You can't."

"Yes, I can."

"They'll be looking for anything you do, any reason to get rid of you."

"Let them try."

"Ange…"

She heard the concern in his voice—

*the fear*

—and she understood where it was coming from. She felt it, too, and as much as she hated to do so, she forced herself to throw off the blanket and get out of bed. The dream was still with her, and though she knew it was ridiculous, she felt nervous about going in today. There would be other nurses and doctors and patients, but just the thought of facing the consultant again filled her with dread.

She didn't actually see the consultant until mid-morning, and Angie had no idea whether he had arrived late or had been busy monitoring someone else. Either way, she was happy not to have run into him until now. They met in the hallway, he coming from one direction, she from the other, and as soon as she saw him, Angie put her head down and moved to the right, intending to pass by.

He moved in front of her to block her way.

Forced to look up, she took in his odd clothes and his blank face, feeling cold just being near him. "Excuse me," she said, flattening herself against the wall and trying once again to pass.

He pressed his shoulder against the wall to block her and, defeated, she moved to the center of the hallway, stood there and faced him.

He looked at her, wrinkling his nose and frowning. "Did you poop your pants?"

"*What?*"

"Did you poop your pants? It smells like you pooped your pants."

She stared at him, stunned into silence. The question was so childish, so unprofessional, so off-the-wall batshit crazy, that she did not know how to respond. Anger was the emotion that replaced surprise, and she immediately turned away—

"Answer my goddamn question!" he screamed.

She whirled around. The other two nurses in the hallway were frozen with shock at his outburst.

"Did you *shit* your fucking *pants*?" he demanded. His entire face was red, contorted with rage.

"No!" she responded.

His features immediately smoothed out. "That's all I wanted to know," he said, smiling. Bowing gracefully, he stepped aside to let her pass.

Shaking, she went into the women's restroom to calm down. In the mirror, her face was drawn, frightened. With trembling hands, she turned the water on and, using her fingers, sprinkled some on her eyes, rubbing it in. The door opened behind her, and she jumped, expecting to see the consultant. But it was only Barbara. "What was that about?" the other nurse asked.

Angie shook her head, breathing heavily. "I have no idea."

"Jesus! We need to report him or something. That was...crazy."

"I know."

"Should we tell management? Or is there someone above that guy we can complain to?"

Angie shook her head. "Let it go."

"But—"

"That company, BFG, has been consulting for my husband's work for the past month. You think this is bad? You should hear some of the crazy stuff that's going on *there*. Those consultants are…" She took a deep breath. "There's something wrong with them. I don't know what it is, but… I think the best thing to do is just wait them out. They'll be gone eventually."

Barbara looked toward the closed bathroom door, her mind obviously on the hallway beyond. "What do you think he's going to recommend? What do you think his suggestions are going to be?"

"I don't know," Angie said, and shivered involuntarily. "I don't know."

---

The smells of a sunny Sunday morning. Eggs and sausage. Bacon. Coffee. Breakfast. The delicious scents wafted through the neighborhood as Craig and Dylan walked to the park. It was a windy day, the first since Dylan's birthday nearly two months ago, and they'd decided to finally try out the dragon kite Angie's mother had given him as a present. Craig carried the oversized kite while Dylan jogged next to him, holding onto his belt when the two of them crossed a street.

They were the only ones at the park, and Dylan was disappointed. He'd wanted their kite to fly higher than everyone else's, and he felt let down as he realized there would be no competition. As soon as they got the kite into the air, however, Dylan's disappointment disappeared. The multi-colored dragon soared over the field, over the trees behind the field, over the street and neighborhood behind the trees. It was higher and farther than they'd ever gotten a kite before, and Dylan shouted excitedly as he played out the line.

"Don't let go," Craig warned him as a gust pulled the kite to the right. "If we lose it now, it'll probably go into someone's back yard and we'll never get it back."

"I know!" Dylan shouted, and looked proudly up at the dragon as it swayed back and forth, now little more than a colorful dot high in the sky.

It should have been a happy day, but even as he stood behind his son, continuing to unspool kite string, Craig could not help thinking about Regus Patoff. The man had visited Dylan's school and was even now at Angie's work. Why? It could not be a coincidence. But what interest could the consultant possibly have in *his* family? There were literally hundreds of people working at CompWare. What would make the consultant focus on an innocuous middle-management employee like himself? Craig had no idea, and that was what frustrated and frightened him.

There was a vibration in his pocket as his cell phone went off. Taking it out, he looked at the screen and saw Scott Cho's office number. On a Sunday? Knowing ahead of time that he would regret it, Craig took the call.

"Where the hell are you?" Scott demanded.

"I'm at the park with my son," he said flatly. "Where should I be on a Sunday morning?"

"Here. At the department meeting I called. Didn't you read your email?"

"On Sunday? No. I promised my wife I wouldn't." Craig clicked off, but the phone vibrated again almost instantly. He considered not picking up, but although Scott probably couldn't get him fired, he could make Craig's life at work a living hell. He answered the phone again. "Hey," he told Scott. "What happened?"

"You hung up on me."

"No. I…"

"Get over here. Now." This time, Scott was the one to hang up, and Craig sighed heavily. "Come on , buddy," he told Dylan. "We have to go."

"Go where?"

"I have to stop by my work."

"But it's Sunday!"

"I know, I know. But it shouldn't take too long." He gestured toward the spool of string. "Why don't you reel it in."

Dylan hesitated. "Is *he* going to be there?"

Craig knew immediately who his son was talking about, and a ripple of cold passed through him. "I don't know," he admitted. "Probably not. I think he's at Mommy's work today. But even if he is, you don't have to see him."

"Can I stay at Raul's? And you can pick me up when you're done?"

That was a wonderful idea. The further away from the consultant he could keep Dylan the better. He tried to keep his voice as even as possible, to not let the relief he felt at the idea creep in. "If it's all right with Raul's parents."

Craig didn't have the phone numbers of any of Dylan's friends. Angie probably did, but calling her at work was strictly prohibited, so after reeling in the kite and walking back home, he looked through her personal address book next to the phone in the kitchen. The number was there, and Raul's family was home, and the boy's mother said she would be happy to have Dylan come over. "Thank you," Craig told her. "I really appreciate this. I wouldn't have called unless it was an emergency—"

"Don't worry about it," she assured him.

"I owe you one," he said.

He got off the phone and told Dylan that he could go over to his friend's house. "I'll try to get back before lunch, and I'll take you and Raul out to Chuck E. Cheese. How does that sound?"

"Yeah!" Dylan said.

But he didn't get back before lunch. He didn't get back until it was nearly four o'clock. Scott wanted to go over the work of every division within the department in detail, and they all had to sit there as their colleagues held the department head's hand on a babywalk through each division's status. This wasn't anything that could not have been done Monday, and Craig was pretty sure it was all for show, but even when he told Scott that Patoff was at Angie's Urgent Care and would not be within ten miles of CompWare today, the department head refused to let them go home.

"Asshole," Elaine muttered as they walked out of the meeting room and down the corridor to the elevators.

No one disagreed.

The sun was starting to go down when Craig finally picked up his son. He apologized profusely to Raul's mother, though he'd called to warn her that he would be late, but she dismissed his apologies and said, "The boys had fun. We should do this again some time."

"I'm sorry," he told Dylan on their way out to the car. "I couldn't get away."

"That's okay, Daddy. I still had fun."

"What'd you have for lunch?"

"Mrs. Rodriguez made spaghetti. And Jell-O. And we got to watch cartoons."

"Did you say thank you?"

Dylan looked offended. "Of course!" There was a long pause. "Was he there?"

"No," Craig said. "I didn't see him."

"Then he was probably at Mommy's work."

"Probably."

Dylan nodded as though he understood, but he was silent as he got into the car, and he remained silent all the way home.

# TWENTY SIX

THE DREAM WAS REALISTICALLY PROSAIC. IN IT, MAT-
thews purposely went to work late, hid in his office for most of
the day, seeing no one, taking no calls, then snuck out of the office
mid-afternoon before going home, drinking himself into a stupor
and going to bed early.

Or *was* it a dream?

Was that what had really happened?

He was not sure. It was hard to tell anymore, and when he
woke up Rachel, sleeping next to him, asked her what day it was,
and found out that it was Wednesday instead of Tuesday, he decided that perhaps it had been both. Maybe it *had* happened, *and*
maybe he had dreamed about it afterward.

He had a slight headache, and the second he tried to sit up,
the intensity of the pain cranked up to ten. Hangover? He wasn't
sure, but he was sure that there was a private meeting of the Board
scheduled for ten, and that he needed to be there. Patoff was not

planning on attending—thank God for small favors—and Matthews wondered whether he should try to talk to the Board members about the consultant. The conference room was wired for sound and would be under video surveillance, but he doubted that every minute in every room was monitored, and there was a better than even chance that Patoff would not find out about the discussion—at least not right away.

Besides, so what if he did? The actions of consultants hired by the Board were a perfectly reasonable topic of conversation.

Patoff was not reasonable, however. Nothing about this situation was reasonable, and Matthews could not shake the feeling that it would be dangerous for him to talk about the consultant behind his back.

Rachel had already fallen back asleep, and he took a long hot shower, got dressed, made himself some strong coffee for breakfast, and headed to the office.

Only three of the Board members showed up for the meeting, and each of them looked the way he felt. Pale, shaky, with bags under their eyes, they filed into the conference room as though they were attending their mothers' funerals. Their newest member, Daniel Lu, was nowhere to be seen, and when Matthews asked if anyone knew whether he was coming or what had happened to him, the others were conspicuously silent. Hogarth Paquenlo's hand was trembling as he picked up his glass of water and took a drink. It seemed obvious that they had encountered the consultant, but how that had happened, or what Patoff had said to them, remained a mystery. He wanted to ask, but was afraid to do so and decided for the moment to go through the motions of conducting a regular board meeting.

"Should we give thanks to Ralph?" Matthews said before they started, but the joke fell flat, and he was immediately sorry he'd said it. Just referencing the consultant brought the man further into the room than he already was, and made it that much more difficult for Matthews to try and coax a little courage out of the cowed men to either side of him.

There was an agenda, and he followed it for the first ten minutes, but he was distracted and the other three men were even less engaged than he was. Finally, he put down the paper in his hand. "If no one else is going to address the elephant in the room, then I am." He took a deep breath. "We made a huge mistake hiring BFG, and I'm truly sorry that I recommended them."

"I make a motion that this meeting be adjourned," Mitchell Lockhart said quickly. His usual gruff and overbearing manner was nowhere to be seen. Instead, his voice was quavering, his trembling hands nervous.

"Seconded," Don Chase hurriedly responded.

"We need to talk about this," Matthews insisted.

Lockhart turned on him. "It *is* your fault," he said. "If you hadn't pushed us to…" He trailed off, eyes darting to the security camera mounted in the corner of the room.

"I think we should vote to terminate the contract," Matthews said. "We can pay them off if we have to, but I think it would be better than going on the way we are now."

"There's been a second," Lockhart announced. "All those in favor of adjourning, say 'Aye.'"

"Aye!" all three said in unison.

"What happened to you?" Matthews asked, looking at them.

Lockhart fixed him with haunted eyes, an expression mirrored in those of his colleagues. "It's your fault," he said, and, grabbing his papers, hurried from the room.

Matthews stood as the rest of the Board departed rapidly. Alone in the room, he could not help wondering what exactly the consultant had said or done to the men to make them so skittish.

No, not skittish.

Terrified.

He had never seen anyone so bone-deep frightened, and their fear made him afraid. It was not as if he wasn't scared already, but seeing the normally rough and loutish Lockhart pale and shaking, cowering at the mention of Patoff's name, left Matthews feeling both fearful and helpless. This was his company, but he was no longer in charge of it. Formerly a lion proudly at the head of a pack, he was now a mouse scurrying alongside, trying not to draw attention to himself. He had hoped to enlist the support of the Board in ousting BFG. But whereas they'd previously been slow to see any sign of problems and had sided with Patoff against him, now they were petrified by Patoff, too intimidated to even *think* about defiance.

He could see no way out of this.

Distracted, taking no notice of the employees he passed, Matthews left the conference room and took an elevator to the top floor. Walking to his office at the end of the hall, he told Diane to hold all his calls and let no one in. He closed the door behind him, sat down at his glass-topped desk and swiveled around in his chair to gaze at the campus far below, something that always cleared his mind and helped him think. Frowning, he suddenly pivoted back around. He'd seen something on his desk, something in his peripheral vision that had not immediately registered.

A snow globe.

Sure enough, the object sat unobtrusively atop a closed ledger on the left side of the desk as though it was nothing more than a paperweight that had always been in that spot. He leaned forward to look at it more closely. The base was brass, an ornately carved stand with clawed feet at each corner of a rococo square, on top of which sat a glass sphere depicting a scene of violent depravity. Matthews picked up the globe, the movement causing a ripple of red glitter at the bottom that could have symbolized either a river of lava or a tide of blood. Peering within the watery world, he saw a naked man strangling a Lady Godiva-esque woman on a miniature horse as he entered the horse from behind. In back of him, another woman, sitting on a stool made of severed body parts, had her face buried in his buttocks.

Grimacing, he shook the globe. The red glitter dispersed through the water, making droplets of blood that fell upon the participants.

He put the object down. How had it gotten here? He knew *who* had brought it here, but he did not know when or how. In his mind, he saw Regus Patoff sneaking into the building in the middle of the night and making his way up here in complete blackness, without the aid of flashlight, his eyes glowing in the dark like a cat's.

Matthews scanned the room. His office was one of the few places left that was not under constant observation by security cameras, and for once he wished that the room *was* monitored. He would like to be able to see what had happened, and would like to have video proof of Patoff's incursion into his private domain, something that he might be able to use against him.

The door suddenly swung open of its own accord, bringing with it a tangible and instantaneous drop in temperature. Patoff strode into the office, throwing a paper-clipped stack of papers down on his desk. "Sign these," he ordered.

Feigning a calm he did not feel, Matthews picked up the papers, glancing at the top sheet as he did so. "What are they?"

"None of your concern," the consultant said dismissively. "Sign them."

"I'm not—"

"*Sign* them."

Matthews signed. He felt weak and pathetic as he flipped each page and found the blank line on which he was to affix his signature. Knowing that it made no difference, he didn't even bother to read what he was signing, because he was fully aware that despite any objections he might have, he would only end up being bullied into doing exactly what he was doing now. It left him more dignity if he signed without reading, pretending this was one of those meaningless formalities in which an underling places inconsequential documents before him that require rote signatures.

He finished, handing the papers back. "Anything else?"

Patoff smiled. "As a matter of fact, there is. Based on our preliminary findings, we've compiled a list of the six most inessential employees, those who will definitely not be needed after the restructuring. Ordinarily, they would be part of the first round of layoffs, but thanks to early identification, we have the opportunity of pressuring them to quit. This will save us money—"

"I'm not pressuring anyone to quit," Matthews said, gaining back some of his self-assurance. "These are loyal workers. They deserve to at least be able to collect unemployment—"

"They don't deserve *shit*." Patoff glared at him. "Weak-minded, weak-willed losers who've been dragging this company down. They deserve to be dropped in the ocean without a lifejacket."

"I'm not going to do that to any of my workers. In fact, I'm going to authorize generous severance packages for anyone who has to be let go."

Without even bothering to respond, as if Matthews had said nothing and was not even there, the consultant turned and walked out of the office. The door closed behind him, *slammed* shut, though Patoff had neither touched it nor looked at it. Matthews exhaled deeply, a feeling of relief flooding through him now that Patoff was gone. He practically collapsed in his chair, leaning back in it and swiveling around to face the window. Below, a man and woman walked along the sidewalk through the campus, deep in discussion. He could not see who they were from this height, but he felt protective of them just the same. It was his responsibility to remain strong and get his company through this nightmare. BFG would leave eventually, and in the interim, he needed to shield his workers from Patoff and his minions to the best of his ability. He'd done a crappy job so far, and it was high time that he stepped up to the plate.

He turned back around—and all of his confidence disappeared. There were *two* snow globes on his desk now, though there was no way that could possibly be. Gingerly, he picked up the new one. Inside the glass was a small perfect replica of his own head, with the bottom of his neck red and ragged, as though it had been chopped off with a blunt hatchet.

Was this supposed to be a warning? A threat?

He didn't know, but the resurgence of resolve that he'd felt had disappeared completely, and he spent the rest of the day locked in his office, praying that the doors would not fly open and Patoff would not return.

—⊗⊗⊗—

He and Rachel were supposed to meet their friends the Sternhagens at Mr. Chow for dinner, but Matthews wasn't in the mood, and he begged off, claiming that he had extra work he needed to complete. To reinforce the lie, he parked himself in front of his computer all evening. He told Rachel that she could go—was *hoping* she would go—but she called the Sternhagens and rescheduled, leaving him to keep up his charade until it was time for bed.

Still, it was better than going out. He didn't feel like seeing people tonight, was not sure he would be able to make small talk and pretend that everything was okay, and it was far safer to just stay home and hide.

He called it quits around ten o'clock, having spent the past three hours doing nothing, staring at his email queue and periodically refreshing the page, trying not to look at the steadily increasing number of messages in his inbox.

Rachel was in bed, watching the Food Network or the Cooking Channel or one of those other useless cable stations she liked so much. Bobby Flay was visiting a little restaurant called Rudell's Smokehouse in the picturesque seaside town of Cayucos on California's central coast, raving about the smoked albacore tacos. Green rolling hills rose up behind the town, and in front of it the ocean was as blue as the sky. That was where Matthews wished he was right now, rather than here in grimy dog-eat-dog Los Angeles, and it made him wonder if maybe it was time to retire, to pack it in and spend whatever years he had left travelling, relaxing and enjoying life. Did he really have the same fire in his belly now that he did twenty years ago? Probably not, and while he loved his company and was proud of how it had grown, the desire to spend all day every day on CompWare business had definitely lessened.

Who was he kidding? He wasn't tired. He was scared, afraid to work at his own company, afraid of the consultants he had hired, afraid, afraid, afraid…

"You're quiet tonight," Rachel observed.

"Long day," he said.

"You should take some time off."

"I was just thinking the same thing," he told her.

In the old days, hearing that he'd had a long day, she would have relieved his pressure with some generously proffered oral sex, but now she simply gave him a quick peck on the cheek and rolled over to sleep. He lay where he was, listening to the television, staring up at the flickering blue light on the ceiling and wondering when exactly his life had gone off track.

He was almost asleep, in that hazy twilight existence where words being spoken by characters on TV in the fading real world were being incorporated into his encroaching dreamlife, when he was awakened by knocking at the front door. He sat up groggily, swung his legs off the bed, and suddenly realized that he shouldn't be *able* to hear any knocking up here. Such a thing wasn't possible. Sound didn't carry that way, from the front door to a bedroom on the opposite side of the house.

The noise came again, and it sounded like someone with a sledgehammer was trying to break down a wall.

Goose bumps popped up on the back of his neck, raced down his arms.

"What's that?" Rachel muttered, only half-awake.

"I'll check," he said, but his gut already knew what it was.

*The consultant.*

This time, he was more frightened than angry. He wanted to be able to act as he had the last time Patoff had shown up unannounced, wanted to project power and strength, to once again order the consultant off his property and warn him not to come back, but he remembered how the contents of his desk had floated up into the air, the way his office door had opened and closed by itself, and was afraid of what might happen if he angered the man. He imagined windows being shattered, furniture smashing against walls, Rachel's snow globes exploding into shards of glass and droplets of water.

Grabbing his robe from on top of the hope chest at the foot of the bed, Matthews pulled it on, slid into his slippers and made his way out into the hall, closing the bedroom door behind him. The knocking had stopped for a moment, but it returned with a vengeance, not knocking but *pounding*, so loud that he could practically feel it in his gut. He hurried downstairs, thinking that he should fire his home security company and wishing for the first time in his life that he was the kind of person who owned guns. He had no idea what he was going to do when he confronted the consultant.

He reached the bottom of the stairs and strode toward the entryway just as another round of pounding started up.

He could see the oversized door on the opposite side of the foyer in front of him, and down here the noise was as loud as thunder, not the sound of someone knocking on a door but the sound of a cannon going off.

He reached the entrance and the pounding stopped.

Matthews took a deep breath.

And did nothing.

He was afraid to open the door, and as he stared at the white wooden rectangle before him, the dominant thought in his mind was a desperate wish that it be strong enough to withstand the mounting pressure from outside.

The pounding came again, only this time it was from somewhere at the side of the house. The laundry room? He thought of the consultant running around the building, knocking on each door in turn, and the image frightened him far more than he would have thought possible. There was a specificity to it that made him think it was true, as superstitious as he knew that to be, and in his mind, he could see the consultant, bright bow tie perfectly in place, dashing from door to door, smiling his soulless smile. For what possible reason Matthews could not even hazard a guess, but then he could never tell why Patoff did what he did.

He remained where he was, staring at the front door, not chasing down the sound, hoping that if he waited this out, the man would leave.

The pounding moved to what sounded like the pool room, then around to the kitchen. How long was this going to last?

*Go away*, he thought. *Go away!*

Matthews jumped as something banged against the front door.

He had to put a stop to this,—

*or it might go on forever*

—had to go out there and confront the consultant instead of hiding here like a scared little girl. He wasn't brave enough to open the door, but he did it anyway, telling his fingers to punch in the security code for the alarm, forcing his hand to turn the lock, twist the handle, push.

The porch was empty.

Thinking he might have just missed the man, and gaining courage from the fact that there was no one on the stoop, Matthews hurried out to the drive, looking around. Motion detector lights switched on by the side gate and the garage, but there was no sign of anyone other than himself. Holding his robe tightly closed, he walked around the side of the house, shouting "Who's there? Come out now!" A quick, rough tour of the grounds immediately adjacent to the house and garage convinced him that he was all alone, and ten minutes later, he was back inside.

He hadn't put on the alarm or locked the front door during his impromptu search, and for a brief, horrifying second, he wondered if the consultant had used the opportunity to sneak into the house.

With a sick feeling in the pit of his stomach, he rushed upstairs to the bedroom, but Rachel lay still asleep and unmolested. To set his mind at ease, however, he locked the front door, set the alarm, checked all of the other doors and went through every room to make sure no one had gotten in and was hiding.

Back in the bedroom, he took off his robe, stepped out of his slippers and got into bed. He closed his eyes, trying to will himself to sleep, but his ears were alert, his mind wide awake, and he remained vigilant for the next two hours, waiting for the return of the knocking, until finally he dozed.

# TWENTY SEVEN

ANOTHER DAY, ANOTHER MEETING.

Craig met Phil and Elaine in the elevator on his way down to the first floor. This wasn't a meeting for departments, divisions, supervisors or even all general employees, but was a gathering of seemingly random CompWare personnel assembled for some unspecified and probably pointless purpose.

"Those consultants sure love meetings, don't they?" Elaine said.

Craig didn't respond but glanced in a very obvious manner at the camera mounted in the corner of the elevator. Elaine nodded her understanding, and the three of them stood in silence until the doors slid open.

There were cameras in the lobby, and Craig wondered if the intent of all this conspicuous surveillance was to purposely make people paranoid in order to cow them into submission. It was definitely working on him, and he looked down at the floor as he spoke, not wanting his lips to be read, and mumbled, not want-ing his voice to be heard. "Anyone hear about Jim Rodman in Ac-counting?"

Phil felt no need to hide. "He quit, right? I heard he trashed BFG in his exit interview." Phil chuckled. "I respect that."

"That's not what I heard," Elaine said quietly.

"Me, either." Craig glanced over at his friend.

Phil frowned. "I'm not sure I want to hear this."

"He disappeared," Elaine said. "Vanished. Didn't take anything with him. His wife called work, work called home, but no one's seen him for three days. The police are searching for him now."

Phil did not respond.

"I heard he was on the list," Craig admitted, still looking down. "The consultants wanted to get rid of him."

"And I guess they did," Phil said.

They were silent as they walked into the conference room. There were seats available, but the turnout was far greater than Craig would have expected from the sparse crowd in the lobby. The three of them took adjacent seats near the aisle, and they wait-ed quietly with everyone else for the remainder of the invitees to show up. On the stage at the front of the room, Regus Patoff stood staring out at them, completely still, hands clasped behind his back, smiling.

Over the next five minutes, people continued to trickle in, and at some point Patoff must have decided that everyone who was supposed to be here had arrived, because he cleared his throat loudly and moved behind the podium.

"Good morning!" he announced. "I trust we will have an ex-cellent meeting. Praise the goodness of Ralph." He briefly lowered his head.

Craig looked over at Phil, who rolled his eyes.

"You have all been chosen to participate in this meeting based on demographic desirability regarding the subject at hand. In short, you are a representative cross-section of the company. I have asked you here to inform you about one of our newest initiatives and to get your feedback." The consultant, still smiling, scanned the room. When his eyes met Craig's, there was a *flicker*, and for a brief fraction of a second, Craig saw Patoff more clearly, like a holographic picture when it hit the right angle and the image suddenly became three dimensional.

Then the consultant's gaze moved on, and Craig wasn't quite sure *what* he had seen. He'd had an impression of great age, a sense of something profoundly inhuman. That was crazy, he knew, but a part of him thought that it made perfect sense.

"With the alarming obesity epidemic in this country, there has been a renewed national focus on establishing and maintaining healthy eating habits," Patoff said. "CompWare has a rare opportunity to become a leader in this movement and get out ahead of the trend. Which is why we are proposing what we've dubbed our 'healthy employee initiative.'" He held up his hands as though someone had objected, though no one had. "I know, I know, this seems outside the purview of our mandate. But our aim isn't entirely altruistic. For one thing, the company could stand a little good publicity. We make sure this is leaked to the trades and the mainstream press, and CompWare comes out looking like an enlightened and environmentally conscious enterprise concerned about the well-being of its employees. Which, under the present circumstances, would greatly benefit the company's public profile, because, as I'm sure you all know, in regard to stocks, perception is everything.

"On a less theoretical level, obesity and health-related issues cost this company an estimated two million dollars annually in lost wages, decreased productivity, increased insurance costs and sick time allocations. What the 'healthy employee initiative' would do is provide, through a series of incentives and disincentives, a framework by which employees could maintain good health and wellbeing. The details are still being worked out, but BFG and CompWare's top management both see this as a win-win for individuals and for the company."

Finished, he stared out at the gathered focus group, smiling.

After several awkward moments of silence, Craig stood. "Are you asking for our input on this idea?"

Patoff's smile disappeared. "No. I'm just telling you what's going to happen."

"You don't want our opinion?"

"I don't give a shit about your opinion."

Craig looked around at his fellow employees, all of whom appeared not only confused but nervous—with the exception of Phil who seemed defiant. "Then why are we here?" Phil asked.

Patoff grinned. "Good meeting," he said. "Thank you for coming. Have a nice day."

The lights switched off and the conference room was suddenly thrown into darkness. For a few brief seconds, Craig saw the consultant's eyes glowing in the gloom. Then they blinked and were gone, and he knew somehow that the consultant was gone, too. Along with everyone else, he grabbed for his cell phone, turning it on, and by the weak illumination of a dozen small screens, they made their way to the door. Once the door was open, light from the lobby was let in, and someone found a switch, flipping it on. As he'd known, the stage was empty.

"What was *that*?" Elaine asked.

"A waste of time," Phil said angrily.

Looking up at the cameras, Craig said nothing as they walked over to the elevators and headed back to work.

———∞∞∞———

Lupe glanced up at the familiar sound of Craig's footsteps on the faux marble floor, aware through her peripheral vision that Todd was immediately noting the interruption in her typing. Craig was aware of it, too, and he glared at the observer as he stopped to chat with Lupe. "Hey," he said, "Lupe is my secretary, and her job is to pay attention when I talk to her. I do not want her doing busywork when she's supposed to be listening to me. Do you understand?"

Todd said nothing but entered something on his tablet.

Shaking his head in annoyance, Craig leaned against the side of her desk. Leisurely, he explained what had happened at his meeting, and made disparaging jokes about healthy eating. Lupe knew he did it to irritate the observers, and they both shared a conspiratorial smile when Todd and Mrs. Adams frowned disapprovingly and began typing intensely on their pads.

"By the way," Craig told her, "I don't want you calling him 'Todd' anymore." He motioned toward her observer. "He doesn't look like a 'Todd' to me. He looks more like a stool sample. Don't you think he looks like a stool sample?"

"I really couldn't say," Lupe replied, trying to hide her smile.

"Well, I do. So please call him 'Stool Sample' from now on. Okay?"

The smile broke through. "Yes, Mr. Horne."

"This is highly inappropriate," Mrs. Adams said.

Craig looked at her on the way into his office. "Your job is to *observe*, Mrs. Adams. Not to render opinions. I am Lupe's supervisor, and she will do as I ask."

Returning to her typing was more pleasurable after that, and Lupe was half-tempted to address Todd by the moniker "Stool

Sample," but she wasn't brave enough to go through with it. Just the thought made her giggle, though, and old Stool Sample marked that down on his pad.

She had never had a set break time—Craig had always been flexible about things like that and had allowed her to break whenever it was convenient—but ever since the observers had arrived, she'd taken her morning break from ten to ten-fifteen because it was easy to keep track of that way, and she didn't want to be accused of staying away from her desk for too long. Thanks to those cameras in the restrooms, she'd also taken to combining her bathroom visits with her scheduled breaks so she could go over to the office building across the street and avoid the consultants' surveillance. Today she'd been holding it in for some time before ten o'clock rolled around.

Lupe stood up and poked her head into Craig's office. "I'll be back in a few minutes," she said. "If any calls come in, you can either pick them up, or allow them to go into voicemail and I'll answer them when I get back."

Craig nodded absently, and she walked down the corridor to the elevator. Todd had given up trying to shadow her, was content now to simply remain at his station and time her absences, but she wished that this time he had tried to follow along. She imagined herself turning on him and saying, "Stool Sample, you are not allowed to monitor my free time." The idea made her smile.

"*Lupe.*"

She was downstairs, crossing the lobby, heading toward the smoked glass doors of the entrance, when she heard her name called over the loudspeaker. She stopped, looking around, unsure of what to do or how to respond.

"*Lupe.*"

She recognized the voice now.

Regus Patoff.

"*Where are you going?*" The question boomed out as though emanating from the man behind the curtain in *The Wizard of Oz*.

She wasn't sure how to respond.

"*Speak up!*" he ordered.

"I..."

"*Louder! So I can hear you!*"

"I'm going across the street!" She was practically shouting. Heads turned to glance in her direction but no one dared stop to find out what was going on.

"*Why?*" Patoff demanded.

She didn't want to answer.

"*WHY?*"

"I need to use the restroom!" She reddened, embarrassed to be making an announcement of it.

"*For what purpose? Urinating or defecating?*"

Angry, she resumed her walk across the lobby. "That's none of your damn business!" she shouted as the door automatically opened in front of her and she stormed out.

Lupe was shaking as she hurried down the steps and strode across the parking lot. Her mouth was dry, and she had a difficult time catching her breath. She could not believe that had just happened, and her fuming mind considered calling the police, the *Los Angeles Times* or one of the local TV stations with their investigative reporters, thinking that this would be perfect for sweeps week.

During a break in traffic, she ran across the street and went into the lobby of the multi-story office building opposite Comp-Ware. The first floor was home to a law firm, an accounting firm and some sort of direct marketing business. Opposite the elevators were the restrooms, and she hurried into the women's, going into the first stall and closing the door behind her. Pushing up her skirt and pulling down her underwear, she sat on the toilet, started to pee—

And the stall door opened.

Startled, Lupe cried out, hands immediately pushing down her skirt to cover her exposed lap.

It was the consultant.

He stood before her, blocking the stall's exit, belt unbuckled, pants unzipped and open, penis hanging out. His organ was grotesque—red and blotchy, S-shaped and far too large—and he stepped forward, holding it in his hand. She tried to scream, but the second her mouth opened, before a single sound came out, he was shoving it in. His penis was rough and dry, tasting of dirt and rot, its twists and curves contacting odd parts of her mouth as he began to slide it in and out. "Oh yes," he whispered creepily. "That's good."

She wanted to bite it off but dared not. Accidentally, she scraped him with her teeth, and he slapped the side of her head. Hard. "Do it right," he ordered harshly.

Crying, she covered her teeth with her lips and remained unmoving as he continued to push himself slowly in and out.

"Oh yes," he repeated. "That's good."

His penis stiffened. She was filled with horror as she realized he was about to climax, and before she could even begin to prepare herself…it happened. Thick sperm, ribbons of it, hit the back of her throat and slid down. She wanted to throw up but was denied the opportunity because he was still ejaculating, holding the back of her head as his freakish erection continued to violate her mouth, his slimy discharge hot and burning, gushing in impossibly copious amounts.

Finally he pulled out, degradingly wiping the last few drops on her nose and cheeks. He tucked his monstrous penis back between his legs and pulled up his pants to hold it in place.

She was gasping for air, and he patted the top of her head. "Good meeting," he said, grinning. "Maybe you'll be able to keep your job."

He started to leave, then returned, poking his head around the corner. "You could stand to lose a few pounds, though. I suggest you come back to the program next week and weigh in."

He left again, and, sobbing, Lupe pulled up her panties, turned around and threw up into the toilet. She could still taste him in her mouth, and she continued to vomit until her stomach was empty and the only thing her convulsing stomach could bring up was a thin dribble of mucous and saliva. Flushing, she made her way over to the sink, where she washed her face and rinsed her mouth out with water from the faucet.

*AIDS*, she couldn't help thinking. *What if he has AIDS?*

By the time she returned to CompWare and her desk, she was ten minutes late, something Todd—Stool Sample—noted instantly, although, at this point, she didn't really care. She wanted to tell Craig what had happened, but didn't know how, knew she should report it to the police, but was afraid to do so. She was filled with an almost constant desire to spit and went through an entire box of Kim Wipes in the next hour and a half, using the oversized tissues to collect, absorb and wipe away the accumulated saliva in her mouth.

Before the beginning of lunch, she walked into Craig's office, closing the door behind her to keep Todd and Mrs. Adams from hearing.

"I'm quitting," she said.

At first, Craig thought she was joking. He started to make a bantering reply, but the expression on her face must have convinced him of the seriousness of her intent. "Really?" he said.

She nodded.

He was shocked. "So you're giving your two-week's notice?"

"No. No two-week's notice. This is it. I'm not coming back after lunch."

"But you won't even get your severance!"

"I don't care," she said. "I have to get away from here."

He stood immediately, coming around the desk. She thought he was going to try and hug her, and she stepped back involuntarily, not wanting to be touched. Obviously sensing her mood, he backed off, and her eyes filled with tears at the thought that they wouldn't be working together anymore.

"Lupe?"

She couldn't meet his gaze.

"What is it? What happened? Whatever it is, I'll—"

"There's nothing you can do," she said.

"Is it the consultants? We can wait them out..."

She shook her head adamantly. "I can't work here anymore."

"Lupe..."

She burst into tears, and though flinching at the initial contact, she finally let him hug her.

"You can tell me," he said. "Whatever happened, whatever it is..."

She shook her head against his shoulder, and gathering herself together, she sucked in her breath and pulled away. "I can't."

"Just tell me," he pressed. "Does it have something to do with the consultants?"

She found herself nodding. "But I'm quitting. I'm not waiting them out. I can't."

"I understand," he assured her. "But just listen, okay? I have an idea."

"What?"

"They're going to leave eventually, right? So what I'll do is talk to Broderick in HR and see if I can get you a leave of absence or something. If that's not feasible, I just won't fill your position. I'll take a temp if they force me, but I'll keep the position open. Once BFG's gone, you can apply again, and I'll make sure you get it." He put his hands on her shoulders. "You can't leave me now. We're supposed to be in this together."

Through her tears, she smiled at him, and he smiled back, giving her shoulders a slight squeeze. "All right then."

"But not until they're gone," she told him. "I can't…"

"I know."

She took a deep breath. "Thank you."

"Go out there, grab your stuff, take what you need. I'll do what I have to do, and once I figure it out, I'll give you a call."

"What if—" *HE calls*, she was thinking, but couldn't complete the thought.

Craig seemed to know what she was trying to say. "I won't call from here. I'll call from home. So you can check your caller ID and know it's me."

"Thank you," she said again.

"I'll go out with you. Make sure Stool Sample and Nurse Ratched don't cause any problems. Then we'll walk out to your car."

There were no problems, and Lupe let him know how grateful she was for all of his help as she got into her Camry.

"I'll call," he promised. His face darkened. "But if it's from CompWare or a number you don't recognize…"

"I won't answer."

He smiled. "Where else can I get this?" He moved his hand back and forth between them, indicating a connection. "That's why we can't break up the team."

"You're a good boss, Boss."

It wasn't until she got home that her stomach started feeling weird.

*AIDS*

No. That wouldn't show up so quickly. But there were probably a lot of other diseases that might. God knows what that freak could have infected her with. It was time to pull her head out of the sand, face reality, go to the hospital and have herself tested for… everything.

A cramp hit her hard, causing her to double over and cry out. The pain was intense, as though a knife had been shoved into her abdomen, and Lupe barely made it over to the kitchen sink before she started throwing up.

She closed her eyes tightly, knowing that if she saw the vomit in the sink, it would make her throw up even more. Just the thought of it caused her to heave again.

There was something wrong.

There was *always* something wrong if a person was throwing up, and she knew the reason why this was happening right now, knew what she had swallowed, but that wasn't all that disturbed her. The *feel* of the vomit was also freaking her out. There seemed to be things moving in her throat and mouth as she puked into the sink, and she opened her eyes to see an assortment of small squirming sluglike creatures amidst the disgorged contents of her stomach. She felt still more of them in her mouth and throat as she spewed again, and began screaming even as she was throwing up. This was what had come from his sperm.

The stabbing pain in her abdomen intensified, and Lupe involuntarily doubled over, her head hitting the sink's faucet handle. Blood was suddenly spurting from her forehead, and she backed off, holding a hand to the wound in order to suppress the bleeding, staggering away from those impossible monstrosities in the sink, not caring that she was now spitting up on the front of her blouse and the floor of the kitchen.

Not all of the creatures, apparently, were sluglike. One with sharp insectile limbs scurried out of her mouth and down her neck. She fell to the floor, weakened legs giving way beneath her, blood flowing down her face as she removed the hand from her forehead to bat away the sperm-spawn scuttling around her neck. Sobbing, her will broken, Lupe slumped on the tile. She was no longer vomiting, but those creatures continued crawling up her throat, gagging her. She flopped about, attempting in vain to suck air into her lungs, using a hand to try and clear her mouth, but her strength was ebbing and she was vomiting again, sickened by the repulsive feel of rubbery slime on her tongue.

Degraded, humiliated and alone, she died.

# TWENTY EIGHT

TO:      All Employees

RE:      Nutrition and Health

Studies have repeatedly shown that good nutrition is the key to good health. In an effort to promote wellness within the CompWare community and to reduce worktime lost by sick leave, a series of nutritional guidelines have been drawn up by health experts and are being provided to all employees. While adherence to these guidelines is strictly voluntary, personnel who adjust their eating habits to accommodate the suggested recommendations will be given preferential consideration if layoffs become necessary between employees of equivalent position. To make the guidelines easier to access, a downloadable app is available to all CompWare employees that not only lists low-fat, low-carb, low-calorie food suggestions, but enables users to scan the bar codes of prepackaged food items to determine their nutritional content.

Reading this email constitutes acknowledgement and understanding of the nutrition and health suggestions made herein.

Thank you.

*Regus Patoff*

Regus Patoff
BFG Associates
For Austin Matthews, CompWare CEO

# TWENTY NINE

L UNCH.

They'd picked a place at random, a hole-in-the-wall Mexican joint in a slummy area east of the freeway, a place they'd found after driving up and down various side streets to make sure they weren't being followed—a ridiculous precaution, perhaps, but it made them both feel better.

"I spent all damn morning in a meeting," Phil said on the way. "They called me in early, and I didn't even get to eat breakfast. I'm starving."

It was the only real thing they said to each other until they arrived, since both of them were paranoid about the car being bugged. *This is no way to live*, Craig thought, and he wondered if he was one of the people being targeted for downsizing now, if the consultant was instilling this paranoia within him, hoping it would pressure him into quitting.

Now he was being paranoid about being paranoid.

The small restaurant was crowded, so they took turns ordering, one going up to the window while the other guarded the small table they'd commandeered near the door.

"So what was the meeting about?" Craig asked as they waited.

"Nothing," Phil said. "What are they ever about? That asshole just likes to hear himself talk."

"So no news?"

"Not that they're sharing."

"You know," Craig said, "they didn't even have our programmers work on that nutrition app. They brought it in themselves. I don't know if they bought it off some vendor or if they have their own in-house programmers, but no one from CompWare worked on it."

"Are you having your guys analyze it, in case..."

"Yeah," Craig said tiredly. "For whatever good it'll do. It's like *Lord of the Flies* among the programmers now. Everyone's afraid their jobs are on the line, so they're throwing each other under the bus so they'll be the last man standing."

His number was called, and he walked up to get his food. On his way back to the table, Phil's number was called. Craig had just bitten into a tortilla chip when Phil put his tray down on the table and said, "You know who Tom Waits is?"

"I've heard of him." He tried to cut his friend off. "This isn't one of your boring music analogies is it?"

Phil ignored him. "In the 1970s, Tom Waits put out these amazing albums: *The Heart of Saturday Night, Nighthawks at the Diner, Small Change, Foreign Affairs.* Jazzy, kind of beatnik things, totally unique, especially for then. As anti-trendy as you could get. At that time, he gave this interview where he said he'd rather play for a bunch of derelicts at a union hall than a crowd of hip college kids with coke spoons around their necks. Well, in the eighties, he changed his style completely, became a critic's darling and he's spent the rest of his career playing to hip, trendy college students."

"The point?" Craig prodded.

"Sometimes things happen. We start out pure and end up becoming exactly what we didn't want to become."

"Do you mean me?" Craig was still confused.

"I mean *us*. Look what we're doing now. Look what we're going along with. We took the blood test. We don't wear tennis shoes. We wear gold shirts. You ordered a taco *salad*, for Christ's sake…"

"Wait a minute," Craig said. "How do you know about that Tom Waits interview? You had to be, like, one."

"I read it online."

"You spend your free time looking up old music interviews from when you were a baby?"

"The internet is a wonderful tool."

Craig picked up another tortilla chip. "'Tool' is *exactly* the word that comes to mind."

"That's not the point I'm making. What I'm trying to say is, despite our rebel stance, against our will and without us even knowing it, BFG's already changed us. The only question is: what comes next?"

Craig thought about that. As much as he hated to admit it, Phil was right. He thought he'd been fighting the consultants, but he hadn't been immune from their influence. He *had* been forced to conform. He'd gone on that dog hunt at the retreat, had had his blood taken, allowed himself to be monitored by camera, was watched daily by an observer, and, as Phil had pointed out, was wearing uncomfortable shoes, a gold shirt and was about to dig into a taco salad he'd ordered instead of the deep-fried chimichanga he'd really wanted to eat.

He thought of that dead dog made into a meal, of Tyler's freak electrocution, of Jess Abodje's wheelchair speeding out into traffic, of everything else that had happened and was still happening. Was he complicitous in any of it? He didn't want to think so, but the circumstances were starting to make him believe otherwise. He should have been more aggressive in his opposition to the consultants, more assertive.

"I know that face," Phil said, biting into his burrito. "Stop beating yourself up."

"I should've—"

"What? You should've what?"

Craig shook his head. "I don't know."

"You're a cog in the machine. You're a division head. And you've done a damn good job of protecting your division, which is what you're supposed to do. Do you know how easy you guys have gotten off compared to most?"

"We're content providers. They need us."

"Maybe," Phil conceded. "But at least you're fighting the good fight. Me, too. We're limited, we're constrained, but given the state of affairs, we're doing pretty well." He paused. "What I want to know is: where's our illustrious leader? Where's Austin Matthews in all this? Listening to you after that retreat, I thought we had him in the bag. But I haven't seen hide nor hair of the guy since. And all of those memos, if you haven't noticed—and I know you have—are signed by Patoff *for* Matthews."

Craig nodded. "I've noticed."

"He's a ghost in the machine. I'm thinking he's on his way out."

"It's *his* company."

"Not since it went public. He has to report to the Board now, and after that merger fiasco, they might be inclined to do whatever BFG says."

"Inclined?"

"*That's* the interesting part. Because I think the consultants are a little more forceful than that." Phil sipped his soda. "First of all, I need to point out that *you're* the one who should be doing this. You're the computer geek; you're the one whose family's being stalked. This is really your bailiwick. But, whatever. I've been doing some more research."

"Not on your own computer?"

"The library's. I'm not entirely dim. But I've been going as deep as I can. Not just articles and press releases, but stock reports, SEC filings, Google searches of individuals, any damn thing I can find."

"And what *did* you find?"

Phil looked grim. "Bad shit. ProTech, for example. BFG consulted for them last year. They were on the verge of going under, and after implementing BFG's recommendations, they not only got back on their feet, but their stock price tripled. Now they've practically cornered the market on USB adapters and niche tech like that." He leaned forward conspiratorially. "But here's where it gets interesting. Because, since then, there've been an unbelievable number of violent acts associated with the company. Nine former employees committed suicide. That's nine *hundred* times the average for tech businesses. One man and two women committed *murder. Three* people from *one* company within the past *year*. What are the odds of *that*? The women are both in jail, awaiting trial. One killed a rival at another company, one killed her husband. The man murdered another ProTech employee, then killed himself, so, technically, he's part of the murder *and* suicide statistics.

"Bad luck? Coincidence? You might think so, right? But the pattern holds. It's true for four of the five companies I've investigated. Shockingly high rates of violence, completely unexplainable, all *after* BFG consults for them."

Craig felt chilled. He believed it. Every word. He thought of Angie. Maybe he *should* have supported her idea to quit her job. "So what do we do?"

"One thing we need to do—and you can help with this—is get the information out there. Maybe someone else has put all this together, but even if they have, it's not readily available. I'm thinking Better Business Bureau, Attorney General's office, newspapers, *60 Minutes*. Hell, corporate ratings sites. I want to get the word out but not have it traced back. Just in case. That's where you come in. Is there some sort of filter, some way to make my posts and emails anonymous so that even a group like BFG can't trace it back?"

"Sure."

"Because these guys don't fuck around."

"We create a fake account, from an offsite computer, someplace with an IP address that has nothing to do with us or CompWare, write the email, run *that* through an anonymizer, send it on time delay set for an hour when we're both verifiably at CompWare and engaged in other work." He was thinking aloud. "Sure. We can do it."

"I have another plan, too," Phil said. "A way to ferret out even more information."

"You've been a busy little bee, haven't you?"

"You know my watcher? John?"

"Yeah."

"We take him out after work today, get him drunk and see if we can't loosen his lips a little."

"I don't think they're supposed to fraternize with us."

"They probably aren't," Phil agreed.

"So why would he?"

"I don't know. But this one...he seems different to me. Not as committed. Disgruntled even. We haven't really talked or anything, it's just a sense I have, but I honestly think that if we played this right, we might be able to have a real conversation with him. And maybe get some inside information, something that might help us."

"After work, huh? I'll have to call Angie and tell her I'll be late. Dylan's definitely not going to like it."

"It's for the greater good."

"Yeah, that argument always works with second graders. By the way, in all your research, did you ever find out what BFG stands for?"

"Still no idea," Phil admitted. "But that's something else we can ask."

They finished eating, and Craig refilled his cup before heading back to work. He arrived at his office with several minutes to spare. "Early!" he announced, pointing to Mrs. Adams. "Mark that down." He walked in, closing the door behind him.

He wasn't quite sure how Phil intended to even broach the topic of socializing with his observer, let alone extend an invitation without the whole thing being caught on surveillance, but halfway through the afternoon, Craig received a call from his friend. "This is a long day," Phil said without preamble. "Want to get something to drink after work?"

Craig's heart was pounding. He felt the way he had as a child when he tried to lie to his parents. "Sure," he said with false nonchalance.

"Great. Talk to you later."

*Smart*, Craig thought. No mention of either the observer or a location where they might go.

Without further communication, they met in the parking lot shortly after five. Phil was alone, and Craig immediately assumed that things had fallen through, but his friend said John was parked in the visitor's lot on the north side of the campus and was going to follow them to O'Gill's Pub. Phil was obviously being careful and taking precautions. He didn't want any of the cameras trained on the lot to see the observer with them. Although Craig wondered how the meet had been arranged without any of the cameras and microphones in the building picking it up.

Phil left first, Craig following behind, and they drove through the visitor's lot, Phil honking once to alert the observer before their little caravan headed out onto the street.

At O'Gill's, the three of them were awkward with each other. The observer was obviously ill-at-ease, Phil was trying too hard to make him feel comfortable, and Craig was on the sidelines, odd man out. Attempts at forging a personal connection with John through questions about family, friends and general interests fell flat, but after a couple of beers, they did manage to initiate a conversation about jobs and work. Although John warned them that even if he had information about CompWare, he could not legally or ethically tell them anything, the observer did reveal that he himself had been recruited by BFG after working for a firm that the consultants were analyzing. He'd only been on the job for a couple of months, but it didn't seem to be a good fit, and…

The observer cut himself off. The implication was that he would like to quit his job at BFG.

But was afraid to do so.

Worried, perhaps, that he'd said too much, John told them he had to leave and hastily put down his beer without finishing it. "Is this enough?" he asked, pulling a ten out of his wallet.

Phil waved him away. "We got this," he said. "You're our guest."

"Well…thanks," John told them and hurried off.

Craig looked over at his friend, eyebrow raised. "So what do you make of *that*?"

"He's scared."

"Of what?"

"Patoff, I assume."

"We didn't learn much today."

Phil was silent for a moment. "Maybe, maybe not," he said.

———— ⧉ ————

John knew he'd made a mistake even before leaving the bar. He hadn't really said anything, hadn't given away any trade secrets, but The Consultant wouldn't want him speaking to civilians about *anything*. He'd been ordered—*warned*—to keep everything on a strictly professional level, and he was well aware that even this minimal amount of contact was forbidden. It had felt good to talk to someone, though. Because he was starting to regret ever taking this job. Yes, he needed the work, but even with as limited a perspective as he'd been granted, John knew that BFG was not...normal. His own duties might be fairly ordinary and straightforward, but he was well aware that he was unable to see the whole picture, and he had no idea what The Consultant did with the information he and the other monitors provided.

Although he was pretty sure it was being used for something... wrong.

Because The Consultant was wrong.

The Consultant scared him.

He shouldn't have met with the subjects, and, walking out of the bar, John told himself that he'd learned his lesson. From now on he wouldn't—

"Where do you think you're going? Or, more importantly, where are you coming *from*?"

The Consultant stood on the sidewalk, a slight smile playing across his mouth though his eyes remained incongruously hard and steely. John's knees felt weak. It had been stupid for him to think that he could get away with it and that The Consultant would not know. The man knew everything, and if he had not been so distracted, John would have realized that.

He looked down, afraid to meet the man's eyes. "I know. I'm fired."

"Did you think you would get off that easy?"

No. He hadn't. He'd been *hoping*, but deep down he had known that any punishment delivered by The Consultant would not be so benign.

His heart was hammering crazily in his chest, and he considered just taking off, running down the street as fast as he could, like a little boy chased by bullies. Then The Consultant's arm was around his shoulder and the chance was gone. Leading him up the sidewalk, The Consultant acted as though they were old pals, good buddies out for a friendly stroll. But the hand on his shoulder had a grip of iron, and John knew that even if he tried his hardest, he could not get away.

They turned right at the end of the block, moving onto a less crowded street, John's muscles tensing even more as potential witnesses grew fewer in number. Hard hand still on his shoulder, The Consultant steered him into an alley that ran behind the first row of buildings—

Except there was no alley.

He was in the CompWare building, and he was all alone. He could still feel phantom pressure on his shoulder, but The Consultant was gone. He was standing by himself in a dim corridor that looked like the floor on which he'd been working, only...

Only the corridor was too wide. And the doors were wrong. The lights, even if they had all been on, were not where they should be in the ceiling and did not give off the illumination of ordinary fluorescents.

This was a *different* version of CompWare. The way The Consultant wanted it to be? The way The Consultant intended to make it? John wasn't sure, but either could be correct.

Where *was* he, though?

Slowly, cautiously, John moved forward. To his left was an elevator, and he pushed the inset button on the wall next to the closed metal doors, thinking he would go downstairs and get out of here. He was aware even as he pushed the button that it was the wrong shape, a triangle instead of a circle, but that realization did nothing to prepare him for what he saw when the bell dinged and the elevator doors slid open.

For there was no elevator behind the doors. There was nothing. Only an impenetrable blackness that seemed to stretch outward to infinity.

The sight terrified him for reasons he could not say, and he turned away—

—to see that the corridor was no longer empty. At its far side, where distance and dim lighting had conspired to shroud the end of the hallway in gloom, were a group of dark figures milling about. In between, halfway, was a torch implanted in the floor and, next to the torch, a man's head impaled on a stick.

Panicked, John turned the other way and ran. The building was silent—the only noise his own heavy footsteps and heavier breathing—and the number of doors in the walls to either side of him grew increasingly sparse even as their size increased and the wood from which they were made grew ever darker.

The silence was broken by the sound of children singing. An old song he recognized from Sunday school: "He's Got the Whole World in His Hands." Grateful that he was not alone, relieved to encounter something as safe and wholesome as a children's choir, he hurried toward an open lighted doorway at the end of the corridor from which the singing seemed to come.

But the words, he realized as he drew closer, were not what they were supposed to be:

*She took the whole thing, in her mouth*
*She took the whole damn thing, in her mouth*
*She took the whole thing, in her mouth*
*She took the whole cock in her mouth*

He reached the doorway. The singers weren't children. They were mutilated men, castrati who stood naked and exposed on a low wooden stage. He thought he recognized one of them: Steve Portis, a floor manager from his previous job, the place where he'd been working before BFG eliminated his position. "Whenever Ralph closes a door, He opens a window," The Consultant had told him with false bonhomie before offering him the job with BFG, and shortly after he'd jumped ship, his old company had filed for bankruptcy. Were all of these men from firms that BFG had not been able to save?

*She took the whole thing, in her mouth...*

Who was *she*? he wondered, and imagined a woman on her knees, with bloody mouth and lips, biting off the genitals of men lined up before her.

He turned away from the room, but the blackness that had been behind the elevator doors had infiltrated the corridor and was spreading toward him. The sight was overwhelming, and in the face of such implacability, the lighted room seemed warm and welcoming, the castrated men comforting and reassuring. He turned back, stepped inside and closed the door to keep out the blackness.

Movement against the far right wall captured his attention. He hadn't seen anything there before because the door had blocked his view. But there *was* a woman on her knees. And her mouth *was* bloody. And as the singers on the stage went into a new song that sounded like "Onward, Christian Soldiers" but was not, John watched the woman waddle toward him, mouth open and smiling.

He looked over at Steve Portis, singing with the others.

It was better than that empty darkness in the hallway, he thought.

And he braced himself as the woman, bloody mouth still wide open and grinning, unbuckled his belt, unbuttoned and unzipped him, and pulled down his pants.

———

Patoff was waiting for Craig and Phil in the lobby when the two of them walked in to work together the next morning. As always, he was smiling, though his eyes were dead and flat. He straightened his bow tie. "May I have a word with you gentlemen?"

"You may!" Phil said in an exaggeratedly chipper voice.

The consultant frowned, but his expression of disapproval lasted only a second. "It has come to my attention that you went out after work with one of our BFG consultants, specifically John, who was assigned to observe your daily routine, Mr. Allen. Although you may not have been aware of the policy, our consultants are not allowed to fraternize with the subjects of our studies. It's unethical, and in violation of both the employment contract they have with us and the contracts we have with our clients. As a result, John will no longer be observing you. He has been terminated."

*He has been terminated.*

What did *that* mean? Craig glanced over at Phil, who was clearly startled by the news.

"Wait a minute," Phil said. "You can't fire him just because—"

"I can. I'm sorry, Mr. Allen. You should have considered the repercussions of your actions before inviting him to socialize with you. As I said, he has been terminated."

*Terminated.*

There was that word again.

*How* did Patoff know they had met after work, Craig wondered. Had they been followed? Had their conversation somehow been bugged? None of the possible options were reassuring.

"Oh, and Mr. Horne?" The consultant said, turning to him. "Your secretary won't be coming back."

Craig had a sudden sick feeling in the pit of his stomach.

"It seems she found a job…elsewhere. So there's no need to hold her place anymore. Although if you think you can do without a secretary, those funds might be used to spare some of the other employees who are on the chopping block."

*Chopping block.*

He didn't like that imagery, and the moment Patoff left with an overly friendly wave, Craig whipped out his cell and tried to call Lupe. He called her home phone first, and after a single ring, three discordantly toned beeps assaulted his ear, a recorded woman's voice informing him that "The number you have reached is no longer in service." Quickly, he hung up and called Lupe's cell phone. It rang five times before sending him to voice mail.

The expression on Phil's face must have been a mirror of his own since its stunned numbness reflected back at him exactly the way he felt. Saying nothing to each other, they split up, Phil taking the elevator to his floor, Craig walking up the stairs to his own.

Attempts throughout the day to reach Lupe were unsuccessful, and after work he drove over to her house, but the shades were closed, the door locked, and no one answered the bell.

At home, he went directly into the kitchen, where he popped open the tab of a much needed beer.

"What's wrong?" Angie asked, but he didn't want to say, wanted to keep it all as far away from his family as possible, and he shook his head, indicating it was nothing, then put down his empty can and went out to the living room to help Dylan with his homework.

# THIRTY

THE GLASS HAD LONG SINCE BEEN CLEANED UP FROM the floor, the framed painting repaired and replaced in its spot on the wall as if nothing had happened, but Matthews could not help thinking about the way the picture had flown off the wall and crashed to the floor. He could still feel that abominable hum in his ears and the splitting headache it had caused, could see in his mind his pens and pencils floating out of their Lucite holder and hovering in the air. Most of all, he could recall with perfect horrifying clarity how the consultant had stood there with his eyes closed, the cause of it all.

*What was he?*

Matthews was not sure he wanted to know.

What he *did* want was for all of this to be over.

Pausing, he stared at the blank computer screen on his desk. An idea had come to him, and he wondered why it hadn't occurred to him before. It was so simple and so obvious. Instead of trying to fire BFG, he could just tell Patoff that the job was over, thank him for his help, pay him off and say goodbye. The Board might not like it (or what was left of the Board) and his ass would be on the fryer because he was the one who'd started the ball rolling with these consultants to begin with and CompWare would have wasted a lot of money for nothing, but it would be worth it to be rid of BFG. As Craig Horne had pointed out to him at the retreat, there was no need for consultants to begin with. Everything he and the Board wanted could be done in-house with salaried employees. So while the money they'd spent on BFG would be essentially thrown away, there wouldn't be any additional expenditures.

He felt almost happy as he buzzed Diane.

"Yes?" the secretary said.

"Get me Mr. Patoff, please."

"On the phone?"

"No, ask him to come in."

There was a pause, and when she spoke he heard the nervousness in her voice. "Okay, Mr. Matthews."

He clicked off. That nervousness would soon be a thing of the past. Everything would return to normal. He turned on his computer and checked CompWare's stock price. Up fifty cents. Nowhere near what it had been before the merger collapsed, but definitely not enough of a crisis to justify BFG's continued involvement. He leaned back in his chair. He had overreacted initially. There'd been no real reason to call in consultants at all. This was a situation that could have been managed by existing executives and easily weathered by the company. Hell, look at their game sales. Through the roof.

This was all his fault. He had panicked. And now they were where they were.

What he still didn't understand was how the executives of so many other firms, men he knew and trusted, could have given BFG such glowing recommendations. Had it been a concerted attempt to sabotage CompWare? Or could their experiences really have been so different?

No.

He thought of Morgan Brandt at Bell Computers and how he'd been frozen out of his own company.

Something else was at work here.

The door to his office opened and Patoff strode in. Had Diane even had time to call the consultant? Matthews didn't know, but the man was here now and though he hadn't had time to prepare what he was going to say, he stood and faced the consultant. "Mr. Patoff," he began, "I'd like a word with you."

"Of course."

The consultant was smiling in a disquieting manner, but Matthews forced himself to remain cool, calm and act as though he was in charge. "I would like to thank you for your service. BFG has been a tremendous help to us during a very difficult period of adjustment, but I think we have everything we need from you. You've done far more than we asked for or expected, and have helped put CompWare back on a stable and profitable path. We're going to take it from here, but in appreciation for all you've done, we're going to give you a ten percent bonus beyond the amount originally agreed on in your contract."

The consultant was still smiling. "I would beg to differ. Our task is nowhere near complete."

Matthews' heart was pounding. He tried to tread carefully. "As much as I respect your opinion, that decision is not yours to make. It is mine."

The painting on the wall wiggled.

"As I said, we are so grateful—"

There was a tapping sound on the top of the desk.

"—for your assistance at this trying time." He was aware that he was speaking too fast. "You've done a fantastic job, and we would be happy to recommend BFG to—"

"As a matter of fact," Patoff said, as though he was in the middle of a completely separate conversation, "I've been thinking that we may need to *extend* our time at CompWare. The problems here are systemic and not easily remedied. Much more time may be required before we can resolve all of the issues facing your company."

"How long?" Matthews asked, and hated himself for the whiny note of subservience he heard in his voice.

"It's hard to say," Patoff responded as a pen floated up from the desk and suddenly whipped backward, slashing Matthews across the forehead and drawing blood. The consultant chuckled. "I'll let you know."

He strode out of the office, the door slamming shut behind him, and Matthews used a Kimwipe to pat the blood seeping from his forehead. He held the oversized tissue in place and made his way over to his private bathroom. The wound felt worse than it looked, but it was definitely noticeable, and he took some Neosporin out of the drawer, rubbed it on the cut and applied a Band-Aid. A jumble of thoughts were struggling for supremacy in his head: frightened theories about how the consultant could do what he did; paranoid notions about what the man wanted and why; pipe dreams about going to the police and charging him with assault; concern for himself, his company, his workers and his wife.

Fear was his overriding emotion, however, and it superseded everything else, ensuring that he would remain impotent and do nothing.

Matthews opened the bathroom door, walked back out to his office—

And saw someone sitting in his chair.

His heart gave an involuntary start.

At first he thought it was Patoff come back, but though the chair was swiveled away from him, facing a window, he could see that the figure in it was shorter than the consultant and dressed in a dark cowl made of some heavy rough burlap-type material. Both observations made him uneasy. The costume was completely incongruous in these surroundings, and the fact that the person in his chair was almost small enough to be a child was just plain creepy.

He made sure his voice was appropriately angry and authoritative. "Who are you and what are you doing here? This is my office."

The chair spun around, and the thing in it smiled at him, an impossibly huge smile that took up most of the bone-white face, leaving little room for the dark piggy eyes and the snake-slit nose.

Matthews cried out, stumbling backward. The bathroom door handle hit his spine, causing a searing flash of pain, but he was afraid to take his eyes off that abomination in his chair, and without looking behind him, he moved to the right, still backing away, hoping to get back in the bathroom where he could close and lock the door before calling Security.

The chair turned around once again, facing away from him.

Matthews glanced quickly at the office door, thinking he should make a run for it. The door was closed, but it was on the opposite side of the room from his desk, with plenty of open space in between. Unless that little freak could move like lightning, Matthews should have no problem getting out of the office and away.

Unless the door was locked.

Patoff had been the last one in and out of that door, opening and closing it with his...powers, and it wasn't inconceivable that when Matthews reached the door he would find it sealed shut. Unable to open it, he would turn around and see that horror smiling its face-spanning smile as it scuttled across the floor toward him.

The chair moved a little to the right and Matthews managed not to scream as he ran into the bathroom and shut the door. There was a phone between the sink and the toilet—one of those little luxuries he'd never used—and he picked it up, punching in Diane's extension. "Call Security," he ordered her. "There's an intruder in my office."

"Right away." She hung up, and he did too, closing his eyes as he leaned against the wall. He could probably go out there now, because he knew that as soon as one of the guards opened the door, his office would be empty, leaving everyone to think he was crazy.

Sighing, he opened the bathroom door.

It was still in his chair.

He slammed the door and locked it, breathing heavily. Moments later, he heard his name called out by a male voice, heard the office door open—it was unlocked!—and heard Diane's short sharp cry of fear.

It was still there.

He felt braver with others around, and he opened the bathroom door, stepping out. His eyes briefly took in Diane and the two security guards but then focused on his desk chair and the figure sitting there.

The dummy.

For it was not a living being that was in his seat now—although he knew it had been very much alive only moments before—but what appeared to be a ventriloquist's dummy. The white face was similar to the one he'd faced, but the mouth was not smiling and was in proportion to the rest of the face. He recognized the figure as a character from one of CompWare's fantasy games and assumed that, if confronted, Patoff would claim that it was part of a marketing strategy to advertise the program.

"I must have overreacted," Diane said, covering for him.

He shot her a grateful look before addressing the Security team. "Yes, you probably didn't need to come, but I'm glad she called you. Better safe than sorry, right?"

The guards nodded. They were looking at the dummy, not as though they had been called here on a false alarm, but as though the object was indeed dangerous and they were afraid of it.

Matthews kept his voice calm. "Take that out of here, will you? Throw it away or do whatever you want with it."

The guards looked at each other, as though deciding between them which would have to touch the object, and the older, burlier one on the right stepped forward and picked up the figure. He handled it gingerly, and when it spoke, saying something in high-pitched gibberish that had to be part of the game, they all jumped, the guard holding the dummy nearly dropping it. There was nervous laughter all around.

"Thanks, guys," Matthews said, ushering them out of his office.

He followed them out to Diane's desk, and neither of them said anything until the Security men were gone.

Diane let out a heavy breath. "What was *that*?"

He shook his head. "I don't know."

"Did Mr. Patoff bring it in? He stormed right past me, but it didn't look like he was carrying anything in his hands."

"No," Matthews said.

"I can see why you thought it was a person. That thing was huge."

"And creepy."

"And creepy," she agreed.

He almost told her the truth but at the last second decided against it. This was farfetched enough as it was. He didn't want his secretary thinking he was seeing things that weren't there. The two of them had worked together for a long time and had a lot of respect for each other, and he didn't want that to change.

She looked at him. "When is he going to go?" she asked. "Mr. Patoff. When's he going to be done?"

"I don't know," Matthews said.

"Soon, I hope."

"I hope so, too."

# THIRTY ONE

CRAIG WAS IN THE MIDDLE OF HIS USUAL MID-MORN-
ing BFG spam purge when Angie called. Dylan's school was having another early release day, and she wouldn't be able to pick him
up because she'd been called in to the Urgent Care to sub for three
nurses who hadn't come to work. "I can't leave until five or six at
the earliest, so you need to get him."

"Okay," he told her.

The two of them had discussed this before. Neither of them
understood these school schedules that kids had now. When
he was little, they'd had three months off for summer and, with
the exception of Christmas, Easter and a few scattered holidays,
they'd attended class straight through from the Tuesday after Labor Day to the first week in June. But summer was now down to
two months, and the school year was broken up by furlough days,
teacher in-service days, early release days and late start days. It was
a ridiculous patchwork that caused havoc with every working par-

ent he knew, forcing far too many of them to waste vacation time picking up their kids on shortened days like today.

Ordinarily, he would have just taken his lunch an hour late and picked Dylan up then, but Mrs. Adams was still "observing" him, and he was pretty sure BFG would frown on such an informal arrangement. So, just to be on the safe side, he officially informed Scott Cho of his plan.

"I'm going to have to report this," the department head said disapprovingly.

"I'm using my lunch hour."

"You can't just *decide* when your lunch hour is. You have a specific assignment, and that is when you have to eat."

"Then I'm taking personal time," Craig informed him. "The way everyone does. Including you."

"I still have to report it," Scott insisted.

Craig was disgusted. "Do what you have to do."

He ate lunch at his desk—a microwaved burrito and a Dave's Buttermilk Twizzle from the vending machines—and made sure to keep the door open so Mrs. Adams could see that he continued to work through his meal. When the time came to pick up Dylan, he let the programmers know that he would be out for an hour or so, and also informed Scott that he was leaving. He didn't say a thing to Mrs. Adams, and the observer didn't ask, just continued to type into her tablet.

It was odd not to have Lupe here, and without even a temporary secretary, Craig set his phone to go straight into voicemail while he was gone.

He and Dylan returned less than forty minutes later, more quickly than he expected, and found Patoff waiting, conferring with Mrs. Adams at the secretary's station outside his office. The consultant clapped his hands upon seeing them. "Perfect! Your little girl's here for Bring Your Daughter to Work Day!"

Dylan did not take the bait, and Craig was proud of him. He was a little less enthralled when he looked down at his son's face and realized that the boy was scared. The consultant was smiling at Dylan, and Craig stepped between them. "Don't you have work to do?" he asked pointedly. "CompWare didn't hire you to chat with employees and joke around with their children."

"Just so," Patoff said. "In fact, I'm here to invite you to a meeting to discuss inter-office email protocols." He made a show of looking at his watch. "The meeting starts in five. Third floor conference room. No children allowed, of course." He cast a faux sympathetic smile toward Dylan.

Ignoring the consultant, Craig took his son's hand and walked into his office, closing the door behind him. He didn't want to frighten Dylan any more than he was already, but he needed to make sure his son remained safe.

He wished Lupe was here.

"Dylan," he said. "I have to go to a meeting. I don't know how long I'm going to be, but until I come back, I want you to stay here in my office. Don't let anyone in. I'm going to lock the door behind me. Just sit there at my desk. I'll set up some games for you, and you can play until I get back."

Dylan, too serious, nodded. "Okay, Daddy."

"And don't open that door."

"I won't. Daddy?"

"Yes?"

"Can I get a drink out of your refrigerator?"

Smiling, Craig mussed his hair. "Of course. Get whatever you want."

"I can get it myself?"

"Sure."

The fear of only a few seconds before forgotten, Dylan dashed over to the small refrigerator, opened the door, sorted through the contents and pulled out a grape Propel Zero. "All right!"

Craig felt a little better. He set up his computer so that the menu offered several different age-appropriate games, all of which Dylan had played before. "Okay," he said. "I need to go."

"Don't open the door," Dylan said, anticipating his next sentence. "And don't let anyone in. I know." He hopped onto the chair behind the desk and spun it around, before stopping it and facing the keyboard and computer screen.

Craig laughed. "Good boy. You going to be okay here by yourself? It's the first time we ever left you al—"

"I'll be fine, Daddy. I'm just going to play."

"Okay, then. See you soon." He put on a brave front, but the idea of leaving Dylan by himself made him nervous, and he knew he was going to catch hell for it from Angie later. He closed the door, locking it behind him, and glared at Mrs. Adams. He expected her to follow him, the way she usually did, but she remained seated, and he wondered if that was what Patoff had been talking to her about, if they had something *planned*. The thought of it almost made him go back in, get Dylan and bring his son with him to the meeting, even though the consultant had specifically said children were not allowed.

But his office was locked, he had the only key, and if Patoff was going to be conducting the meeting, his office was probably the safest place for the boy.

Shooting a last glance at his closed office door and the seated observer stationed outside it, Craig started down the hallway.

He would have felt a hell of a lot better if Lupe was here.

His dad told him not to leave the office, but he'd been gone a long time and Dylan desperately had to go to the bathroom.

And the door to his dad's bathroom was locked.

He'd been holding it for a while now, but if this went on much longer, he was going to have an accident. *That* hadn't happened since kindergarten, and Dylan, remembering how embarrassing it had been, did *not* want that to happen again. He tried to make his brain forget about it by focusing on the game he was playing. He crossed his legs, pressed down on his lap, even got up and walked around, but he was nearing the end of his rope. He *had* to go.

Dylan walked over to the door, turning the lock, knowing he was disobeying what he'd been told and feeling guilty about it. He was hoping to see that his dad had arrived back at exactly the same time he opened the door. No such luck. There was only Mrs. Adams, the mean woman in the chair outside, and she was staring at him with the blank face of a statue.

His gut reaction was to slam the door, lock it and stay inside the office, but it was an emergency, and he stepped out tentatively. "I have to go to the bathroom," he told Mrs. Adams.

She smiled, and the smile scared him. It reminded him of Mr. Patoff's. She said nothing but typed something on her pad.

"Do you have a key to my dad's bathroom?"

She stared at him silently.

"Do you know where another bathroom is?" he asked.

She didn't answer, and when it became obvious that she wasn't *going* to answer, he walked past her, stopping to look both ways down the corridor. To his left, he saw a man talking to a woman, and he hurried over to them. The woman looked at him as he approached. "Do you know where the bathroom is?" Dylan asked.

"Why don't you show him, Bill?" the woman said.

The man nodded, looking down kindly. "It's over here, sport." He led Dylan down the hall before gesturing to a door with a plaque showing the white stick figure of a man on a blue square. "Are you okay? You want me to go in with you?"

"No, thanks," Dylan said, hurrying in.

He made it just in time.

Afterward, he washed his hands in the sink, having fun with the automatic soap dispenser and the motion-activated faucet. There was music in the bathroom, boring old man music, although Dylan didn't notice it until it shut off. After several seconds of silence, there came an announcement over hidden speakers. "*Dylan!*"

He jumped at the sound of his name.

"*Dylan!*"

Recognizing Mr. Patoff's voice, he quickly moved away from the water and grabbed some paper towels to dry his hands.

"*There's someone who wants to play hide-and-seek with you!*" Mr. Patoff's voice was teasing.

He was hoping the man who'd brought him here was still waiting outside, but when Dylan hurried out of the bathroom, the hallway was dark. There were no lights in the ceiling, just torches on the walls, flickering flames creating pockets of pulsating illumination that made some areas blurrily light and others utterly dark.

That was impossible. This wasn't a fairytale castle. It was a regular building. How could there be torches?

He didn't know, but there were.

There were also no people. He was the only one here, and that was scary.

"*Dyl-an!*" It was Mr. Patoff's voice again, sing-songy, as though he were playing, having fun. "*It's hide-and-seek time! The dwarf's finished counting! He's looking for you!*"

The dwarf?

Dylan looked around frantically, trying to remember which way he'd come. Everything was different, even the directions seemed off, and he wasn't sure how to get back to his dad's office. There was movement down the hall to his right, and he turned his head to see, by the flickering light of the torches, the tall shadow of a very short man.

He ran in the opposite direction, hoping this was the right way. Nothing looked familiar. The ceiling, walls and floor were dark gray, and he didn't see any office doors or secretaries' alcoves, only a series of branching hallways that made him feel as though he were in a maze.

From behind him came a terrible high-pitched giggle.

*The dwarf.*

Dylan ran faster, tears blurring his vision. He managed not to cry out, though he could feel a scream of pure terror building in his chest. He kept running straight, not turning down any of the offshoot passageways because the bathroom had been along the same corridor as his dad's office. He was afraid that he was running in the wrong direction when he saw the widened section of hallway where his dad's office was located. It was farther away from the bathroom than it should have been, but he recognized it, and it looked regular.

Mrs. Adams was sitting in her chair, grinning at him. "Better hide," she said. "He's coming."

Sobbing, Dylan ran through the doorway into his dad's office, where all was as it should have been. He closed and locked the door.

The lights went out.

"*Daddy*!" he screamed, afraid to move.

From beneath the door came the flickering light of a torch.

"*Daddy*!"

The doorknob rattled.

And his dad stepped into the office.

The lights were on again, and he could see through the open doorway that that weird castle-like place with the torches was gone. Everything was back to normal.

Dylan hugged his dad, crying.

"What is it, little buddy? What's wrong?"

"I had to go to the bathroom…and everything was dark…and there were torches…and I got lost…and a dwarf was playing hide-and-go-seek with me…and…" He didn't know how to explain everything so that it made sense, but even though his dad couldn't really understand what had happened, he seemed to *believe* it, and Dylan felt so grateful that it made him cry even harder.

His dad held him tightly. "It's okay," he said. "I'm here. I'm here…"

⟋⟋⟍

Angie could feel the tension in the Urgent Care as she signed in. Outwardly, it was a typical weekday: the waiting room full, overwhelmed nurses hurrying from exam room to exam room, doctors pausing between patients only long enough to log reports. But there was…something *else* this morning, an uncomfortable feeling in the air, a sense that medical treatment was not the only thing happening here.

She initially put it down to the presence of Patoff but was surprised to learn that he wasn't here today. There *was* a consultant from BFG on the premises, but no one had seen him since opening, and from what Hannah, one of the full-time weekday nurses, said, they should all be grateful for that. Angie found it hard to believe that he could be creepier than Patoff, but when she turned around seconds later and came face-to-face with the man, she let out a small involuntary cry and immediately changed her mind. With a shaved head, a gold hoop earring and a scar on his right cheek, he looked more like a criminal than a consultant. The man smiled at her, and she saw that his teeth had been filed down until they were the size of a child's.

"Terence," he said, introducing himself, and his voice was as rough as his appearance. "I'll be observing today and making notes for Mr. Patoff."

Angie nodded an acknowledgment, and he pushed past her into the office.

"Told you," Hannah whispered.

Like the other nurses, Angie attempted to stay out of the consultant's way, which was easy because he popped up only periodically, disappearing throughout the latter half of the morning for long stretches of time. His presence could be felt, however, whether he was there or not, and everyone acted as though they were tiptoeing through a minefield.

Weekday staff was different than the weekend staff, and Angie knew only two of the nurses and one of the doctors. Ordinarily, that would not have been a problem, but by the fifth patient in, she began to have the distinct impression that her presence here was not entirely welcome. She'd been called in because the Urgent Care was understaffed, yet the doctors and nurses with whom she interacted treated her like an unwelcome intruder. Even Hannah, who had seemed so helpful and accommodating at the beginning, was now formal and distant in their brief interactions.

Handed a chart at the front desk, Angie opened the door to the waiting room. "Frank Rocha," she announced. "Frank Rocha?"

A mild-looking middle-aged man stood up from one of the far seats and walked over.

Angie held open the door for him. "How are you doing today?" she asked as she took him to the scale at the end of the hallway

"I'd be better if I wasn't here."

She chuckled, marking down his weight. "We'll try to have you out as soon as possible." Leading him into exam room three and closing the door behind her, she motioned for him to sit down on the exam table as she checked his chart. "Sore throat, huh? Well, let me take your temperature and get your blood pressure, Mr. Rocha, and then we'll get the doctor to come in and see you."

"*I* don't have a sore throat," the man said. "*You're* going to have a sore throat after you suck my cock."

That was a rude and completely inappropriate joke, and she was about to tell him so when she saw that he was unbuckling his pants. He *wasn't* joking.

Angie immediately placed the digital thermometer back in its sheath and walked out of the exam room, her pulse racing. She needed to report this, and she walked up the hall toward admissions, looking for Hannah. The door to exam room one was open, and she glanced in as she passed by, seeing one of the doctors standing in front of the elderly woman whose vitals she had taken only moments before.

"She was rude to me, doctor. She treated me like I…" The patient's voice fell silent as she saw Angie passing by.

*Were they talking about me?* she wondered.

Hannah wasn't at the front counter, so Angie told the nurse there what had happened. Hannah was paged, but before she arrived, Angie saw the man—Frank Rocha—pass by the admissions desk and walk through the waiting room toward the exit. She considered stopping him, but at this point the best strategy was probably just to let him leave. The head nurse arrived seconds later, and Angie explained what had happened.

"Do you want to file a report?" Hannah asked.

Angie shook her head. "No."

"Good. Get back to work."

Her rhythm was off after that. It was as though she were returning to nursing after an extended absence and was not quite up on current procedures. Everything she did took longer than it should have, and she found herself overthinking what usually came naturally.

Her first patient after a short lunch was a grotesquely overweight man with an upturned piggish nose who had come in after experiencing anal bleeding. She checked his signs, then gave him a gown and waited outside while he put it on. It seemed to take him an extraordinarily long time to change, and after nearly ten minutes, she rapped lightly on the door. "Mr. Mouzon? Are you ready for me to come in?"

There was some sort of response, but she couldn't make out what it was, so she opened the door a hair. "Mr. Mouzon?"

She could hear the man crawling around the small exam room, his bare feet and the palms of his hands slapping the floor as he grunted like an animal.

One of the doctors came up behind her, taking the chart from her hands. "Is the patient ready?"

"Yes," she said, hoping that this time she would have a witness.

The doctor opened the door, and Angie followed him in. The patient was sitting on the exam table, and she could hear the rustling of sanitary paper as he shifted in his seat to look innocently over at them. "Hello, doctor," he said. "Nurse."

Angie stared at the man, saw the dust on his hands from the floor. It occurred to her that she was being set up, that these patients were plants, sent to the Urgent Care by BFG to test her.

But why? It made no sense.

Although that didn't mean it wasn't true.

Odd incidents continued to plague her throughout the day, and by late afternoon, her nerves were jittery and pretty well fried. She had never been so stressed out by a day of work, and when a delivery of bandages arrived shortly after three and she was asked to unpack the cartons and restock the supply closet instead of bringing in a pale, frighteningly severe woman from the waiting room, she was grateful for the respite.

Emerging from the supply closet, Angie found the entire staff waiting for her in the hallway. No, not the entire staff. Hannah wasn't there. Neither was anyone else she recognized. The people standing before her were all unfamiliar, and she thought that maybe the consultants had rigged this entire day as a test for her, that she had been called in to face fake patients and fake nurses and fake doctors in order to…

No, that was just being paranoid.

One of the doctors she hadn't yet worked with—*Dr. Benjamin*, according to his nametag—stepped forward. "You've had a great first day," he said, and it sounded as though he were reading from a script. "We'd like to take you out to celebrate."

She put down the empty boxes she'd been planning to take out to the dumpster. "We still have patients to—"

"There are no more patients."

Indeed, she saw now, all of the exam room doors were open, as was the door to the waiting room. There were no patients to be seen. How was that possible? She glanced up at the clock above the front desk. It was six-ten!

That couldn't be.

"You've had a stellar first day," the doctor said.

"This *isn't* my first day," she told him. "I work here every week-end. Before my son was born, I worked full-time at St. Jude's. I've been a nurse for over twelve years." She wasn't sure why she felt the need to justify herself, but she did.

She realized that there was no sign of the consultant, that she hadn't seen him all afternoon. "Where's…Terence?" she asked.

"He's gone."

The doctor was speaking slowly and evenly, as though to calm down an emotionally disturbed patient. The entire staff, she saw, was looking at her as though they were planning to commit her to a mental institution.

"Come with us to celebrate."

She was suddenly filled with a terrible apprehension, a premo-nition that they were *not* going to take her out to celebrate.

"I'm leaving," Angie said, and strode quickly down the hall, through the open doorway into the waiting room, and outside. She didn't bother to sign out, didn't look back, and as soon as she hit the parking lot, she dashed around the rear of the building to where she'd left her car. She expected to be followed from the front, expected to see doctors and nurses streaming out the employees' entrance in the back, but she made it into her car unmolested and after fumbling for several seconds with her key like the protagonist in a bad horror movie, she got the car started and took off. Her heart was hammering crazily in her chest, and she didn't feel safe until she was several miles away in the heart of traffic.

*What the hell was that?*

She had no idea, but there was no way she was going to let it happen again. Maybe she *was* being paranoid, but she was filled with the certainty that if she had not gotten out when she did, something bad would have happened to her.

She thought of Dylan and Craig, and decided that she wasn't going back to the Urgent Care. Ever. This wasn't a career, it was a job. A part-time one at that. She received no benefits, was not dependent on the Urgent Care for anything but extra money, and she knew that, with her experience, if she quit, she could easily get a job somewhere else. Nurses were always in demand.

The decision was made as quickly as that, and the second she knew that she was quitting, Angie felt relieved, lighter, more at ease. She hadn't realized until that moment how stressful her job had become, how much she had begun to dread it, and the freedom was wonderful.

She'd email her notice tomorrow.

Craig and Dylan were waiting for her at home, with Chinese takeout from Pick Up Stix, and she was so happy to see them both, that she gave each of them a huge, hard hug, Dylan first, then Craig.

Craig chuckled. "What's that for?"

"I quit my job."

"What?"

She looked at Dylan. "Go into your room for a few minutes, okay? I need to talk to Daddy."

"But the food's getting cold! We've already been waiting!"

"It'll just be a minute. I'll call you when we're done, okay?"

"Okay," he said reluctantly.

She waited until he was gone and she heard him moving around in his room at the other end of the house before explaining to Craig what had happened. "It was after six o'clock when I came out," she said. "Six o'clock! There are three missing hours there!"

He nodded grimly.

"You need to quit, too," she said.

"I can't," Craig told her.

"You know how when you see a movie with people living in a haunted house, you always say they should get out, that they're stupid if they stay? That's us. Here. Now. Our jobs are the haunted house, and we need to get out."

"You already did. But I can't. Not yet. Not until I have another job lined up. This isn't a movie, it's real life, and we have bills to pay. There's no way we can make the payments on this house with what we'd get from Unemployment. And what about insurance? There are practical considerations."

"Then we sell the house."

He was getting frustrated. "It's not that simple! First of all, neither of us wants to sell the house, do we? And what would we do? Have a garage sale, sell everything and move into some crappy apartment? What if no one wants to buy the place? What if we *can't* sell it? Huh? We need to just calm down…"

"Those consultants are dangerous. And scary. People are dying and disappearing and—"

"I know," he told her.

"Well?"

He sighed. "I can wait them out. I just need to…keep a low profile, stay out of the line of fire until it's over."

"But you're not doing that, are you? You and Phil are on some noble crusade—"

"I will."

"You *have* to. You have a family."

"I know."

She hugged him, spoke into his neck. "I'm worried. I'm scared."

"Me, too."

She pulled back. "We could just make a clean break, have a new start."

He put a hand on her shoulder, looked her in the eye. "We'll talk about it," he said. "We'll figure out our expenses and see what's feasible. I don't think we'll be able to, but…we'll see. If you can get another job, maybe we can… I don't know. We'll figure things out, see what we can do."

"They're dangerous," she said.

He held her gaze. "I know." He took his hand from her shoulder. "But right now we have a starving boy and some Chinese food that's getting cold. Dylan!" he called.

Their son came racing out, grinning.

Angie felt herself smiling back at him.

And knew she'd made the right decision.

⌘

Angie's jostling shoulder woke him from a sound sleep. "Get it," she mumbled, and as Craig drifted up from a nightmare back into the real world, he heard the faux analog ringtone of his cell. He sat up, suddenly wide awake. How was that possible? He always turned his cellphone off before going to bed. Reaching over to the nightstand, he clumsily picked up the phone, his fingers working by sense memory as he pulled it to his ear. "Hello?" he croaked.

"What are you doing? Why aren't you responding?"

He was confused, his mind unable to make sense of the words. "What? Who is this?"

"This is Regus Patoff. I'm calling because one of your programmers sent you an email attachment well over an hour ago, and you still haven't looked at it."

Anger was cutting through the fog. "It's the middle of the night!"

"Are you a part-time employee or a full-time employee? When you are contacted by CompWare in regard to a business matter, you are expected to respond within a reasonable time frame."

"I was asleep! It's—" He looked at the clock. "—two fifteen!"

"That's no excuse."

"I'm—" *Going back to sleep*, he intended to say, but Patoff cut him off,

"—going to read that email and its attachment right now," the consultant finished for him.

The line went dead.

Slowly, Craig placed the phone back on the nightstand. Angie was awake, and she'd obviously heard enough to know what the call had been about. "This is bullshit," she told him. "You're an employee, not a slave. They don't own you. You work your allotted hours, and the rest of the time is your own."

He sighed, rubbing the side of his face. "That doesn't seem to be the way it works anymore."

"Just because they have the *ability* to contact you twenty-four hours a day, doesn't mean they *can*. You need to call the labor relations board or the wage and hour commission or whoever's in charge of this stuff. It can't be legal."

Maybe it was, maybe it wasn't, but Craig knew that official complaints through recognized channels would not mean anything to Regus Patoff. He thought about Dylan's experience at CompWare, Angie at the Urgent Care, and part of him thought that he should just quit right now, collect unemployment and look for another job. But an even stronger part of him refused to give up, vowed to fight, to stay standing and not let himself be run off.

He pushed away the covers, getting out of bed. "I'll be back," he said. "I'm just going to check it out."

"Craig…"

"I'll be right back."

Moving quietly so as not to wake up Dylan, he walked across the hall to his office, turning on his laptop. He could have done it on his phone, but with Patoff being so insistent, he wasn't sure what he'd find, and he didn't want Angie to see—just in case. As it turned out, the email was from Huell Parrish, but while Craig had received it after midnight, the time sent was listed as three-thirty in the afternoon.

The attachment was an official acknowledgment of a pre-approved programming update that the two of them had discussed earlier in the day.

Patoff had called and woken him up only to fuck with him.

Angie was waiting up when he returned, but he assured her that it was nothing and told her to go back to bed. He crawled under the covers, turned onto his side, and held her arm when she snuggled next to him and draped it over his shoulder. He closed his eyes, tried to clear his mind, thought of nothing.

But no matter what he did, he couldn't fall back asleep.

# THIRTY TWO

MATTHEWS SIDLED NEXT TO DIANE'S DESK, PRETEND-ing to sort through a sheaf of papers in his hand. What he had to ask her, he didn't want overheard. Which was why he wasn't using the phone or the intercom, why he was making sure that they were the only two people within earshot before he spoke.

"See if you can find me the home phone number and address of Morgan Brandt," he said in a low conspiratorial tone.

She obviously sensed his anxiety because she answered in a similarly subdued manner. "The Bell CEO?"

"*Former* CEO," he said.

He didn't have to say anymore. She nodded her understanding and told him softly, "I'll write it down and bring it in to you."

"Thanks." Still looking at the papers in his hand as though searching through them for specific information, he walked back into his office.

Several moments later, Diane came in. "Found it," she said, handing him a Post-It note. "It's the most recent I could find. Hopefully, it's up to date."

He smiled at her. "You're a lifesaver."

There was obviously something more she wanted to ask, but she seemed to sense intuitively that he did not want to talk, not here, not now, so she left, closing the door behind her.

He glanced at the address. He recognized the street. It was in Bel Air. A neighborhood close enough to his own that it made Matthews wonder why the two of them had never socialized outside of work. He considered driving over there and showing up at Brandt's house, but there were probably security gates, and it would obviously be better to phone first and give the man some warning.

He definitely didn't want to call from his office, not even using his cell phone, so he told Diane he was going out, and waited until he was on the road, making a hands-free call from his car. The phone rang ten times, twelve times, twenty times, the rings continuing long after voicemail should have answered. Matthews didn't even think about terminating the call, however, and he was rewarded when the phone at the other end was finally picked up. There was no voice, only silence, but he could tell there was someone there, and he proceeded as if this were a routine call and nothing out-of-the-ordinary was happening. "Morgan? It's Austin Matthews."

"Austin?" Brandt's voice sounded weak and tired, *old*, with nothing like the dynamic authority Mathews was used to hearing.

"Yeah!" He put some false cheer in his voice. "I heard you weren't with Bell anymore, and I thought I'd check in with you, see what's doing."

There was a long pause. "It's about BFG, isn't it?" Brandt said. "It's about *him*."

Suddenly given the option to tell the truth, Matthews took it. "Yes," he admitted. "It is."

Silence on the other end.

He pressed on. "I was wondering if we could meet, if I could talk to you in person. I have some questions, and I'm not sure I want to—"

"Talk over the phone?" Brandt said in his old man's voice.

"Exactly."

"I understand."

"I'm on my way home, and I'm in the neighborhood. I thought I could stop by your place."

Another long pause.

"Do you still live off Summit Ridge? I'm over on Oak Pass."

Silence.

"It won't take long. A few minutes. I just want to…talk."

"Are you alone? You're not *with* anyone?"

"I'm alone. In my car. I didn't want to call from work, and I don't want to call from home. I know I'm taking a chance even here, but I have questions."

Brandt was apparently satisfied. "Okay," he acquiesced.

"I'll be there in ten minutes. Do you have a gate or anything…?"

"Use the intercom. I'll buzz you in."

They said goodbye, hung up, and Matthews mused about what must have happened to make Brandt so fearful. He was frightened himself—and paranoid—but even after everything he'd seen, he hadn't sunk to Brandt's level.

*Although it might be only a matter of time*, he thought. Shivering, he turned up the radio to distraction level, concentrating only on the music as he pulled onto the onramp of the freeway.

Brandt's estate looked…sick. It was the only word that fit. The iron fence surrounding the property was a pale gray instead of the shiny black it should have been, and the landscaping had reverted to wildness. Shrubbery was not only overgrown but underwatered, the exotic once-carefully manicured plants now untamed and shapeless, green leaves drying out to brown. The gardeners had obviously been let go, which explained the grounds, but Matthews could think of no reason why the house itself looked so dilapidated. He cruised slowly up the drive, parking at the top of the slope next to a dirty Mercedes whose tires were connected to the cement by spiderwebs.

Ringing the doorbell, he was told via intercom to come in, the door was unlocked. It took his eyes a moment to adjust to the dimness of the interior. No lights were on in the entryway and all of the shades were drawn. A flickering bluish light emanated from an arched doorway to the right, and Matthews walked into the most depressing room he had ever been in. There was no furniture save a recliner in which Brandt sat, and a small table next to it. The only illumination came from a flat screen TV mounted on the wall and turned to CNBC.

"Austin?" Brandt said weakly, peering at him through the gloom.

"Morgan," he greeted his friend. There were a lot of questions and comments he had, but he sensed the emotional fragility of the situation and decided to pretend for the moment that there was nothing unusual going on. What he wanted—what he *needed*—was information about BFG.

Brandt didn't beat around the bush. "*He* put me here."

"Patoff?" It felt weird saying the name aloud.

"I'm the one who brought him on board. I *hired* BFG." Brandt struggled to put down the foot rest and scoot forward in his chair.

"They were supposed to just streamline operations, make us more competitive. Like they did for all those other tech companies." His frail voice was filled with regret. "Their references were stellar."

"I know," Matthews said. "*You* gave them a great recommendation when I called."

"I knew by then," Brandt said quietly. "But I was afraid to tell the truth."

In the light from the television, Brandt's face looked odd, swollen. Matthews had the impression that he was suffering from some type of skin disorder, that the darkness was purposefully meant to hide his appearance.

*He put me here.*

"What *is* the truth?" Matthews asked. "What does he want? I've tried firing him, I've offered to buy out his contract, but he won't go. It's like he has some sort of…I don't know, *mission.*"

"Oh, he does." There was a long pause. "Do you know how many permanent full-time employees BFG has?"

Matthews shook his head. "I have no idea."

"One. Regus Patoff. Owner and operator. He hires other people on an ad hoc basis, but only for specific tasks, things he doesn't want to do himself or doesn't have time for." Brandt's voice had gotten a little stronger. "That's his goal, for BFG and for the companies he consults for—to pare down the number of workers."

"I got that," Matthews admitted.

"I'm not sure you do. Before he—" Brandt spread his arms to indicate his surroundings. "—put me out to pasture, he *talked* to me." There followed a short coughing fit, and Matthews had the distinct impression that Brandt was suggesting that the physical state he was in was a direct result of that talk.

"His goal," Brandt continued, "is to create what he calls the 'perfect company,' an organization so lean and mean, so expertly put together, that it can be run by a single person, with no other workers. He hasn't reached that goal yet, but he'll never stop trying. He did it with Bell; he's doing it with CompWare." Brandt coughed again. "That's *all* he cares about. He's worked for corporations that he's driven into the ground, others that have tripled their stock prices and profits. Doesn't matter to him. All beside the point. The objective is manipulating departments and people, input and output, purchases and products, to get to the point where the company can run on its own, with just that one employee. And he takes the long view. He might hire *more* people. Or expand departments. But those are just temporary detours on a road that goes in one direction."

"He doesn't like anyone to interfere with his plans," Matthews noted.

"Oh no, he does not." Brandt let out a sickly chuckle.

"A woman quit, a woman he wanted to get rid of, but she exited on her own timetable, not his, and he went crazy." Matthews was not sure how much of this he wanted to tell, but he decided to press on. "He stormed into my office, and suddenly things started flying off the walls and floating off my desk."

"He has power," Brandt said grimly. "I don't know what it is or where it came from—I don't know what *he* is or where *he* came from—but he's not human. That's one thing I'm sure of."

"So what do I do?"

"If I knew, I wouldn't be here." Brandt coughed. "Bell was my company. And now it's not. If you're not careful, you'll find yourself in the same situation." He sighed. "Or maybe even if you are careful. It depends on Patoff's plan. And only he knows what that is."

"There's no way to stop him?"

"Not that I know of."

"Have you tried talking to anyone else?"

"No. In fact, I probably shouldn't be talking to you right now. But I know you. And…" He trailed off for a second. "…it's partly my fault you're in this mess. I gave BFG a good reference when you asked. I *knew* what was going on. I was just…afraid." Struggling, Brandt sat up further, leaned to the left, reached over to the wall and flipped on the room's light.

Matthews gasped. He'd known there was something strange about Brandt's face, but he was still shocked to see the extent of deterioration. For the man barely looked human. His forehead and cheeks were swollen so badly that his eyes could barely be seen; they were little more than slits peering out from between folds of flesh. Beneath his wide, flattened-out nose, his mouth had been twisted into a grotesque grimace exposing overlapping teeth, the lips bulging.

*Acromegaly*, Matthews thought, although Rondo Hatton had never looked anywhere near this bad.

It was not only the distorted shape of Brandt's face that was so disturbing, however. The skin itself seemed to have been transformed. It was scaly and lizardlike around the nose and cheeks, furry in an almost feline way on the chin.

"Jesus," Matthews breathed. "What happened?"

"The consultant happened." Brandt flipped off the light, fading back into the shadows, and Matthews welcomed the darkness. "You don't want this to happen to you. So my advice? Lay low, keep quiet, stay out of his way."

"But it's my company. And I intend to keep it."

"That decision's not up to you anymore. It's up to *him*."

# THIRTY THREE

EVERY DAY NOW STARTED WITH A MEETING.

Before the arrival of the consultants, Craig would not have thought that *anyone* enjoyed meetings more than Austin Matthews. But the CEO was a piker compared to Patoff. The consultant lived and breathed meetings, seemed to draw strength and energy from them, and he used the get-togethers to unveil major policy changes as well as to announce inconsequential minutiae. Everything seemed to be equally worthy of meeting status in his eyes, and while BFG's initial assemblies had been with workers of a specific class or particular job definition, they now seemed thrown together completely haphazardly with employees of little or no commonality.

The one constant was that Craig seemed to be invited to all of them.

At least the observers were gone. Cameras were still in place, had continued to multiply in fact, but somehow they were easier to ignore and felt less restrictive than an honest-to-God person sitting there taking notes and monitoring everyone's every movement. On the flipside, no one trusted anyone anymore. Other employees were now suspect, and in crowds larger than two or three close friends, people were wary, not certain where the others' loyalties lay, worried that one of them might be a conduit to BFG. Craig had no idea if this was intentional or not, but it was like living with the Hitler Youth, and tension was ratcheted up so much that most employees preferred to spend their time at the office alone, working—which may have been the point.

But no one could be alone at a meeting.

Today's was an anomaly. It consisted entirely of supervisory personnel and had an actual purpose: an announcement that CompWare would soon have its own cafeteria.

Patoff stood in front of a professional draftsman's detailed conception of a light, airy restaurant. "While it is too early to draw conclusions on many of CompWare's business practices and operations, our study shows that, on average, employees return from lunch a minute to three minutes late. Which means that, in the course of a year, the company loses approximately a day's work from each employee. With three hundred and sixty-eight employees at present, that's a loss of three hundred and sixty-eight days, more than a year. Having a cafeteria onsite will put a stop to that, in fact will quite possibly result in employees taking shorter than allotted lunches. It will also allow CompWare to control the portion size and nutritional content of its employees' lunches, which, in the long term, will lead to a healthier, happier and more efficient workforce. A win-win!"

"When is this cafeteria supposed to be completed?" Sid Sukee asked.

"Oh, it's done," Patoff said, and Craig was surprised to hear that. Everyone seemed surprised. There'd been no indication that any sort of construction or remodeling had been going on in the building.

"The official grand opening is Monday, but we're going to give you a sneak preview today. Are you ready to take the tour?"

People started standing up, gathering their things.

"I *said*—" The consultant was glaring at them. "Are you *ready* to take the *tour*?"

"Yes," they responded. "Sure…Of course…Yes…"

"That's better." He smiled. "Come with me."

They followed Patoff out of the meeting room to the elevators. Craig was surprised to see that, even after everything that had happened, the consultant still retained some of his original charm for some of the women. He conspicuously flirted with two of them and spoke of personal matters with three others, matters he'd obviously discussed with them several times before and that he gave a good impression of caring about. The remaining supervisory staff, however, was wary, suspicious, and kept a wide berth. Not wanting to be stuck in an elevator with the consultant, Craig, Phil, Elaine and a stream of others, under the pretense that it would be faster, took the stairs down to the second floor, where Patoff had said the cafeteria was located.

If any of them had thought they'd have a difficult time finding the eating area without Patoff to lead them there, that fear was put instantly to rest the second they opened the stairwell door. For the entire second floor seemed to have been converted into a massive high-end restaurant. Gone were the nearly identical corridors and rooms found on every floor above the first. In their place was a gigantic open space filled with light and plants and access to windowed views. Craig could not remember exactly what department had been stationed on the second floor, but it had obviously been moved elsewhere. His eyes took in the blond wood tables, spacious booths, potted ficus trees and ferns. Behind the long counter where food would be served, the kitchen was wide open, visible to all behind a glass wall.

"It seats four hundred," Patoff was saying, as he came out of the first elevator with the initial group of supervisors. "Even without staggered lunch hours, there's room in here for every employee as well as visiting clients." He nodded at those who had taken the stairs and at the employees still emerging from the stairwell. "We have a few more stragglers," he said, nodding toward the elevators. "Once everyone's here, we'll get started."

How had they all missed this? Craig wondered. It had taken a tremendous effort to redesign an entire floor, yet no one had seen any workers, trucks or materials. No one had heard any noise or smelled any dust or paint. Whoever had previously occupied the second floor had not said a word, so there'd been no news from the rumor mill.

How was that possible?

"What are the prices going to be like?" Phil asked.

"The cafeteria will provide a free lunch to all employees," the consultant said, and there was a murmur of surprised approval. "Of course, a minimal pre-tax cafeteria fee will be deducted from each employee's paycheck in order to subsidize these meals. This has already been approved by the Board, and not only will it provide everyone with a lunch, but it will act as an incentive to eat healthy. Since you'll be paying the fee anyway, why bring a leftover greaseburger from home when you can have a nutritious meal here for free?"

"If we're paying a fee, it's not free," Phil pointed out.

Patoff beamed. "Exactly!"

Both elevators opened and the last batch of attendees emerged awestruck onto the second floor.

"Shall we?" the consultant announced, and led them through the cafeteria, showing off the seating arrangements, allowing them into the clean spacious kitchen, going over proposed menus with the head chef, who joined them for the tour. Patoff, as usual, was acting as though he was in charge of the company, and Craig couldn't help wondering where Matthews was and why he wasn't the one showing them around.

*Ghost in the machine.*

It was all very impressive, Craig had to admit, and even he was looking forward to eating here. It would be very convenient—despite the fact that they would be under constant surveillance.

"One other thing before we adjourn," Patoff said as he gathered everyone before the elevators. "It has been decided that it would be more advantageous for the ongoing benefit of the company if all supervisory personnel were married. Studies have shown that a stable homelife leads to less volatility at work and a more logical, less rash decision making process on the part of the employee. Put simply, the presence of a spouse allows an individual to focus more of his or her attention on work rather than dating and socializing.

"Now, obviously, we can't *force* anyone to get married. That would be illegal. But let me assure you that, as we contemplate culling the ranks, that will be one of many factors that could be considered."

Jonah Kosinski, a manager from the Finance department, spoke up timidly. "Does that mean I need to start looking for a wife?"

Patoff laughed. "Of course not. But if you are involved with someone and in a serious relationship, perhaps you should consider taking the plunge. If you are not currently involved with anyone, then we will be offering a dating service that can match you with compatible individuals within the CompWare family, or in one of the many other companies and corporations for which BFG consults. Strictly voluntary, of course, but, as I said, a stable homelife can lead to a stable work life—and stable employment." He clapped an overly familiar hand on Kosinski's back. "Just something to keep in mind."

The consultant smiled and waved as the elevator door opened behind him. "Thank you all for coming."

The milling group began to break apart, some going into the elevator with Patoff, others taking the second elevator, still others taking the stairs. Craig found Phil. "There go my divorce plans," his friend said, smiling.

"Pretty nice," Craig said, nodding toward the cafeteria.

"We're paying for it." He looked around. "How much do you think that 'fee' is going to be? My guess is a lot more than a few cents per paycheck."

They waited by the elevators. "I noticed Matthews wasn't here," Craig said, keeping his voice low.

"I actually saw him this morning," Phil said. "I got here early, thought I'd get a little something done before the meeting, and we rode up a few floors on the same elevator. Looked a little worse for wear, maybe, but not the Howard Hughes figure I was expecting."

"At least he's not…"

"Dead?" Phil finished for him. "I thought exactly the same thing."

One of the elevators opened, and they got inside. "Still no word of Lupe?" Phil said.

Craig shook his head, glancing up at the small surveillance camera in the corner.

Phil nodded his understanding, and they rode the rest of the way to their respective floors in silence.

———— ✖ ————

Craig had set up a meeting of his own after lunch. The final OfficeManager updates were near completion, and he wanted Huell and his team of programmers to give him a live demo so he could make sure everything was copacetic before giving Scott Cho access. Unfortunately, five minutes before the scheduled demo, he got a call from Regus Patoff requesting that he attend a meeting on the fourth floor. It was in a room with which he wasn't familiar, and when he arrived, he saw ten people he didn't know seated on folding chairs, watching Patoff set up an outdated TV and VCR combo on a tall metal cart. Craig sat down on a chair in the back row. Moments later, two other people sat next to him.

"Thank Ralph you could make it," the consultant said to them, smiling. He adjusted his bow tie. "I have to step out for a moment, but I want you to watch a little video for me. Afterward, we will discuss it." He turned on the television, turned on the VCR, walked past the seated employees, turned off the room lights and closed the door as he left. There was a minute of silence and a blue screen until the video came on.

An old Bill Nye video about dinosaurs.

What was the point of *this*? Craig looked around. It was hard to see in the dark, but by the light of the screen he was able to tell that the men and women around him were focused intently on the goofy lab-coated science teacher talking about the Age of Reptiles. None of them seemed fazed by the video, none of them were making fun of it or questioning it. They were just watching.

He had never seen any of the people here before, and he wondered if they were BFG employees instead of CompWare workers, if he was being set up somehow.

It was a twofer. After the half-hour dinosaur program, they had to sit through still another Bill Nye show, this one about the solar system. Patoff returned at the end of the video, flipping the lights back on and passing out to everyone a pencil and thick sheaf of papers affixed to a clipboard. "Please fill this out," he said. "And make your answers as detailed as possible."

Craig didn't know what to expect. He felt as though he was back in junior high, and when he saw that the top page was a worksheet about dinosaurs, he assumed that BFG was testing their memorization skills or comprehension. But the second page had nothing to do with Bill Nye or the videos. It was a detailed questionnaire about dreams, asking for descriptions of recent nightmares, even referencing specific people, places and objects to see if they appeared in any of the dreams. He flipped through the other pages: one contained questions about sexual fantasies, one about preferred modes of death, one about torture.

A soft hand touched his shoulder, and his head jerked up to see the smiling face of Regus Patoff. As always, the consultant's eyes were hard and dead. "Answer every question to the best of your ability."

"And if we don't?" Craig challenged him.

"Then you will be terminated."

*Terminated.*

As always, there seemed to be a deeper meaning to the word, a menacing hint that it denoted more than being fired. Craig wanted to get up and walk away, wanted to storm out dramatically and make a scene, but he lacked the nerve. He settled for writing short fake answers to those questions that required them and randomly checking the boxes of those that were true or false. He was the first to hand in his clipboard, and he left without saying a word.

It still felt strange coming back to an empty desk where Lupe was supposed to be. He had contacted her family—her parents and sister—and confirmed that she was missing, and he'd contributed what he could to the police report, telling the investigating officer that she had had suspicions about one of the consultants at work. Not wanting to be sued,

*or worse*

he hadn't mentioned Patoff specifically, but his hope was that a police investigation would turn up evidence against the consultant. He knew the likelihood was that Lupe was…gone. But there was still a chance that it could be something less severe than he feared, and he chose to believe that that would be the ultimate outcome.

He was just about to call Huell and set up another OfficeManager demo when Scott Cho came in, furious. "And where were you for the past hour?" Scott demanded.

"I was at a meeting."

"*I* called a meeting!" the department head bellowed. "For everyone! All divisions!"

"I'm sorry."

"*Sorry*? I couldn't even reach you!"

Craig looked at him calmly. "Maybe I should tell Mr. Patoff that you think your meeting is more important than his."

Scott blanched. "I didn't mean *that*," he said, some of the belligerence gone from his voice.

"Then leave me alone and let me do my job," Craig told him.

"I am *still* your boss. And I will not tolerate any insubordination!"

Craig sighed. "I'm not being insubordinate. I'm trying to meet with the programmers about the OfficeManager updates, which I will then show to you. But if you want to waste time with this…"

Scott strode off, scowling. "Just do your damn job," he said.

At home that night, Craig was helping Dylan with his math homework (had *he* studied fractions this young? He didn't think so) when his son suddenly stopped writing and looked up at him. "Daddy?"

"Yes?"

"I think you should get a new job."

Frowning, Craig looked over his head at Angie, but she raised her eyebrows and shook her head, indicating that she knew nothing about this.

"Why do you say that?" he asked.

"Mr. Patoff."

"Mr. Patoff?"

"What if he makes *you* play hide-and-go-seek? Dylan paused. "With that…dwarf." Craig heard the tremor in his son's voice.

He put a hand on his son's shoulder. "Don't worry. I'll be fine."

"Mommy quit. Why don't you quit, too? We can move to New York."

Craig smiled. "New York? Where did that come from?"

"I don't know. But we can move there."

"But all your friends are here. And our home is here." He turned Dylan so the two of them were facing one another. "Mr. Patoff *is* a scary man," he admitted. "No one likes him. And you and Mommy need to stay away from him. I'm going to stay away from him, too. But he won't be here forever. Once he finishes his job at my work, he's going to move on to someplace else, and then he'll be gone forever. We just need to wait a little while longer."

The look of doubt on Dylan's face was so comical that it was all Craig could do not to laugh.

"I'll be fine," he promised.

Dylan looked seriously into Craig's eyes. "I worry about you, Daddy. I don't want anything to happen to you."

It was the purest expression of love Craig had ever experienced, and he gave his son a warm hug. "Don't worry, little buddy. Nothing'll happen to me." Over the boy's shoulder, he caught Angie's eye. She didn't look convinced, and he smiled at her, trying to appear reassuring. He was worried himself, but he couldn't let them know that, and he prayed that what he'd told Dylan was true: that the consultant would soon be gone.

# THIRTY FOUR

ANTHONY GENERRA FINISHED WASHING HIS HANDS and looked at himself in the men's room mirror, frowning. His tie was slightly askew, tilting left, though it had been perfectly in position when he'd left home. He adjusted it, made sure the tie clip held it in place and backed away from the mirror to check from afar.

He looked good.

*Look good, feel good, do good, be good*, he thought. It was a motto learned from his father as a child, and one he'd always tried to live by.

He was an overachiever because of his father, although that result was probably unintentional. A Republican congressman, his dad had so consistently stressed his pro-life bona fides that Anthony's brother Basino, knowingly born with Down syndrome, had been treated as a saint—at Anthony's expense. It was Basino who was a blessing to the family, who had taught all of them so much about compassion, who was so loving and life-affirming that he made every day a joy. Anthony, by contrast, was just ordinary, not an inspiration, and despite all of his academic accomplishments over the years, he'd always kind of gotten lost in the shuffle. Even here at CompWare, he'd ended up being just another face in the crowd, one of the many talented, top-of-their-class professionals hired by the company.

Until The Consultant chose him to be one of His helpers.

*This* was what he'd been made for. He was perfect for this job, and The Consultant had *known* he was perfect, but Anthony still didn't understand *how* the man had known. Frustrated by his lack of career progress despite his significant personal achievements, Anthony had, for the last few years, begun...acting out. But he'd kept all of that secret, had never mentioned any of his extracurricular activities to anyone.

It had started simply enough with responses to wrong numbers or telemarketers who called him at home at inconvenient times. He would tell a caller that Anthony Generra was dead, that he had killed him. Or he would pretend to be an Anthony Generra who was deaf or mentally disabled.

Then there'd been the boy at McDonald's.

That was when he'd upped his game. He'd been reading the newspaper and having a cup of coffee one morning before going to work. A family of tourists, probably from Texas, judging by the dad's Longhorns t-shirt, walked into the fast food restaurant. Or, in the case of the kids, *ran* into the restaurant like whirling dervishes. They were big, loud and obnoxious, all of them, and despite the numerous empty tables in the dining room, the mom and her brats plopped themselves down in a booth right next to his while the dad stood in line to order at the counter.

"Wash up," the mom ordered, and all three kids ran to the bathrooms. The mom carried her little baby with her into the woman's room, where her little girl had already dashed in, and the two boys ran into the men's room. One of them came out almost immediately, hands still dripping wet, and yelled triumphantly as he sped back to the table.

"Little boy," Anthony said, motioning him over. He'd remembered an old Emo Phillips joke about hitting a crying baby in a movie theater, and that had given him an idea.

The kid shot a look at his dad, still in line, and apparently deciding it was safe, ran up.

"What's your name?" Anthony asked.

"Devon."

"Devon what?"

"Devon Sanderson."

Anthony spoke softly. "Now listen to me, Devon Sanderson. And hear me good. If you don't quiet down and stop making so much noise, I'm going to kill you."

The boy's eyes widened, and he made as if to run.

"Don't you move a muscle, Devon. You just stand there and listen. Because if you don't stop yelling in this restaurant, I will not only kill *you*, but your brother and your sister and your parents and even that little baby. I just escaped from prison, and I don't want any attention drawn to me. So if you keep up this racket and the cops come, I will slit your throat from ear to ear. Do you understand?"

The boy nodded fearfully.

"Now," and Anthony delivered the coup de grâce, "get the fuck back to your table and don't you dare look in my direction again."

He didn't. The boy was silent throughout his breakfast, his eyes steadfastly avoiding Anthony's direction. Twice, his mother asked him if something was wrong, and both times Devon shook his head. Anthony waited until the family was about to leave, then he got up himself, walked over to the exit and held the door open for them, nodding knowingly at Devon as he passed.

He watched the family drive off in their minivan, smiling to himself.

It had given him a feeling of power to deceive the boy so thoroughly, a warm sensation that was utterly satisfying.

A week later, at another fast food restaurant where a fishbowl sat on the counter so that customers could drop in their business cards for a chance to win a free lunch, he had reached in and pulled out several cards at random. One was for a man who ran a tow truck service, and he called that number from a pay phone at an AM/PM mini-mart during his lunch hour, putting on his most threatening voice. "Do you know who this is?" he asked when the man answered the phone and identified himself.

The tow truck operator possessed the defensive belligerence of the easily annoyed. "Should I?"

"Last week, you towed a vehicle with over two million dollars of my product hidden in its frame. That vehicle has now been impounded by the police."

He said nothing else, let the silence drag out.

The tow truck operator made a tentative noise indicating that he was about to speak, then cleared his throat and tried to speak again. His reply, when it came, was timid and deferential. "I...I wasn't aware of any of this."

"I am extremely displeased," Anthony told him, leaving an unspoken threat hang between them.

"I...What...I..." The man was fumbling around, unsure what was being asked of him. Did Anthony want him to pay back the two million? Was he supposed to get the car back?

372

"I want my product," Anthony said. "Tomorrow. Bring it to dock thirty-two at nine p.m."

He had no idea if there even *was* a dock thirty-two or, if there was, at which port it would be located.

The tow truck man was equally confused. "Is that in San Pedro or—"

"Nine p.m."

"Wait! Wait! I need to know the type of vehicle and—"

Anthony hung up the phone. He waited a few moments to see if the man would try to *69 the call, but the phone did not ring. He imagined the tow truck driver frantically searching through his records of last week's work, trying to find a vehicle that had been impounded by the police. Grinning to himself, he walked into the AM/PM and got himself a 32-ounce Coke before heading back to work.

That had been just the beginning.

There had been many more incidents, and the amazing thing was that somehow The Consultant had known about all of them.

It was the reason, in fact, that Anthony had been recruited.

When The Consultant requested an interview, Anthony saw that the man was in possession of a complete file on him. But instead of consulting its contents and asking pertinent questions, He had smiled at Anthony and pushed the manila folder across the table for him to read. *Everything* was in there. The boy at McDonalds. All of the phone calls. Transcripts of conversations. Where this information had been obtained, He wouldn't say, but it was obvious that Anthony had been under surveillance for quite some time. And it was just as obvious that The Consultant admired what Anthony had done. Smiling, He said, "That priest shakedown was particularly funny. I laughed my ass off when you did that."

Anthony wasn't sure how to respond.

"Thank you," he said.

The Consultant took back the folder, leaned forward. "Let's get down to business, shall we? One of my associates recently disappeared, and I'm looking for someone to take his place. John was an observer, but the observer phase of our study ends today, and now I need someone with a slightly different skill set, someone to take a more, shall we say, *active* role on my behalf.

"I feel that your talents have been wasted here at CompWare. Up to this point, you've been merely one of many cogs in this giant machine. What I'm offering you is the opportunity to be an engine at BFG."

"What does that mean?"

The Consultant had smiled broadly. "It means," He said, "that I will be hiring you to do what you do." He tapped the folder meaningfully.

He'd been given carte blanche.

There was no official job description, no assigned duties. The Consultant provided him with information: names, phone numbers, email addresses, home addresses, spouses' names, children's names, parents' names, friends' names, pets' names. But he was never told what he could or could not do with that information. He was left entirely to his own devices, encouraged to do whatever he wanted to whomever he wanted in any way that he wanted.

After the first week, The Consultant had called a meeting with him and had told Anthony, "*Now* you are living up to your full potential."

And he was.

Anthony finished straightening his tie, smiled at his appearance in the mirror. *Look good, feel good, do good, be good.*

Well, maybe not *do* good.

He chuckled, checked his watch.

It was time to get to work.

⸺◦∞◦⸺

Hector from the mailroom dropped off the usual boxful of correspondence on Diane's desk outside Mr. Matthews' office, and, as always, it sat untouched for several minutes while she finished what she was doing. Finally turning her attention to the mail, she separated the envelopes into three categories: junk, business and personal. As usual, about half of the mail was addressed to Comp-Ware, the other half to Mr. Matthews personally.

But this time, there was also an envelope addressed to her.

That was odd.

Opening it, Diane saw that it was some sort of bill. A credit card bill, apparently, though why it had been sent here rather than to her apartment was a mystery. She glanced down at the charges.

$186,000.

Her heart almost stopped. That couldn't be right. This was a mistake. It had to be. Or a sick joke. That was more than her entire remaining mortgage. She looked over the bill. Current charges: $63.49. That was about right. But the outstanding balance carried over from last month was $185,936.51.

That was impossible.

The phone rang, and she answered it, still staring at her bill in disbelief. "Mr. Matthews' office."

"Hello," the man on the other end of the line said. "May I speak to Diane Bellows?"

"This is she. How may I be of assistance?"

"I'm calling in regard to your Visa balance…"

"I was just about to call you," Diane told him. "There must be some mistake."

"I'm afraid not. You currently have a balance due of one hundred and eighty-six thousand dollars—"

"That's not possible."

"This bill is past due, and if the charges are not paid in full by the end of business hours on Friday, I'm afraid our only recourse is to start proceedings against you."

"I didn't do it!" she said, panicked. "It's fraud or identity theft. Someone got my number and used it to—"

"You are responsible for the charges, ma'am. The card agreement is in your name, and if you read the terms on the back of your statement, you'll find that your responsibilities in regard to this matter are spelled out very clearly."

Diane took a deep breath. "I need to talk to your supervisor. Someone who can make decisions. There's been a huge mistake here. I need to go over all of my individual purchases with someone and—"

An idea suddenly occurred to her. "Wait a minute. A hundred and eighty six thousand dollars?" My credit limit is three thousand. How did charges over that amount even get on there?"

"We would like to know that as well."

"It's impossible. There's some sort of computer glitch on your end."

"We require immediate payment of one hundred and eighty-six thousand dollars."

"Even if I *did* owe that much, which I don't, I still wouldn't have to pay the whole thing at once. I'd have to make a minimum monthly payment. That's how you guys make your money, charging fees and interest."

"That time is past, Ms. Bellows. You have been delinquent in your payment for over a year—"

"What?" Diane was shouting. "This is crazy! You're making a huge mistake! There's *obviously* been a computer error. I've *never* been late with a payment in my life!"

"Our records say otherwise, Ms. Bellows."

Diane hung up the phone, her hands shaking. She didn't know what to do. She probably needed a lawyer or something. Maybe she could talk to Mr. Matthews, see if he could get Legal to help her—

The phone rang again.

It was an outside line, and she knew it could be someone important, someone for Mr. Matthews, someone who had business with CompWare, but she had the feeling that the call was for her, that it was the man from the credit card company.

Instead of answering, she pressed the mute button and watched on her console as the little red light blinked in silence. It finally stopped, but only for a moment. It started blinking again as another call came in. Diane knew that she couldn't ignore the problem forever, that she needed to deal with the credit card company—

*by Friday*

—but she needed to talk to someone higher up. This was obviously a gigantic mistake, and all she had to do was tell the truth and get things sorted out.

She stared at the blinking light, thought of picking up the phone, but realized that she was afraid to talk to that man again. Something about his unflappable persistence frightened her.

Maybe she *would* talk to Mr. Matthews about her problem. He'd been acting a little odd lately, but she'd been his secretary for over a decade and she knew he'd want to help her.

She pressed the mute button a second time, and the phone started ringing again. She picked it up. "Mr. Matthews' office."

"Ms. Bellows?" said the credit card man.

She hung up the phone, trembling.

———◦◦◦◦———

Huell was not happy. No, it was more than that. He was pissed. He squirmed around in his seat, trying and failing to get comfortable.

Someone had switched chairs on him. The one behind his desk looked exactly the same as his old one, even had the same crack on the left armrest, but this one was smaller. The seat was so narrow that he had to wedge himself in, forcing his body into a painful angle that was bound to play hell with his bad back. Was this a joke? Was someone trying to tell him he was too fat? He knew he had gained a few pounds lately, but that was his own damn business, and, besides, it was completely understandable. He'd been under a lot of stress lately, what with taking over the OfficeManager project after Tyler's death, and when he was stressed, he ate.

But that didn't give anyone the right to prank him about it.

This was illegal. It was harassment, that's what it was, and, damn it, he was going to find out who was responsible. Twisting his hips sideways and pushing himself up using the armrests, he managed to struggle out of the chair.

Rusty walked by, probably on one of his three thousand trips to the bathroom. Huell called the technical writer over. "What was that manual update you gave me?"

Rusty looked confused. "When? Recently?"

"This morning."

"I haven't sent out an update for weeks. I've been working on testing and redocumenting OfficeManager."

"Yeah? What's this, then?" Huell picked up a paper-clipped set of papers from his desk. "You think that's funny?" The technical writer looked confused. Exasperated, Huell turned to the second page, tapping his index finger on the headline *Suicide Instructions*.

"I…I didn't write that!"

"Then who did? You're the only tech writer we have."

"I don't know, but it wasn't me."

"Bullshit!"

"Huell…"

"You call me Mr. Parrish from now on."

Rusty walked away, shaking his head. "Whatever."

Rusty might be weaselly enough to write idiotic things like "Suicide Instructions," but there was no way he had the where-withal to pull off a subtle trick like switching an office chair. That required someone with more focus and determination.

Huell started walking around the programmers' workstations, trying to figure out if one of them was behind it. He had his doubts, but—

He stumbled, nearly falling, tripping over a leg that had been thrust into the aisle. Recovering, he turned to see Lorene glance briefly in his direction. "Whoops," she said. "Sorry."

Huell confronted her. "You tripped me on purpose!"

Lorene looked up innocently. "Whatever do you mean?"

"That's it," he said. "I'm reporting you to Craig. I don't want you on this project anymore."

"Wittle baby's going to cwy to Daddy," she responded in a whiny girlish voice. Her tone hardened and she fixed him with a laser stare. "Like the pussy that he is."

"Fuck you, bitch."

"No, fuck you. I know you're the one who erased the new updates I created."

He glared at her. "Yeah? Well, you were trying to get me fired by making my computer access porno sites."

"That doesn't even make any sense."

"Doesn't it?"

"Asshole."

"Stupid dyke." He started to walk away, then turned on her. "And, besides, you changed my chair, didn't you?"

"Changed your chair?" She rolled her eyes crazily and pretended to be manipulating steel balls in her left hand. "It was the strawberries," she said in a terrible Humphrey Bogart voice.

"It doesn't matter. You're off this project."

"Go to hell."

Huell was about to storm off when Rusty reappeared. "Have you ever thought," the technical writer said, "that they're *trying* to get us to fight with each other, that they're pushing our buttons, *knowing* how we'll react?"

"Shut the fuck up," Huell told him.

"Yeah, douche," Lorene said.

"The consultants—"

"Both of you just stay the fuck out of my way," Huell said. He made a quick tour around the cubicles then ended up back at his own workstation. It could have been any one of them, he decided.

He needed to stay on his toes.

Nobody could be trusted anymore.

———— ❧ ————

Julio Ortiz was the first of the day shift custodians to arrive, and he was early enough that he was able to chat for a few moments with Maria, one of the cleaning women on the night shift and one hell of a fox. He was pretty sure she was illegal—why else would someone who looked like her have such a crappy job?—but that was a point in her favor. Maybe she was looking for a green card marriage. In his fantasies, the two of them got hitched so she could become a citizen and, while they were pretending to love each other, they *actually* fell in love. He knew that was more a movie plot than something that would happen in real life, but even if things didn't pan out that way, he was still willing to be in a sham marriage with her.

As long as she helped pretend the marriage was real by performing her wifely duties.

None of this was anything he ever brought up with her, though. Their conversations, short as they were, were always about work and things in general, and all of that romantic stuff stayed where it belonged, in his head.

After Maria left, he was still early, so before clocking in, he walked over to the row of boxes next to the tool room and checked his mail. Traffic and the snooze button on his alarm had led to him to be a minute or two late almost every day this week—which was why he'd made a special effort to get here early today—and he hadn't checked his mailbox. He was surprised to find that it was nearly full.

That was strange.

The only mail he usually got in his box was the union newsletter once every two months.

Julio pulled the stack of papers out, sorting through them. They were all nearly identical: single lines of type in the center of a blank sheet.

"*I know where your parents live,*" said one.

"*I know where your sister lives,*" said another.

"*I know where you live.*"

"*I know the name of your dog.*"

"*I know the code for your alarm.*"

Beneath the stack of papers was an envelope, and in the envelope were photographs. His parents eating breakfast in their kitchen. His sister naked in the bathtub of her apartment. Himself, asleep in his bed. His dog, Armando, eating a raw hot dog from the hand of the man taking the picture.

"What the hell…?" Julio said aloud.

He looked into the boxes next to his to see if similar messages had been given to anyone else on the custodial staff but saw nothing. How long had these been piling up? he wondered. Had someone put them all in at once or had they been inserted one each day?

And who had done it?

And how could anyone have possibly taken those pictures?

Julio considered himself a pretty brave man. He had never run away from a fight, and even as a child, he had stepped in to help kids who were being bullied, no matter if the bullies were gang members. But he had never come up against something like this before, and he was more afraid than he had ever been in his life.

He tried to tell himself that it was a joke, but he knew it was no joke. He tried to tell himself it was one of the other custodians, but he knew it wasn't one of the other custodians. He didn't know *who* it was, but whoever—

*whatever*

—was behind this, knew everything about him and could do the impossible.

*Diablo*, his mama would say, and though he thought he'd grown out of that sort of childish superstition, he crossed himself.

He jumped a mile when Akeem walked into the basement a second later, and he forced himself to smile when his friend laughed and said, "A little nervous today, aren't you?"

"Yeah," he said. "I guess I am."

# THIRTY FIVE

"CHECK THIS OUT," PHIL SAID, PUSHING A PAPER across Craig's desk.

"What is it? A memo?"

"Read it."

---

TO:     Human Resources Senior Supervisory
        Personnel
RE:     New Hires

It has been determined that preferential consideration should be given to potential hires who are not married or are, at the very least, childless. In today's competitive work environment, the presence of children in an employee's life invariably results in a loss of productivity on the part of that employee. Until a companywide standard can be established and corresponding rules implemented, it is strongly suggested that any new part-time, half-time, full-time or contract workers engaged by CompWare through the Human Resources department not be married and not have children.

*Regus Patoff*

Regus Patoff
BFG Associates
For Austin Matthews, CompWare CEO

---

"How did you get this?" Craig asked.

"I have my sources."

"But weren't they just saying that we *had* to be married?"

"Supervisory personnel," Phil reminded him. "These rules are for *non*-supervisory employees."

"That seems random."

"They're just fucking with us. Probably trying to pressure certain people into quitting or retiring or something." He pushed another paper across the desk. "I have something else," he added. "I'm not sure how real it is, and there's no way to authenticate it, but check it out."

Craig picked up what turned out to be a printed list of names, dozens of them, in small print, arranged alphabetically in five columns. "What's this?"

"Supposedly, it's the people who are going to be fired, laid off, let go, downsized, rightsized, whatever you want to call it."

"The list?"

"The list."

Craig scanned the paper. "Lorene's on here," he noticed.

"There's a lot of names you'll recognize. From your division *and* mine. I haven't done any calculations, but it definitely seems like some enemies of the state have been targeted and are going to lose more people than others. Your group, of course, is relatively safe because, well, you're necessary. You create content."

"Huell, too?" Craig said, still reading. "Lorene and Huell are two of my top programmers."

"What I want to know is: how are they going to do this? Is it going to be gradual or done in one fell swoop?"

They were both silent for a moment, each of them able to read between the lines.

*Was anyone going to die?*

How had it come to this? Craig wondered. How had it gotten to the point where the two of them were wondering if any of their co-workers were going to suffer some mysterious accident or illness, yet neither of them were even contemplating going to the police or quitting their jobs or...*doing* something? For all of their defiance, they were little more than passive bystanders, watching what was going on and hoping that none of it touched them personally.

Capitulation was a slippery slope, and they were already sliding down to the bottom.

It was all for Dylan and Angie, Craig told himself. That's why he was doing this. And it was. He didn't want to rock the boat too hard and have Patoff come after his family. But it was also easier to stay out of it, and he realized that for some time he had been putting up with much more than he should have due to an optimistic hope that BFG's presence here was temporary, that the consultants would be gone soon.

That's all it was, though. A hope.

He saw no indication that BFG would be leaving anytime in the immediate future.

"It's almost lunch," Phil said. "Want to try the cafeteria? It opens today. And we're paying for it."

"Sure," Craig said, handing back the list.

"No, that one's for you. I made a copy."

"And what exactly am I supposed to do with it?" Craig said.

Phil frowned. "What do you mean?"

He sighed. "Nothing. Let's eat."

They were in a full elevator on their way to the cafeteria, when a Zen-like bell tone issued from the overhead speakers, followed immediately by an announcement made by a woman's voice so mellifluous it sounded like that of a professional broadcaster rather than another CompWare staffer: "Attention all employees. The lunch hour has begun. Outside doors to the building will be locked until lunch is over. Those who have brought their own lunches may eat at their desks, in the break rooms or in the cafeteria. Those who have not brought their own lunches should proceed immediately to the cafeteria, where healthy food options are available for all."

"Huh," Phil said, eyebrow raised.

"We're going to be locked in? I hadn't heard about that," Craig admitted.

No one on the elevator had, and though everyone was cautious and circumspect in their reactions, the consensus seemed to be that this was not a desirable development. It was unsettling to know that they were prisoners here at work, and while Craig understood the more-efficiency-greater-productivity rationale, it didn't make it sit any better with him.

The doors opened on the cafeteria floor and though he had seen it before, Craig was once again blown away by the sight of the open, airy restaurant. As much as he hated to admit it, the consultants and whoever they'd hired to build this place had done a wonderful job. It was truly impressive, even more so when filled with people. The well-designed space easily absorbed all comers and managed not to seem crowded no matter how many arrived.

"So do you want a salad, a salad or a salad?" Phil asked as they approached the wide serving area. "Jesus. They really are taking this healthy food thing seriously, aren't they?"

Craig settled on a taco salad with iced tea, then took his food over to a small table next to a bushy planter, Phil following after. There were tables of all configurations—single seaters, doubles, those that sat four, six, eight, all the way up to a long banquet table that looked as though it could easily seat twenty—and each managed to impart a sense of privacy for their diners, though Craig knew that was an illusion.

The food was good and, even though a "fee" was being taken out of their paychecks, not having to pay directly for lunch made it seem free. The entire experience was atypically pleasant, the second floor an uncharacteristically calming oasis amidst the ratcheting tension that had enveloped the rest of the building. The atmosphere was so enjoyable and relaxed that Craig almost felt as though he could speak freely here to his friend, that the two of them could have a private conversation. But that would be a mistake. He glanced up to see cameras on the ceiling, between the large powerful lights and the inset speakers from which issued agreeable music. The planter next to them, he realized, could easily hide a directional microphone.

Phil, he could tell, was thinking the same thing, and the two of them kept their conversation free of content as they ate, commenting on the cafeteria, on the food, not mentioning a word about what was really on their minds.

The rest of the day was spent discussing a relaunch of OfficeManager with Sales and Promotions, and dealing with the astounding number of intra-division feuds that seemed to have metastasized within the past few days. At the top were Huell and Lorene, who were practically at each other's throats, and as he tried separately to calm each of them down, he hinted, without spelling out anything specific, that perhaps they should try to be on their best behavior because their jobs might not be that secure. He didn't want to say anything to them about the list, but he did want to give them a heads up. They were too angry, however, too focused on each other to pick up on anything so subtle as a hint. Ditto for three of the other programmers who came to him with complaints.

It was after five by the time he finally got out of his office and made his way downstairs. He assumed that Phil had already left but was surprised to meet his friend in the lobby. "How was your afternoon?" he asked.

"Sucked. Yours?"

"That's as good a description as any."

Walking out the front doors with a group of other employees, they passed a man in a suit standing in front of the building and wearing a brown paper bag over his head. There were two eyeholes in the bag and a wide smile drawn in felt pen. Craig turned toward Phil. "That's—" *weird*, he was going to say.

And then the gunfire started.

—◦◦◦—

Matthews had not gone in to work today. He'd had a dream—a *nightmare*—about Regus Patoff standing in the middle of his office while furniture flew around him in a circle, and it had freaked him out enough that he'd decided to stay home. After his alarm rang, he shut it off and went back to sleep, not waking up until it was nearly ten. Rachel was off with one of her friends, her clubs or her charities, and he made himself a simple brunch, then decided to give himself a treat, spend the day on the links and not think about work at all.

The scheme was actually somewhat successful. He called up his brother-in-law, and the two of them spent the afternoon at a course so exclusive that they shot 18 holes without encountering another party. Afterward, they had a few drinks at the clubhouse before going their separate ways.

It was a relaxing afternoon, and even if he wasn't able to put CompWare entirely out of his mind, he did enjoy himself, and was glad he'd made the decision not to go in today.

Rachel was back when he got home, but she was in the spa, and he wasn't in the mood to join her. Instead, he went into the media room, made himself a martini at the bar and turned on the television. A reality show was on, a gaggle of Botoxed blondes screaming at each other in what looked like an expensive restaurant. Did Rachel really watch this shit? Matthews switched over to the local news, where an overendowed woman was delivering the coming week's weather forecast. Immediately afterward, a swooshing sound issued from the speakers as a "Breaking News" graphic appeared on the screen. One of the petty crime stories that local stations used to boost ratings, no doubt, and Matthews wouldn't have paid any attention to it were it not for the word "CompWare" that jumped out at him.

Immediately, he grabbed the remote and cranked up the volume.

A lone gunman had entered the CompWare building approximately fifteen minutes ago, at the end of the business day, and had opened fire on employees in the lobby before he was taken down by an armed security guard. Although unconfirmed, reports were that six people were dead and three seriously injured.

How had he not instantly been informed of this? Matthews whipped out his cell phone. Was it off? No. Had someone called Rachel at home? No, because she would have told him.

"What the hell…?" he fumed.

Security footage from the building had already been supplied to the TV station, and it showed a man with a brown paper grocery sack over his head entering the lobby, pulling a handgun from the back of his belt and opening fire at random. It was difficult to tell from the angle of the camera, but it appeared as though a big smile had been drawn on the paper bag.

"The suspect has been identified as Mitchell Lockhart," the newscaster said.

Matthews sucked in his breath, shocked. *Lockhart*!

"Mitchell Lockhart is apparently a member of CompWare's board of directors. It is unknown at this time whether—"

Matthews' cell phone rang. He answered it immediately.

"Are you watching the news?" It was Regus Patoff.

"I shouldn't *have* to watch the news. Why wasn't I informed of this right away?" he demanded.

"I'm informing you now."

"After it's already on every station…" He used the remote to flip through channels.

"Well," Patoff said smoothly, "if you had *deigned* to come in to-day, you would have been on top of this. But as you chose to shirk your duty, BFG had to make an executive decision in your stead."

"I'm not just in the chain of command," Matthews bellowed, "I'm at the fucking *top* of it!"

"That's the type of fire and dedication we were hoping to see from you," the consultant told him. "Maybe you should have been the first call. My apologies. Anyway, since I have you here on the phone, I thought we could discuss the situation. From a PR standpoint, of course, this is a disaster. At the same time, everyone knows there are lunatics out there these days, and this could garner CompWare some sympathy in the public eye. Luckily, the victims all seem to be individuals we were planning to lay off anyway, so there should be little or no impact on our revised general plan, or, indeed, on company productivity—which is why they were on our list to begin with…"

He zoned out, the consultant's voice a vague drone in his ear. Six dead and three injured. And by Lockhart! It was inconceivable.

No. It wasn't.

It wasn't, and that's what upset him the most. This was par for the course these days, and the fact that all of the victims had been on BFG's hit list couldn't be a coincidence.

*Ultimate plan.*

The anger he'd felt was softening into fear.

On TV, paramedics were wheeling out stretchers.

He was suddenly aware, by the singsong cadence over the phone, that Patoff had noticed he wasn't paying attention. "Austin, what are you thinking of? Austin, where is your mind? Austin, what are you thinking of? Austin, where is your mind? Austin…"

"I'm right here."

Patoff chuckled. "But you weren't, were you?"

"Yes, I was," he lied.

"That's part of your problem. You see on your TV there how things are getting out of hand? You need to be a little more hands-on in your management style. *If* you want to maintain control of your company, that is. And *if* you want BFG to recommend your continued tenure. I suggest we have another management retreat so we can hash things out, re-establish boundaries with your staff."

Matthews said nothing. He thought of Morgan Brandt.

"The big question is," Patoff continued, "why you're on the phone with me, watching this unfold on television, when you should be *there*. It is supposed to be your company, isn't it?"

Matthews terminated the call, hearing the consultant's mocking laughter in the seconds before his phone switched off. The ass-hole was right. He *should* be there.

He quickly headed toward the bedroom to put on an appropriate suit.

He'd come up with some platitudes for the cameras on the way.

———— ∘∞∘ ————

"Thank God!" Angie was out of the house and on him before Craig had even closed the car door. She hugged him so tightly it hurt. "I was afraid…" She couldn't even finish the sentence.

"Are they showing it on the news?" he asked.

"Every channel."

"You didn't let Dylan—"

"No, he's in his bedroom, playing with his computer."

"I was outside when it happened," he told her. He'd said all this over the phone, but he repeated it anyway. "Phil and I just missed the guy. He was walking in while we were walking out. I thought it was weird that he had a bag over his head, and when I turned around to look..." His voice trailed off. "How many victims are they saying?"

"Six dead and three injured."

"That's what they said on the radio, too."

"It's stayed pretty stable for a while, so hopefully that's it."

"No names yet?"

She shook her head.

Craig held his hand out in front of him. He was shaking more now than when he'd actually been on the scene. A delayed reaction, he assumed.

"Do you think—?" she began.

He knew what she was asking without hearing the rest of the question. "I don't know," he told her.

But he did.

He did.

# THIRTY SIX

HE MISSED LUPE.

Craig had known he would—she'd been his secretary since he'd started working at CompWare—but the loss was on a much deeper level than expected. He could complain to Phil about work when he saw him, could talk to Angie when he got home, but he and Lupe had been in the same place at the same time, and it was that minute-by-minute dissection and discussion of events as they occurred that had forged such a strong bond between them. He had no one he could immediately bounce ideas off of anymore, and he missed that solid sounding board far more than he thought he would.

He remained in contact with Lupe's parents, her brother, and even her sleazy ex-boyfriend, but no one had heard from her. She was officially a missing person, but Craig had not told the police his real suspicions. He hoped they would discover evidence of foul play on their own, evidence that would lead to BFG, but, coming from him, it would sound too crazy and unbelievable.

And it might put him in jeopardy.

He saw Patoff in the middle of the day, glad-handing his way through the floor, greeting everyone by name. The vibe was different than it would have been a few weeks ago, however, and those he greeted responded nervously, carefully, while others scurried out of his way, not wanting to be stopped and singled out. Craig was out of his office, looking through Lupe's desk for a stapler, and the consultant smiled at him as he passed by. "Are *you* still here?" he asked, and laughed.

Later, at lunch, sitting alone at what had become their usual table in the cafeteria while Phil went back for seconds, Craig was startled when Patoff sat down across from him. He hadn't seen the consultant walk up—the man had just appeared—and his sudden presence caused Craig to jump. The consultant laughed. "Nervous, are we?"

Craig faced him head on. "No. Why should I be?"

Patoff smiled. "I don't know. Why should you be?"

There was something going on here below the surface, a reason for this conversation that Craig didn't understand. The consultant never did anything without a purpose.

He took a bite of his salad, intending to ignore the man, but looking into that soulless face, he put down his fork and said, "Why?"

"Why what?" the consultant asked innocently.

"Why me? Why were you at my son's school and my wife's work?"

An expression of sympathy, perfectly composed and utterly fake, crossed the man's features. "I was sorry to hear that she quit. She was a very competent and dedicated employee."

"Why?" Craig pressed.

Patoff shrugged. "I was hired to consult. I do the jobs I am hired to do."

"And it's a complete coincidence that you were hired by my son's school and my wife's medical group?"

"Apparently."

He gestured around the crowded cafeteria. "What about other people here? Are you at their spouse's workplaces, too?"

"BFG is very busy," Patoff conceded with a smile.

Phil returned with a veggie panini and a refilled coffee. He looked from the consultant to Craig, then sat down in a chair at the side of the small table.

"Phil!" Patoff said. "How goes it?"

"All right." Phil casually picked up his sandwich as though this was the most ordinary thing in the world. "To what do we owe the honor?"

"We're just having a little informal lunchtime chat. Life's not all work and no play. Sometimes it's nice to relax and…socialize."

"Didn't you specifically tell us that we were *not* to socialize with BFG consultants? Right after you fired my watcher, John?" Phil took a bite of his sandwich, chewing slowly as he waited for a response.

"Exactly so, Phil. But that phase of the study is over."

"And now we're all friends?"

"I would very much like to be," Patoff said, smiling. Again, the proper form of the smile was in place, all of the elements warm and friendly, but the sentiments beneath were ice cold and hard.

Neither Craig nor Phil said a word, and the three of them sat for several minutes in uncomfortable silence, Phil eating his sandwich, Craig finishing off his salad, Patoff watching them and smiling.

"Well," the consultant said finally, putting both hands on the table to push away his chair, "I guess I'd better get back to work." He stood, started to turn away, then paused and looked at Craig. "Speaking of work, I suspect that your lovely wife will have a somewhat difficult time securing employment—since the fucking bitch is a lying quitter." Patoff's normally placid face was contorted, the rage in his voice audible. For the second time, Craig thought he saw something he wasn't supposed to see, the skull beneath the skin, a glimpse of something not at all human and very, very old.

The consultant turned, striding through the cafeteria toward the exit, and Craig realized that the revelation had been entirely inadvertent. Patoff never did anything unintentionally, but his anger had been exposed, and he'd left quickly so as not to reveal more of himself. Angie quitting had obviously left him furious. Her spur-of-the-moment decision had been completely unpredictable, something for which he had not prepared, and she had upset his plans enough that he had made a special trip out here today to confront Craig.

Sort of.

Because nothing had really happened. A rude remark, a vaguely threatening manner…these were nothing. The consultant could have done much worse. But why hadn't he? Why, Craig wondered, was he still alive? And why hadn't Angie been attacked? Others had fallen victim to accidents, had committed suicide, had died in unnatural, implausible ways. Why had the two of them been spared?

For the first time, he thought that there might be rules to this game, lines that the consultant couldn't cross. He had no idea what they were or why they should inhibit the consultant, but he was beginning to suspect that the man wasn't free to do whatever he wanted.

Perhaps the consultant could kill only those people his study had deemed unnecessary to the viability of the company, the people the company no longer needed or wanted, the ones who had been slated for—

*termination*

—and anyone else was off limits. As crazy as it might be, perhaps Patoff could only harm people on the list. The idea seemed plausible to him, and Craig couldn't wait to tell his theory to Phil.

But that was going to have to wait. The cafeteria was a hotbed of surveillance, as was the entire building, and there was no way for the two of them to get off campus without arousing suspicion until after the workday ended at five.

Phil watched Patoff leave. "That was fun," he said drily.

Craig laughed. It was a tension-relieving laugh, Phil's comment only funny because of the circumstances, like a lame joke told in church, but it lightened Craig's mood, as did his newfound hunch about the limits of Patoff's authority.

He returned to the sixth floor feeling oddly good, and the afternoon was very productive. He even managed to get ahead of schedule and assemble a skeleton team for a new as-yet-unspecified first-person shooter game. Unfortunately, Phil was nowhere to be found after work, though his car remained in the parking lot, and when Craig tried his cell, the call went directly to voicemail. He considered hanging out, either waiting by his friend's car or sitting in his own car and listening to the radio until Phil showed up, but there were security cameras trained on the parking lot, too, and he thought it would probably be more prudent to leave.

At home, Angie was putting together what looked like a pretty spectacular Mexican meal, while Dylan had finished his homework and was playing on his computer. Craig told Angie about his lunch and his suspicion that the consultant was not free to act entirely as he wanted. "He was really pissed that you'd quit, you could tell that he was thrown by it, and while he wanted to punish me, he couldn't. I'm…protected, I think. You are, too, because you no longer work at the Urgent Care. My guess is that you're the only reason he took that job to begin with, and now that you're gone, he's stuck with it."

"What about Dylan?" Angie said worriedly. "It doesn't seem like he's safe."

"Isn't he? No one's touched him. He's been scared, yes. We've *all* been scared. But no physical harm has come to him. Or any of us. And, believe me, that's not true for everyone."

"I know," Angie said softly, and he knew she was thinking of Pam.

He held her shoulders, looked into her eyes. "I think we're going to get through this."

Angie breathed deeply. "I hope so."

Craig got himself a can of Coke out of the refrigerator and went out to find Dylan. He tried giving his son a big hug, but the boy squirmed out of his grip. "Leave me alone, Daddy!" he objected, eyes on his computer screen. "I'm about to be eaten!"

Smiling, Craig sat down on the bed and watched Dylan play until Angie called them for dinner.

Halfway through the meal, the phone rang. Angie didn't want him to answer, but he had to, just in case. "Hello?"

It was Phil.

Craig was relieved it wasn't Patoff, but he knew his friend wouldn't be calling just to chat, so it was with a sense of trepidation that he said. "What's up?"

Phil spoke carefully, obviously worried that someone was listening in to their conversation. "I was wondering if you could come over for a few minutes. We just got a new flat screen for the bedroom, and I need some help installing it."

That was a lie. Phil *had* talked about buying a new TV, but he was far handier than Craig, and even if he had just purchased a new flat screen, he'd need no help hooking it up. As for mounting the set on the wall, his wife Josie, a fitness freak, was twice as strong as Craig and would be of much more assistance.

No, Phil wanted to talk.

About CompWare.

"Sure," Craig said. "I'll be over after we finish dinner."

"Thanks."

"See you soon."

"Okay. Bye."

The cadence of their conversation was stilted, and anyone listening in would know that something was off, but if they were being monitored by a computer using word-recognition software, nothing would appear amiss, and the call would not be red-flagged.

"You need to read to me!" Dylan said when he put the phone down.

"I will," Craig told him. "And don't worry. I won't leave until you're in bed asleep."

"Will you check on me when you come back?"

"I always do."

Dylan happily dug into his enchiladas. Angie shot Craig a worried look, and he tried to smile reassuringly, but he could tell that she was still concerned. "I don't know what it is," he told her honestly.

"Do you have to go over there?"

"I'll make it quick."

An hour later, Dylan was in bed, and Craig was off. Phil lived a good fifteen minutes away, but there was no traffic on the freeway, and on the street he hit a string of green lights, so he made it there in ten. His friend had obviously been watching for him because Craig had not even knocked on the door or rang the bell when Phil called out, "Come on in! It's open!"

In the center of the living room floor was an unopened box containing a 60-inch plasma TV. Phil sat on the rug before the box, an X-Acto knife in his hand. He had not started cutting open the box, and he glanced up as Craig entered.

The house was still and silent. "Where's Josie?" Craig asked.

"I sent her out. Told her to have a girl's night with her friends. She's a civilian. I don't want her involved."

Craig would have talked everything over with Angie even if BFG hadn't consulted for the Urgent Care, but he understood that Phil and Josie had a different sort of relationship. He nodded.

Phil took a deep breath. "Something's been bugging me. For a long time now."

Craig smiled. "Only one thing?"

"His name. It never seemed right to me, never seemed real. It was familiar, somehow, but I couldn't seem to place it."

"It sounds like it might have a Russian origin."

"It's not his name," Phil said quietly.

"Regus or Patoff?"

"Both."

"How do you—"

Phil pointed, his finger touching cardboard.

Craig looked closely at the side of the box, at the small words beneath the name of the product that indicated it was registered with the U.S. Patent Office: Reg. U.S. Pat. Off.

*Regus Patoff*

He suddenly felt cold.

Who the hell was this guy?

*What* was this guy? That's what he really wanted to know, and he looked over at Phil, who was nodding grimly. "I saw that when I was getting ready to open the box."

Craig said aloud what, until this point, he had only thought. "I don't think he's human."

It should have sounded absurd, laughable dialogue from a bad horror movie. But in this place, at this time, with everything that had happened, it sounded eminently reasonable and frighteningly true.

The house around them suddenly seemed too dark, a perception that Phil obviously shared because he stood and started turning on lights, moving from the living room to the dining room to the kitchen to the hall. "How hasn't this come up before?" Phil wondered aloud as he returned. "BFG's consulted for companies far bigger than CompWare. *Name* corporations. Are you telling me that none of them did their due diligence and conducted a thorough background check? This is something that should have come up." He shook his head, exhaled deeply. "Jesus."

"What do we do?" Craig asked.

"I don't know. If this were anyone else, we could call the attorney general's office, but…" He left the thought unfinished.

Craig plunged in. "I think we might be safe," he said. "I mean me and you. Personally." He explained his lunchtime revelation, how he suspected that the consultant had to work within boundaries and couldn't just do whatever he wanted, how he thought the man could physically harm only those employees the company no longer needed and how anyone else was off limits. "It fits," he said. "It makes sense. And it explains why we're still here."

Phil looked thoughtful, and Craig realized what a relief it was to have his friend thinking again. That stunned and passive Phil who'd been sitting blankly in front of his TV box had frightened him, and he felt better knowing that it was once again the two of them against Patoff.

"Maybe we can use this," Phil said. "Not to stop him, of course. We can't do that. But maybe we can mitigate the damage."

"How?"

"I don't know yet. But we have the list. And we know something he doesn't want us to know, doesn't *know* we know." He pointed to the words on the box again. "That's valuable, that's ammunition."

*Reg. U.S. Pat. Off.*

"We're still in the game."

# THIRTY SEVEN

THE ANNOUNCEMENT WAS MADE OVER SPEAKERS throughout the building at four forty-nine, eleven minutes before quitting time: "*All senior staff please report immediately to the third floor conference room for a mandatory meeting. This includes all vice presidents, department heads, division heads, managers and supervisors. Repeat: a mandatory meeting for all senior staff in the third floor conference room.*"

Craig's phone buzzed, indicating an incoming text message, and when he looked at it, he saw: "Senior Staff Meeting. Third Floor Conference Room. 4:50."

The same message popped up simultaneously on his computer.

It was bad enough that he was coming in on weekends, that his lunch hour had been co-opted and he had to spend the entire day within this building. Now he had to stay late for some pointless meeting?

The third floor conference room wasn't even big enough for that many people. How were they all going to fit into such a small space?

He shut off his computer, gathered up his stuff and made his way to the elevator, where he encountered Scott Cho, waiting in front of the closed metal doors. "Thought you were going to look over the new updates," Craig said. "I sent them to you two days ago, and you haven't even opened the email."

"I have a lot more on my plate than just proofreading the fixes to your screw-ups," the department head snapped. "I'll get to it."

Elaine arrived, and Craig talked to her until the doors opened, ignoring Scott. Sid Sukee ran up at the last second, sliding in just before the doors closed. "Anyone know what this is about?" he asked.

"No," Craig said.

"Well, it better be fast. I have things to do. Got a hot date with one of your programmers." He grinned.

"Huell?"

Sid frowned. "Asshole."

The doors opened, and the four of them made their way toward the conference room, which, Craig noticed immediately upon arriving, was now entirely devoid of furniture. All chairs, tables and equipment had been removed. One of the walls had been pulled aside to reveal a floor-to-ceiling window, which was a surprise to him because he hadn't known that the walls *could* move or that the room *had* a window.

The place was crowded already, and within the next few minutes, it filled completely. Craig faced the front of the room where Matthews stood next to Patoff, the CEO appearing drained and drawn, as though he'd recently survived a life-threatening illness. From their body language, the relationship between the two did not look like one of employer and contractor, or even equals. Rather, Craig realized with a sinking feeling in the pit of his stomach, it appeared to be one of master and servant, with Patoff definitely the former and Matthews the latter.

Without so much as glancing at the CEO, the consultant raised his hands for silence, though the room was already quiet and very few people were talking. "We've called you here," he announced, "because you will be going on a management retreat this evening."

"Another retreat?" Branford Weiss from Legal said. "In the mountains?"

Patoff gestured outside. "No. Here. On the campus."

Craig peered out the window and saw that, on the grounds below, high temporary walls had been put up. From this angle and altitude, it looked like a rat's maze. When had this happened? He'd been busy all day, hadn't gone outside or had an occasion to look out the window, but when he'd arrived this morning, the campus had been clear; there'd been no sign of any of this.

People were glancing at each other in confusion, no one really sure what to make of Patoff's announcement.

"How long is this going to take?" Elaine asked.

"It's a two-day retreat."

"And we're going to be, what, camping down there?"

"Yes, you are."

"Starting tonight?"

"Starting now."

"Then we need to be able to go home and get our things. Our clothes, our toothbrushes…"

"You won't need any of that."

Parvesh Patel took out his cell phone. "I'll call my wife, have her…" He frowned. "There's no signal."

"That is intentional. The whole point of the retreat is for you to get your priorities straight, to make you aware of how much more important your job is than your home life."

"And I thought you wanted us to be married," Phil said sarcastically from the far corner.

The consultant turned on him. "Indeed, we do, Mr. Allen. But there is a time and a place for everything, and if you are spending sixteen hours out of every twenty-four at home, and only eight hours at work, you need to make sure that those eight hours count for something, that you are not distracted, that home and family time doesn't bleed into your work hours. You need to remain focused, which is why all phone signals have been blocked."

Now there was a lot of conversation. Supervisors were appealing to their managers, who were complaining to department and division heads. The consultant remained above the chaos, smiling serenely, seeming to take particular joy in watching Matthews flounder about, ineffectually trying to justify enforced attendance of the suddenly announced retreat to all of the employees who were pleading with him to postpone it.

"I need to let my wife know where I am," Craig said, addressing Patoff directly. "She'll be worried. So will my son."

The consultant shook his head. "No, they won't." He smiled. "I'll stop by and tell them where you are."

Panic welled within him. "No ," he said, "you don't need to."

Patoff's smile widened. "I *want* to."

Objections and complaints had reached a cacophonous pitch, and once again the consultant raised his hands for quiet. "Enough!" he shouted. The room lapsed into silence. "This is the beginning of your two-day retreat. It has already started, and in a moment we are going to start with the team-building exercises. But first, let us bow our heads and give thanks to Ralph." He clasped his hands together in prayer, and though no one followed suit, the room remained respectfully hushed, and the consultant's voice rang out clearly. "Dear Ralph, bless our efforts and make them successful. Amen."

There were actually a few scattered "amens" in return, though Craig suspected that those saying the words had shot off some kind of prayer to the Judeo-Christian God (probably to get them out of this) rather than asking "Ralph" to let them have a successful retreat.

Patoff clapped his hands. "Speed Conversation!" he announced. "Places!"

It had been awhile, and getting into position was awkward, but eventually they stood once again in two concentric circles that covered most of the conference room. This time, Matthews did not participate but remained next to the consultant.

Craig was staring into Scott Cho's hostile face as the whistle blew.

"I fucked your wife's dirty asshole," Scott said. "And she *came*."

Craig laughed. The taunt was so stupid and childish that he could have no other response, and he was still laughing when the whistle sounded again and the outer group moved on.

"When I French kissed your wife, her mouth tasted like penis," said Neal Jamison from Finance. "She must suck a *lot* of cocks."

So this was going to be a theme. The only question Craig had was whether the consultant had fed the game's participants their lines or whether he had manipulated them into thinking the ideas were their own. He looked over at Patoff, but the man was gazing off in another direction, a blank expression on his face.

The taunts continued, and he was tempted to respond in kind. But, he reasoned, that was probably what the consultant wanted, so he made an extra effort to stay above the fray. The truth was that the relentless insults began to wear him down after a while, but soon it was his turn to speak his mind as the conversational circles turned, and he used the opportunity to repeat, "We don't work for BFG. We work for CompWare."

The speed conversation ended.

"Downstairs and outside!" the consultant ordered.

Within ten minutes, they were all gathered on the sidewalk border between the parking lot and the campus on the side of the building. A funneling entrance that started wide and narrowed as it went in to the grounds had a big white *Welcome* painted on the left wall and *CompWare Management Team!* painted on the right.

A man emerged from within, blinking against the weak late afternoon sun like a person who'd been held in captive darkness for weeks.

It was Dash Robards.

The guide looked far different than he had at the camp, as though he had aged decades in the past months. His haggard face was thin and pale, his clothes torn and ragged. "Come on," he said tiredly, one limp hand beckoning them forward. "Let's get this show on the road."

Craig, Phil and Elaine happened to be near the front of the pack, and they stepped up. Patoff, Craig noticed, had disappeared, though he had no idea when the consultant had left or where he'd gone.

"What are we supposed to do?" Elaine asked Robards as they approached. This close, the guide looked in even worse shape than he had from a distance. There were visible cuts on the backs of his hands, and poorly healed burn scars on his worn face. His straw-like hair was an ill-fitting wig.

"Just continue on in," Robards said. "You'll know what to do."

The three of them, followed by a line of other management personnel, pressed past Robards, through the opening between the *Welcome* and the *CompWare Management Team!* On the other side of the temporary wall was the maze they had seen from above, though the three passages leading outward from the entrance each looked wider from this vantage point. They picked the middle one and walked in.

Craig did not recognize any landmarks of the CompWare campus. He didn't see the sidewalk that passed through the center of the grounds nor the fountain to which it led. Instead, they marched over grass between walls that looked like marble rather than plywood and on which grew ivy, morning glory and other vines.

"I thought he said we'd know what to do," Elaine said.

"Keep walking," Phil told her. "And be thankful we're not hunting dog for our dinner."

No one was behind them. Had everyone else chosen the other pathways?

The maze seemed bigger than the campus, though that was not physically possible, and they continued on, down long straight stretches, around corner after corner after corner. Fifteen minutes in, it was Craig who suggested that they turn around and retrace their steps. "This is going nowhere," he said. "And no one's following us. I think we picked the wrong way."

"Who cares?" Phil said. "You want to participate in one of Robards' pre-planned activities? If we're off the radar, so much the better."

"Yeah," Elaine agreed. "Let's see where this goes."

Craig shrugged. "All right."

Ahead, the path branched off. They chose the right fork, which ended at a small meadow that Craig didn't recognize and had never seen on CompWare property. It was surrounded by the maze wall, and in the center was a picnic table topped with at least a dozen bottles of spring water. Phil immediately walked over, sat down, picked up a bottle, unscrewed the top and started drinking. Craig and Elaine did the same.

They sat there for several minutes, speculating about the purpose of this "retreat," knowing that BFG had to have ulterior motives, but unable to come up with a plausible reason for why it had been sprung upon them so suddenly, why it had to take place right here, right now. Craig was about to ask the other two about their speed conversations, when a fleeting shadow passed over Elaine's face as she looked behind him. There was a sharp, slashing intake of breath, and he turned quickly to look over his shoulder but saw nothing. Elaine's eyes were wide. "What was *that*?"

Phil had seen it, too, though apparently not as clearly. "I don't know. It moved too fast."

"An animal, maybe?" The hope in her voice could not mask the fear.

Craig peered around the small meadow. "I didn't see anything. And if there was an animal, where did it go? There's only the one entrance. Unless it jumped over the wall."

"It just kind of—"

"Disappeared," Phil finished for her.

This time Craig did see something. A dark flash that sped behind Elaine. He wasn't sure where it had come from or where it went, saw it only for the second that it was in his sightline, and when he tried to look in the direction it had been travelling, he saw nothing, as though it had vanished into the air.

"Let's get out of here," Craig said.

There was no argument. They each grabbed an extra bottled water from the table to take along, and headed out the way they'd come.

In the sky above them, the sun went down.

——∞∞——

Austin wasn't back by dinnertime.

He'd warned her that this might happen. The management re-treat was scheduled to last two days, and he told her he'd probably be able to get out of it, but he'd also cautioned that he might end up stuck there with everyone else. So she'd known this was a possibility.

She just hadn't allowed herself to believe it.

As she'd done obsessively since first finding that horrid snow globe, Rachel Matthews walked through the first floor of the house, carefully examining all of the globes in her collection.

She didn't like Austin being gone. He'd told her she could in-vite her sister over. Or a friend. He'd even offered to station a secu-rity guard outside the residence or have one of the help spend the night if she wanted. But none of that had seemed necessary.

In the daytime.

However, now it was night, and she was all alone, and just the thought that she might run across a snow globe that portrayed perverted scenes like the other one gave her the willies. She'd al-ways loved this house, but tonight it seemed too big, and every-where she looked she saw hiding places where *other* snow globes could be stashed.

The doorbell rang.

Rachel jumped. *The doorbell?* That was impossible. The gate was locked and the perimeter alarm set. The motion detector should have spotted anyone making his way up the drive to the front of the house.

Making *his* way?

How did she know it was a *him*?

Because she did. She was afraid she knew *exactly* who it was, and that was why she did not answer the door, why she hurried quickly upstairs, locking herself in the bedroom. She ran over to the bed. Her first impulse was to call 911, and after only a second's hesitation, she decided to do exactly that. The worst that could happen was that the police would come out and discover it was a false alarm, which might be embarrassing, but at least she would know that she was safe.

She picked up the phone off the nightstand.

There was no dial tone.

He had cut the lines.

Her breath coming in ragged gasps, heart thudding in her chest, Rachel realized that her cell phone was downstairs, on the hall tree, in her purse.

The doorbell rang again.

She quickly went over her options. There were only two as she saw it. She could go downstairs and get her phone. Or stay up here and wait him out. In her mind, she imagined pulling the phone out of her purse just as he opened the front door and grabbed her. It was safer to remain where she was, Rachel decided. At least it would make an attack more difficult, because even if he did get inside the house, he would have to find her, and then he would have to break down the bedroom door to reach her.

Just in case, she started looking around for a weapon. Hurrying into the bathroom, she opened the top drawer, dug through the jumbled items and took out the scissors she sometimes used to trim her bangs.

She walked back into the bedroom feeling slightly more confident. If he—

*The Consultant*

—really did intend to harm her, he would have to find a way past the locked and bolted front door, then past the locked bedroom door. The second he entered the bedroom, she would be on

414

him with the scissors, so it seemed pretty unlikely that he would be able to do much damage.

Still, she was frightened, and she took up a place to the left of the door, ready in case he should come in.

The front bell had stopped ringing, and for a brief moment she allowed herself to hope that he had gone away, but then came the sound of a crash from somewhere downstairs. And another. And another.

He was destroying her snow globes!

Furious, Rachel turned the lock, threw open the door and hurried down the steps, scissors held high. She expected to see him picking up her globes and throwing them to the floor, but instead he stood in the center of the living room as around him, one by one, pieces of her prized collection floated up from the shelves and tables on which they were sitting and then dropped, shattering. He turned to look at her as she entered the doorway, and the scissors were pulled from her hand by some unseen force, the pressure yanking her index and middle fingers back hard enough to make her cry out.

The scissors clattered to the floor, one last snow globe fell, and the consultant walked slowly toward her. "Mrs. Matthews," he said, smiling. "I'm so glad we've found this time to talk."

"Talk? About what? The way you're destroying hundreds of dollars' worth of antiques?" She was aware that her voice had come out weak and wobbly.

"No. I want to talk about CompWare. I understand you're one of the majority shareholders."

"I have nothing to do with that," she tried to assure him, backing up. "Austin's the one who—"

"Your name is on everything."

"Only for tax purposes."

"So you're useless," he said, talking more to himself than her. "Just as I thought."

"I'm—"

He looked at her, and her vision grew foggy, the room swirling about her, everything becoming hazy and indistinct. She wanted to run away but found that she could not move. Her body felt as though it had been encased in cement; her mind could not command even a single muscle. Gradually, her vision cleared. She was frozen in place next to a smiling Santa Claus and a gang of happy children, all of them encased within a glass dome. The world beyond the glass was a distorted blur, though she could make out specific elements of her living room, blown up to gargantuan size.

She understood where she was.

What she was.

And around her fell the snow.

---

Where was Craig?

Angie was trying not to seem worried in front of Dylan, but she *was* worried. Craig always called if he was going to be late, and he was so late tonight that she'd had to feed Dylan dinner before his father came home. They *always* ate dinner together. She'd called his number at work several times, called his cell phone even more, but in both instances she'd been transferred directly to voice mail. And he had yet to call back.

Something was wrong. She knew it deep in her bones, and though she pretended nothing was the matter as she read Dylan a story, in her imagination she saw Craig dead in a car crash, lying on the side of the road, his head cracked open and bleeding into the asphalt.

The doorbell rang. She was so tense and keyed up that the sound made her cry out and drop the book she was reading.

Dylan laughed. "It's only the doorbell, Mommy."

She was already rushing across the room, her heart pounding crazily, certain that it would be a policeman on the porch, a policeman sent over to tell her that her husband—

She unlocked and pulled open the door.

Regus Patoff stood behind the screen, smiling at her. "Hello, Mrs. Horne."

She slammed the door in his face. Gasping for air, she looked frantically around to make sure Dylan was still in sight. He stood in the center of the room, confused and frightened.

"Go away!" Angie shouted through the closed door.

"I'm here on behalf of your husband, Mrs. Horne."

*Craig's dead!*

The thought, unbidden, flashed into her mind, where it would not be dislodged.

"What do you want?" she demanded.

"Your husband just wanted me to let you know that he will be gone for the next two days. He is on a retreat, along with other senior staff members."

Against her better judgment, she opened the door a crack. "Why didn't he call?"

The consultant smiled. "Because I wouldn't let him."

A chill passed through her.

"He should be fine." The consultant was still smiling. "If he does what he's supposed to do. May I come in?"

"No." She fixed him with a laser stare, her face between the wooden door and the screen door, pitching her voice low so Dylan wouldn't hear. "And if anything happens to him…"

"It'll be his own fault." The consultant chuckled, pretending to tip an invisible hat in her direction. "Have a nice night. And day. And night. And day. And try not to think about it."

He turned, making his way down the porch steps and up the walkway to the street.

⸺∞⸺

There was light in the maze, though Craig was not sure of its source. Directly above, he could see the stars and, looming above the wall on the left, the illuminated windows of the CompWare building's upper stories, but there were no lamps or bulbs of any sort along the walls of the maze.

Still, they could easily see where they were going, though some areas were darker than others, and the three of them remained on edge, ready for the return of that shadow-thing that had flashed through the meadow. It continued to surprise him that they had not encountered more people. Dozens of senior staff members were roaming the partitioned campus, so it would have been only natural to run into some of them now and then, but the place was like a ghost town.

And then it wasn't.

Another pathway intersected the one they were on, and four supervisors from Finance passed in front of them. "Hey," Phil said in greeting, but the others ignored him and kept walking.

"Shouldn't have had garlic for lunch," he joked.

At a dead-end up ahead, they came across Daisy Chung from Phil's department, naked on her hands and knees, grunting like an animal as Garrett Holcomb entered her from behind with vigorous, violent thrusts. Both looked over as the three of them approached, but neither seemed to mind being seen, and they kept on doing what they were doing as though no one else was there. In another alcove, two men Craig had seen around but whose names he didn't know, were engaged in a vicious fight, their clothes ripped, both of their faces bloody, one man biting into the arm of another, who was repeatedly kicking the first man in the groin.

"What the fuck," Phil said.

"Knock it off!" Elaine shouted at them. "You're at work, not in a cage fight!"

The men ignored her.

"Should we try to stop it?" Craig wondered.

Phil shook his head. "Not our problem."

The situation had deteriorated far more than any of them would have thought possible, and it occurred to Craig for the first time that someone might die tonight.

Maybe that was what the consultant wanted.

*You'll know what to do,* Robards had said.

Apparently, that was truer for some people than others. The three of them were still wandering around aimlessly while others were engaged in acts of increasing debauchery.

What were things going to be like in another 24 hours?

And where *was* Robards?

They needed to stay away from all this, wait it out. Already, though, his stomach was starting to growl, and he wondered if they were going to be provided with dinner or breakfast or lunch, or anything other than bottled water.

"Let's get out of here," Elaine said disgustedly.

"I wonder, if we just left, if anyone would notice," Phil mused. "I don't see any cameras anywhere. Or guards. Why don't we try to make our way back to the beginning, go home and get a good night's sleep, then come back later?"

They were so lost and the maze so impossibly large that Craig doubted they could find their way out, but he liked the plan and so did Elaine. The face of the CompWare building allowed them to get their bearings, and from it they figured out in which direction they should be heading. The building wasn't visible from all points within the maze, but they could probably see it often enough to use it for navigation, and they backtracked a few yards, then entered a passageway to their right that led to another path heading in the direction they wanted to go.

Turning a corner, they passed an alcove taken up by what looked like a dining room table. Sitting on top of the table was a paper grocery bag with two holes cut out for eyes and a too-large smile drawn underneath in felt pen.

Next to it was an ax.

Elaine's voice was hushed. "Is someone supposed to pick that up?"

"Not me," Craig assured her.

"Me, either," Phil said. He looked toward the table. "But I'm wondering if we shouldn't tear up that sack and hide the ax somewhere. Things are getting kind of crazy here. Someone might actually be tempted to, you know, *do* something with them."

"Go ahead," Elaine encouraged him, and he ripped up the bag, dropping the pieces on the grass. Tipping over the table so the top side was leaning against the wall, he hid the ax behind it.

"Let's go."

Ahead was one of the gloomier segments of the maze. It wasn't so dark that they couldn't see, but it was definitely in shadow, and when Craig saw someone walking toward them, he could not immediately tell who it was.

He had a bad feeling about that.

Phil and Elaine must have had similar thoughts because they all slowed down, waiting in the light for the figure to approach.

It was a man with the face of Alfred E. Neuman.

Craig experienced a tingle of fear. He had never liked the *Mad* magazine mascot. He knew the figure was supposed to be comical, but there was something about that perpetually grinning gap-toothed mouth that had always creeped him out and set him on edge.

It was impossible to tell who was behind the mask. Craig thought he might be able to deduce an identity from the body type, but the tall powerfully built man's physique did not look like that of any software company executive with whom Craig was familiar.

The figure walked by them without stopping, without slowing, without acknowledging their existence.

Craig looked at Phil and Elaine without speaking, then continued on, leading the way. The passage passed through the shadows, then turned left briefly before heading back in the direction from which they'd come. He looked for a cross-corridor that would set them back on course, and when he found one, he took it.

And immediately stopped.

On the ground before him was the bloody body of a man.

Robards.

The guide's face was contorted in an expression of agony, mouth and eyes both wide open. The body lay on its side, unmoving, blood still flowing from fresh wounds and seeping into the grass. One of the legs had been almost severed but was still attached to the thigh by a thin strip of muscle and skin. Organs spilled out from a hacked open stomach. Neither of the arms had hands.

An ax lay on the ground at Robards' feet, its blade glistening with red, and, next to the ax, stood a man with a grocery sack over his head, a sack with two holes cut out for eyes and an over-large smile drawn on the brown paper.

How was that possible? Phil had torn up the bag.

Maybe there were more of them. Maybe they were scattered around the maze, just waiting to be picked up and used.

Craig took all of this in, seeing it, thinking it, processing it in seconds, then he was rushing forward and so was Phil, both of them acting instinctively to subdue the man before he could reach down and pick up the ax again. Phil, faster and more lithe, ran to the side and, in a move he must have stolen from movies or TV cop shows, grabbed one of the man's arms and then the other, twisting them behind him. The man did not seem to be putting up a fight, was docilely going along, but Craig punched him in the stomach just to be on the safe side and ripped the bag off his head, staring into a horrifyingly familiar face.

Austin Matthews.

# THIRTY EIGHT

THE NEXT SEVERAL HOURS WERE A BLUR. ALL PHONES were supposed to have been confiscated, but someone somehow had called the police, and the campus and parking lot were awash in pulsing blue and red light from the phalanx of patrol cars that had descended upon CompWare. By the time a stunned Craig, Phil and Elaine had staggered out of the maze, pushing a submissive Matthews before them, half of the retreat participants were huddled in a confused mass to the side of the entrance, one of the women topless, several of the men bruised and battered.

It was nearly two in the morning by the time Craig arrived home. Angie had been asleep, but the sound of the unlocking and opening door awakened her, and she greeted him in the living room with a baseball bat in hand. She put it down gratefully when she saw that it was him, and hurried to give him a hug. "I thought you were Patoff."

"No."

"He came by to tell me that you were at a retreat and wouldn't be back for days."

Though exhausted, Craig explained what had happened, looking over her shoulder periodically to make sure Dylan was not up and listening, and she shook her head, growing more and more incredulous. "Austin Matthews?" she said. "He *killed* someone with an *ax*?"

"Apparently."

"My God."

Craig took a deep breath. "I'm wondering if this is the end of it. Patoff was nowhere to be found, and I'm hoping he just…took off."

"That doesn't seem likely," she pointed out. "He runs a major consulting firm with a serious reputation and major clients. This might give him a black eye and some bad publicity, but there's no way it'll bring him down. Besides, didn't you say you thought this was what he wanted, that it was probably intentional? He's not going to be blamed for anything that happened tonight. He's going to *use* it."

Craig sighed. "You're right, you're right."

She hugged him, pressed her cheek against his. "It's late. You're tired. Come to bed."

"Bed sounds good," he admitted.

"Come on."

The alarm woke him at six. It was still a work day, and though Angie told him that he hadn't gotten enough sleep and that he didn't have to go in because he was still supposed to be on the retreat, Craig got up anyway.

Robards' murder and Matthews' arrest for it was the top story on the local morning newscasts. Craig flipped back and forth between NBC and ABC, CBS and Fox, astounded by how either BFG or CompWare's own publicity department had kept everything but the bare bones outline of the story away from the press. What should have been a PR nightmare seemed like little more than a random tragedy, the kind that occurred daily in major metropolitan areas.

At work, police had cordoned off the building and forensics experts were inside looking for…something. Employees were milling about the parking lot in groups that mirrored their work units. Craig walked over to where the programmers stood.

"What's going on?" Huell asked as he approached.

Craig told them what had happened last night, but that news was common knowledge, and it turned out that the programmers were more up to date on what was happening than he was. He learned that Scott Cho and three others had been arrested on charges of assault and attempted rape, and two supervisors had been charged with indecent exposure and public lewdness.

All of them had been on Phil's list of targeted employees.

"Scott arrested?" Rusty said. "My heart bleeds for him."

Several of the programmers laughed.

No one was laughing in the gathering of Legal employees on the opposite side of the row. In fact, it had suddenly grown very quiet over there, and Craig walked across to see what was up. Tom Scheer, the head of the Legal department, was on the phone to someone, and the other lawyers, paralegals and secretaries were gathered around him in hushed silence. Craig tapped Fred Green on the shoulder. "What is it?" he asked.

"Austin Matthews," Fred said. "They found him dead in his cell. Suicide. Tom's trying to get more details."

Craig was stunned.

"He smashed his head against the wall."

The picture in his mind was far more vivid than he wanted it to be, and Craig hurried back to the men and women of his own division to tell them the news. As taken aback as everyone had been by the fact that Matthews had murdered Robards, they were even more stunned to learn that the CEO had committed suicide. Craig was, too. He kept seeing Matthews the way he'd looked when the bag had been torn off his head, his face grimacing in pain from being punched in the stomach, his eyes blank and…not there. Though he didn't know *how* or *why*, he knew *what* had compelled the CEO to kill both the guide and himself.

The Consultant.

The news was spreading across the parking lot, groups of people growing quiet as they learned what happened, and gradually, everyone began pushing toward the front of the building. Moments later, Gordon Webster, vice president in charge of product development, and, apparently, the senior staff member on the lot, mounted the building's steps, holding a cell phone to his ear. At the top, he faced the parking lot and called for attention. When the chatter died down, he provided a quick rundown of everything that had happened at the retreat last night and beyond, giving a brief description of what was known about Matthews' death.

"So everyone go home," he said. "There's nothing that can be done here today. You all have the day off. Come back tomorrow."

"Are you in charge here?" someone shouted out.

"I am in charge."

"Of the entire company?"

Webster hesitated slightly. "No."

"Then who is?" someone else wanted to know.

Webster looked out at them, his face expressionless. "Regus Patoff," he said. "BFG."

———◈———

There was no keeping this out of the press. Not only was it on the nightly newscasts, but it was the top story on the front page of the *Los Angeles Times* the next morning. Craig had expected to hear from Phil, but his friend hadn't called, nor had he answered the texts Craig had left him. It wasn't until Craig saw his friend in the CompWare parking lot before work that the two of them had a chance to speak.

"Where were you?" he demanded.

"He called me last night at home," Phil said quietly.

"Patoff?"

Phil nodded.

"He's done that to me, too. What'd he want you to do? Check your emails at one in the morning?"

Phil shook his head.

"What, then?"

"He just wanted to talk."

Craig frowned. "That's weird."

"We talked from midnight until three."

"Jesus! About what?"

"I don't know," Phil admitted. "Nothing. Everything. It was more a soliloquy than a conversation. *He* did all the talking. I just listened. I can't even remember what it was about, exactly, but it was amazing."

"Amazing? Is that really the word you want to use?"

"He's different than we thought. He's…he's different."

Craig was growing concerned. "He's different, all right. Whoever he is. *What*ever he is."

"He wants to meet with me this morning."

"Why?"

Phil shrugged. "To talk, maybe. I don't know."

Craig reached out and put a hand on his friend's shoulder. "Are you all right?"

"I'm fine."

"Something's up. What aren't you telling me?"

Phil shook his head, but Craig knew there was something wrong. He looked into Phil's eyes, saw an unnerving blankness. Had his friend been corrupted or co-opted? He would not have thought that possible, but the fiery defiance that had always been an essential part of Phil's nature no longer seemed to be there, and in its place was an uncharacteristic equanimity. The man standing before him this morning was not the same person with whom he had gone through the maze.

"What time are you supposed to meet with him?" Craig asked.

"Now. Eight o'clock. First thing."

"I'm going with you."

Phil didn't object, but he didn't exactly agree, either. There was a disconcerting passivity to his manner, and Craig accompanied his friend inside the building, the two of them getting into a crowded elevator. Phil pushed the button for the seventh floor.

Was that where the consultant had his office? It made sense. It was where he had conducted interviews and where the blood tests had been taken, and Craig wondered if BFG had commandeered the entire floor.

The elevator stopped at each level. They were the only two employees left by the time it reached the seventh floor, and they exited into a dim hallway that stretched to the left and right seemingly farther than the length of the building. "His office is room seven hundred," Phil said, looking in both directions. "I'm not sure where that is."

"Let's try this way," Craig suggested, pointing to the left. "On the other floors, lower numbers are over here."

They saw no one. There was noise, but it wasn't the sound of people talking or the usual background Muzak. It was more organic, as though they were passing through the body of an animal and could hear simultaneously the beating of the animal's heart, the gurgles of its digestive system and the working of its lungs.

A cat slunk by them, hugging the corner where the wall met the floor, only it wasn't exactly a cat. It was long and thin, moving with a feline grace, but there was something unnatural and disturbing about the creature, and Craig could not look at it for more than a few seconds.

Reaching the first door, they both stopped to look at the posted number. To Craig's surprise, it was 700. Phil reached for the handle, turned it, pushed open the door, and the two of them walked into what looked like the waiting room of a doctor's office. Chairs lined three of the walls, the corners taken up by triangular tables on top of which sat *Highlights* magazines and copies of *People* and *Sports Illustrated*. The fourth wall contained an open window next to a closed door. A somber-looking elderly woman seated behind the window frowned at them and asked in an unfriendly voice, "May I help you?"

"I have a meeting with Mr. Patoff," Phil told her.

The door opened, and the consultant himself came out, hand extended, all smiles. "Indeed you do! Indeed you do!" He pumped Phil's hand, then looked over at Craig. "I wasn't expecting you."

"I came for moral support."

Patoff—

*Reg. U.S. Pat. Off.*

—smiled at him. "I'm afraid this is a private meeting."

"That's okay. I'll wait."

"Don't you have work to do?"

It was one of those trick have-you-stopped-beating-your-wife questions. "I'll get it done," he said simply.

"I'm sure you will." The consultant turned away from him and put an arm around Phil's shoulder, leading him into the office. "Let's step inside, shall we?"

The door closed automatically behind them, and Craig sat down in one of the chairs. For a while, he watched the closed door, expecting it to re-open at any time, listening intently on the off chance that he could hear part of the conversation going on within. Fifteen minutes passed. Twenty. A half hour. Bored, he picked up an issue of *People* magazine, flipping through the pages. He hadn't read one for years and, looking at the abundance of photos and paucity of text, thought that it had been dumbed down even further than it had been before—if that was possible.

He ended up going through all of the magazines in the waiting room, even the *Highlights* (and was glad to see that Goofus and Gallant were still around). He'd read everything he'd wanted to read and even some things he hadn't, and Phil still hadn't come out. He waited several more minutes, then stood and walked over to the window. "How long do you think they'll be in there?" he asked the woman.

She smiled meanly. "Fuck off," she said.

He leaned forward, speaking quietly. "No, you fuck off, you ugly old bag."

He jumped back as she slid shut the window and it barely missed his face. Kicking the wall, he sat back down.

And waited.

Three hours later, Phil emerged from the meeting looking stunned.

"Praise Ralph!" the consultant called out before the door to his office closed.

Neither of them spoke until they were in the darkened corridor and walking back toward the elevator. "So," Craig said finally, "what happened? What'd he say?"

"He said a lot of things."

"Like what?"

"He told me that the happiest day in history was February eleventh, nineteen seventy-seven. That was the only day where more people were happy than miserable, more good things happened than bad. There were more births than deaths, more promotions than demotions, more marriage proposals than divorce decrees. I asked him how he knew that, and he said he has access to a lot of statistics, a lot of information. He does, too." There was a long pause. "February eleventh, nineteen seventy-seven was the happiest day on earth. It was the day Jethro Tull released their album *Songs from the Wood*.

"And it's the day I was born."

Craig frowned, feeling worried. "Phil?"

His friend stared blankly at him.

"He could be making this shit up. He probably is. You know that."

Phil shook his head. "He has a lot of information."

"Maybe so, but…"

"There are *patterns* here, Craig. We don't see them because we don't have access to all the data, but Patoff *does*. These are the patterns that control our lives, that determine success or failure, that make us what we are. Do you know why he called this meeting with me today? He's looking for a replacement for Matthews. Someone to run the company."

"Run the company? He doesn't make that decision. The board does. And, no offense, but they're not going to choose a division head from Sales to be CEO when there's plenty of people above you in the hierarchy. In fact, they probably won't even choose anyone from in-house. There'll be a search committee—"

"I've been chosen. He offered me the job."

"It's not his to offer."

"I'm fated to do this."

"*Luke.* It is your *destiny.*"

Phil didn't even crack a smile. "I think it *is* my destiny. All roads have led to this. Patoff has shown me—"

"That's not even his name," Craig said.

"Your name is not who you are."

"So are you going to change *your* name? Are you going to call yourself General Mills and lead our army into the future?"

"You do not understand."

"Understand what? Jesus, Phil—"

"Not Jesus. Ralph."

"You're not even making any sense!" Craig forced himself to stop and take a deep breath. "Look, if you were made the CEO of CompWare *last week*, that would have been amazing. It would have meant that we won. We've been fighting against these bastards the whole time, and right now you'd be in a position to dump the consultants and get things back on track. But from where I stand, it seems like you drank the Kool-Aid. Don't you remember what happened to Jess? To Tyler? To Lupe, for God's sake? Remember hunting the dog? Remember the other night? I mean, shit, look around at this *floor*. Does this look even remotely like any software company you've ever seen? This isn't normal. This isn't right."

Phil looked at him flatly. "Your attitude leaves a lot to be desired."

"Patoff's a monster, Phil. You used to know that."

"I suggest you go home, take the rest of the day off and think about what you're saying."

The elevator doors opened. Craig got in, pushing the button for the sixth floor. "No offense, Phil, but you're not my boss."

"I am now."

"I'm not taking your word for that. Until I get official confirmation that you, Phil Allen, have somehow, for some reason, been promoted over everyone else to take over as CEO from Austin Matthews, *who committed suicide after killing Dash Robards with an ax*, I'm going to assume that you're still in Sales and I'm in Programming."

The elevator stopped at the sixth floor, and Craig got off, ignoring Phil and heading straight down the corridor without looking back. He passed by Lupe's empty desk and walked into his office, closing the door behind him, feeling more alone than he ever had in his life.

# THIRTY NINE

CRAIG CHECKED HIS MESSAGES IMMEDIATELY UPON waking, though he had promised her he would stop doing that, and Angie could tell by the expression on his face that the news was not good. "What is it?" she asked.

"Phil *is* the new CEO. It's official."

"I assume the fact that he didn't call to tell you is not a good sign."

Craig sighed. "I don't know what's happened to him."

"So what are you going to do?"

"Play it by ear."

She put her hand on his arm. "I think you should quit."

He nodded. "It's occurred to me," he admitted.

"People are *dying*."

"I know. I was there. But…"

"But what?" she said, starting to get angry.

"Phil's in charge now, and maybe—"

"Phil's not Phil!" She gripped his wrist. "You have a family to think about."

Craig got out of bed, putting on his bathrobe, and Angie did the same. "You're not going in today?" she said. From down the hall, she heard Dylan stirring in his room, already awake.

"I have to." He walked over to the closet, picking out clothes.

"Craig," she pleaded.

Dylan jumped through the doorway. He was wearing Superman pajamas, which always made him act in a manner he thought heroic. "What are you guys arguing about?"

"We're not arguing," Angie said.

"I heard you."

"We're not arguing," Craig seconded.

"Okay." He didn't really seem to care. "What am I having for breakfast? We have a math test today."

"How about an omelet?" Angie asked him. Craig headed toward the bathroom to take his shower.

"And toast!"

"And toast," Angie agreed. She patted him on the back. "Now go get dressed, and I'll start making your food."

Craig had squirmed his way out of that conversation, but she wasn't about to drop the subject, and she wouldn't give in without a fight. As soon as he finished his shower, she was going to guilt him into quitting his job—and if she had to use Dylan to do it, she would. Walking into the kitchen, she bypassed the light switch and opened the shades above the sink. The room faced the morning sun, and she preferred natural light. She moved over to the breakfast nook, pulled open the shades—

And saw Regus Patoff standing next to the window, staring in at her.

Angie managed not to scream, but she bumped her hip on the table and stumbled over the legs of one of the chairs in her effort to get out of the kitchen. She ran down the hall. "Stay in your room!" she ordered Dylan, closing his door.

"Why?" He sounded scared, clearly aware that something was wrong.

"Just stay there!" she shouted as she hurried into the master bathroom. Craig was standing on the rug in front of the shower stall, toweling off. "He's here!" Angie said in as low a voice as she could manage. "Patoff's standing in the front yard staring into the kitchen window!"

Still wet, hair wild, not bothering to put on underwear, Craig pulled on his pants and ran toward the front of the house. "Stay with Dylan!"

Dylan was safe in his room; there was only the one door that opened into the hall, and his window faced the back yard. "Stay there!" she ordered her son again, rapping on his door as she rushed by. "Don't come out!"

She wasn't about to let Craig face the man by himself, and she hurried into the kitchen directly behind him. The consultant was gone. He was not at the window by the breakfast nook or peeking in through the window above the sink. Craig leaned over the counter, looking through the glass in both directions. "I don't see him." There was relief in his voice but also wariness.

A knock sounded at the front door, a jaunty shave-and-a-hair-cut tapping on the wood.

She hadn't expected this to be over, had known the consultant would pop up again, but she jumped anyway.

"Stay back," Craig said as they passed into the living room. He motioned toward the hallway entrance, and Angie took up a position there, a mother bear guarding her cub. She wished she had some sort of weapon in her hand.

"What do you want?" Craig shouted through the closed door.

The door opened of its own accord. She knew it was locked—she'd checked the deadbolt herself before going to bed last night—but the door swung wide, and through the screen she could see the consultant looking in at them. He had always been an odd-looking man, but something about his appearance this morning seemed even stranger than usual. Ordinarily tall and thin, he now looked even taller and thinner, his usually light brown, almost-orange hair now a brighter orange that matched his bow tie. His mouth was smiling but, as always, his eyes were not. Even through the dusty mesh of the screen door, she could see their hard intensity.

He bowed in a comically formal manner. "Regus Patoff, at your service."

"That's not your real name," Craig said flatly.

He chuckled. "Isn't it?"

"So I assume you're registered with the U.S. patent office?"

The consultant took an exaggerated look at his watch. "It took you this long? I'm disappointed." He leaned forward. "So what does BFG stand for?"

"I don't know. Yet."

"If you don't know that, you don't know anything. And—tick tock—I'm afraid that your time is almost up."

Angie's control was holding, though it was only through a sheer effort of will that she herself had not screamed after the door opened. *I should be calling 911*, she told herself. *I should be calling the police.*

"Why are you here?" Craig demanded.

"I just wanted to make sure you were coming in today. I was passing by, on my way to the office, and I thought I'd stop in and check on you. Maybe you want to carpool?"

"No."

"But you are coming in?"

"Of course."

"Excellent! Excellent! There are big changes afoot, and I wanted to make sure you didn't miss anything."

Craig said nothing, simply stared at the man.

"I'll take my leave, then." He looked past Craig at Angie. "You'd better get busy making Dylan's omelet. A boy needs protein before a test."

And then he was gone.

He didn't disappear, but somehow she didn't see him turn around and walk away, and in what seemed like only seconds after his last words, he was on the sidewalk in front of the house.

Craig closed the door, locked it.

"Oh my God," Angie breathed. "Oh my God."

They both hurried down the hall to check on Dylan, who was sitting on the floor, still tying his shoes. "Is it over?" he asked, looking up. "Can I come out now?"

Craig picked him up, and Angie gave him a kiss on the cheek. "You can come out," she said.

"Is my breakfast ready?"

"Not yet. But I'll make it right now."

Dylan looked from her to Craig, and she saw an understanding in his eyes that shouldn't have been there. "Was it Mr. Patoff?" he asked.

"Yes it was," Craig said. "But he's gone now."

There was a pause. "Is he coming back?"

"No," Craig said. "I'm going to talk to him today and tell him he's not allowed to come over to our house."

The answer satisfied Dylan, who smiled with relief, but when Angie looked at her husband, she saw an apprehension that mirrored her own. Shooting him a supportive glance, she gave her son another quick kiss, then went out to the kitchen to make breakfast.

———o**o———

It was mid-morning, and Angie had just finished vacuuming when Craig walked into the house. He'd left for work only a few hours ago, after a whispered fight conducted out of Dylan's hearing, and she hadn't expected to see him until the end of the day.

"Did you quit?" she asked hopefully, wrapping the vacuum cleaner cord around the hook below the handle.

"Phil's giving me a week off."

She raised an eyebrow. "Is that a reward or a punishment?"

"Who the hell knows?"

"What happened?"

"I went up to see Phil as soon as I got there. I thought I'd congratulate him and sort of...see where he was at, how he was. I should've called first because when I went up to Matthews' office, he wasn't there, and when I went to his regular office, he wasn't there. I asked his secretary where he was, but she was crying and packing up her stuff because he'd fired her."

"Phil?"

"Yeah. In fact, when I got back to my desk, I found an email on my computer announcing that six people from my division were being furloughed, and six others were being cut down to part-time. I called Phil at his old number, left a message on his voicemail, then sent him an email, asking to talk to him. I went down to talk to the employees who were being cut, but none of them were there; they'd been told not to come in. I called Human Resources but got a voicemail. The programmers were all up in arms, the ones who were left, wanting to know what was going on, and I had to admit that I had no clue. Scott was still in jail, for all I knew, and I couldn't find anyone who could tell me what was happening.

"Phil showed up, and he was happy, excited, acting as though everything was normal. I tried to ask him about the furloughs, about the hours being cut, about his own secretary, but he pretended he didn't know anything about it. I said it must be BFG, but he wouldn't take the bait. He ignored that and only said that he'd call HR and look into it. I played along because he was acting like Phil again—but he wasn't. It was in his eyes, it was…" Craig shook his head. "It was like he was a pod person or something. He told all the programmers to get back to work, and we walked back up to my office, and he said he had something to do but would get back to me about the furloughs and everything.

"He did get back to me about an hour later. Called me on the phone and told me to take the week off. I asked why, and he said there was some restructuring going on, and all supervisory personnel were being asked to take a short vacation."

"Maybe you'll be laid off," Angie said hopefully.

"Maybe," he conceded, "but it didn't sound that way."

"And you don't really want that."

"No, I don't."

"Why not?"

"I don't know. Part of it's because I don't want to give up; I don't want to let *him* win. But part of it's because BFG will be gone eventually, and if I can maintain contact with Phil, keep him from completely drifting away, we might be in a position to roll back this craziness and do some good."

"That's bullshit and you know it."

Craig didn't respond.

"Quit."

"I can't."

Angie started pushing the vacuum cleaner over to the hall closet.

"I have to see this through."

She ignored him and went into the bathroom, where she started cleaning the sink, shower and toilet. Fifteen minutes later, she came out to find him in the living room parked in front of the television. "Is this what you're going to do all week? Watch TV?"

"I don't know. Do you have any other suggestions?"

She stopped for a moment on her way to the kitchen and looked at him. "Send out résumés," she said.

"Maybe I will," he told her.

But she knew he wouldn't, and she wasn't sure if that made her more angry or afraid.

# FORTY

THE PARKING LOT WAS LESS THAN HALF-FULL WHEN Craig arrived at CompWare a week later, and he found out when he went upstairs to check in with HR that fully a third of all employees were being laid off or furloughed. Michelle Hagen, the woman behind the counter, was the one who told him that, and though she kept glancing up at the camera in the corner, she made no effort to censor herself, and though he didn't ask, he had the feeling that she was one of the employees affected.

She told him as well, after looking at his file on her computer, that his hours would be changing next week, that his entire division would be working from eight at night to five in the morning rather than from eight in the morning until five in the afternoon.

"That doesn't make any sense," he said.

She looked at him levelly. "Nothing does."

The corridors of the building were curiously empty as he made his way back to the elevators, and the sixth floor seemed almost completely unoccupied. He'd intended to call Phil and hear from the horse's mouth exactly what was going on, but his friend—

*(was he still his friend?)*

—was sitting in Lupe's chair outside of his office when he arrived, waiting for him. "Craig!" Phil said welcomingly. "Glad to have you back!"

Craig motioned toward the empty hallway. "What's going on here?"

"We're implementing some of BFG's suggestions to streamline the company. I really think it's going to work out."

"How's it going to work out when you're cutting programmers?"

"I told you before, I think we should be expanding into devices. Software's a limiting market, particularly in regard to your area: games. If we can control all aspects of the gaming experience, if we provide content that is only usable on our proprietary devices and we tap into the gullible public's endless willingness to shell out for upgrades, we'll be able to explode our market share. Besides, it's not like we're picking on your division. We're cutting across the board. Sales, my old stomping ground, has been reduced by a third."

"That makes it even worse. We need people to create product, and we need people to sell product or we won't be making any money."

"Oh, we'll be making money."

"But with fewer workers?"

"A company is like a machine. All of the parts need to fit together in order to achieve maximum efficiency. What we're building here is a leaner and meaner machine."

"Do you hear yourself?"

Phil leaned forward excitedly. "I have a revolutionary idea for a new device aimed at teenage boys. The average 18-year-old has ten to twelve erections every day. We could harness this natural energy and use it to power a handheld device. Each expansion of the penis would generate a charge that would be stored in a battery. They'd never need to plug it in; it would run off their own bodies. For women and girls, we could connect a charger to their toilet. Just as dams are used to generate electricity, each flush would cause the water to turn a turbine embedded in the base, generating electricity that would be used to recharge the battery. We'd be pioneers in the field of sustainable energy."

Craig looked at him. The ideas were not just ridiculous, they were crazy. He was about to say just that—in as circumspect a manner as possible—when a sharply dressed man with a short clean haircut, a man Craig didn't know but who looked vaguely familiar, walked up to Phil. "Patel has been taken care of," he stated.

Craig didn't like the sound of that. "Parvesh Patel?" he asked.

Phil nodded. "Parvesh has met with an unfortunate accident," he said, a smile playing around the edge of his lips.

Craig froze. Phil and Parvesh had never gotten along, but he couldn't believe that his friend would actually cause physical damage to be inflicted on another person, no matter how much he disliked him.

*The consultant would.*

Yes, the consultant would. And had.

Now Phil had, too.

Things had apparently gone far off the rails in the week he'd been gone.

"Thanks, Anthony." Phil said. "You can make phone calls if you want."

The other man smiled, and Craig didn't like that smile. "My favorite thing to do," he said, and left the way he'd come.

Was Phil brainwashed? Drugged? Possessed? What could have caused the change in him—a few telephone calls and a long meeting with the consultant? It seemed impossible, but the proof was right there. Part of him blamed Phil, but part of him didn't, since he knew his friend was being manipulated by a power neither of them could understand.

The Consultant.

*Reg. U.S. Pat. Off.*

"Let me talk to him," Craig said.

"Who?"

"You know who. Patoff. Or *whatever* his real name is."

Phil's expression hardened. "Why do you want to talk to him?"

"I have a few questions."

"You can ask *me*. I know you resent it, but I *am* the CEO."

"I don't resent it," Craig said.

"But…?" Phil prompted.

He paused, then decided to answer honestly. "But what do you know about running a major company? I certainly couldn't do it. And I have my doubts that you can, either. But that's not what I want to talk to Patoff about."

"What is it, then?"

Before he could answer, an announcement came over the speakers. "Will Craig Horne please come to Mr. Patoff's office immediately?" The words seemed to echo in the empty corridor.

Craig looked up at the camera through which the consultant had obviously been monitoring their conversation, then over at Phil, who had paled considerably. *He's afraid*, Craig thought, and in a weird way, he considered that a good sign.

The message repeated, and the two of them stared at each other for a moment. Craig asked, "Is his office still on the seventh?"

"As far as I know," Phil said, and that hint of uncertainty was also a good sign.

They walked into an elevator together, though neither of them spoke. Craig pressed the button for the seventh floor, and when Phil didn't press one of the other buttons, he assumed they would be visiting the consultant together. But when the doors opened on a dingy darkened corridor, he was the only one to step out.

He turned around, intending to say something to Phil (though he didn't know what), but the doors closed and he was left alone.

The seventh floor had deteriorated since he had come here with Phil. The hallway, if possible, was even dimmer than before, lit only by occasionally recessed fluorescents that emitted a faint sputtering light. The walls were peeling, the floor torn up. Whereas the hallway had previously appeared to stretch farther than the length of the building, it now seemed far too short, dead-ending immediately to his right and extending to the left only as far as room 700, the consultant's office.

The strange organic sounds that had pulsated behind the walls, above the ceiling, beneath the floor, were still audible but muted, as though the body in which he found himself was dying.

Craig walked down the shortened hall toward the office, stepping slowly and carefully over the broken floor, trying not to trip, keeping an eye out for that cat thing that had been slinking around here before.

The door opened before he reached it, and he thought, absurdly, of Willy Wonka. In the Gene Wilder movie, the door to the chocolate factory had opened in the same way. It was not through any mechanical means but magically, and Craig had the sense that the same thing was happening here. He hadn't set off any motion detector; this wasn't an automatic door. It was a regular door, and it opened because the consultant had made it open.

The waiting room had changed. It no longer looked like part of a doctor's office. Gone were the chairs and magazines, replaced by a jumbled pile of discarded office supplies. Drawn on the walls, in tiny obsessive detail, were flowcharts and organizational diagrams so complicated that it was impossible to tell what they were supposed to represent, or where one ended and another began.

The old secretary was nowhere to be seen, the frosted window in front of her work station closed, but the door next to the window swung open of its own accord, and Craig walked back to the consultant's office, skirting the edge of the absent secretary's circular desk and passing through an open doorway into a well-lit room the size of a school auditorium. At the far end was a window, and in front of the window a small nondescript desk, behind which sat the consultant. Other than that, the room was empty.

Except for the blood.

There was blood on the floor and on the walls, a tremendous amount, an impossible amount, some of it dried but most of it fresh and wet, and he had to walk through it to reach the consultant's desk. He considered not doing so, staying where he was, forcing the consultant to either come to him or shout at the top of his lungs in order to be heard, but even as the thought entered his head, he was being drawn forward, a force not unlike magnetism pulling him toward the far off desk. His shoes almost slipped in the blood, and the smell was nearly overpowering, but he managed to stay upright and not vomit as he approached the consultant.

From somewhere far off came the sound of singing. A children's song of some sort.

He reached the desk. Wearing a crimson bow tie that matched the shade of the splattered walls and floor, the consultant nodded at him. "Thank you for attending this meeting."

"This isn't a meeting!" Craig spat out. "Everything isn't a meeting!"

"Oh, but it is. Life is nothing but a series of meetings, and I called *this* one in order to discuss your bitter jealousy over Mr. Allen's promotion to CEO, and to determine whether that jealousy will impair your work performance and jeopardize your continued tenure with the company."

"Bitter jealousy?" he said. "I'm not jealous at all."

"Aren't you?"

Craig looked at the man with dawning understanding. Phil's promotion, he realized, had been nothing but a tactical move on the consultant's part, a way to drive a wedge between himself and his friend. The two of them had probably been the closest thing to a threat that BFG faced, and the consultant had made a concerted effort to separate them.

But how had Phil succumbed? How could he have been so weak?

He couldn't help feeling disappointed. *He* could not have been recruited, and he wondered how the man had known that Phil was the weaker link.

"I'm happy for him," Craig said, looking the consultant in the eye. "And I'm hopeful that having one of our own in that position will lead CompWare in a better direction."

"That is a hope we all share." The consultant was suddenly all business. "Now, starting next week, the entire operation here will be on a nighttime schedule. This will cut down on the commute time for employees as they won't be on the road during rush hour, and it will cut down on electricity costs since CompWare will be operational during non-peak hours, thus providing the company with a lower utility rate."

"But that's not why we'll be working at night," Craig said.

"No," the consultant told him. "It isn't."

"Are you trying to get people to quit? Is that it? Because I'm not going anywhere."

"If I wanted to get rid of you, there are far more effective methods."

Craig became exceptionally aware of the sticky blood beneath his shoes, the red all over the walls. But he didn't back down. "You don't intimidate me."

"I'm not trying to," the consultant said innocently.

Craig confronted him. "So why are you doing all this? You're running this place into the ground. People are *dying*."

"People die everywhere, every day. That's life."

"You didn't cause this kind of damage at any of those Fortune 500 companies you consulted for."

Patoff seemed pensive. "We do what's best for each individual business, based on needs, resources, financial status, a whole host of variables."

"You went to my son's school. My wife's work."

"We're thorough." He swiveled in his chair, looked out the window. "This is the saddest time," he said softly. "When it's all winding down, coming to an end." He seemed to be speaking more to himself than to Craig. "I honestly thought we had a chance here, an opportunity to streamline operations and create a perfect company."

He swiveled the chair back around, brightening a little. "Maybe we still do," he said. "Maybe I'm getting ahead of myself. Sometimes Ralph works in mysterious ways."

"I'll bite," Craig said. "How do you create a perfect company?"

"A company is like a machine. All of the parts need to fit together in order to achieve maximum efficiency."

He recognized those words. That was what Phil had told him. Verbatim.

"Our job is to make those parts fit, to take out what's unnecessary, to file down gears so they mesh, to rewire when required. The ultimate goal? Speaking plainly: a corporation without workers, an entirely self-contained entity."

"You're crazy."

"It's not always possible," the consultant conceded. "But that's the goal, that's what we're after." He looked out the window again. "I really thought CompWare might be..." He trailed off.

"I'm leaving," Craig announced.

"Good meeting," the consultant said. "Good meeting. And with Ralph's blessing, maybe CompWare *will* be the one."

"And we'll all be fired. Or dead."

"Ralph willing." The consultant laughed to show he was only joking—but they both knew that he wasn't.

Craig turned away, walking back through the blood and out the door, heading down the short dark hall to the elevator, leaving red footprints behind him.

On Tuesday, the two remaining members of the Board were found dead in their respective houses, one the victim of a home invasion robbery/murder, the other having slipped in the bathtub and hit his head.

On Wednesday, Elaine told him that she'd landed a job at a rival software development firm. She'd taken a pay cut, but was relieved to be out. Scott Cho and the other employees who had been arrested after the fatal retreat were officially fired.

On Thursday, six divisions were condensed to three, with a total of twenty-four people laid off.

On Friday, in a freak accident in the CompWare parking lot that was "breaking news" on all of the local stations, six employees were killed, three others sent to the hospital in critical condition.

And when Craig checked the target list Phil had given him, all of them were on it.

# FORTY ONE

CRAIG SLEPT IN LATE MONDAY MORNING, WAKING UP when Dylan came in to give him a hug before Angie took the boy to school. Craig wanted to be well-prepared for his new shift, didn't want to give anyone a reason to question his competence, ability or loyalty, and though he wasn't really tired, he forced himself to take a nap in the afternoon, shortly after picking up Dylan at three. He instructed Angie to wake him at six, so he could eat dinner before heading off to work.

"I'll wake you up, Daddy!" Dylan offered.

"Okay," Craig told him, smiling. "Don't forget."

"I won't!"

But no one woke him, and it was after seven when Craig finally got up on his own. He noticed immediately that the house was dark. And silent.

*Something was wrong.*

He jumped out of bed. "Angie? Dylan?" Passing quickly from room to room, he saw nothing out of place, nothing out of the ordinary, but he didn't see his wife or son either. Maybe they'd gone to the store and lost track of time, he reasoned, or had car problems on their way back. He knew that was highly unlikely—by now, Angie should have been helping Dylan with his homework and making dinner, and if she *had* gone somewhere, she would have woken him up to tell him—but he still managed to almost convince himself that their absence had a perfectly sensible explanation.

Until he saw what was lying on the kitchen counter.

A business card.

He knew even before picking it up whose it was, and when he looked at its face, he saw what he expected, two words printed above three letters:

*Regus Patoff*

*BFG*

Below that, on the bottom left of the card, was a phone number, and Craig immediately picked up his phone and called it. There was no ring, only a recorded message that clicked on after a moment of deep eerie silence. "The voice mailbox of Regus Patoff is full."

The connection was severed.

This time, Craig called Angie's cell phone. *Pick up*, he thought as he finished punching in the numbers and put the phone to his ear. *Pick up*.

Her phone sounded from somewhere else in the house, its distinctive *Brady Bunch* ringtone unmistakable.

She never went anywhere without her cell.

He found her phone, and her purse, on the floor next to the couch in the living room. His first instinct was the call the police—but Angie and Dylan had only been gone a couple of hours, not the 24 or 48 required to be a missing person, and he knew the police would do nothing and tell him to wait. The consultant's business card was still in his hand, and he knew where he needed to go.

He scribbled a quick note—on the off chance that they *did* return—and left it on the couch where it would be seen, before locking the front door and heading out.

⌘

Lights illuminated the CompWare parking lot, revealing more cars than Craig was expecting. The building itself seemed underlit, and though he knew that the people inside were just starting their work shift, CompWare appeared closed and empty. It was only seven forty-seven, and he wasn't scheduled to work until eight, but he was still apparently the last one here, and the sound of his heels on the asphalt seemed loud as he dashed across the parking lot toward the front entrance.

The maze was still up, he saw, and he shivered. Was it now going to be a permanent part of the CompWare campus? He wouldn't be surprised, and he paused for a second before going up the steps, wondering if Dylan and Angie had been taken there. Somehow, he didn't think so, and he hurried the rest of the way up and through the doors into the lobby.

The lobby had changed. It was dark and lit by torches spaced far apart on spectacularly dirty walls. Guards were stationed around the perimeter, all of them wearing black militaristic uniforms, all of them holding automatic weapons in their hands, all of them wearing brown paper sacks over their heads. Craig expected to be stopped and quizzed as to where he was going, but no one moved as he made his way over to the elevators.

He considered going to the seventh floor but instead pressed the button for CompWare's top level, intending to confront Phil, knowing he had a better chance of getting answers out of his friend than he did the consultant.

There were nearly a dozen frantic employees in front of the CEO's office when he arrived, all of them talking over each other. Most, he saw with a sinking feeling in the pit of his stomach, were waving business cards in the air exactly like the one he held in his own hand. Phil's new secretary—Matthews' old secretary, Diane— was crying, repeating over and over again, "I don't know where he is! I don't know where he is!"

"What's going on?" Craig asked, walking up.

"My husband—"

"My wife—"

"My daughters—"

Like Angie and Dylan, their family members were missing and what had been left in their absence was the consultant's business card. Craig pushed his way through the crowd until he was standing before the secretary's desk. "Diane," he said calmly. "You must have some idea where he is. Did he come in today?"

"He was in his office when I got here," she told him. "He's always here early."

"And where do you think he went?"

She remained flustered. "I don't know! It's impossible to know where he goes or what he does. He's been saying crazy things for the past week, talking about programs that predict violent deaths and apps that find prostitutes and smart phone screens made from plant extracts and protective covers made out of skin…I don't know!"

"Calm down," Craig said reassuringly. "It's all right." He patted her hand on the desk. "Did he say anything about using *people* for…something?"

Diane wiped a tear from her eye. "Maybe. He's said so many crazy things…" She thought for a minute. "He said the cafeteria was closing since there were no meals between dinner and break-fast, and people working at night wouldn't need lunches anymore. I wasn't spying, but I overheard him talking on the phone about that—to *him*—and he said, 'We can put them there.' Maybe that's what you're looking for?"

It made as much sense as anything else.

"Okay," Craig announced. "I'm going to the cafeteria. Anyone who wants to can come along. If we don't find anything there, I say we search the building."

"It'll be faster if we split up," said Carlos Baldonado from Research.

"It's safer if we stay together," Hetty Johnson from Sales countered.

He didn't want to stand here and argue. "Okay, those who want to go off on their own, start here on the top floor. The rest of you, come with me."

He was going to the cafeteria, though he knew the most logical place to start would have been on the seventh floor. But he didn't want to believe that Dylan and Angie could be there. He saw in his mind that monstrous room with its crimson-splattered walls and floor sticky with blood, and felt the bleakness of despair pushing itself into his thoughts. He pushed back, pushed it away, and led all of them except Carlos and another man he didn't know to the elevators.

Everyone was panicked and outraged, talking over each other, but from what he could tell, the circumstances of each were remarkably similar to his own. While sleeping in preparation for the new nighttime work shift, family members had disappeared, and upon awakening, the employees had found the consultant's business card.

457

It took two elevators to hold them all, but luckily both arrived at once, and they rode down in tandem to the second floor.

Where the cafeteria had been was a stark industrial landscape. Gone were the ficus trees and ferns, the open kitchen and light wood tables. In their place, large metal gas tanks lined the walls and steel girders slanted from dark ceiling to torn-up floor. Dim dirty light filtered in from grimy windows, revealing a shadowed network of tubes, ducts and pipes. A single light bulb stood on a metal tripod in the center of the huge room, and as Craig made his way toward it, he saw that the cord from the light ran across the ground to an area where a group of men, women and children were standing in narrow stalls, electrodes and wires attached to their heads.

There were gasps all around as everyone seemed to notice the sight at once, and then the names of wives, husbands and children were being shouted as employees rushed across the open space to find the members of their families. Craig was running, too, looking for Dylan and Angie, and he found them next to each other in the middle of the group. They were restrained within their stalls, arms affixed to metal bars with plastic ties, and he pulled the electrodes off their heads and used the most jagged key on his ring to saw through the thin plastic fasteners, freeing Dylan first, then Angie. Others were doing the same, and the light bulb on the tripod slowly dimmed as its power source was disconnected.

Craig didn't know how such a thing could work or why anyone would want it to—

*human batteries?*

—but he was certain it was one of Phil's new lunatic ideas, and his focus right now was getting his wife and son out of the building.

He hugged Dylan tightly. "Are you all right, little buddy?"

Dylan nodded, faking a small smile, but he didn't answer and his eyes remained blank.

"What happened?" Craig asked Angie as he pulled her out of her narrow cubicle.

"I don't know," she said. "I should, but I can't remember." She put a protective arm around Dylan, kissing the top of his head. "Everything's all right now," she told him. "We're okay."

"I found Patoff's business card in the kitchen."

"I knew it had to be him, but…I can't remember. I don't know how we got here or what happened at home. I don't even know the last thing I remember. I was just…there. Then I was…here."

"Well, we need to get you out of here now," he told them. "As fast as we can. And then go to the police." He looked around at the others, some of whom had freed their loved ones, others who were in the process of doing so. One woman remained alone, with no one to help her, and she was struggling against her bonds, begging for someone to let her out. "Stay here," Craig told Angie, and pulled the electrodes off the woman's head, sawing through her bonds with his keys.

The light bulb finally went out completely.

In the pale illumination offered by the grimy windows, everyone more than three feet away looked like a silhouette. "We need to go!" Craig announced loudly.

"You're coming with us, right?" Angie said. Her lip was trembling. Dylan stared at him mutely.

He put an arm around both of them. "Yeah. I'm coming."

"This way!" he called out, leading everyone toward the stairwell. He didn't trust the elevators and thought they had a better chance of getting out more quickly if they took the stairs.

After the darkness of the second floor, the light in the stairway was jarring. He blinked against the brightness, wiping his eyes, and started down, one hand on the metal railing, the other holding tightly to Dylan's hand. They made it to the first landing, then continued to the bottom, where Craig opened the door that led to the lobby.

The stair door was hidden off to the side, next to the restrooms, but Phil was waiting when they emerged. He stood before them, an expression of triumph on his face. He was wearing a bow tie, and his hair had been cut short. The effect was disconcerting, as though he had been possessed by the consultant, and the words that he spoke did nothing to dispel that impression.

"Trying to escape?" he said.

Craig looked at him. "Escape from what? This is where I work."

"And them?" Phil motioned toward Angie and Dylan.

"My wife and son were kidnapped and hooked up to a light bulb in what used to be the cafeteria. And so were all these other people." The growing crowd pushed him forward as everyone from the second floor came through the door. "What's gotten into you?"

"You are my sworn enemy," Phil said softly.

Where was *this* coming from? Craig moved a step closer, motioning for those behind him to head toward the lobby exit. The armed uniformed guards who had been there on his way in had decamped to another part of the building, and, remarkably, the doors were unguarded. If he could keep Phil distracted, the others might be able to make it out safely and call the police. From the corner of his eye, he saw a line of people hurrying toward the doors. Angie was holding onto his sleeve, but he pulled away from her and, without taking his eyes off Phil, gestured frantically for her and Dylan to leave.

It was only for Dylan's safety that she took their son and left. Otherwise, he knew, she would have remained right where she was.

Phil looked at him with hatred. "Patoff *told* me."

"Told you what?"

"About *you!*"

"Where is Patoff—or whatever his real name is?"

Phil stared at him in silence.

"Where is he?"

"The consultants are leaving. They've done their job."

"*He*," Craig said. "Not *they*."

Phil sounded forlorn. "We're on our own now. We're all alone." His voice was filled with sudden fury. "BFG failed!"

"Good," Craig said. "That's what we wanted, remember?"

His friend—

*ex-friend*

—shook his head as though trying to free it from confusing thoughts.

The lobby was starting to fill with workers entering from the elevators and stairwell. As though summoned by a dog whistle audible only to them, they arrived individually, in pairs and in packs.

*Packs?*

Yes, there was something almost wolflike in both the way they arrived and immediately began circling in, and in the nearly identical expressions on their faces. It wasn't all of them, of course, but too many for comfort, and Craig saw that the lobby entrance was now blocked to him.

But at least his family and the others had gotten out.

And were hopefully calling the cops.

From elsewhere in the building came the staccato sound of automatic gunfire.

"There's nothing left for us," Phil said.

"You're talking nonsense," Craig told him.

"CompWare wasn't worthy."

He almost made a *Wayne's World* joke, but he could tell from Phil's face that it would not be appreciated. "I'm glad BFG's leaving. Now we can get back to doing what we're supposed to do: create software packages." He attempted a rapprochement. "And you're in charge."

Phil didn't take the bait. Behind him, the lobby was getting crowded. As in the parking lot the morning after the retreat in the maze, when they had learned of Austin Matthews' suicide, the CompWare employees had separated themselves by department and division. There seemed a competitive aspect to it this time, however, as though workers remained within their own group not because they felt more familiar and comfortable with their immediate coworkers but because they didn't want to associate with people from *other* groups. It was almost a hostility, and Craig wondered what the consultant had done or said to obtain that result.

"You are my sworn enemy," Phil said again, softly, threateningly.

"I've had enough of this shit." Craig tried to push past the other man, but Phil moved to block him. Other employees—salespeople and personnel from Phil's division—massed behind Phil protectively, and Craig saw that many of them had in their hands office supplies that could be used as weapons: scissors, staplers, letter openers, laser pointers, box cutters, sharpened pencils, metal rulers.

"A fight to the death!" Phil announced. "Programming versus Sales!"

Craig frowned, confused. "What?"

As if on cue, the various factions in the lobby stepped back, forming a rough perimeter around the open middle section of the floor. Phil's Sales force fanned out around him like one of the gangs from *West Side Story*. Craig looked over at the programmers, who were standing together some ways off to his left. They seemed just as baffled as he was.

"No one's fighting anyone!" Craig declared.

"Fight or die," Phil said, and his smile made it clear which one he'd prefer.

"We don't even have any weapons!" Huell shouted.

"What the fuck is going on?" Rusty muttered to no one in particular.

Not all of the gathered employees were in lockstep, Craig noticed. For every brainwashed gung ho would-be soldier, there were two noncombatants who were frightened, bewildered and wanted nothing more than to get out of the building. Indeed, several employees *had* left the lobby and were sprinting across the darkened parking lot, following Angie and the others, but that avenue of escape was no longer an option. The uniformed guards were back, faces still hidden by paper bags, and they stood with their cradled weapons in front of the doors, ready to repel anyone who attempted to flee.

"Everyone get back to work!" Craig announced loudly. "Just stop this nonsense and go back to your desks!"

"Attack!" Phil cried.

Those competing commands led to a chaotic free-for-all in which charged-up salespeople attacked programmers who were trying to get to the elevators, while individuals from other divisions and departments joined in the fracas, either trying to protect those who were being assaulted or assailing people themselves. Craig could only hope that the police would arrive soon, because this could not continue for long without resulting in serious injury.

Or death.

That was what the consultant really wanted.

Phil came at him, an expression of irrepressible rage etched deeply into his ordinarily placid face. Phil was one of the few assailants without a weapon, and because of that, Craig was able to go low and bring him down, tackling him around the waist and throwing him into the swinging door of the women's restroom. Lisa Goldberg, wielding a wooden clipboard she held by its metal clasp, attempted to protect her boss and swung at Craig's head as he got to his feet. He easily sidestepped her, causing her to tumble on top of Phil, and he quickly grabbed a broom from one of the custodians, swinging the long stick in front of him in order to clear a path through the melee. Several men and women ran past him, pushing through the stairwell door and hurrying upstairs in an effort to get away from the violence.

The rampage had spilled out through broken windows and glass doors onto the campus and was now a genuine riot. Dozens of people were fleeing into the maze chased by pursuers who seemed to have found actual weapons: baseball bats, axes, knives, swords. One of the cars in the parking lot appeared to be on fire. Inside, computer terminals from the security station were being thrown to the floor and smashed. Mild mannered employees who had never even had the temerity to call in sick before were now purposefully destroying company property and aggressively battling with coworkers.

Throughout it all, the bag-headed guards remained in place and unmoving, and Craig couldn't help wondering what would provoke them to action—and what would happen then.

The swinging broom had cleared a path for him through the brawling crowd, and he reached the programmers, who were surprisingly unhurt, given the fact that they'd been attacked by Sales and had had no weapons. Only Rusty appeared to have been seriously injured, and he sat on the floor with his back to a wall,

464

holding a wadded-up woman's blouse to a wound on the side of his face. Several of the programmers were very large, however, and while very little of that bulk was muscle, it had obviously aided in repelling Phil's people.

Where was Phil?

Craig looked toward the restrooms, but the area was filled with struggling secretaries and paralegals, and he couldn't tell if Phil, or anyone else for that matter, was behind the fighters.

Both Huell and Benjy were clutching letter openers they'd taken from their attackers, and Craig sidled up to them. "So what do we do now?" Huell asked.

Lorene appeared at his side. "The front door's open and not exactly guarded," she said. "If we can make our way over there and slip between some people, we can probably get out."

"Good idea," Craig said. "You guys do that. My wife's out there somewhere—probably far down the street by now—and I'm sure she's called 911. The cops should be here soon. In the meantime, I'm going to see if I can stop all this before someone gets killed."

"How?"

"By going straight to the source."

"Patoff?" Benjy said.

Craig nodded.

"I'm coming, too."

Four of the programmers decided to accompany him. Several others had already taken off, and Hong-An chose to stay and help Rusty get outside so he could be ready for transport when an ambulance showed up, but Huell, Cuong, Lorene and Benjy went with him on a stealth mission across the lobby, where the crowd was thinning out, the fight being taken outside and up the stairs. Phil may have started this battle, but it had long since grown out of those confines. Employees weren't fighting for or against Phil, they were just fighting, egged on by circumstance to wanton destruction. Papers were flying everywhere, more glass was shattering, smoke from the fires was drifting over all.

Heading to the elevators, they gathered converts along the way, much more than Craig could have ever expected or predicted, angry employees who somehow figured out where the programmers were going and wanted in on it. It was a lynch mob, and he was at its head, and though he should have had qualms about that, he did not.

An elevator arrived, the doors sliding open to let out a battered, bloody group of terrified men and women who immediately ran screaming along individual trajectories into the heart of the increasingly smoky lobby.

When the doors of the adjacent elevator opened seconds later, no one ran out. The people inside this elevator were dead, piled on top of each other in such a way that there was no space between them, fitted together like pieces in a jigsaw puzzle so that they formed a wall of heads and feet and arms and torsos, many of them naked, most of them bloody. He recognized quite a few of the corpses, and sadness threatened to overwhelm horror as he looked into the lifeless eyes of Matthews' secretary Diane. A pink Facilities and Equipment form had been stapled to Diane's forehead, and Craig didn't have to move closer and read it in order to know what it said.

These people had been surplused out.

Sickened, Craig entered the first elevator, along with everyone else who could fit inside. There were nearly a dozen of them, with an equal or greater number left out, and before the doors slid shut, Craig told the others to follow as soon as they could.

Staring up at the lighted numbers above the door, he had no idea what they were in for, what they would find. This was a foolhardy move, a strategy conceived entirely without logic or reason. But with all that had happened, he was still alive, had remained relatively untouched, and he believed that to be because the consultant had other plans in mind for him. He needed to take advantage of this protection and confront the consultant directly—

*kill him*

—before the police arrived and his chance was lost. Still holding onto the broom, he asked Julio Ortiz if he could swap the broom for a claw hammer the custodian was carrying. A frightened Julio acquiesced, and Craig hefted the hammer in his hand as the elevator doors opened.

The seventh floor.

It had changed yet again. He wasn't sure what he had been expecting, but it had been along the lines of what he'd encountered last time—floors and walls covered in blood—or what he'd found on the second floor—industrial darkness and people hooked up to electricity. It definitely was not the sight that greeted them as they stepped off the elevator. For they found themselves in a generic business office: CompWare without the modernist touches. A single room the size of a football field, it was well-lit and divided into cubicles by metal-framed partitions. The room walls and partition walls were a uniform off-white, and both the floor and acoustic ceiling panels were the slightly lighter color of unlined paper. Craig smelled smoke, but the whiff of it was faint, as though seeping in from another world, and the dominant odor was of printer ink and toner. Muzak issued softly from speakers situated in the ceiling next to air-conditioning vents.

"We stay together," Craig said.

There was a musical ding behind them as another elevator arrived, and those employees joined Craig's group as they hugged the wall to the left, walking past the warren of cubicles, searching for the consultant.

Why had he come up here? Craig asked himself. What did he hope to achieve? The consultant was not human, was beyond human, and there was no way he could hope to fight against something that possessed the sort of power wielded by the consultant. He should have tried to get out of the building, find his family and wait for the police.

But he hadn't.

Something had compelled him to search out the consultant, something had drawn him up here, and he wondered if he was unknowingly doing the consultant's bidding.

So far, the cubicles they passed had been empty, but that changed. A temporary partition wall blocked the way forward, forcing them to turn right and walk down an aisle between open workspaces. Here, the cubicles were populated by people who appeared to have died at their desks. At one, Anthony, Phil's new right-hand man, the one who had brought the news of Parvesh's unfortunate "accident," lay dead in a chair, frozen in place, eyes wide open, face contorted in agony, phone held to his ear. Next door, the "doctor" who had taken the sample for his blood test was slumped lifelessly over his workstation, one hand clutching a hypodermic needle. The trail of dead continued as they made their way up the aisle, all of them men and women Craig recognized as being affiliated with BFG.

He saw Mrs. Adams, his observer, lying on the floor with her legs splayed and her skirt hiked up.

The instrumental Muzak had disappeared sometime in the last few minutes, replaced by a church spiritual, "Will the Circle Be Unbroken," that sounded as though it were being sung in a nearby room by a live choir. Only...

Only the words were wrong.

*May the bastards*
*All be broken*
*Right damn now, Ralph*
*Right damn now*

"What the fuck?" Huell said under his breath.

Craig looked over the tops of the partitions, trying to see if there were any doorways in the wall that might lead to another room where the choir could be singing. The idea of a cappella singers in an office made no sense at all, and even as he scanned the side wall, the singing voices faded away, replaced by a generic instrumental version of "Girl From Ipanema" from the speakers in the ceiling above.

Ahead, the labyrinth of cubicles ended, and the office beyond was an oversized version of a *Mad Men*-era executive suite, with low Danish modern tables, blocky chairs and sofas, and bland hotel art framed on walls that were spaced so far apart a four-lane highway could fit between them. At the far end, barely visible, was a gigantic wooden desk.

Craig could see in the structure of this office the bones of that terrible bloody room where he had faced the consultant before. Its size and the placement of the desk were roughly the same, as though one room had been superimposed over the other, and Craig wondered if what they were seeing was real or if their minds had been clouded to *think* this is what they were seeing.

Or had he been misled last time?

Maybe the office and the abattoir were both real.

"What do we do?" Lorene asked, but Craig didn't answer, just kept walking forward.

Behind him, those employees who had come up from the first floor followed in single file, like children on a field trip. Their presence gave him courage, and his gait grew quicker and more assured as he proceeded across the massive office. In front of him, the desk was no longer a desk but a strange creature of approximately the same color and size. It was as though the tableaux at the far end of the room had become less hazy and was growing sharper the closer they came to it, only the desk had been well-defined to begin with. The object had not grown clearer with their approach, it had *changed*, and it was changing still, moving from all fours to two legs, standing, and though it was not in any way, manner or form human, Craig knew that it was the consultant.

Craig stopped. He was still several yards away but was afraid to get any closer. In his hand, he clutched the hammer tightly. The others who had been walking behind, spread out next to him, holding tightly to their own weapons.

The consultant stood before them, naked, his body a grotesque grayish brown, leathery skin covering a skeletal structure more raptor than man. His face was horrible: cold lizard eyes above a beaklike nose and hard lipless mouth. The age Craig had briefly sensed in him before was now evident to anyone who looked at him.

Craig took the offensive. "What are you?"

"I've had many names."

"Oh, this is going to be one of those conversations?"

The consultant smiled in a manner that was far too wide and revealed teeth he should not have had.

"You destroyed our company."

There was a chorus of assent.

"*BFG* didn't destroy your company," he said. "*You* did that."

"You got rid of half our workforce," Craig countered. "Whoever you didn't lay off, you *killed*."

"When you arrived to work tonight, this was CompWare. If you had gone to your offices and workstations, if you had done your *jobs*, it would still be CompWare. But you threw a tantrum, like spoiled children, and you fouled your own workplace."

There was a truth to that, Craig knew, but it was a partial truth. The riot downstairs had only hastened what was going to happen anyway. The consultant had put them on this path. He had not been able to turn CompWare into the perfect company he wanted, so its fate held no interest for him. He didn't care what happened to it, and it seemed to amuse him to watch it devolve.

"You're a failure," Craig said.

The consultant nodded in agreement. "I am."

Someone off to the right—Benjy?—threw a stapler at the monster. It stopped in midair, hanging suspended in space for several seconds. Without taking his eyes off Craig, the consultant caused the stapler to whip back twice as hard and twice as fast as it had been thrown originally, hitting Benjy in the side of the head, then Cuong, both of them going down, screaming. Beneath, the floor trembled as though they were experiencing an earthquake.

The smile came again, and Craig glanced briefly away, unable to face all those teeth.

"You are a worthy adversary," the consultant said. "I've had my eye on you from the beginning. I even admire the way you've handled your buddy's completely unwarranted ascension to the head of this dying firm. It's why I called this meeting today. I thought the two of us should have a discussion."

Craig met those cold reptilian eyes. "We have nothing to discuss. And you didn't *call* me here."

*But he had, hadn't he?* That was why Craig had come upstairs instead of going out to join his family. He felt disoriented, as though he were not in charge of his own thoughts. He was aware that Lorene and several other people had coalesced around Benjy and Cuong to make sure they were okay, and he felt guilty that he'd made no effort to check on their injuries himself. They were only up here because of him.

He shook it off. "I assume you're done here? You're leaving?"

"Almost time," the consultant conceded. "A few more loose ends to tie up…"

"Like what?"

"Like you." The consultant was changing. Although he had not put on clothes, he was now wearing a business suit: gray pants, white shirt, red tie and gray jacket. He was faceless. Smooth skin covered the flat area where his features should have been. This, Craig suspected, was his true appearance, his real self. The monster from moments before had been their projection of him made flesh, but the consultant was not that sort of cartoon evil. His malevolence was more subtle, more insidious. He corrupted from within rather than from without, and the faceless businessman in front of them was the perfect embodiment of what he really was.

"I'm inviting you to join the team, to become a part of BFG."

The consultant had no mouth and so could not speak, but his voice sounded clearly in Craig's head, and it was obvious from the expressions on their faces that the others could hear him, too.

"Never," Craig vowed.

"There are benefits—"

"Never."

The faceless man shrugged. "It is your choice."

Benjy and Cuong were jerked into the air and slammed into the ceiling, their feet kicking the faces of those administering to their wounds as they rocketed upward. The air suddenly felt thick, heavy, and a swirling wind caused everyone's hair to stick up straight.

Without thinking, acting purely on instinct, Craig rushed forward. They all must have had the same impulse because everyone was rushing the consultant simultaneously, and before the wind could grow, before others could be hurled into the ceiling or thrown against a wall, they were upon him, makeshift weapons pounding, hacking, slashing. Craig raised his hammer and brought it down, claw-end first, on the consultant's right arm, feeling a satisfying crunch as metal sank through flesh and hit bone. Then he was jostled aside as other employees pushed their way in, eager to administer their own personal justice.

Falling onto his stomach, Craig crawled out of the dogpile. The consultant's voice in his head was silent, the wind was gone and the thickness of the air had dissipated. The only noises in the office were the grunts and cries of attacking employees.

He looked up at the ceiling, saw nothing, then looked down and saw Cuong's and Benjy's lifeless bodies lying in a contorted heap on the floor.

The sounds of violence were becoming more disturbing—*wetter*—and Craig stood. "Stop!" he ordered. He wasn't anyone's boss other than the programmers, but the mob listened to him, the fray petering out as employees backed off and separated. The consultant's body lay there, bloody and unmoving.

But it wasn't the consultant's body.

It was Phil's.

That was impossible. Craig had been staring into that blank face as he'd pounded the arm with his hammer. It had been the consultant's. And Phil was downstairs somewhere or on another floor. There was no way the two could have been switched.

But the proof lay before him.

The consultant was gone.

And Phil's dead body, cut and beaten by his fellow workers, was on its back, eyes in the battered face staring upward into nothingness. Craig was reminded of a figure on the cover of some album, but, try as he might, he could come up with neither the name of the band nor the title of the record.

*Phil would know*, he thought, and a profound sadness settled over him. He realized at that precise moment just how much he would miss his friend.

Legs giving way beneath him, Craig sat down hard on the floor, grateful for some reason for the pain that shot through his body as his butt landed on the ground.

Huell tried to lift him up by his arm. "Are you okay?"

And Craig started to cry.

# FORTY TWO

HOLDING TIGHTLY ON TO DYLAN'S HAND, WITH HIS
other arm around Angie's waist, Craig stood in the parking lot
with several of the programmers and others who had accompanied him to the seventh floor. He watched the police round up
dazed rioters while firemen attempted to put out myriad blazes
on the CompWare property and in the building. He felt drained
and empty, sad and shell-shocked, but underneath all that was a
deep abiding sense of relief. It was over. It may have ended badly,
may have ended *horribly*, but it had ended, and that brought him a
surprising measure of peace.

He looked up at the building, counting up to the seventh floor,
and was gratified to see flames shooting out from shattered windows. He wished the consultant was up there, but he knew that
wasn't the case. He didn't know how he knew, but he did, and his
hope was that the firemen would put out the blaze quickly enough

to preserve whatever the hell that floor had become. The second floor, too.

There might be enough evidence left for the authorities to go after the consultant or at least destroy the reputation of BFG.

Who was he kidding? The consultant would just change his name and the name of his firm.

He never had found out what the acronym BFG stood for, he realized.

*If you don't know that, you don't know anything*, the consultant had said.

What did that mean?

Craig didn't know. He looked at the burning ruins of the CompWare campus, wondering if this could have been avoided, if there were something he could have done to prevent all of this death and destruction. A brown paper bag skittered along the ground, propelled by the breeze, two eyeholes cut in its face.

What had happened to the guards with the automatic weapons?

There were so many questions to which he didn't know the answer, to which he might *never* know the answer.

He squeezed Dylan's hand, held Angie tighter.

This was what was important. This was what mattered.

He saw Rusty being wheeled into the back of an ambulance. Phil was dead, Matthews was dead, Benjy and Cuong were dead, and so were God knew how many others. Those remaining were now jobless, every last one of them unemployed, though he couldn't help thinking that they were better off unemployed than working for what CompWare had become.

He stared up at the night sky, the stars made invisible by the lights of the city and the illumination of the fires.

And the consultant? Craig wondered. Where was the consultant?

But he knew the answer to that one, didn't he?

His eyes focused again on the burning seventh floor.

In a meeting.

The consultant was in a meeting.

He was always in a meeting.

Praise Ralph.